I0742183

# When The Church Bells Ring

## A Greek Adventure

Annell St. Charles

Red Penguin
BOOKS

*When the Church Bells Ring*

Copyright © 2025 by Annell St. Charles

All rights reserved.

Published by Red Penguin Books

Bellerose Village, New York

ISBN

Digital 978-1-63777-813-5

Print 978-1-63777-814-2

No part of this book may be reproduced in any form or by any electronic or mechanical means, including information storage and retrieval systems, without written permission from the author, except for the use of brief quotations in a book review.

*also by annell st. charles*

<u>Novels</u>

**The Georgia Ayres Series:**

*The Chances We Take*

*The Things Left Unsaid*

*The Choices We Make*

*The Hearts We Trust*

<u>Photography</u>

*Sunrise on Hilton Head Island: Coligny Beach*

*Island Life*

*Hilton Head Island: Sunrise, Sunset, and the Beauty Between.*

<u>Poetry</u>

*The Clam Shell*

# a message to the reader

Greece is a country with a unique history that goes deeper than I ever imagined. I first visited there in the late 1980s, shortly before marrying my Greek-born husband, Costas Tsinakis. While "digging" through the facts about its history and culture, I uncovered much about it by reading about and visually observing the findings from numerous archaeological explorations displayed in both museums and within the local sites that allow a visitor to get a first-hand look at what has been discovered. Although I have never studied the field of archaeology, it was an unavoidable inclusion in this book in order to properly tell the tale.

I have not had the opportunity to explore the entirety of this magnificent country, but I imagine it's impossible to go anywhere in Greece without coming across these remnants of historical treasures. In this story, I have limited my description to what I have witnessed and experienced in Athens, as well as the islands of Andros and Santorini.

This book is a work of fiction. But like most books of that genre, it was inspired by a lot of facts. In that light, I ask the reader, especially any Greek-born readers, to forgive me for occasionally taking creative liberties with the facts. For example, there truly is a Tower of Bistis, but it was never a site of the type of archeological exploration I have described within this book. I suppose you could say I was expressing wishful thinking because, unfortunately, the Tower is abandoned and falling into ruin rather than being rescued.

The key archaeological dig sites I describe on both Andros and Santorini are real, but I have at times used freedom of expression in my depiction of them.

The hotel in Apoikia still stands in that village. I have stayed there and enjoyed the experience, but it is true that it has seen better days. I hope that by including it here, it might increase in popularity with hikers out exploring one of the nearby Andros hiking routes. That could, in turn, lead to a resurgence in its former glory as a grand site for pleasure and entertainment.

The tavernas I mention in both Apoikia and Stenies are a couple of my favorite spots to eat and never disappoint with their succulent offerings. My mouth is watering just thinking about it ...

There is indeed an estate called *Ktima Lemonies* in the village of Lamyra, on the island of Andros, as I have alluded to in the book. However, I have unfortunately never had the opportunity to visit it. What I have described herein resides only in my imagination. I hope to remedy that some day.

Overall, it is my hope that this story will inspire my readers to take a journey to this fascinating land, or to return if you have been lucky enough to have ventured there before, and to discover for yourself how beautifully the past and present can co-exist.

*To my Greek-born husband, Costas Tsinakis, who introduced me to this fascinating Country many moons ago, and instilled in me a deep appreciation for its history and culture. Thank you, my love. Efcharisto, aghapi moo.*

*My heartfelt thanks to the villagers of Apoikia who have welcomed this foreigner/xenos into their lives, their homes, and many of whom have become dear friends. I particularly want to recognize my sisters-in-law, Anna and Yota, who have graciously allowed me to stumble my way through speaking a little Greek and who, most importantly, have made me feel very much a part of their family. Efcharisto poly! And to the new friends I have met through our time at Omilos, you have enriched my life.*

# one

I was sitting in a rocking chair on the porch of a mountain-top cabin looking out over the Great Smoky Mountains National Park in Gatlinburg, Tennessee. The view was a hazy purple with a tinge of pink where the setting sun was taking a dive into obscurity. The person sitting next to me was encouraging me to take a hike down the mountainside before darkness set in, but I was unsure whether or not I had the strength, both physical and mental, to handle the up and down challenges of a mountain trek.

I wasn't sure why I was afraid. Walking had been my daily passion for as long as I could remember. But there was something disconcerting about the idea of heading out into the unknown. *Kind of like my life in recent years*, I thought to myself.

"The unknown can quickly become the known if you allow courage to override your fear. Be brave and follow your heart."

I turned to regard the person sitting next to me. Had they really spoken out loud the thoughts that were in my mind? I couldn't see them clearly because their face was hidden in shadow. But there was something oddly reassuring about their presence. I felt comforted, and I was just about to shake off my fears and stand up when the chair I was sitting on suddenly began to wobble, causing me to struggle to keep from falling out.

*"Ladies and gentlemen, you are advised to please make sure your seat belts are firmly secured in preparation for landing.*

*"Kuries kai kurioi, sas simvoulevoume va vevaiotheite oti oi zones asfalias sas einai stathera stereomena kara tin protimasia yia prosgeios."*

The announcement startled me awake from my dream, and I struggled to sit upright, jostling the arm of the passenger next to me, who turned to me with a slight grimace.

"Ugh. I don't think I slept more than a few minutes. I hope you fared better." She looked at me questioningly.

For a moment, I wasn't sure where I was. The dream had seemed so real, but as I glanced around me, I realized I was sitting on an airplane surrounded by strangers. I wiped the sleep from my eyes and held my wrist up close to my face. The dial read 8 a.m. I had started my trip very early the morning before, departing from San Francisco with a stop in Atlanta, which, including a four-hour layover, meant I had been traveling a total of fourteen and a half hours. I had reset my watch before leaving Atlanta, so I quickly did the math to adjust for the 7-hour time difference in Greece.

I groaned. "According to my body clock, it's 1 a.m. No wonder I'm so tired. The last thing I remember is eating dinner and then trying to watch that crazy movie they were showing. *9 to 5*, I think it was called. I guess I must have dozed off sometime after that, and I dreamed I was in the East Tennessee mountains. Must have something to do with the fact that Dolly Parton was one of the main characters in the movie." I yawned and stretched my arms, trying hard not to make a repeat assault on my seat mate. *Seat mate?* It suddenly occurred to me that the seat next to me had been unoccupied before I dozed off.

The person next to me must have read my mind. Or at least caught the look of alarm on my face. She looked at me apologetically. "I hope you don't mind. Originally, I was sitting a few rows back, but the man in front of me was insistent on reclining his seat as far back as possible. I felt he was practically lying in my lap. The flight attendant saw my predicament and told me there was a spare seat up here. I jumped at the chance to move. You were asleep when I came up, so I didn't have a chance to alert you to my presence." She reached into her pocket and held her hand out to me. "You missed breakfast. It wasn't much, but I kept this little cake if you'd like to have it." She inched her offering, or should I say, *peace* offering, closer to my face.

I smiled. "No problem. I wasn't even aware you were here until I woke up. Sorry for hitting you." I glanced at the packet she was holding and felt my stomach growl in response. I lifted it from her hand. "Thanks. I guess I am sort of hungry." I eagerly tore open the plastic wrapping and bit into the cake. It was soft and moist with a lemony twang. "Umm. That's actually really good." I shoved the remainder into my mouth.

She smiled warmly. "Is this your first time visiting Greece?"

I nodded, afraid to speak in case I let loose a shower of cake crumbs with my response.

"Me too. I've booked a hotel in Athens for the next few days, and then I'm off to meet a friend in Rome. She's been there for a couple of weeks already, so she should have things well sorted out by the time I arrive."

I reached for the bottle of water I had tucked into the seat back in front of me and took a sip before answering. "I have a cousin who lives in Athens. Unfortunately, he's away on a business trip, so I'll have to fend for myself until he returns. My plans were kind of last-minute." I took another swallow of water.

"Will you be staying in his place?"

I shook my head. "I didn't want to impose on him since I didn't give him much notice that I was coming. I did ask for his help with booking a room at a hotel. It's in some place called *Plaka*. He said I can just take a taxi there from the airport."

"Plaka. That's where I'm booked also. What's the name of your hotel?"

I reached into the backpack I had crammed under the seat in front of me and pulled out my cell phone, scrolling through the information I had typed into the notes section. "It's called Hotel Central. That doesn't sound very Greek, but it's supposed to have a view of the Acropolis from the rooftop."

She nodded. "I've heard of it. In fact, I almost booked a room there myself, but my friend suggested another one called the Hotel Hermes. If I remember correctly, it's very close to the one where you'll be staying. In fact, we could share a taxi if you'd like."

I hesitated for a moment. Even though we had shared close quarters on the plane, I was asleep for most of that time, and I had no idea who she was. I tried to glance at her discreetly. She looked to be a few years older than my twenty-three, although I wasn't very good at guessing people's age. She was dressed comfortably in faded denim jeans and a dark-blue, button-up blouse with a cream-colored sweater wrapped around her shoulders. Her feet were clad in sensible sneakers that matched the color of her jeans. Her auburn hair was pulled back into a ponytail that appeared surprisingly intact despite the number of hours we had been traveling. All in all, she seemed harmless and, to be honest, I felt relieved at having someone help me navigate transport to my hotel.

Even though my cousin had been living in Greece for several months, he hadn't been terribly helpful when I told him I was coming for a visit. In fact, to be totally honest, I wasn't sure if he would be happy to see me or be put out by the whole idea. We had been pretty good friends as kids growing up in the same neighborhood, but I lost touch with him for several years after high school. A chance encounter on Facebook, where he popped up as a friend suggestion, enabled us to begin to get reacquainted, albeit virtually. Still. There was a lot of water under that bridge, as they say, and I had no idea if seeing him again would be a blessing or a curse.

I twisted the cap back on my water bottle and nodded at her gratefully. "Sharing a taxi would be great. Truthfully, I've been more than a little worried about how I would find my way around. Especially since my command of the Greek Language is limited to *Kalimera*, good morning, and *Pou einai n toualeta*, where is the bathroom."

She smiled. "Both are very helpful expressions to know. I took an online course to try and learn a little Greek before coming, but I can't say my command of the language is much better. Hopefully, there will be enough Greeks who speak English to let us get by." She held her hand out for a shake. "I'm Shelly Bainbridge, by the way."

I gripped her offered hand. "Jesse. Holloway. Jesse Holloway. Sorry. I guess I'm not quite awake yet." I rolled my eyes as I thought, *I must sound like a complete idiot!* Another announcement interrupted our exchange, reminding us to raise our seat backs and put away our carry-ons in preparation for landing. I lifted the window shade and peered out. The sky was beginning to be lit by the rising sun, which cast shades of pale pink and blue on the horizon. In the distance, I could see the outline of mountains that appeared dim and bare of vegetation, reminding me of the hills around my home in California. Their smoky appearance, which was likely a result of the smog I had read about that was common around the capital city of Greece, was also a vague reminder of the Smoky Mountains—an image that brought back to mind my pre-landing dream.

I felt my stomach clench as I remembered the uncertainty with which I had viewed the possibility of a mountain trek, which seemed silly in retrospect. After all, hiking in the Smokies was something I was quite familiar with. What was it that I had been so worried about? I scrunched up my face as I tried to recall the details of the dream. All I could bring to mind was the fear that had gripped me, eased by the reassuring words of my unknown dream partner. *What was that all about?* I wondered. Maybe it had to do with the changes I was likely to face in the days that lay ahead of me. After all, I had taken on the role of a *stranger in a strange land* with barely a glance backward. While that wasn't a position I was completely unfamiliar with, I couldn't say it was something I embraced without apprehension either.

I had been living in the Bay Area for the past three years. Seven, if you counted the four I spent as a student at UC Berkeley. But California wasn't my *real* home. I was born in Nashville, Tennessee, but sought greener pastures after high school, landing me in the not-so-green hills surrounding Berkeley. I had become fascinated with history as a high school student, and Berkeley had one of the best history departments in the country. I had been toying with the idea of continuing on there for a master's degree in archaeology after completing my undergraduate studies. For some inexplicable reason, I had become fascinated with archaeology at a young age, and UCB was supposed to have a top-notch archaeology program. However, an offer to teach history at a local high school gave me the opportunity to pay off my student loans before adding to them with more years of education. The idea of continuing my studies was still simmering in my thoughts, but I had decided to put it on the back burner for now.

My stomach lurched as the plane landed with a jolt, and I heard what sounded like a mouse squeak from the seat beside me.

"My! That was a bit rough." Shelly wiped her hands on either side of her face, smoothing the already neat bundle of hair away from her cheeks.

The PA system sputtered its greeting as the plane's landing gear attempted to bring it to a halt.

*Ladies and gentlemen, we would like to welcome you to Athens, Greece, where the time is 9:25 a.m. The flight attendants will be coming through the cabin one last time to collect any items you would like to discard. It has been our pleasure to serve you. We hope the next time you decide to travel, you will choose Delta Airlines.*

*Kuries kai kuroi, tha thelame vas as kalosopisoume stin Athena Ellatha opou I ora einai epta kai eikosi pende. I perasoun apo tin kampina yia telutaia ora gia va sillexkete opiathipote antikeimena thelete va aporripsete, itan hara mas na exthpiretisoume. Elpizoume oti tin epomeni ora pout ha apofasisete va taxithepsete tha epilezete tin Delta Airlines.*

The plane taxied for another several minutes before pulling up to our gate. The overhead light, indicating it was safe to get out of our seats, dinged on at the same time an announcement reminded us to be careful when opening our overheads in case someone's errant bag toppled out.

I unhooked my seatbelt and looked around, deciding to stay put for a while rather than risk getting elbowed or body slammed by one of the other passengers who were frantically attempting to collect their belongings while simultaneously claiming every inch of aisle space.

Shelly looked at me with raised eyebrows. "Blimey! It's amazing how adults can suddenly turn into ill-behaved adolescents! I thought I was well rid of this when I left teaching."

"You were a teacher, too?"

"Yes. *Was* being the key word. I slogged through a half dozen years of primary until I finally admitted to myself that teaching was NOT my cup of tea. I've been working in real estate since then. Started as a secretary and worked my way up to managing my own sales. I love the freedom it gives me. Like being able to take this trip. I never had more than a few weeks free as a teacher. Even though summers were supposed to be time off, the salary of a primary teacher in Great Britain was barely sufficient to cover expenses. I had to teach summer school, as well, to make ends meet. The real estate market has been gloriously booming in GB the past few years, so I can afford to take time away fairly often. Of course, that means I have to hold tight to my pennies. Can't just jump at the most luxurious accommodations."

It was interesting to hear her take on teaching, and I nodded at our mutual experience. "I must admit that teaching is not my first passion either. But the teacher salaries in California are pretty good. I've been able to make a sizable dent in my student loans and still save a little extra for trips like this."

"Good for you. It sounds as though you have things well in hand."

I nodded hesitantly as we settled back in our seats to wait out the mass exodus. What she said was true, to some extent. I seemed to be heading in the right direction financially. But beyond that, it was anyone's guess how things would end up.

When the crowd finally began shuffling towards the exit doors, I looped my arms through my backpack and stepped out into the aisle behind Shelly, who had already pulled down her carry-on bag from the overhead compartment. Her bag was reasonably sized, but I noticed she still struggled under the weight of it.

She smiled at me as she placed her bag in the aisle in front of her. "You were smart to travel light. I have a fear of losing my checked bags, so I tend to overpack my carry-on."

I shifted my backpack and nodded. "I may have the opposite problem. I was afraid of bringing too much, so I may have left behind some essential things. Hopefully, Greece has some shops where I can pick up some extras if I need to."

We spent the next half hour following the herd of passengers embarking from our plane as we wove our way through Customs and on to the baggage claim area. We were quickly surrounded by what looked to be several hundred people, as passengers from other arriving flights blended into the throng of arrivals. Finding the correct baggage claim area proved to be no small task since the arrival board notifications were listed in Greek. Luckily, Shelly spotted a couple of other passengers who she recognized from our flight, and we followed them to the appointed location. After another half hour of waiting, our bags finally appeared on the belt, and we quickly pushed our way through the crowd to claim them, lifting them onto the baggage cart Shelly had been smart enough to grab as we passed through the arrival lobby. With her two checked bags and my one, plus her carry-on, we could easily fit them on the cart.

"Whew!" She stretched before grabbing the handle of the cart. "Ready to find a taxi?"

I nodded, but my mind was full of doubt as I looked at the growing crowd of people pushing carts and towing bags toward the exit doors.

Shelly pointed to our left. "There. I see a sign that I believe says there are taxis outside that door."

I looked in the direction she was pointing and could see the word *ταξί* clearly displayed. "That looks enough like the word *taxi* that I think you may be right."

We headed in the direction the sign indicated and exited the building, quickly spotting a line of people next to what appeared to be a taxi stand. At least ten taxis, recognizable by their standard bright yellow coloring, were idling next to the line, and an official-looking man was calling out in Greek to those waiting, indicating which taxi they were to approach. As each taxi pulled away from the curb, another quickly moved into place.

Shelly tapped me on the arm. "Come on. Over here." I hurried to follow her lead as she pushed our cart to the end of the line.

The number of people waiting for taxis in front of us was considerable, so it was several minutes before we finally reached the front of the line. We hurried to stow our luggage in the trunk of our assigned car with the help of a burly but affable-looking driver before scooting into the back seat. The driver climbed into the front and turned to look at us. "Where you go?"

We glanced at each other with wide eyes before Shelly answered. "Two Hotels in Plaka on a street called Apollonos. The Hotel Central and The Hotel Hermes."

The driver grunted, which I hoped meant he had understood. I looked around the inside of the taxi. A string of round beads with a tassel on the end hung from his rearview mirror. A second chain held what appeared to be an eye with bright blue and white circles surrounding a black dot. Subtle strains of music emanated from his car radio, which he hummed along with, occasionally adding his voice to what I assumed were Greek words.

I glanced out the window as he pulled onto a busy road that looked like an interstate. Cars were zipping along at a rapid pace, but the driver appeared unfazed as he maneuvered his way into the line of ongoing traffic.

I turned to look out the window, spotting the same barren, hazy-looking mountains in the distance. On either side of the highway were an assortment of businesses that, from what I could gather based upon the images that decorated their fronts, ranged from hotels to furniture stores and what appeared to be bakeries. The signs were all in Greek. I don't know why I was expecting to see English descriptions, but there were none in sight. Instead, the lettering appeared to be a combination of *GREEK* Greek and *LATIN* Greek, which is how I thought of the use of both the Greek and Latin alphabets to describe the contents of the businesses we passed.

Shelly appeared to be equally enthralled by what she was seeing out the other side of the cab. "Do you think the Greeks believe that non-Greek speakers will be able to understand what the signs say just because they changed the way the letters are written? It's still Greek to me!" Her eyes sparkled as she choked down a laugh.

"I don't know, but I wish they would translate everything for us. My head is spinning from trying to figure out what I'm seeing."

"You no speak Greek?"

I looked up to find the driver staring at me from the rearview mirror.

"Uh, no. SHE speaks a little, but I'm afraid I'm completely lost." *Lost in translation,* I thought to myself, remembering a movie I once saw about a traveler attempting to comprehend what he was seeing and hearing during a visit to Japan.

He nodded his understanding, causing his mustache to jiggle up and down. "No problem. Most Greeks speak little English. If not, we use hands." He held both hands up with the palms flat in the universal language of *What can you do?*

I smiled at his reflection, which reminded me of either an otter or a Wild West cowboy, neither of which was very familiar, but still felt oddly reassuring.

Shelly poked me in the arm with her finger. "Did you see that?" She pointed out the front window. There was a motorcycle ahead of us with a wooden crate attached to the back holding what appeared to be chickens, or at least some sort of feathery creatures. A young woman was perched on top of the crate with her arms wrapped around the upper back of the driver.

"Oh my god! I hope she has a tight grip!" I laughed.

The rest of the ride was mostly uneventful, except for the abundance of automobiles on the road and the smell of fuel and dust that flowed in from the open windows. At one point, I started to ask the driver to roll up the windows and turn on the air conditioner, but after examining the inside of the car, which appeared tattered and old, I decided that either request would be futile.

After about 20 minutes, we left the highway and began to weave our way up and down a series of small streets. On occasion, I caught a glimpse of what appeared to be an ancient building with pillars and crumbling walls mashed up against a more modern edifice. At one point, the driver pulled to a stop despite the line of cars behind him and pointed to the right. *"Ei Akropoli."*

Shelly and I both leaned to the right to catch a better look. My breath caught at the image of a foreign and yet familiar building perched on a distant hill. I recognized it immediately as the Parthenon, which sat on a high point of rocky land referred to as the Acropolis. I was familiar with the image because a replica of the same structure sat in a park in my hometown of Nashville, Tennessee, although, in that case, it sat on flat land rather than a hill.

When I was a teenager in Nashville, the steps of the Parthenon were the chosen locale of many after-school and weekend gatherings with my high school friends. At the time, I didn't pay much attention to where it came from and why it was sitting in the middle of what was known as Centennial Park. I just knew that it was a cool place to hang out. Now, looking out the window at the real thing, I remembered that the Nashville Parthenon was built as part of Tennessee's 1897 Centennial Exposition, celebrating Tennessee's 100th year of statehood. Apparently, when the Exposition was being planned, Nashville decided to take advantage of its nickname, *Athens of the South,* by building the world's only exact-size and detailed exterior replica of the original temple in Athens, Greece. The initial plan was to tear down the structure at the conclusion of the Centennial Exposition, but so many residents of Nashville protested that idea that, instead, a rebuild of the decaying original structure occurred.

After its completion in 1925, the Nashville Parthenon became the site for the display of paintings and sculptures and the occasional musical or theatrical event, eventually adding a 42-foot replica of the statue of Athena in 1990, which still stands in the interior of the main room.

As a teenager, I had spent many afternoons and weekends with friends, enjoying the shaded exterior of the structure while we traded life stories and regaled one another with sing-alongs to a tune led by one or more of us strumming away on an acoustic guitar. And every Christmas, I remembered it as the site of a large-scale, lighted Nativity scene that one could enjoy either from the grassy area just below the display or while parked in a car in the nearby lot. Sadly, the Nativity scene disappeared just before my senior year. Word had it that the city felt it was just too expensive to maintain. I later learned it had been sold to a firm in Cincinnati, Ohio, which only kept it a couple of years before discarding it into a rubbish heap.

Those memories were both sad and sweet, and I took a slow breath in an attempt to control the emotions that filled me as I looked at the amazing sight just outside the car windows. I noticed a line of people snaking their way along the hillside as they made their way to the famous structure, while others were strung out in various locations, both near and far from the top. The pillars that surrounded the Parthenon appeared to glow in the rapidly rising sun, which also served to illuminate the crumbling remains that were held aloft by scaffolding.

Shelly pointed out the window, "I read they've been working on restoring it for years. It looks like they still have a long way to go."

The driver nodded at us from the rear-view mirror. "Greek way. Work little. Look at work. Rest. Have food. Sleep little. Drink coffee. Work little more." The driver, whose name badge proclaimed he was named Yiorgos, chuckled. "But only if government say okay. Most of time, they say wait more. Before finish one job, more work to do."

He pulled away from the curb in response to the honking protest of the drivers waiting none too patiently behind our stopped vehicle. He waved his hand in disgust. "*Malakas. Everyone trelos!*"

Shelly leaned over and whispered, "I don't have the nerve to translate the first word he said, but I believe the second one means *crazy*." She covered her mouth to suppress a giggle.

We continued to weave our way through the congested streets until he finally pulled to a stop. "Hotels. Central, Hermes." He gestured quickly to the right and then left before hopping out the door.

Shelly and I scurried to follow suit. I grabbed my backpack from the floor in front of my feet and stepped out onto the curb. Yiorgos placed the remainder of our baggage on the sidewalk and then stood behind it with an expectant look on his face.

"What do we owe you?" I asked.

"*Saranda evro.* Forty euros."

We reached into our respective purses and pulled out some money, quickly pooling our resources to provide the total he indicated. Shelly held out an extra five euro note. "For you, Yiorgos. Thank you for the ride."

He looked at the offered bill in surprise. "Not necessary. Greeks no expect tip."

She pushed the note closer to him. "Please."

He shrugged before taking the money. "Okay. American way."

"Actually, I'm British. But tipping is something we're used to, like the Americans."

He tugged on the front of his cap before climbing back into the taxi. As he drove off, Shelly and I looked around at our surroundings. "I guess this is where we say goodbye," I commented.

"I suppose so. Or perhaps you'd like to meet up a little later for a drink or something to eat?"

Her suggestion pleased me, especially since the thought of finding my way around Athens alone was more than a little intimidating. "I'd like that!"

"Good. I fancy a shower and a bit of kip first, so why don't we plan to meet in front of your hotel at ..." she glanced at her watch, "one o'clock?"

"Perfect." I waved goodbye as I headed toward my hotel.

# two

The Hotel Central was a pleasant surprise. From the outside, it appeared simple and similar to any standard hotel I had seen in the States, but inside was a whole different story. Subtle strains of music greeted me as I stepped inside the air-conditioned interior. The lobby was small but tastefully decorated in fresh tones of cream and yellow, with comfy-looking chairs and sofas positioned in front of a large screen television. Cut-out shelves along the walls held sculptures of ancient-looking figures lit by soft overhead lighting. Fresh flower arrangements adorned marble-topped, wooden tables that sat next to the seating, and a bowl of fresh fruit was placed prominently on the check-in desk, where a young woman around my age stood behind the counter.

"Welcome to the Hotel Central. How can I help you today?"

Her greeting was in English, which I supposed meant she was more used to non-Greek-speaking visitors than native speakers. Or maybe I just looked like a tourist.

I stepped up to the desk and set my backpack on the floor next to my roller bag. "Hi. I have a reservation."

She smiled at me warmly. "Name, please?"

"Oh, yeah. Jesse. Jesse Holloway." *There I go again, stumbling over getting out my full name!*

She looked at the computer screen in front of her. "Yes. For three nights. Is that correct?"

I nodded.

"We have you booked into one of our standard rooms with a double bed." She paused for a moment as she studied the screen again. "Unfortunately, your room is not available now. The previous renter left the water running in the tub when he went upstairs to the roof garden, and the water overflowed. We have someone trying to dry it out now, but I'm afraid it will not be ready until late afternoon, at the earliest, and all of our other standard rooms are taken." She glanced quickly at my forlorn expression before studying her computer again. "However, I can give you an upgrade to one of our superior rooms. For the same price, of course."

My sleep-deprived brain was already struggling with the news that my room was flooded, so I wasn't sure I heard her correctly. "I'm sorry. What did you say?"

She smiled at my obvious confusion. "None of our standard rooms are currently available, but we would be happy to upgrade you to one of our superior rooms so as not to inconvenience you. Would that be acceptable?"

"Yes! That would be ... amazing!" I could feel a slow blush rising up my throat as I stuttered my reply.

She nodded as she pulled something out of the drawer below her desk and placed it on the counter in front of me. "Here is your key card. Just wave it in front of the screen on the door to your room. Your room number is 424. There's an elevator just behind you that will take you to the 4$^{th}$ floor. A complimentary breakfast buffet is available on the second floor each morning from 7 until 10:30." She glanced at her watch. "In fact, I believe it will still be open for a few more minutes if you'd like to stop there before you go to your room. There is a rooftop bar that opens at 11:30, where you can buy drinks and light snacks until 6 pm. After that, the full menu is available until 11 p.m. The rooftop terrace has a wonderful view of the Acropolis and the surrounding area. It is especially beautiful at night when the lights are on. Is there anything else I can help you with today?"

*Free breakfast and a rooftop view. Had I heard her right??* "No. That all sounds wonderful!"

She smiled in response. "Excellent. Please let me know if there is anything more I can do for you. I hope you enjoy your stay."

I nodded as I collected my things and headed toward the elevator. I pressed the button for the second floor as she had suggested, depositing my bags against a wall as I hurried to check out the breakfast offerings. Many items appeared to have already been depleted, but I was able to gather a reasonable array of treats from those that remained. I carried my plate to a table near a window and proceeded to dig in. The food on the plane had been sparse. Especially since I missed the breakfast offerings. A waiter appeared with a bottle of cold water, which he poured into an empty glass.

"Room number, please?"

"Um, let me think. I've just checked in." I pulled out my key card and searched for the number, but not finding one, I resorted to checking the receipt I had been given at the reception desk. "424." He quickly jotted down the number on a notepad.

"Welcome to the Hotel Central. Can I bring you anything else to drink? Perhaps a coffee?"

"Coffee would be great. With a little milk, please." He bowed slightly as he headed off in the direction of what I assumed was the kitchen, returning shortly with a small silver tray that held a cup of coffee and a small pitcher of milk. I speared another bite of food from my plate and held up my fork. "This is so good. What do you call it?"

"*Fourtalia*. It is like an omelette or an Italian frittata. This one is our specialty. It is made with eggplant, spinach, and tomatoes."

"Umm. It's delicious."

He smiled. "It is my favorite also." He pointed to another item I had selected. "Be sure to try the *Spanakopita*. Spinach and feta in filo pastry. A Greek tradition. Enjoy your breakfast." He turned to walk away, leaving me to continue filling my mouth and my stomach with the savory and sweet treats. When I had finished, I dug in my bag for a few euros and placed them on the table beside my empty plate. Even if it wasn't customary to tip in Greece, as the taxi driver had explained, I knew that any server anywhere in the world would likely be pleased by the gesture.

I collected my bags and took the elevator to the fourth floor, pausing outside the appointed room to wave my card in front of the door as the front desk attendant had instructed. I pushed open the door and stepped inside. The curtains were closed, causing the room to be dimly lit. I crossed the room to pull them aside and was immediately greeted by a view of the Acropolis on a hill just to the left. The open curtains revealed a balcony that fronted the view, and I pushed aside the sliding door and stepped outside.

"Wow. That's incredible!"

The view defied description. Not only was I treated to a full-scale image of the Parthenon, but there was also a panoramic view of the entire hillside and the city below.

I re-entered the room, leaving the door open behind me to allow the pleasantly cool air to circulate inside. I quickly scanned the room. It was decorated with simple but stylish furniture of a modern design. A clever use of mirrors along one wall gave the impression that the room was much larger than it was. A small desk was tucked into one corner with a flat screen television mounted on the wall above it. I strode across the room and opened another door that led to the bathroom. It contained a large marble-topped vanity along one wall with an enclosed shower stall at one end. A plush-looking terry cloth robe hung on the wall just outside the shower, and a selection of complementary toiletries was placed on a tray next to the sink. There was also a hair dryer mounted on the wall on the other side of the sink.

I turned from the bathroom door and looked around the room again. Its beige and gray tones gave it a clean and fresh appearance, and the double bed with its white spread and four plump pillows looked extremely inviting. I glanced at my watch and did a quick calculation, deciding I had enough time for a short nap before meeting Shelly. Just to be sure, I called down to the front desk and asked the receptionist for a wake-up call in an hour. That would give me enough time for a quick shower before meeting Shelly. I took off my clothes and slipped between the sheets, luxuriating in their cool softness. The last thing I remember before sleep overtook me was the image of the Acropolis reflected in the mirror in front of the bed. *I could get used to this,* I thought, as I turned and pressed my cheek into the fluffy softness of the pillow.

---

"Jesse! Jesse! Over here!"

I had just stepped outside the front doors of the hotel when I heard Shelly call my name. I scanned the sidewalk and spotted her standing in front of a building across the street. I waved and looked both ways before jogging across to join her.

"There you are. Did you rest well?" she asked.

"I did. My room is so nice, and it has a view of the Acropolis. How about you?"

She frowned slightly. "I'm afraid I didn't do as well. The hotel is nice enough. Welcoming and cute. But my room is tiny with a large bed that takes up much of the space. But it's good enough for the amount of time I'll be there, and apparently, there's a rooftop garden that serves food all day long, and a bar in the lobby. They offer a buffet breakfast each day, but unfortunately, it had stopped serving by the time I got checked in. There was a rather wordy gentleman in front of me who took too much time getting settled. Luckily, the nice lady behind reception offered me a box containing a few snacks to carry up to my room. I would have loved a cup of tea, though."

I glanced around at our surroundings. "Maybe we can find someplace nearby that serves tea."

She pulled a folded map out of her purse. "I picked this up in the hotel. It has a list of places of interest in the area, as well as shops and restaurants of various types." She unfurled the map and pointed at one spot. "This is where we are. If we walk in this direction," her finger moved to the left, "we'll be close to a pedestrian street called the *Peripatos* that's just below the Acropolis. There are supposed to be several cafes in that area."

"Shall we head there then?" I asked.

She looped her arm through mine. "Let's! I can't wait to explore the city."

We spent the next hour roaming around Plaka, occasionally stopping to browse in one of the many tourist shops that lined the streets. As the brochure had indicated, there were several restaurants where people were being served food that *looked* delicious and smelled even better. Eventually, we stopped at a small sidewalk café tucked away on one of the side streets overlooking some ancient ruins. We were scanning the posted menu when a waiter spotted us and showed us to a table. We had barely sat down before another young man appeared with a pitcher of water and a basket of bread.

"*Kalos erthate. Me lene Nikos.*"

Shelly and I looked at each other blankly before she shrugged at him with a smile. "Sorry. We don't speak much Greek."

He smiled. "No problem. I say welcome, my name is Nikos. This is menu with specials for today. Here you will find English." He turned the menu over with a flourish. "I bring something to drink first?"

My nap had revived me, so I decided to treat myself. "I would like a beer. What would you recommend?

"*Mythos.* Is good Greek beer." He turned to Shelly. "For you?"

"I don't suppose you have English tea?"

He gave her an apologetic look. "No, sorry. Perhaps a coffee?

Shelly sighed and held her hands up in an imitation of the cab driver's expression. "Why not? With cream and sugar, please."

"I suggest a *frappe*. Very nice when is warm like today."

"That sounds perfect. Thank you."

He nodded and walked away.

Shelly picked up the menu and began reading it while I tried to discreetly glance at the plates of the other diners seated nearby. There was a wide assortment of foods on display, but I was particularly intrigued by a table covered with several small plates being shared by the couple sitting there.

"Why don't we order some things and share them?" I asked.

Shelly put down her menu. "Great idea. We can ask the waiter to bring whatever he recommends."

When the server returned with our drinks, we requested his help in selecting an assortment of foods to share.

"*Mezedes.* Good choice. I bring most favorite ones."

While we waited for him to return, Shelly opened one of the brochures she had picked up during our walk. "It says here that Plaka is an old historical neighborhood clustered around the northern and eastern slopes of the Acropolis, full of narrow, cobblestone streets lined with tiny shops selling an assortment of jewelry, clothing, local ceramics, and a wide variety of souvenirs to take home." She laid down the brochure. "No kidding. This place is like a never-ending, open-air shopping mall."

I glanced at one of the stores to our left that had attracted a large cluster of people intent on purchasing one of the baseball caps or brimmed fedoras on display. I suspected their interest was in large part due to the sun that had been increasing in intensity as the day progressed. "I think I'd like to buy a hat before we set out again."

Her eyes followed my gaze. "Good idea. The receptionist at my hotel said it's supposed to be even hotter tomorrow. After that, let's go check out those ruins." She pointed across the sidewalk to a sunken area that appeared to be full of the remnants of buildings in various stages of deterioration.

I stood to get a better look. "Great idea." I sat back down and took a long sip of my beer. "Not bad. How's your coffee? What did he call it?"

"Frappe, I believe. It's actually quite good. Cool and refreshing, with just enough milk and sugar."

Just then, the server arrived with a large tray containing dishes of various sizes that he placed in the middle of our table.

"Here you have slices of fresh *aggouri*, Kalamata olives, *dolmades*, *tomates*, *keftedakia*, feta, and grilled halloumi tyri, *kolokithokeftedes*, and *tsatziki. Kalo orexi!*"

We stared at the assorted dishes in wonder. "I'm not sure what he said, but it all looks and smells delicious!" Shelly picked up her plate and began to fill it with the selections.

I followed her lead, spearing what I guessed was some type of meatball with my fork. "We can read the translation on the menu, but for now, I'm willing to let my taste buds tell me what I'm eating."

For several minutes, we munched on the various items, signaling our mutual delight with an assortment of groans and head nods. When I finally had my fill, or to be precise, MORE than my fill, I sat back in my chair with a contented sigh. "That was delicious! I had no idea Greek food was so good!"

Shelly finished chewing her last mouthful and folded her napkin, placing it sideways on her plate. "I can't eat another bite. Well, I COULD, but I'm determined not to."

The waiter returned and gestured to our mostly empty dishes. "You like the food?"

I patted my full stomach. "Everything was SO good."

He smiled as he began to collect our plates. "I bring something else? Perhaps a coffee?"

I glanced at Shelly, who shook her head. "No thanks. Just the check."

"Two or one?"

"One. My treat." I said.

Shelly started to protest, but I stopped her with a wave. "It's the least I can do. You rescued me at the airport from what would have likely been a *lost-in-translation* adventure, and kept me company while we explored this area. Treating you to lunch, or maybe this is considered an early dinner, is the least I can do."

"That's so kind of you, but the feeling is mutual. It's not much fun to be in a foreign city alone. I've had to do it a few times and, believe me, it is much more pleasant to share it with someone else."

The waiter returned with our bill and two small plates containing slices of bright red watermelon. "*Karpouzi.* Something refreshing to end meal."

Shelly and I both smiled our thanks and dug into the juicy fruit, our fullness suddenly dissipating in anticipation of its cold sweetness. It was delicious, as anticipated, and we finished every bite.

We spent the rest of the afternoon roaming around Plaka after first stopping at the kiosk we spotted earlier in order to purchase lovely fedoras. Shelly chose one in creamy white with a black band, and my selection was a golden tan with a white band. We promptly plopped them on our heads and nodded at our images reflected in the window of a nearby shop.

"We look properly spiffy!" She remarked.

I grinned. "If that means that we look pretty darn good, I agree!"

We spent the next half hour or so wandering among the ruins we had spotted across from our restaurant, before heading out to explore more of the area. At one point, we came across the pedestrian street Shelly had mentioned. Its name, *Dionisiou Aropagitou,* was posted on a stone wall at the beginning. It was an interesting street. Dotted with a good number of shops and restaurants, but also bordering what appeared to be a residential area with apartment buildings scattered along one stretch.

A big draw to the area, which is likely why there were large crowds of pedestrians all up and down the street, was its location just below the Acropolis. At one point, we stopped near an entrance to the famous hill and gazed upward at the route that would lead to the Parthenon itself. The pathway up to the top looked daunting, to say the least, and we hesitated before venturing farther.

"What do you think?" I asked.

She lifted her shoulders. "It's something we simply MUST do, but perhaps tomorrow? I'm afraid my full stomach and jet lag have caught up with me."

"I agree. Let's plan to meet up again in the morning before it gets too hot."

We sauntered back the way we came, enjoying the view of ancient buildings and an assortment of businesses clearly designed to capitalize on the tourist trade that filled the avenue. I looked with particular interest at the numerous rooftop restaurants that all appeared to offer an equally impressive view of the Acropolis and the surrounding area.

Eventually, we found our way back to where we had first started the day and looked with some relief at the sight of our hotels.

"What a wonderful day!" Shelly leaned to pull me in for a hug. "I couldn't have asked for a more congenial companion."

I returned her hug, finding myself suddenly feeling a bit shy, which wasn't really like me. Most of the time, I was open to meeting new people and making new friends at the drop of a hat. A teacher characteristic, I imagine. But with Shelly, I found myself in awe of what a special person she was, and I hoped our blossoming friendship could continue growing. That is, if we could find a way to stay in touch. "It was a lot of fun exploring the area with you. Thank you so much for suggesting it."

"If you were serious about getting an early start tomorrow, I could meet you at your hotel at, say, half past nine?"

"That sounds perfect. See you tomorrow."

She headed toward the door to her hotel as I turned to enter mine.

When I stepped into the lobby, the receptionist waved me over. "You had a telephone call, and I have written down the message for you." She handed me a folded piece of paper.

I thanked her and walked over to a chair and sat down before opening the note. It contained a message from my cousin, Matt, welcoming me to Athens and informing me that he would be returning the next evening and would get in touch with me the following morning.

The message left me both pleased and nervous. It had been a long time since we had seen each other, and I hoped our reunion would be pleasant, but I wondered what he would say when he called. Would he invite me to stay with him, or suggest another arrangement? I hadn't made any plans yet for the rest of my stay in Greece, thinking that I would just *play it by ear* once I spoke with him. That was probably a very foolish thing to do given my unfamiliarity with the country and my limited resources. However, I had read there were some inexpensive ways to visit a few of the Greek islands, which sounded like an exciting possibility.

All of the uncertainties about the remainder of my stay were daunting, to say the least, and since I had no way to resolve them until we had spoken, I decided to try and put my mind at rest, at least for the night. Right now, there was a very comfortable bed waiting for me that I intended to put to good use!

# three

I woke up the next morning feeling somewhat refreshed despite the long trip and little sleep of the past two days. I stretched my arms overhead and squinted at my watch. 8 a.m. That meant I had slept at least ... eleven hours! *Could that be right?* I had never been what you would call a sound sleeper, but I guess the combination of a long flight, the large lunch/dinner I had consumed, and several hours of walking had helped.

I swung my legs over the side of the bed and stood, walking to the window so I could pull aside the curtains. I gazed out and was greeted by the same vision I had gone to sleep with—the Acropolis, in all its shining glory!

I was looking forward to getting a closer look at it later that morning, and I smiled in anticipation. But first, a shower was in order, and then I wanted to get downstairs in time to take advantage of the free breakfast buffet before the selections were as limited as they had been when I arrived.

When I stepped off the elevator on the second floor, I was greeted by the same waiter who had served me the day before.

"Room 424. Yes?"

"Right!" I looked at him appreciatively.

"I am Yanni. Today we have a special treat. Homemade *loukoumades*. They are like the doughnut you have in America, only just the middle. I will bring you some fresh from the oven if you like."

"I'd like that very much. And a coffee, please."

"Americano or Greek? Or perhaps espresso?"

I hesitated before answering. I hadn't tried a Greek coffee yet, and I was a little intimidated by how to drink it. I had heard it was strong and bitter, with a pile of what could only be described as *brown sludge* on the bottom of the cup. "I guess I'll try a Greek coffee. With milk and sugar."

"It is most usual to drink without milk, but I will bring some for you."

He walked away, leaving me to choose a place to sit before helping myself to the breakfast offerings. I returned to the table to find a small cup of coffee and a plate of doughnut holes, at least that's how I thought of them. The round part that would have been in the middle of the doughnut had it not been cut out. I picked one up and took a bite, closing my eyes in enjoyment at the warm sweetness. They were soft in the middle with a slightly crispy outside that had been drizzled with honey. *Delicious* was the only way to describe them. I sat before lifting my coffee to take a sip. The first taste made my lips pucker, and I quickly added a little milk before trying it again. *Better.* I added a little more sugar and sipped again. *Not bad.* Not good, really, but different. And different was, after all, what I was looking for from this trip. Not necessarily *out with the old and in with the new,* but I was eager to try new things and broaden my scope of the world.

I occupied the next several minutes sampling the other breakfast treats I had selected before taking another sip of the coffee. Sure enough, I found myself looking down into a pile of the *sludge* I had read about.

"My *yiayia*—grandmother—can tell your fortune by looking in your cup." I looked up to see Yanni leaning over my cup. He reached down and lifted it, turning it upside down on the small saucer that accompanied it, rotating it three times before turning it right side up again. "She looks at the images in the cup to see what is in your future."

I peered down at the cup. "All I see is a mess. Can you see anything there?"

He shook his head. "I do not have her gift." He reached into his back pants pocket and pulled out a cell phone, raising it to take a photo of the sludgy smear inside the cup. "I will show it to her. Perhaps tomorrow I can tell you what she sees? It may be difficult for her to read because of the milk, but I will try."

"That would be great. Tomorrow's my last full day here, so I'll be sure to come down in time for breakfast."

After returning to my room to freshen up and grab my hat and sunglasses, I headed down to the lobby to wait for Shelly. I sat down on one of the couches and leafed through a magazine I picked up from a nearby table. Greek was printed on one side of each page with the English translation on the other. I had just finished an article about the relatively new Acropolis Museum when I heard my name.

"Sorry I'm a few minutes late. I slept so well last night that I had a hard time getting up." She looked over my shoulder at the magazine. "That looks interesting. I spotted that museum while we were exploring yesterday. Perhaps we should head there first thing or, better yet, wait until the sun gets too hot to be outdoors."

"Apparently, it has a nice café where you can eat and look at the Acropolis. That seems to be a standard thing in this area: eating with a view."

She nodded. "I took in the view from my hotel's roof last evening. It was such a lovely treat." She pulled on her hat and tugged it firmly against her head. "Shall we?"

This time, we headed out in the opposite direction from the previous day, which took us to an area called Monastiraki, replete with numerous rooftop bars and an ancient Byzantine Church. From there, we wandered past the ruins of a Roman *agora*, or meeting place, eventually finding our way to the top of Areopagus Hill. The climb wasn't long, rising only a hundred meters or so in height. But it required us to mount numerous stone steps. When we finally reached the top, we sat down on a stone bench and quickly downed two of the four bottles of cold water we had purchased at a kiosk at the start of our hike.

I allowed my eyes to scan the 360-degree view from the top of the hill. "It's absolutely breathtaking."

Shelly nodded her agreement. "Even better than I imagined." She stood and pointed to the right before turning slowly in a circular motion as she indicated what could be seen beyond our vantage point. "There's the Acropolis, Lycabettus Hill, the agora we passed on our way here, and, over there, the Athenian coast.

She sat back down before continuing. "Where we are now—Areopagus—is also known as Ares Hill. It was named after Ares, the god of war. St. Paul was supposed to have preached up here. And after the battle of Marathon, a messenger from Athens ran all the way from Marathon to Athens, where he announced victory against the Persians from the top of this hill before keeling over and dying. I guess the run was a bit much for him."

We sat in silence for a while, sipping on more water and fanning ourselves with our hats. Finally, Shelly pointed to the southeast. "There's the Parthenon and the Theater of Dionysus. Just below that should be the Acropolis Museum. Shall we venture up to the Parthenon now before it gets any hotter? Afterward, we can stop by Dionysus and then go to the museum."

I looked back down at the view and the Parthenon perched on the opposite hill. *So close, yet so far away,* I thought. I stood up and tucked the rest of the water in my backpack. "Sounds like a plan. I'm ready."

The walk from Areopagus to Acropolis was relatively short, allowing us to reach the ticket office in less than fifteen minutes. Unfortunately, there was a long line of people in front of us waiting to buy admission.

Shelly studied her map and then grabbed my wrist and pulled me in the opposite direction of the queue. "Follow me. I read about another entrance near the museum that is usually not as busy, so I used a computer in the hotel lobby this morning to purchase two tickets for us."

I looked at her appreciatively. "What a great idea!"

We hurried to the side entrance, passing the Dionysus Theater along the way, and joined a considerably shorter line waiting to pick up their pre-purchased tickets. Once we had them in hand, we followed the directions printed on the back of a flyer we were given to make our way in the direction of the Parthenon.

Getting to the actual Parthenon took much longer than either of us had anticipated, since there was so much to see along the way. We first visited several of the sites described on the flyer, including the Temple of Athena Nike and the Erechtheion, also known as the Temple of Athena Polias.

My only familiarity with the name *Nike* was associated with the sneakers of the same name, which would have been a welcome addition to my wardrobe for this hilly outing instead of the sandals I had chosen to wear. In this case, I read that the name referred to the goddess of victory in Greek mythology, worshipped in hopes of successful outcomes in war. The Erechtheion was dedicated to both Athena, the goddess of wisdom, and Poseidon, the god of the sea. All in all, we were in very good company!

As Shelly and I continued to make our way up the southwest slope of the Acropolis, we came across a large, open-air theater full of stone seats known as the Odeon of Herodes Atticus. Shelly and I climbed to the top seats where we gaped in awe at the semi-circular structure.

"Can you imagine what it looked like originally? Apparently, it was able to hold at least 5,000 people who came to attend political rallies." Shelly glanced down at her brochure. "It says here it used to have a three-story stone wall along the front, and a wooden roof."

I looked at the open area that now made up the entirety of the structure. "What happened to it?" I asked.

"It was destroyed by invaders in 267 AD. Since then, it has been used to host open-air concerts and theater productions."

"Cool. Can you imagine attending a concert here? I bet the acoustics are fantastic."

When we left the Odeon, we backtracked to the Parthenon, stopping just below the steps to gape in awe at the sight of the magnificent, but crumbling, marble temple that had also been built to honor Athena. *The lady sure made an impression on the ancient Greeks.* I smiled at the thought.

I nudged Shelly and pointed to the row of columns that stretched across the front and sides of the Parthenon. "Do you see how the columns get smaller in diameter from the bottom to the top? I first noticed that on the replica we have in Nashville. I thought it was just a fluke when I saw it there, but, apparently, it's a true representation of the original. The inside of this Parthenon is bare. In fact, you can see all the way through it. That's quite a bit different from the Nashville Parthenon, which is enclosed by stone walls and features a huge, floor-to-ceiling statue of Athena on the main level that fills up a lot of the inside space. The statue is painted gold, and there are several stone sculptures lining the nearby walls."

Shelly placed her hands on her hips and leaned back as she gazed upward at the structure. "I believe originally there was a similar statue of Athena here and quite a large number of the stone sculptures you're referring to. That was, of course, before the building sustained massive damage." She paused for a moment. "I'm hesitant to bring it up, but I suppose you know what happened to most of the sculptures that were inside?"

I shook my head in confusion.

"Lord Elgin sold them to the British Museum in London in the early 1800s. That was after a large number were destroyed by the Venetians, who were fighting with the Turks for possession of the Parthenon. Apparently, there are some sculptures that ended up in Paris and other places, and several are also right here in the Acropolis Museum. The Greeks have never forgiven the British for keeping the ones they bought."

"I can see why. No offense, but that hardly seems fair."

"No offense taken. In fact, I find it rather embarrassing to be associated with a country that wouldn't step up and do the right thing."

We spent several more minutes walking around the outside of the Parthenon before venturing down the hill to the Theater of Dionysus. It was built into a natural hollow on the southern slope of the Acropolis, and, as Shelly informed me from one of her ever-present brochures, was reported to have been the first theater in the world. We had both grown quite tired by the time we arrived there, but since admission was included in the cost of visiting the Acropolis, we felt we should at least stop for a look.

In a similar way to Herodes Atticus, Dionysus was a semi-circular structure with stone seats built into a hillside. Originally, it was said to be much larger than Herodes, capable of holding over 17,000 people in its prime. Now, it appeared much smaller in comparison.

We paused at the top of the theater and gazed at its surroundings.

Shelly checked the brochure and read out loud. "The Theater of Dionysus was the very first theater in the world, dedicated to Dionysus, who was the god of wine making and ecstasy." She wiggled her eyebrows. "Can't go wrong with THAT combination!"

I laughed. "It certainly is impressive. I can't imagine attending an event that would have been able to fill the original space completely. Do they still have productions here now?" I asked.

"Not as many as at Herodes Atticus." She pointed toward the front. "Isn't that interesting? There are several marble chairs up there with back supports. I suppose they were used by the highest-ranking attendees."

"Sort of the VIP section." I chuckled.

"You're quite right!"

We sat in silent awe of our surroundings for a few more minutes until my stomach let loose an embarrassingly loud noise.

"Oh! I'm so sorry!" I covered my face in embarrassment.

"Don't be. That gives me an excuse to suggest we head to the museum. It may not have been as insistent, but my stomach has been talking to me for the past hour! Plus, I'm feeling rather knackered. Something to eat and a respite from walking sounds like just the ticket."

By the time we reached the museum, which, luckily, was only a few minutes away, I was practically dragging my feet from exhaustion. We entered the air-conditioned building, which perked me up considerably, and found our way to the café. A waitress greeted us as we entered, and showed us to a table with a view of the surrounding neighborhood and the Acropolis. She laid two menus on the table and indicated she would return with some cold water.

We studied the menus and, upon her return, ordered two glasses of white wine and a large Greek salad. The wine arrived first. It was smooth and sweet and refreshingly chilled. Our salad arrived next in a large bowl containing a generous amount of ripe tomato wedges, crisp cucumbers, plump Kalamata olives, a little green pepper and onion, with a thick slice of oregano-sprinkled Feta perched on top. I dished some onto my plate before tearing off a chunk of bread from the basket the waitress had also brought, dipping it into the juices on the bottom of the salad bowl.

"Umm. How can something so simple taste so incredibly delicious?" I asked.

The waitress returned with a plate containing little meatballs, called *keftedhes* in Greek, and a generous portion of fried potatoes. I added some of each to my plate before trying one of the potatoes.

"These fries are great." I forked another couple and shoved them in my mouth.

Shelly nodded. "They call them *tiganites patates,* which means fried potatoes. Of course, in England we call them chips."

I shrugged and speared another few, along with a chunk of meatball. "Reminds me of the lyrics of that old song ... *'You say potato and I say potahto.'* Whatever you call them, they're delicious! And I don't miss the ketchup I would usually squirt on them in the least."

"Try a little squeeze of lemon. I saw someone at another table doing that, and it's really quite good."

I picked up a hunk of the lemon surrounding the edge of the plate and spritzed some over a couple of fries, tasting one before adding a more generous amount. "Um. It's not something I would ever think of adding, but I have to admit it works."

We continued to munch our way through the offerings while enjoying the view outside the wall-to-wall windows, and chuckling as we overheard the people at the tables around us attempting to pronounce the Greek words on the menu. Eventually, Shelly pushed her plate away and scooted her chair back from the table. "I'm going to find the loo."

I nodded at her retreating back, snagging a few more potatoes before tossing my napkin onto my plate.

"Can I bring either of you anything else? Perhaps a coffee?"

I looked up at the smiling face of our waitress and shook my head. "Not for me, but do you have English tea by chance? I'm sure my friend would love one of those."

"Yes, we have Earl Grey tea. I'll bring some right away." She began to gather up the assorted dishes and walked away just as Shelly was returning.

I looked at her with a smile. "Good news. They have English tea. I asked the waitress to bring you some."

Her eyebrows rose in surprise. "Really? I'm pleasantly surprised. But I guess I shouldn't be. I'm sure they have a lot of international visitors to the museum."

I nodded. "By the sound of things, I think that's true. I believe I'll also visit the toilet." I rose to leave.

"It's back there. Just outside the door we entered and to the left."

I made my way in the direction she indicated, glancing to either side as I walked. There was an interesting array of sweets displayed in a counter to the right of the exit, making me regret my full stomach. A gift shop was located just outside the exit, and I reminded myself to stop in to have a look before we left.

When I returned, I was surprised to find Shelly talking to a man standing next to our table. She waved as she spotted me.

"Jesse! I'm glad you're back. I want you to meet someone."

I watched the man standing there as I approached the table. He appeared to be in his late twenties or early thirties with light brown hair that hung over his forehead and dark brown eyes that peered back at me curiously. He was taller than me, which wasn't saying much given that I was only 5 feet 5 inches in flat feet, but I guessed that he exceeded my height by another half foot. I looked away from him as I approached, aware that his intense yet friendly look had not wavered.

"Jesse Holloway, meet William Harris. He heard us talking earlier and picked up on my accent. It turns out, he's originally from Reading, which is a town near my family home in Maidenhead. Both are in Berkshire, which is just outside London. William, Jesse is from the States. California, most recently, but she lived in Tennessee before that. Nashville, I believe?" She looked at me questioningly.

I hesitated before answering. I was finding it hard to break free of the gaze of the man standing in front of me, which made me feel both nervous and embarrassed. Finally, I swallowed and nodded. "I grew up in Nashville, but I spent several years living in Knoxville, which is in East Tennessee. I moved to California to go to college and have been working there as a teacher for the past few years."

"And what is it you teach, Ms. Holloway?" He smiled in a way that was both encouraging and teasing, leading me to guess he had picked up on my nervousness.

"History. Although archaeology is my passion. I hope to return to grad school someday to continue my studies. Once I pay off my student loans, that is." *TMI, Holloway. No need to tell this stranger your life story!*

"A fine plan. I have an uncle who is an archaeologist. As he has put it more than once, *it's a grand occupation if you don't mind dirt and sweat,* which has never seemed to bother him. He's working on a dig in Greece now, which has brought me to this fair land."

Shelly spoke up. "William, or *Wills* as he has indicated he prefers to be called, arrived in Greece a fortnight ago. He has been apprising me of some of the key sites in this area, although I told him that, unfortunately, I'll be heading out to Rome tomorrow. Since you'll be staying on a while, perhaps the two of you would like to chat about some of his discoveries." She looked at me with a slight smile.

His gaze returned to me. "I'm staying at a hotel near Syntagma Square. My uncle is presently in Santorini, but he'll be returning in a few days, and I'll join him then. In the meantime, I'm available if you would be interested in taking a bit of an excursion." His raised eyebrows suggested he was waiting for my reply.

I hesitated before responding. His idea was intriguing, but at the same time, I felt uncomfortable committing to seeing him again on my own. "I'm checking out of my hotel tomorrow, too. At least, I think I am. I have a cousin who lives in Athens. He's returning tonight and indicated he would phone me tomorrow morning. I have no idea what I'll be doing after that."

Wills nodded and took his cell phone out of his pocket. "If you don't mind, I'll just send you my contact info. That way, if you find yourself free, you can message me." He held his phone out so I could type my name and number into it.

I entered my information and handed the phone back to him.

He returned it to his pocket, swiping the hair back that had fallen over his forehead as he leaned toward me. "Well then, I'll be off. Shelly, it was a pleasure to meet someone from the homeland in such an unexpected place. I hope the remainder of your travels are delightful."

"Thank you, Wills. And I wish the same for you."

"Jesse." He tipped his imaginary hat and sauntered away in the direction of the exit door. Shelly looked at me with a smirk.

"He's a bit cheeky, I admit. But he seems like an affable chap. And quite nice looking. Do you fancy seeing him again?"

I frowned at her question, uncertain how to respond. "Maybe. He seems nice enough. But then again, I don't know him. I'll just wait and see after I talk to my cousin. Everything's up in the air for me until then."

"Of course." She stood and placed her hands on her hips, stretching her back from side to side. "Time to get a move on. I want to have a good look at the museum, and then I'm afraid I need to pack."

I took a final sip of water and stood, as well. "Sounds good to me but, if you don't mind, I'd like to stop in the gift shop before we head upstairs. I really should pick up a few things to take to friends back in the States, and maybe something for my cousin."

"Good idea. Perhaps I can find something for my friend in Rome, as well."

The next morning, I was awakened early to the unexpected sound of rain splattering on my balcony. I pulled open the shades and stuck my head out to peer down at the street below. Rain in June must not be very common, given the frantic, rain-avoiding behavior of the locals dashing about.

I stepped back inside, leaving the balcony door partly open to allow a faint breeze to enter the room. The smell of rain was pleasant. And the mingled scent of some sort of flower enhanced its appeal. *Honeysuckle?* I tucked that thought away until I could ask someone who might know the answer.

I entered the breakfast area a short while later, which seemed more crowded than usual. I was scanning the room in an attempt to locate a place to sit when I felt someone tap me on the shoulder. I turned to find my waiter from the previous two days standing there.

"I have a table for you. Please follow me." He proceeded to lead me to a small table in the corner at the far end of the room. "We are busy today because of the weather. I will bring your coffee in a moment." He bowed slightly before leaving.

I sat down at the table and glanced around the room. There was a fairly long line gathering at the buffet table, causing me to get up as quickly as I had sat down in order to join the line. After making my selections, I returned to my seat to find Yanni standing nearby. He turned to look at me as I approached.

"My yiayia—grandmother—is here with me today. I told her about your desire to have your coffee read, and she wishes to see it directly. She is waiting in the kitchen. I will bring her out when you finish your breakfast, if that is okay."

"Oh! How nice of her to come. Yes. That will be fine." He nodded and walked away with a slight smile. I glanced down at my coffee cup, noticing it was the same small serving of Greek coffee I had tried the day before. I decided not to add milk and sugar to it in case that would throw off his grandmother's ability to read the cup. I sipped it carefully, grimacing slightly at the bitterness before pushing it aside. I set about sampling the breakfast offerings, which, as before, contained a generous assortment of sweet and savory treats. I had just finished my last bite of feta with a bit of tomato when Yanni reappeared.

"Would you like anything else this morning?" He asked.

I shook my head. "It was delicious as usual."

"*Endaxi.* I will take these out of your way." He made a stack of my plates and silverware. "I'll bring my yiayia now. Perhaps you will finish your coffee." He nodded at my half-full cup.

I lifted the cup and took two more sips before placing it back on the saucer. I wasn't sure if I was supposed to follow the ritual he demonstrated the morning before, of placing it upside down and turning it three times, but I decided to wait for his grandmother. I could feel my heartbeat increasing as I stared at the cup. *Must be the caffeine,* I thought. Which was at least partly true.

I looked up as I heard a sound. Yanni was pulling out the chair opposite me. "This is my yiayia, Kiria Makris. I have told her of your interest in having your cup read. She speaks no English, but that is okay. I will stay until she finishes."

I eyed the elderly woman sitting across from me. She had grey hair that hung loosely around her face, stopping at ear level. She wore no makeup, but her face appeared surprisingly unlined. She smiled at me slightly before reaching to pull my cup close to her, repeating the ritual I had first witnessed performed by Yanni.

She turned the cup three times clockwise while spilling out the sludge and allowing it to spread around the entire inner surface. She then poured the excess out from the handle side before overturning the cup onto a napkin. After a few minutes, she turned the cup right side up again and then peered down into the grounds before releasing what could only be described as an exclamation of delight. Yanni spoke to her in Greek, to which she replied with a string of sentences, pointing at various places in the cup as she spoke. Finally, Yanni nodded and looked up at me.

"My yiayia says there is much to see in your cup." He spoke a few words to his grandmother before pointing inside the bottom of the cup. "Here, there is a boat, which means a trip. But it is surrounded by waves suggesting uncertainty." He looked at the old woman for further explanation, and after she replied, he continued, "There is a door, meaning something unexpected. And since it is near the handle, that means the love life." The old woman spoke again, causing Yanni to nod. "Yiayia says there are other images that mean friendship and big change." He paused and looked at his grandmother to see if there was more, but she shrugged and bent her right arm, rotating her hand in a clockwise motion. "That is all she sees."

I struggled to understand what he had told me. "Uncertain travel. That could definitely describe this trip I'm on. But the rest—unexpected love, friendship, and big change—that could mean pretty much anything."

"I understand. The things that can be seen in the cup are not always easy to explain. *Merikes fores.* Sometimes, becomes clear quickly. Sometimes, much longer."

I frowned at his attempted explanation. "But are they ALWAYS right? I mean, have you ever known your grandmother to make a mistake in what she THINKS she sees?"

"Perhaps a little. But when that is so, it is because the person has chosen a way that is in conflict with their heart."

*Well, that's about as clear as mud, or SLUDGE, to be precise.* I smiled slightly and then took a deep breath to try and shake the annoyance from my mind.

"Well, please thank your grandmother for me. Actually," I started to reach into the small purse that I used to carry essentials, but Yanni quickly raised his hand, causing me to look up at him.

He raised his eyebrows and tilted his head backward before

saying *Ohee*. "No. Please. To offer money would offend my grandmother."

I pulled my hand back quickly. "I'm so sorry. The American way, I guess. We always think a tip can fix anything."

"I understand. In Greece, we feel the same about coffee. Or, ouzo." He smiled at his grandmother, who must have understood something about our exchange because she covered her mouth as she suppressed a giggle.

"Well, again, please tell her I really appreciate her time, and I hope her predictions are correct. At least, I THINK I want them to be correct. Honestly, I don't know WHAT to make of it all."

"*Katalaveno*. I understand. I find it best to write down her predictions and then forget about them. If they come true, it will matter then what was said. If not ..." He shrugged and held up his hands in the exact way that the taxi driver had, which I took to mean the Greek equivalent of *what will be, will be*.

"Sounds like good advice." I pushed back my chair and stood, directing a smile and nod of my head to his grandmother. She looked at me warmly and then surprised me by taking my hands in a firm grip.

"*Akolouthise tin kardia sou, koritsi mou.*"

I glanced at Yanni for an explanation. "She say to follow your heart, my girl. That means she likes you."

I could feel heat penetrating my hands and radiating up my arms as the old woman held me in a firm grasp. The feeling was not unpleasant, but it caused my heart to race even more fervently than before. I took a deep breath, giving her hands a quick squeeze before turning to leave. *What an odd encounter*, I thought. Not unpleasant. But, certainly unexpected and a little disconcerting. Just before I left the room, I looked back over my shoulder and was surprised to find the two still gazing in my direction. I gave a little wave before hurrying to the elevator.

When I reached my room, I sat down on the edge of the bed and took several deep breaths to try and calm my racing heart. *She said to listen to my heart. Well, right now the only thing my heart seems to be saying is that it's all shook up.* The old song by Elvis of the same name started running through my mind, and I shook my head to try and quiet it. I picked up a notepad and pen sitting on the bedside table and jotted down the things Yanni had told me his grandmother had said. *A trip. Unexpected love. Friendship and big change. And to follow my heart.* The last item on the list caused me to pause as if I was trying to remember something. Nothing came to mind, so I glanced at the list and then tore the page off the pad before placing it inside my purse. I took a deep breath and let it out slowly. "Come on, Jesse. Don't let a bunch of hocus pocus silliness get to you." At that moment, the room phone began to ring, causing me to jump in surprise. I lifted the receiver from where it sat on the bedside table.

"Hello?"

"Hello, Ms. Holloway. I have a Matt Temple on the phone for you. Would you like to take his call?"

I had forgotten my cousin said he would call me this morning. "Yes, please. And thank you."

I waited for her to transfer the call, anxious to hear from him, but a little nervous, as well. There was a click on the line.

"Jesse? It's Matt. How are you?"

"Matt! It's good to hear from you. How are you doing?"

There was a pause on the line before he answered. "Uh, that's what I just asked you. Did I wake you up?"

I grimaced as I realized how flustered I must sound to him. "No, no. I just came back from breakfast and, frankly, I forgot you were going to call. I'm sorry. I guess I'm still trying to adjust to a new time zone, although I've been sleeping pretty well."

"I'm glad to hear it. Listen. I have to get to a meeting soon, but I wondered if you have any plans later today? The rain is supposed to stop shortly. We could meet for a late lunch or early dinner."

"That sounds good, but I need to check out of my hotel and get situated somewhere else."

"I'm so sorry! I meant to tell you. You can stay with me. At least until you figure out the rest of your plans. My place is not very big, but I have a comfortable sofa that I can use, which would free the bedroom for you."

"Oh, no. That's very thoughtful of you, but there's no way I could put you out like that. Maybe you could suggest an inexpensive place for me to rent near you?"

"No, really, it's no trouble. I should have mentioned it to you when you first said you were coming to Greece. I've just been a little distracted with work things lately. Please. I would like for you to stay with me. It will give us a chance to catch up."

I hesitated before answering. "Well, if you're sure it won't be too much of a bother. But I'll only agree to it if you let me sleep on the sofa. There's no way I'm going to put you out of your bedroom."

He chuckled. "Why don't we wait until you see my place, and then we can decide. What time do you have to check out of the hotel?"

"I believe check-out is at eleven, but I'm sure I could get them to store my things until you want to meet up. I wouldn't mind having a little more time to explore the area around the hotel."

"Great. Why don't I swing by to pick you up at one o'clock? That way, we can come back to my apartment first and get you settled, and then go somewhere nearby to eat."

I glanced at my watch. "One o'clock sounds good. Call me when you're close by so I can come out front to meet you. I've noticed that parking seems to be nearly impossible around here."

"That's pretty typical for Greece. Narrow streets and too many cars. I'll text you when I'm on my way. And Jesse? I really am looking forward to seeing you again."

"Me too, Cuz."

His parting words made me smile, and I hung up feeling reassured that our reunion just might work out.

Since it was a little after 9 a.m., I decided to get my things together and then spend an hour or so roaming around Plaka before returning to shower and wait for Matt to arrive. I took a little time organizing my things, which didn't take very long given how sparsely I had packed, and then headed down to the lobby. As I passed by the front desk, I decided to stop and inquire about storing my suitcase after checking out. The same friendly young lady was working at the reception desk, and she surprised me by offering a late check-out time of 1 p.m., again at no extra charge. That meant I didn't need to come back to the hotel before 12:30 in order to have time to change and turn in my key card.

I headed out the front door with a smile on my face and a spring in my step. It's funny how the smallest things, like the invitation from my cousin to stay with him, and an unexpected courtesy by the hotel receptionist, could turn my mood around so quickly. I paused on the street in front of the hotel. The rain had stopped, as Matt had predicted, and aside from a few puddles here and there, the day appeared to be shaping up nicely. I considered which way to head, finally deciding to return to Plaka to an area called the Flea Market. Shelly and I had gone there briefly on our first day, but there was a lot more to explore, and I still hadn't managed to find a gift for Matt or my friends back home. The items for sale in the museum gift shop had been lovely, but priced too high for my budget.

I made my way to Monastiraki before heading across a wide area paved with stone tiles to an entrance marked by a sign announcing *The Flea Market*. I walked under the sign and entered a maze of pedestrian streets filled with a huge number of shops that carried an array of items for sale. Everywhere I looked were things that captured my attention: clothes, books, street food, jewelry, and souvenirs. In one area, there was also an impressive assortment of both antique and modern household items similar to what could be found in flea markets, or yard sales, as we sometimes called them, in the U.S.

I stopped at one booth that had several racks out front holding items similar to the one I had seen hanging from the rear-view mirror of the taxi we took from the airport. I fingered the colorful strings of beads, intrigued by their appearance. They reminded me a little of the rosary beads we had used in Catholic church services when I was growing up. Except in this case, the beads were much larger with a tasseled end instead of a cross.

"These are *Komboloi,* or worry beads. Would you like to hold them?"

I glanced over my right shoulder at the young man who had addressed me.

"What are they for?"

He lifted one off the rack and held it in his hand, rotating his wrist in a circle so that the beads flipped over the top of his hand before making a loud click as they came in contact with the ones he was holding in his palm. "They are used to reduce stress, or just to pass the time. You will see them in Greece, carried mainly by men." He smiled. "Perhaps to help lower their worries over women." He held out his hand to offer them to me.

"Maybe I shouldn't hold them. That is, if only men use them."

He shrugged. "It is customary for men, but there is no reason for a woman not to hold them."

I took the beads from his hand and felt their smooth roundness before allowing them to sway gently from side to side. I glanced back at the rack and was particularly attracted by a pair with turquoise beads on a black string. I lifted it from the rack and held it out. "I'd like to buy this, please."

He nodded and took the beads from me. "Follow me and I will wrap them for you."

We entered his shop, where he disappeared behind a check-out counter and proceeded to lay the beads on a piece of paper before placing them inside a plastic bag. He handed the bag to me and announced the charge as five euros. I dug into my purse and pulled out a five-euro note, which I laid on a plastic tray that sat on the counter in front of him. I had noticed during my shopping adventures of the previous couple of days that in Greece, it was customary to place payment for purchased items on a tray at the check-out area rather than hand it to the shopkeeper. Likewise, change given to the customer was laid on the same tray.

I thanked the salesman and turned to leave, but was stopped in my tracks by the sight of another item that was also reminiscent of the taxi ride.

"What is that?" I pointed to the item in question, which was a round piece of glass that contained four concentric circles of bright blue, white, and light blue surrounding a black dot.

"Ah, that is the evil eye. It is believed to have the power to keep away evil wishes or curses that may have been placed upon a person. We call this curse *Matiasma*. You may receive it if someone looks at you with jealousy, but also if they give you a compliment."

"Does it work?"

"My yiayia believes so. Me, I don't know. But I carry one just in case." He reached into his pocket and pulled out a keychain that contained a similar symbol to the one that had caught my attention.

The worry beads would make a nice gift for Matt, but these evil eye key chains were small enough to take back to my friends. "How much are they?"

"Two euros each. But I make you a special offer of 6 for ten euros."

"Deal." I pulled out a ten-euro note and started to hand it to him before realizing my mistake and returned to the check-out counter, where I placed it on the tray again. He wrapped the key chains in paper and placed a piece of tape around them.

"Would you like a second bag?"

"No, thank you." He handed the bundle to me, which I slipped into the bag with the worry beads.

"*Kali tihee*. Good luck."

"Thank you. How do you say that in Greek?"

"*Efharisto.*"

"Well then, efharisto." I wiggled my fingers at him as I turned to leave.

"This place is crazy! How do you manage to drive here without scraping all the paint off your car?" I clutched the edge of my seat as Matt inched his way down a street lined with cars parked on both sides and two-way traffic in a space barely wide enough for one car to safely pass through.

"Ha! Believe me, it wasn't easy to get used to. I get the feeling the Greeks weren't expecting to have to accommodate so many cars when they planned the street patterns here. You should see it when a truck comes along. Or a bus! I've had to back up a couple of blocks at times just to avoid a head-on collision."

I gripped the door handle as we squeezed past another oncoming car that seemed intent on forcing us from the road. "How far are we from your place?"

Matt glanced over at me with a smile. "About twenty more minutes. It's not very far, but as you can see, the traffic makes it take more time. I live in an area called *Kypseli*. It's a pretty cool neighborhood. Very walkable, with an interesting combination of old buildings and newer developments. Many years ago, it attracted a lot of the "so-called" upper-class. Unfortunately, as many of them moved away from the city, either to one of the islands or somewhere along the coast, they listed their places for rent, which led to the area becoming overpopulated. Many of the rentals became home to a large number of illegal immigrants who often rented under the guise of only one or two people planning occupancy when, in fact, the residences became inhabited by a half dozen or more."

"The area started to deteriorate after that, but fortunately, in recent years, it has again become one of the most vibrant parts of Athens, with a very diverse population, including a lot of folks involved in the arts. I was lucky to find an affordable apartment there, mainly because one of the guys who used to work at my office decided to move back to New York just before I arrived. The office manager got in touch with me before I moved here and arranged for me to take over the lease."

I looked out the window as he drove. The area we were passing through seemed much more congested than what I had seen during my daily walks. There was a vibrancy about the city, but it also struck me that it could use a good cleaning to spruce up the graffiti-covered walls and dirty sidewalks. I also noticed quite a few dog walkers, some of whom seemed to have no problem allowing their pets to leave their droppings wherever they chose to stop, with nary a poop bag in sight!

This was so in contrast to my neighborhood in California, where there were cans with free plastic bags on practically every corner and signs warning that failure to pick up after one's pet would carry a steep fine. Even Tennessee, which was always a few, or several, steps behind California, had been serious about controlling the disposal of pet waste. With so many people forced to walk during their daily outings in Athens, why in the world wouldn't they have a similar policy? I shook my head as I peered out the window.

Finally, Matt pulled to a stop on the side of a street, edging his tires as close as possible to the curb. "My apartment is just over there. I'm lucky to find this parking place. Usually, I have to stop a few blocks away or pay for a spot in one of the parking garages. You must be my good luck charm!" He smiled at me as he opened his door to get out.

We collected my bag and backpack from his trunk before heading in the direction of an apartment building across the street.

"My apartment is on the second floor. There's a small elevator we can use, or we can just take the stairs."

"The stairs are fine. Luckily, I packed light."

He collapsed the handle of my roller bag and lifted it. I followed him up the stairs, where he stopped outside the door of an apartment in the far corner of a hallway. He set down my case before inserting his key in the lock and pushed the door open, indicating that I should enter first. I stepped into a small entrance area with a desk on one side and a combination chest of drawers and clothes cabinet on the other. Just beyond the entrance was a living space with the sofa he had mentioned tucked up against one wall, with two comfy-looking chairs facing it. Behind the chairs was a round table that I assumed he used for dining. A galley kitchen was located adjacent to the dining area, with a small hallway to one side that led to a storage room with a washing machine. A bedroom and a bath were located at the far end of the hall, which completed my tour of the apartment. It was, in one word, cozy, but not in an unpleasant way.

I walked back down the hall to the living/dining area, noticing a row of windows lining the wall that looked out on the street. There was a door at the far end of the windows, and I walked over to have a look outside.

"You can open the balcony doors if you'd like. The balcony stretches all the way across the wall outside my living room, dining room, and bedroom. I placed a few potted plants out there to help block the view of the apartments across the street, and there's a small table with two chairs in one corner that makes a nice spot to have a morning coffee or late-day glass of beer ... or wine, since I think I recall that's your drink of choice."

I smiled at him, pleased that he remembered that tidbit of info about me. "You're right, although an occasional glass of beer is nice. Especially in the summer."

He gestured to the closet next to the front door. "I cleared a bit of space in the top there for any clothes you want to hang up. There's also an empty drawer just below if you want to put some other things away."

"That's very thoughtful of you, but I'm really fine just leaving everything in my suitcase."

"Okay. But there's really no need to do that. Why not unpack so you can settle in?"

I considered his suggestion. "Well, okay. But I'm really going to insist that I take the sofa to sleep on. Especially since my things will be out here."

He frowned and scratched his chin. "You know, I didn't think about that." He quickly headed down the hall toward the bedroom, gesturing for me to follow. Once inside, he opened the doors to a closet that was built into the wall on one side of his bed and began pulling things out. "Change of plans. I'm going to move some of my things out front so you have space here. I tend to stay up late and leave early, so it makes much more sense for me to sleep on the sofa. Besides, my desk is out there, and it's not uncommon for me to wake up in the middle of the night with an idea that I just have to jot down on my laptop. If you were sleeping on the sofa, I would be too inhibited to do that."

I sighed and raised my shoulders in a gesture of *I give up!* "You win. But I'll have to find a way to make it up to you."

He smiled and put his arm around me in a hug. "How about buying me lunch? I'm about half-starved!"

"Only half?" I said laughingly. "Just let me grab a few things and I'll be ready to go."

---

When we stepped back onto the street from Matt's apartment building, it had grown noticeably hotter, which was likely because the rain clouds had dissipated, leaving behind bright sunshine. I pulled my sunglasses out of my purse and put them on, wishing I had thought to bring my hat, as well.

"I thought we'd walk to a café I like. It's in an area called *Fokionos Negri*. It's hard to tell now, but the area was built over two streams that sort of cut through the middle of Kypseli. The whole area is filled with cafés, bars, and shops, with a lot of trees scattered around that create some welcome shade. There are also green spaces in the middle that are mostly used by dog owners. In other words, I don't recommend setting foot in any of those." He smiled at me knowingly.

"Don't worry. I noticed on our drive here from Plaka that Greeks seem to have an aversion to doggie poop bags." I rolled my eyes.

"Yeah. Be sure you keep an eye out for undesirable droppings on the sidewalks, too. It's gotten a little better in recent years, but it's still somewhat of a problem. After a while, it's just something you get used to."

We walked several minutes before turning right onto a pedestrian street lined with assorted businesses on each side. Even though there were no cars allowed, I noticed several motorcycles parked at various places, and I even had to quickly step aside to avoid being hit by a couple of them.

I looked at Matt askance. "I can't believe they allow motorcycles to be ridden in here. Isn't that dangerous?"

He frowned as he side-stepped the path of one of the offenders. "I wouldn't say it's allowed. It's just something people do here. There's no one to stop them, so the motorcyclists tend to drive and park wherever they want to."

We continued walking along the *mostly* pedestrian street until we reached the end, where it spilled out onto another pedestrian street that looped in both directions. It was a very vibrant area, with a large number of people milling around and occupying seats at various cafés, or just strolling along, seemingly enjoying the shaded walkway. The smell of freshly cooked food was prominent, and my stomach began to rumble in response.

We cut across the middle of the area, which seemed to follow a circuitous route in both directions for several blocks, with green spaces down the middle, as Matt had mentioned, that were occupied by children playing or people walking their dogs. Eventually, we paused in front of a building with a roof and walls that were open down the middle. "This is the Kypseli Municipal Market. I was told that years ago, it was used as a food market. Nowadays, it's a place where you can buy old vinyl records, books, used clothes, handmade crafts, and a variety of other things that pop up from time to time.

"Kind of like a flea market. Cool."

"Yes, but with more upscale items for the most part. And sometimes it's used as an area for local artists and artisans to display and sell their handmade items."

We walked a little farther, finally turning left to cross over to the other side of the green space, then right up a slight hill. We had passed several cafés and restaurants during our walk, all of which seemed to carry a variety of delicious-looking and smelling food, and I was beginning to wonder if we were ever going to just pick one. My hunger had intensified, and I was just short of reaching the point where I would beg for a bite of pretty much anything to quiet my growling stomach. Luckily, Matt chose that moment to stop in front of a restaurant. A sign over the building said it was called *Mezedomaxies*.

"This is one of my favorite spots. The name means something like *appetizer battles*. I don't know what that's all about, but the restaurant serves little plates of food, or *Meze* as they are called, as well as a wide variety of other homemade dishes. Shall we sit inside or out?" He gestured to one of the tables placed just inside the building, each one topped with a red and white checked plastic cover. Several more tables sat outside, shaded by large, beach-type umbrellas with beige cloth tops.

Since the weather was pleasant, I suggested we choose one of the umbrella-covered tables.

Immediately after we were seated, a waiter appeared with two menus that he placed in front of us, after which he began a stream of Greek, causing me to zone out into my *lost-in-translation* mindset. Luckily, Matt appeared to understand as he listened to the waiter's recitation and replied with a few sentences of his own. The waiter nodded and left.

I looked at Matt with awe. "When did you learn Greek?"

"In college. You know I studied in Boston, right? One of my professors suggested I take a course in Greek when he learned I was interested in majoring in tourism. I made that decision well before I learned that my career in baseball wasn't going to happen. I guess I had some sort of premonition. Or maybe it was just my dad's advice that I shouldn't put all my eggs into one basket. Or one career, as it turned out. In addition to Greek, I also studied Italian and Spanish. I'm so thankful I did because knowing more than one language gave me a lot more flexibility in choosing where to work after graduation. At first, I was planning to take a job in Italy in the Tuscany region. But then I got an offer here, and it seemed too good to pass up. At least for now. I'm not sure how long I'll stay in Greece, but I'm in no hurry to move either."

The waiter returned with a small glass pitcher of what I guessed was white wine and two small glasses, followed by a waitress who delivered a basket containing bread, napkins, and cutlery. Matt lifted the pitcher and poured each of us a glass of wine as the waiter returned with two plates stacked beneath a third that was filled with black olives, wedges of bright, red tomatoes, and chunks of feta cheese drizzled with what I assumed was olive oil. Matt placed a plate in front of me and gestured to the food.

"Dig in. I thought we could use something to start with to keep this wine from hitting us too hard."

I tore off a chunk of bread and then forked a bite of feta, pressing the cheese on the bread before using a spoon to drizzle some of the olive oil from the bottom of the plate over the cheese. I bit into the cheese-topped bread and then speared a piece of tomato, sighing as the flavors exploded in my mouth. "Oh my God! I'm always amazed how the simplest foods here taste so delicious."

Matt helped himself to a black olive before forking a chunk of tomato. "I think it's because everything is so fresh. Unlike the States, where we can get pretty much any type of food at any time of the year, here they only serve what's in season. As a result, you're usually eating something that's locally grown."

The waiter returned with two more plates of food, placing them in the center of the table. One appeared to be a mash of something yellow topped with capers, and the other contained slices of something fried. Matt pointed to each with his fork. "This is called *fava*. Cooked split peas mashed together with some oil and lemon, and the other is fried zucchini."

I added some of each to my plate, pausing before tasting them as the waiter reappeared with three more plates of food.

Matt smiled at the waiter and said something in Greek before pointing to one of the plates containing what looked like ovals of ground meat in tomato sauce. "This is one of their specials today. It's called *Soutzoukakia*. It's a type of meatball, or I guess a meat *foot*ball, with onions, garlic, and cumin in tomato sauce. The other plates contain tzatziki and fried calamari. Tzatziki is a yogurt sauce with grated cucumbers and some other stuff, and calamari is squid." He grabbed one of the slices of lemon that ringed the plate of calamari and squeezed a generous amount on top. "I recommend trying some of the tzatziki with the zucchini, but it's also good by itself on a chunk of bread."

I took his suggestion, placing a small amount of the white sauce on my plate before dipping a slice of zucchini into it. The taste was slightly tart in a good way, and I quickly took a second bite. "This is really good." I spooned some fava on my plate and tasted it, and then added some of the meatballs and sauce. "Also, good." I looked questioningly at the calamari. Matt must have read my mind because he laughed and nudged my arm.

"Oh, go on. At least try one bite. Don't worry if you don't like it."

I shrugged and cut off a small piece, studying it from side to side before placing it in my mouth. It was both tender and crispy, and the added lemon gave it a pleasant tang. I cut off another bite and added a smear of tzatziki before popping it in my mouth. "I hate to admit it, but you're right. This is really, really good. In fact, everything I've tried is delicious!"

He laughed and began to fill his plate with each of the delicacies. "This is one of my favorite places for Meze. There are lots of restaurants that serve them, but, in my opinion, this is one of the best."

We ate for a while in silence, making our way around the various dishes with groans of enjoyment. At one point, Matt refilled our wine glasses and held his up for a toast. "*Stin uyeia mas.* That means, to our health. I should have made that toast before we started eating, but I forgot." He clinked his glass against mine before taking a sip.

I followed his lead and took another sip of wine, and then put my glass down along with my fork. I leaned back in my chair and smiled. "Now I can understand why Greeks take a nap after lunch."

"Yes. It's customary to eat a fairly large meal around this time. Sleep for a couple of hours. Have some coffee and then either go back to work or meet friends for a late-night snack. I usually still have work to do, so I often skip alcohol in the middle of the day. Today is special, though." He took another sip and smiled at me.

"I want to know more about your work. Do you have an office near where you live?"

He shook his head. "Unfortunately, it's not that close to Kypseli, but it's not far from the hotel where you were staying. It's in the middle of Syntagma Square, near the Parliament Building and the National Gardens. It's ideally situated for a tourism office because the terminal for the Athens Coastal Tram that takes people to the beaches is near the Parliament, and trolley buses that go all over the city stop across from the entrance to the Gardens. I spend most of my time arranging tours for people who want to get an overview of Athens without venturing out on their own. Sometimes people hear about us and call ahead to book a tour. Other times, they drop in as they wander past when they're exploring the area. My company also specializes in island excursions."

His mention of islands reminded me of my own interest in

visiting one or more of them. "Do you ever get to go along on the excursions?"

"Not usually. Although occasionally I have had to fill in for one of our tour guides who came up sick or was overbooked. My favorite memory was when I got to tag along on a trip to Santorini. It was my first time there, and I was so enthralled with its beauty that I just wanted to sit back and be guided around the island rather than guide anyone else. I hope to be able to go back there someday and explore more of the island."

"I was thinking about visiting some of the islands while I'm in Greece, although I don't know how practical that is. I'm still working on paying off my student loans, so I need to budget myself very carefully."

"I understand. I was lucky. My tuition was covered at Boston College because of baseball. I had no idea at the time that my aspirations in that area would be so short-lived." He shrugged and glanced off into the distance.

Matt had been an all-star outfielder in high school with an outstanding batting average. As a result, he had his pick of several colleges to attend that were more than eager to award him a full ride. I knew something had happened that ended his baseball career, but I wasn't sure exactly what.

"I know you had to quit playing ball, but I'm not sure of the details."

He scrunched up his face. "It was a stupid mistake. I was playing a pick-up game one night with some of my buddies from college. One guy had a few beers before joining us, and he ended up crashing into me as I ran the bases. My right arm was broken in two places. The doctors said I would be able to play again, but I'd probably never be able to hit the ball with as much force or return a high catch with as much speed. It happened during my senior year. Luckily, my guidance counselor, like my dad before him, advised me from the start not to put all of my hopes in the hands of baseball. I chose tourism as a backup plan because it sounded like fun. Imagine my surprise when that *fun* ended up being my career."

"Wow. I didn't know all that. I'm sorry I haven't stayed as up-to-date about your life as I should have."

He shook his head. "Don't worry about it. It's not like I know everything that's happened in your life since elementary school, either. It's sad to say, but if it wasn't for Facebook, we probably wouldn't even be back in touch with each other now."

"Yeah, it's crazy." *And embarrassing*, I thought. I was grateful for the fact that Facebook helped us reconnect, but I vowed not to limit my personal contacts with family or friends to social media platforms from that point on.

The waiter reappeared and started to collect our empty plates. I was a little surprised we had managed to finish everything, aside from a scrap of bread and a little tomato sauce. I guessed that was testimony to how hungry we were and how delicious everything had been.

"Thanks for picking this place, Matt. It was a real treat."

"My pleasure." He glanced over my shoulder. "And if I'm not mistaken, there's one more surprise in store. We both looked up as the waitress set down two small bowls containing what looked like dark, purple fruits in a syrup. Matt lifted a spoon and gestured to my bowl. "Try it."

I dipped my spoon in the bowl and scooped up a bit of the fruit. It was both sweet and tart with a pleasantly dense texture. "Umm. What IS this?"

"Sour cherry spoon sweets. *Vyssino glyko koutaliou.* It's made from fresh sour cherries, water, sugar, and lemon. It's really nice by itself, but my favorite way to have it is over a dish of vanilla or chocolate ice cream." He rolled his eyes in ecstasy.

I took another spoonful. "That sounds incredible, but I have to say this is fantastic by itself." I finished my dish and patted my stomach. "I've only been in Greece a few days, but I can tell I'm going to have to log a LOT more walking steps if I'm going to avoid getting fat."

He smiled at me in amusement. "You've never been fat. Not that I can recall. In fact, in grade school, you were kind of a skinny kid."

I laughed at the memory. "That was a long time ago. It's not so easy staying trim these days. Especially with food like I've been eating so far in Greece."

He pulled a small rolled-up receipt from a shot glass on the table and, after glancing at it, gestured for the waiter to return.

"I'm paying, remember? How much is it?" I asked.

"If you insist. Thirty euros should cover it."

I dug some bills out of my wallet and then handed them to him. "Do you think they have a bathroom I can use?"

He pointed to the front of the building. "Just inside to the left. You'll see the letters WC on the door."

I stood up and made my way inside past the tables and chairs, which were now fully occupied, quickly spotting the door marked WC. I was a little familiar with Greek bathrooms by now, but it still took me a moment to remember that throwing paper of any kind in the toilet was strictly forbidden due to the precarious situation with the sewage system in Greece.

Apparently, at least based upon what Shelly had told me, Greek sewage pipes are only about two inches in diameter, in contrast to those in the United States and Great Britain that average four inches. That was why every Greek bathroom featured a little metal trash can next to the toilet for paper disposal. Occasionally, I forgot and dropped a wad in the toilet bowl, which immediately filled me with guilt. But not enough to make me fish it out. That was not going to happen!

When I returned to the table, Matt was chatting to a different waitress from the one who had helped serve us. They seemed to be engrossed in conversation, causing me to hang back for a minute until the waitress left abruptly. I pulled out my chair and sat back down.

I glanced over at Matt with a smirk. "What was that all about?"

"What? We were just talking about the food."

*Was it my imagination, or did he seem to be blushing?* "If you say so."

He rubbed his hand over his hair, which was kind of funny since he wore it in a buzz cut. "We went out for a while. It was no big deal. At least not to me. But I guess it bothered her when I stopped calling."

I waited for him to continue, and when he remained silent, I nudged him with my foot. "Go on. What's the rest of the story?"

He shook his head and shrugged. "Damned if I know! One minute, we were just having fun. Then the next thing I knew, she wanted me to meet her family. That's a big deal in Greece, given how close families are. Meeting them is like announcing you're engaged or something. I guess I got scared and stopped calling her."

I looked at him aghast. "You mean you never asked her about it? Maybe she was just being polite."

He shook his head emphatically. "No way. I'm sure it was more than that. She was sort of grilling me while you were away from the table. Wanted to know who you are and how long I've been seeing you." He chuckled quietly. "I'm not sure she believed me when I told her you're my cousin."

I thought about what he said. "I can understand how she probably feels. You disappear without an explanation and then show up here with another woman. It makes sense she would be hurt or angry or both."

He smiled sheepishly. "Yeah, I guess so. Anyway. I apologized, but told her I wasn't interested in seeing her anymore. She implied that she didn't believe me or I wouldn't have shown up at the place she works. I told her I came here because of the food, but she didn't seem to buy my explanation."

I shook my head. "Yuh think?! I wouldn't have either. And maybe that's not the only reason you thought of coming here today. Were you hoping to see her again, or were you trying to convince her that it was over by bringing another woman around? One that, of course, she didn't know was related to you."

He crossed his right leg over the left and jiggled his foot nervously. "I suppose the latter, although now I can see that it was a cowardly thing to do. I really do love to eat here, and I've avoided coming back since we stopped seeing each other."

"Sheesh. I thought I'd done some stupid dating things, but that about tops the cake!"

He held up his hands in front of his chest. "Okay, okay. I hear you. But since there's nothing I can do about it now, why don't we get out of here?"

I placed a hand on his arm. "Wait. Why don't you at least go over and apologize to her? Tell her you wish you had been more upfront about how you were feeling, and you hope there are no hard feelings, or however you would say all that to a Greek."

He seemed to think it over and then got up and walked over to where the waitress stood in front of the restaurant. I watched as he gestured for her to follow him to the side of the building, where it was more private. They talked for a few minutes until she threw up her hands and walked away. Matt stood there alone for another minute before returning to the table.

"How did it go?"

"Not bad. But not good, either. She basically said I'm a big jerk for not being honest with her, and that she only wanted to introduce me to her family because she was proud of me. She suggested I find another place to eat from now on."

I smiled. "I can't say I blame her. But I applaud you for trying." I looked around the restaurant. "So, do they have take-out here? It sounds like that's the only way you're going to be able to enjoy this food again. At least as long as she's working here."

"Yeah, you're right. But given how mad she seemed, I'm not

sure how safe it would be to order from here. Not unless I can eyeball how it's packed to go."

I began to imagine possibilities. "Yuck. I guess you're right. Well, I say we leave this joint and go scout out some other options on our way back to your place."

We strolled back in the direction of his apartment, this time taking a slightly different route. There seemed to be a large number of restaurants lined up along either side of the green space that divided *Fokionos Negri*, some of which advertised special foods, such as pizza or burgers, and others that posted specials of the day on a blackboard outside the entrance.

"I don't think you're going to have any problem finding other places to eat around here."

"True. But I've tried several of them already and, although they have some good dishes, none match the quality of what we just ate. I guess I'm just going to have to branch out a bit more."

As we approached the front door of his apartment building, he suddenly paused. "I almost forgot. I need a few things from the supermarket. Do you want me to let you into my apartment, or do you want to go there with me?"

"I'll join you, if that's okay. It'll be fun to see inside a Greek grocery store."

We retraced our route until I saw a sign for the AB Supermarket. Matt grabbed a cart from the front after placing a coin in a slot that released a chain that attached the cart to some others.

"You have to pay to use a shopping cart here?"

"Sort of. Stores have a problem with people stealing carts, so they require you to put a coin in the slot that frees the cart from the chain it's attached to. If you return the cart and reinsert the plug into the chain, the coin is returned. I guess it's mostly a deterrent against theft by people who can't afford to lose even a coin."

My attention was drawn to the front of the store where a woman stood with a small child, extending her hand to passersby in an effort to elicit money. Most people passed her without a glance, and I wondered how long she would have to stand there just to collect a small amount of cash.

I nodded in her direction. "That's sad. I can't imagine having to beg for money just to be able to feed my child." Matt turned to look in the direction of the woman and nodded.

"I know. Unfortunately, some of them are scam artists. They use the child as a distraction, and if someone approaches them with a little money, they often leave with their pocket picked. That's not always the case. But it happens often enough that a lot of people just turn a blind eye."

He pushed his cart ahead of us as we entered the store. Once inside, I was struck by how similar and yet different it looked from grocery stores in the States. There was a rack with baked breads and pastries just inside the entrance, next to a counter that displayed freshly cooked items. Among the baked goods were crispy-looking pastries that appeared to be filled with cheese or vegetables, which reminded me of the spinach pie I had at the hotel. The cooked items ranged from chicken packed with potatoes, tomatoes, and peppers stuffed with some kind of rice mixture, green beans, okra, meatballs, and French fries. If the smell they were emitting was any clue, I guessed they would be as delicious as the other cooked foods I had sampled so far in Greece.

Just beyond that counter was a section featuring a wide variety of cheeses. Three white-coated workers stood just behind, ready to fill orders. Matt approached one of them and placed an order in Greek, causing the woman behind the counter to cut off a hunk of cheese, which she wrapped in paper held together by a rubber band before slapping a sticker on it with the price.

A little farther along the same counter was a display of raw meats and poultry. Matt pointed to what looked like ground beef and indicated how much he wanted. At the very end of the counter was a section with individual containers of olives, both green and black, and some other dishes that held what looked like the spoon sweets we had been served at the restaurant.

We headed to the produce section next. Matt selected some tomatoes, cucumbers, and peaches, placing each in plastic bags that were then given to a man who weighed them and stuck a price sticker on the outside of each bag. I followed him to the store aisles next, where he picked up a box of what looked like square crackers shaped like a small slice of bread, followed by a bottle of white wine in a large, plastic container. He paused and looked around.

"I think that's everything. Unless there's something special you'd like me to buy."

I thought for a moment. "Maybe some yogurt? I usually have some at breakfast."

He motioned for me to follow him down another aisle that carried refrigerated items, opening one door and removing two medium-sized plastic containers. "This is local yogurt. It's really good." He opened a second door and reached in to snag a package of sliced meat. "Might be a good idea to get some ham, too. That way, we'll have the option of making *tost*."

I frowned at his comment. "Toast? Don't you need bread for that?"

He laughed. "Of course. But in Greece, *tost* usually refers to a toasted sandwich made with bread, cheese, and sometimes ham. They even have special toast-makers that press the sandwich flat while melting the cheese and toasting the bread. I like to add a slice of tomato to mine, as well."

He pushed the shopping cart toward the check-out aisles, stopping to grab a loaf of sandwich bread along the way. I stood back and watched as he unloaded the groceries onto the check-out counter. He motioned for me to go to the end of the counter, where the check-out lady was placing the scanned items.

"*Hreeahzeste sakoules?*" The woman at the check-out counter addressed the question to me, and when I looked at her blankly, she turned to look at him.

Matt nodded. "*Nai, efharisto.*"

She grabbed four plastic bags from under the counter and placed them where I could reach. I quickly began bagging our purchases, hurrying as fast as I could as the items began to pile up. Matt scanned his credit card on a device the check-out lady held in front of him, which spit out a receipt. He took it from her and said *efharisto*. She nodded at him and began scanning the groceries placed on the counter by the next person in line.

We each grabbed two bags and left the store.

"That was interesting. Do most people bring their own bags?" I asked.

"Usually. They charge around 15 cents per bag, otherwise. I have several cloth and plastic bags at home that I use, but I didn't think to bring any today."

We made our way back to his apartment, depositing the bags on the kitchen counter.

"I'll just put these things away. Why don't you relax for a while? Take a nap, if you feel like it. I have some work to take care of, and then I may snooze a bit myself."

I wandered down the hall, pausing to brush my teeth along the way, before opening the bedroom door. Matt had closed the blinds in the bedroom before we left the apartment, and the room felt cool and inviting. I pulled aside the covers on the bed, closing the door quietly before slipping off my shoes and shorts and sliding beneath the sheets. It still felt a little uncomfortable to take over his bedroom, but I had to admit that I appreciated the privacy it provided.

As I closed my eyes, I thought about the events that had transpired since I arrived in Greece: Meeting Shelly. Having my fortune read out of a coffee cup. Exploring Plaka. Going to the Acropolis and nearby sites. The last image that came to mind before I gave in to sleep was of the guy Shelly had introduced me to at the Acropolis Museum. William, or *Wills,* I think he was called. He was kind of cute. But also, kind of uppity. Or maybe I was just being super sensitive. Either way, it wasn't likely we would see each other again.

# *six*

The smell of coffee woke me a little while later. At least I thought it was a little while. I rolled over and peered at the clock that sat on a little table beside the bed. 7 a.m. *What? That can't be right!* I looked again and confirmed what I first thought. That meant I had been asleep over ... twelve hours? Man! Jet lag was something. I hadn't slept that many hours since I was a teenager. Or at least since my first night in the Hotel Central, although that night my sleep had been in segments broken up by frequent awakenings.

I stretched my arms overhead and swung my legs over the side of the bed, pulling my shorts on before opening the bedroom door. I looked down the hall toward the kitchen, where the coffee smell was clearly coming from, then decided to make a stop in the bathroom. When I walked into the kitchen, Matt turned to me with a smile.

"Good morning! Can I interest you in some of this?" he held out a full mug of coffee.

I sighed and nodded, taking it from his outstretched hand. "Yes, please."

"There's milk and sugar on the table."

I walked to the table and pulled out a chair, and then poured a little milk into my mug. "I can't believe I slept all night."

"Jet lag is a killer. I remember when I first moved here, I don't think I slept more than four hours at a time for a week. Finally, I was so exhausted I fell asleep when I got off work one afternoon and didn't wake up until mid-morning the next day. Lucky for me, it was Saturday."

I took a long sip of the coffee. "Um. This is good. It's nice to have American coffee for a change. I've only had Greek coffee since I've been here, and I have to tell you, I'm not a big fan."

He smiled. "It definitely takes some getting used to." He gestured at the counter behind him. "Would you like a *tost*?"

I remembered his explanation of what that meant from the day before. "Not right now. Maybe a little yogurt and fruit?"

"Coming right up." He busied himself in the kitchen and then placed a bowl of yogurt topped with fresh peach slices in front of me. "What do you feel like doing today? I don't have to go into the office, so I thought I could show you around Athens. Maybe go to some of the lesser-known spots that tourists don't find unless they sign up with a class A tour guide." He looked up at me with a grin.

"My own private tour? Wow! I'm honored. Except, what'll that cost me?" I smirked at him as I tucked my feet behind the chair legs.

He leaned against the kitchen counter and narrowed his eyes as he took a swig of coffee. "Hmm ... let's see. Dinner and drinks? That should just about cover my usual fee."

"Deal. When do you want to leave? I'd like to take a shower first."

He glanced at his watch. "It's still pretty early. Why don't we plan to head out around 10? That should give us plenty of time to see the sights, and still avoid the worst of the heat and crowds."

I finished my coffee and scooped the last spoonful of yogurt from the bowl. "Do you want to use the bathroom first? I might take a little time to get ready."

"Yeah, just let me pop in there for a minute, then I'll send a few emails while you're getting ready."

By ten o'clock, I was washed, dressed, wide awake, and ready to see what sights Matt had in store for me. I had unpacked my bags as Matt suggested, hanging most things in the closet, or laying them in an empty drawer next to the bed. I picked up the worry beads I had purchased in the Flea Market part of Plaka and carried them to where Matt was sitting at his desk, peering down at his laptop. I held the beads out to him. "These are for you. I hope you like them."

He looked up and smiled. "*Komboloi*. Thanks! I used to have some that I bought shortly after I arrived in Athens, but I lost them somewhere. These are great." He took them from me and flipped them from side to side.

"I'm glad. The man I bought them from said a lot of men carry them in Greece. He suggested that women were the main reason that men use them, seeing as how they are called *worry beads.*"

He laughed and looked down at his hand. "I don't know about that, but I certainly could have made good use of them when I was dating that waitress you met." He tucked the beads in his pocket. "Ready to go?"

I pointed down at the two pairs of shoes I had placed on the floor. "Should I wear sneakers or sandals?"

"Whichever would be more comfortable for walking. We'll be visiting some spots where we'll have to walk some to get around. Bring your swimsuit and a towel, too."

I considered my choices of footwear, finally deciding to grab the sneakers. I picked up my backpack and stuffed my swimsuit, towel, and sunscreen inside, along with a hairbrush, my cell phone, and wallet, before heading out the door of the apartment.

We made our way out of his building, crossing the street to where he had parked his car the evening before. I tossed my backpack onto the back seat and climbed in the front. Matt placed a backpack and a small cooler on the floor behind his seat before getting behind the wheel. He grabbed his seatbelt and pulled it across his chest, firmly securing it before starting the engine. "Ready?"

"Ready!" A wide grin spread across my face. My visit with Matt was turning out to be more fun than I had ever imagined. "Where are we heading?"

"I'm going to take you to the Riviera. The ATHENS Riviera, that is."

I look at him skeptically. "You're kidding, I assume?"

"No, really. The coastline of Athens on the south side is called the Riviera. I guess the name is meant to imply that it's pretty plush, like the French Riviera, or the Hamptons on Long Island. It's about 37 miles long with a mix of villages, suburbs, high-end resorts, and, of course, numerous beaches. It will take us about 20 or 30 minutes to get there from here, depending on the traffic, but I promise you it's worth it. We'll drive along the coast for a while so you can see the sights. Then eventually, we'll stop for a swim and a bite of lunch before venturing on. There's a spot at the end of the drive that I want to show you, but I'll keep it a secret for now."

"I can't believe there are that many beaches close to the city. From downtown Athens, I get the impression that the city is just mile after mile of concrete. And pollution. Don't get me started on the air quality here. I've been ready to pull out my COVID mask every time I venture outside."

We were just a few months past a global pandemic created by an outbreak of the coronavirus disease that started in 2019, referred to as COVID-19. The virus was believed to have started in China, but rapidly spread to other countries across the world. At first, everyone I knew had scoffed at the likelihood that a virus could wreak so much havoc in such a short time, and at such a huge magnitude. But the impact on our daily lives was unmistakable and unlike anything I could have ever imagined. Even now, three years after the start of the pandemic, I felt uncomfortable whenever I found myself in a crowded place, like an airplane or an indoor restaurant. But I was doing my best to be smart, while at the same time trying to live my life in the best way I could.

Even going to school and working as a high school teacher shortly afterward had been a challenge during the pandemic.

Luckily, I had been wrapping up my undergraduate degree before the worst of the outbreak reached the States. But securing a job as a teacher required a quick lesson in virtual teaching since bringing a crowd of young people into a classroom was prohibited. It was a difficult time for both the students and the teachers, but luckily, we had begun to transition back to classroom learning during the past year.

My decision to take a trip to Greece had also been influenced by my forced semi-isolation. I was so tired of worrying about being around other people, so careful to sanitize anything I touched, and so exhausted with explaining to parents why their children had to be distanced from one another both in and out of the classroom, that I jumped at the idea of traveling to another country when my dad suggested it. He had been in touch with his brother, my Uncle Bob, who was Matt's father, and the two of them thought it would be a good idea if Matt and I were reconnected.

In some ways, Greece had been even more locked down than the USA during the pandemic, but things had finally begun to loosen up for them, too, over the past few months. What sealed the deal for me was the fact that one of my friends needed to cancel a trip she had booked, and it was past the deadline for getting a refund, but she was allowed to transfer the airfare to someone else. I guess you could say her misfortune was my good luck.

"Wearing a mask wouldn't be such a bad idea, and you wouldn't be the only one to wear one. If you look closely, you'll notice a lot of people still wear a mask when they're out and about, especially older folks. It's just good sense given the air quality, as you said. Plus, it's essential if you ever take public transportation, like a bus or tram."

"I agree. I wore one most of the time on the airplane, except when I was eating or drinking something. And all the time in the airports. It's hard to shake the fear that consumed us during the worst of the pandemic."

We drove on for several minutes past developments that did nothing to change my mind about my previous impressions of the city. It was crowded and busy, and it made my heartbeat faster just witnessing it from the car window. Finally, we reached the end of the highway and turned left onto a four-lane road that ran parallel to the beach. I rolled down my car window and was treated to a refreshing breeze with a scent of the sea and the flowers that lined the road in several spots.

"What's that flowering bush over there called? I noticed its scent one day when I was walking in Plaka. It reminded me of honeysuckle, but the flower looks a little different."

Matt leaned forward for a closer look. "That's Jasmine. You're right that the scent is similar to honeysuckle, but I find it even sweeter. Honeysuckle does grow in parts of Greece, but jasmine is more prevalent."

I could see several beaches along the side of the road as we drove by. Some appeared quite rocky, while others were covered with brown sand. Each was dotted by beach umbrellas or cabanas, either in an organized fashion that implied a private area or spaced haphazardly by individuals, couples, or groups seeking their own piece of beach.

There were a couple of areas that hosted rather impressive marinas with yachts of various sizes, either anchored to the pier or afloat in the water. Eventually, we drove through a more developed area where I could see large hotels, numerous restaurants, and various other establishments mingled with apartment buildings and private homes. Matt pointed out the front window to our left.

"This area is called *Glyfada*. It's considered one of the most sought-after parts of the coast. As you can see, it has a lot of high-end hotels, restaurants, and stores, as well as several nice beaches. There's also a golf course—the only one in Attica. A buddy of mine from work knows another guy who lives around here, and he invited me to play a round with them one time. Golf is not really my thing, but it was a fun way to spend a day. There's a tram that can bring you here from central Athens. It takes about 45 minutes, which is a little more than it normally takes by car. But at least you don't have to fight the traffic, which can easily add another 15 to 30 minutes to the drive on a busy day."

I glanced out the window to look at a particularly appealing beach. "Is that where we're going for a swim?"

He shook his head. "That's a nice place, but today I thought we'd stop a little farther up the coast at a place called Vouliagmeni Lake. I know it's not the sea, but the water is a mixture of saltwater and fresh, and it stays between 71 and 84 degrees Fahrenheit all year round. The water is also thought to have healing properties. They do charge an admission fee, like most of the beaches up and down the coast, but it's a quiet and peaceful place in a lovely setting. I called ahead and reserved a couple of sun beds for us to use, and they have an outdoor restaurant and beach bar on-site where we can pick up a coffee and snack when we get hungry."

"That sounds perfect. All I want to do today is relax in the sun, swim a bit, and look at nature."

Matt pulled into the far left lane before heading into a narrow drive that led down a short hill. I could see the lake behind a row of trees and eagerly unhooked my seat belt when he stopped the car.

"Let me grab our things out of the back. There's a little platform just over there where you can get a view of the area if you want to check it out while you wait."

I stepped out of the car and headed across the parking lot to the viewing platform. A row of bushes partly occluded my view, but I was in awe of the tall cliffs surrounding shimmering greenish-blue water. A few heads of swimmers were visible in the distance, and off to the far right, I caught a glimpse of beach chairs spread out along a raised deck.

Matt jumped up on the platform next to me. "Pretty cool, huh?"

"Yeah. Although I can't see the whole area from here."

"Follow me. The entrance is just over there."

We walked a short distance to a small building that listed the various entrance fees and information about the services offered. I turned to Matt with raised eyebrows and spoke in a whisper. "Pretty steep prices."

He nodded. "Yeah. But not much different than most of the other beaches in the area. That's one reason this is called the Riviera." He stepped up to the admission window and spoke to the woman stationed there, who held a reader out for him to scan his credit card before handing him two tickets. Matt turned and gestured for me to follow him. "Our lounge chairs are over here. We'll be away from the crowd, but still able to have a nice view of the surroundings."

We made our way to two white cushioned lounge chairs that sat on the edge of the deck near the water. Matt placed our bags on two small tables on either side of the chairs. I removed my towel from my bag and spread it on the chair closest to me, and then looked around for a place to change. Matt must have read my mind because he immediately informed me of the location of the changing rooms that were up a sloped walkway near what appeared to be a café.

When I returned, Matt had settled into the other chair and was checking his phone for messages. He held it up with an apologetic look. "Sorry. I just got a text from the office, so I thought I'd better read it. Apparently, one of the tours I was supposed to lead tomorrow was canceled. COVID still has some people scared of crowds, so cancellations are, unfortunately, not that uncommon. The good news is that now I'm free for the rest of today and most of tomorrow." He grinned and pushed his sunglasses back in place. "Don't you love this view?" He gestured to the scene that stretched in front of us.

The sun was reflecting off the sheer rock wall behind the lake, casting it in a golden glow and causing the water just below to appear to shimmer. Farther to the left, the lake appeared green in the shadows of the rock. I leaned back against the cushions and closed my eyes, reveling in the warmth of the midday sun. I had generously lathered myself with sunscreen in the changing room, but I decided to also pull on the straw fedora I had added to my bag before leaving Athens. I was just about to doze off when I heard a noise next to me. I opened one eye to spot Matt pushing up from his chair.

"I'm going for a swim. Care to join me?"

I glanced at the water, trying to decide if it was more or less appealing than a nap. "Sure. I was about to fall asleep, but a dip in the water sounds good."

I followed him to a set of steps that led down from the deck into the water. As I started down, I noticed a couple of people perched on the steps with their legs in the water, laughing as they looked down at their feet. I nudged Matt as I paused just behind them and spoke in a whisper. "What do you think those folks are laughing at?"

He followed my gaze and smiled. "Look closer. Do you see all the little fish swimming around their feet? They're called *Gara Rufa*. They eat dead skin. Well, they don't actually EAT the skin. They suck the dead cells off and then secrete an enzyme that helps regenerate the skin cells. It's kind of like having a spa treatment. Want to try it?"

I looked at him aghast as I shook my head. "I don't think so. That sounds creepy!"

He chuckled. "Suit yourself. Although I can assure you it doesn't hurt at all, and it leaves your skin looking pretty amazing. It does tickle a little if you're sensitive in that way. But that's all."

I watched the couple for another minute before moving past them so I could step into the lake. The water was wonderful: not too cool, and not too hot. I dipped my entire body in the water up to my neck and began paddling farther out. Matt swam past me using broad strokes that quickly carried him a good distance from the shore. I followed him slowly, gazing upward as I spotted what appeared to be caves scattered over the rock face. Matt turned around and swam back in my direction, raising one hand to send a splash of water in the general direction of my face as he drew close. I lifted one hand to wipe my mouth and was surprised to discover a slightly salty taste.

"I thought this was a lake. Why does it taste like the sea?"

"Because the lake is partly fed from an underground stream that flows from the sea. That helps keep the water fresh and clean, and moderates the temperature too."

Matt turned toward the opposite shore and began to swim away. I tried unsuccessfully to match his strong strokes, finally giving up and allowing myself the luxury of just paddling my arms and legs to stay afloat. After several minutes, he turned and began to head in my direction, pausing next to me as he wiped a hand across his face.

"The water feels great, but I think I'm about ready for a coffee or something cold to drink. How about you?"

"Absolutely." We swam the short distance to the steps leading onto the deck. I noticed that the couple who had been perched there enjoying their 'fish pedicures' had left, and I hesitated for a moment before climbing up onto the deck. I was curious what it would feel like to have a spa treatment by little slimy fish, but not enough to actually try it.

I toweled off and settled back onto the lounge chair.

Matt rubbed his towel over his head and upper body before flinging it onto his chair. "I'll be right back. Would you like a frappe or something with alcohol?"

I considered his question. "Surprise me."

He nodded and turned to walk in the direction of the café.

While I was waiting, I looked around at the variety of people spread out on the lounge chairs, cabanas, and umbrella-covered tables. The majority of them appeared to be regulars based on the casual way they ignored the beauty around them and exchanged greetings with others seated nearby. Now and then, I caught a glimpse of someone peering curiously in my direction and wondered if my status as a tourist was apparent. I guess I was staring a little too long because two men nudged each other and nodded in my direction, causing me to quickly turn my head away.

"Here you go." I looked up as Matt placed a tray on the table nearest to where I sat, containing a small bottle of clear liquid, two small glasses, a metal pitcher with cubes of ice, and a bowl of mixed nuts.

I glanced at the bottle curiously. "What's that?"

"It's called *Tsipouro*. It's made from the wine residue left after the grapes and juice have been separated." He placed a couple of ice cubes in each of the glasses and then unscrewed the bottle, pouring a small amount in each. "See what you think of it. It's similar to ouzo, which I believe you said you've tried, but tsipouro is purer. It's also stronger, which is why it is served in small glasses." He lifted the glasses from the tray, handing one to me before clinking our glasses together. "*Stin eeyia mas!*"

"Whatever you just said!" I took a tentative sip. It tasted slightly sweet with a slow burn as it traveled down my throat to my belly. It wasn't bad. But I couldn't say it was exactly good either. It was just different and unique, which is what I asked for, after all.

Matt glanced at me with a smirk. "What do you think?"

"It's very unusual. Not bad, but not something I can see myself drinking very often."

"It's pretty strong. Most of the time, this is served with appetizers, Meze, like what we had at the restaurant yesterday. It's also fairly common to serve it at after-church gatherings."

I looked at him curiously. "Have you been to many of those? After-church gatherings?"

"A few. One of my co-workers invited me to join him, and I took him up on his invitation once out of curiosity. After every service, the attendees would gather outside on the church patio and pass around trays with tsipouro or ouzo, sweetened Greek coffee, and a variety of snacks. I got the impression that the after-gatherings were as important as the church services themselves. In fact, some people didn't even show up until the service was almost over. And many of them never went inside the church. They just hung around outside the doors until the official service ended."

"I can't imagine doing that. The way you and I grew up, going to the Catholic Church, we would have been excommunicated if we routinely showed up late for Mass. In fact, it was better not to go at all if you were going to arrive late."

He smiled and nodded. "Absolutely. But here, it's perfectly acceptable to arrive any time before the communion, if that's what they call it in the Greek Orthodox religion. In fact, they use a series of church bells to indicate what stage the service is at so people can gauge when they choose to arrive."

I looked at him doubtfully. "Are you serious?"

"Absolutely. There's a different sound depending on where things are in the service. The ringing speeds up when it's approaching Communion. I guess that lets people know they'd better hurry up."

I shook my head in disbelief. "I'd like to hear that sometime."

"Oh, you will. You usually don't hear church bells in Athens except on Sunday or when there's a special occasion. But if you ever go to one of the islands, there are so many churches spread out all over the place that it seems like the bells are always ringing in one place or another. Most of the time, it coincides with the feast day of the saint for whom the church is named."

I took another sip of the drink and followed it with a handful of nuts. "I'd really like to visit one or more of the islands."

Matt was silent for a moment. "I have an idea. I'm supposed to go to Santorini next week to tag along with one of our new travel guides. Check out how she does on the job. Maybe I could arrange for you to come along."

"Really? Santorini is at the top of my wish list. But how could you work that out without it being a problem?"

He looked thoughtful for a moment. "I'm not sure. Let me think about it and I'll let you know what I come up with."

We continued munching on nuts and sipping tsipouro for a while, enjoying the warm sunshine and beautiful view of the water and surrounding cliffs. Finally, Matt looked at his watch and downed the rest of his drink. "We should probably get going if we're going to catch the sunset."

I looked around in puzzlement. "The sun doesn't look like it's going to set for another hour or so."

He stood up and began to collect his things. "True. But we'll need at least 30 or 40 minutes to make it to our next stop. It's a special place I want to show you, known for its sunset views."

I nodded and grabbed my bag. "I'm going to change out of my swimsuit. I'll meet you at the car."

When I returned, Matt had stowed our things in the trunk of the car and was pulling on a clean shirt. I tossed my beach bag in the back seat and climbed in the front. We made our way back up the drive that led to the lake and turned onto the highway again. For the next half hour, we rode in silence, enjoying the view of the sea and beach towns along the way. At one point, Matt turned the car into a pull-off overlooking the water.

"Look over there. That's where we're heading."

I looked where he was pointing and spotted what appeared to be an ancient temple perched on the top of a hill. There was a walking path that zig-zagged up the side, and I could just make out the shadowy images of what looked like a large number of people who were either making their way up the path or who had already reached their destination. "Impressive. It reminds me of the Parthenon, but smaller."

"It's called the Temple of Poseidon, and the land it sits on is Cape Sounion. It was built around 440 B.C., and it's located on the southernmost tip of the Attica peninsula."

"Poseidon. I've heard that name, but I can't recall its significance. Something to do with the sea, I believe."

"Right. In Greek mythology, Poseidon was one of the twelve Olympian Gods and the ruler of the seas and oceans. He's also associated with earthquakes and horses, although the connection between the two is a little vague. As I recall, the ancient Greeks believed that his movements beneath the earth's surface caused tremors and earthquakes that shaped the land.

He is also often shown riding a chariot pulled by horses because, according to mythology, he was believed to have created horses, having produced the first one by striking his spear on a rock. That's why you often see statues of him holding a spear. If you get a chance to visit the National Archaeological Museum in Athens while you're here, you'll see several statues of him.

"According to the myth, Poseidon's son, who was named Theseus, volunteered to be one of the 14 young people who were sacrificed each year to the fearsome Minotaur who lived in the Labyrinth of King Minos of Crete. Theseus promised his father, Poseidon, that he would slay the Minotaur, which would put an end to the sacrifices. Poseidon reluctantly agreed but instructed his son that upon returning home, he should exchange the black sail usually displayed on the ship for a white one to show he was still alive.

"Apparently, Theseus succeeded in killing the Minotaur with the help of the daughter of King Minos, who was named Ariadne. The night before they were to return to Athens, the God Dionysus appeared to Theseus in a dream, instructing him to abandon Ariadne on the island and return home without her. He was so distraught at having to obey the wishes of the god that he forgot to change the black sail to a white one. As a result, when his ship showed up in the waters below the Temple, Poseidon saw the black sail and threw himself off the cliffs into the sea in grief. It is believed that this happened at Cape Sounion, which is why the temple is named after Poseidon."

"Wow! You really know your Greek mythology. I'm impressed!"

He smiled as he pulled the car back onto the highway. "Just part of my job. As a tour guide, you have to know everything that the tourists may, or may not, be interested in hearing about."

We drove for another 15 minutes or so before turning onto a road that eventually led to the top of the hill containing the Temple. There were a large number of buses and cars parked along the road and in the lots nearer to the Temple. Luckily, Matt found a vacant spot close to a café that sat just below the entrance. We made a quick pit stop at the restrooms located inside the café and then stood in line to buy the tickets that would allow us admission to the grounds surrounding the Temple.

There were large, stone steps leading to the top in some places, interspersed with sandy paths. We headed up what appeared to be the shortest route, quickly positioning ourselves on a stone bench overlooking the sea and the setting sun. I glanced upward at the Temple. Its stone pillars were cast in a warm, golden tint from the sun's rays. I noticed several people taking photographs either with their phones or more sophisticated cameras, and I pulled out my iPhone to capture as much of the view as possible.

There were a couple of boats in the water below where we sat. One appeared to be a fishing boat, whereas the other seemed chartered just to allow its passengers to view the sunset colors. As the setting sun became more prevalent, a hush settled over the crowd of people surrounding us. I looked at Matt appreciatively and leaned over to speak to him in a whisper.

"This is so cool! Thank you for bringing me here today."

"You're welcome. I've been a few times before, but it's always a unique experience."

We sat a while longer, enjoying the changing colors as the sun continued its descent. Finally, Matt nudged my arm.

"I think we'd better be going. It gets really dark when the sun finally sets, and once this crowd gets moving, they'll have the way down backed up for some time."

I followed him as we made our way to where the car was parked. After we made our descent, we turned back onto the highway that had brought us there and drove for a short distance before Matt pulled off into a parking lot.

He pointed to the building in front of us. "Are you hungry? I thought we could grab some dinner before heading back to Athens."

I laughed as, predictably, my stomach voiced its response. "I guess that answers your question."

We headed inside, where a waiter showed us to a table on a patio overlooking the darkening sea across the road. He handed us two menus before inquiring about our drink orders. I asked for a glass of white wine, while Matt chose a beer. I opened the menu, which, like a couple of other ones I had encountered in Athens, was printed in both Greek and English.

"This must be a popular spot for tourists. Have you been here before?" I asked.

"Just once. I brought one of the tour guides from our office to acquaint him with the route to Sounion. We stopped here on the way back for a bite to eat." He opened his menu. "I remember the food was pretty good."

We studied the menu for a few moments until the waiter returned with our drink orders. I closed my menu and looked over at Matt. "Why don't you order for us? I'm having a hard time deciding what to choose."

"Okay." He rattled off several selections in Greek, while the waiter pressed buttons on what appeared to be an electronic pad before nodding as he turned to walk away.

"As I said before, your Greek is impressive. At least I think it is. For all I know, you may have just ordered us a pile of dirt and some rocks."

He laughed. "I promise you I ordered something tastier than that, although there have been a couple of times when I've mixed up my Greek words and embarrassed myself pretty bad."

"Really? Give me an example."

He took a sip of his beer. "Um, I'd rather not. The only one that comes to mind right now is pretty bad. It was something I said to someone on a date once that came out completely different from how I intended. Just suffice it to say, I learned the difference very quickly!"

I had no clue what he meant, but I decided not to push it based on the look on his face. Instead, I busied myself looking around at the other tables of diners. I could detect a smattering of English being spoken by at least half of the people, who also seemed to be studying their menus very intently. Waiters passed by on their way to deliver plates of food to nearby tables, and I sniffed appreciatively at the smells they left behind. I also noticed that every table seemed to have one plate of food that I instantly recognized.

"Did you order French fries?" I asked Matt.

He glanced around and smiled. "Of course. *Tiganites patates.* You'll find them on most menus in Greece. They're cooked in olive oil, which I suppose makes them a little healthier, but also delicious."

I remembered my previous impression of the fries I had tasted and nodded my agreement.

The waiter chose that moment to deliver our food. The promised plate of French fries arrived first, accompanied by a bowl of Greek salad prepared with the customary bright, red chunks of tomato, black Kalamata olives, slices of cucumber, and a thick slab of feta cheese resting on top. Two more plates were laid next to these. I recognized the first as the stuffed vine leaves I had tried before, but the other puzzled me. I pointed to it with my fork.

"What's that? It looks strange."

"That's an experiment for your taste buds. It's grilled octopus in a vinegar sauce with onions and capers." He picked up a cut half of a lemon and squeezed it over the plate. "It's better with some lemon." He cut off a piece from the long, knobby tentacle and placed it on my empty plate. "Try it and see what you think. If you don't like it, don't worry. I'll be happy to eat your share."

I frowned as I studied the chunk he had served me. I had to admit it didn't look at all appetizing, but I decided to push myself outside of my comfort zone as I speared the piece and swirled it around in the sauce before placing it in my mouth. It was chewy. Tough, almost. But with a nice tangy flavor.

"Not bad. The sauce is really good."

Matt held a basket of bread in my direction. "Try a piece of this dipped in the sauce. I also ordered some of that yogurt sauce we had the other night. You might enjoy some of it combined with a bite of octopus and bread."

I followed his advice and layered the three tastes on my fork. "You're right. The combination is delicious." I quickly prepared another taste and placed it in my mouth.

We ate in silence for a few minutes, filling our plates from the various dishes. The Greek salad was good as always, and the vine leaves, which Matt informed me were called *dolmades,* were stuffed with a rice and herb mixture and covered with a creamy, lemon sauce. I had to admit that the French fries were my favorite. They were crispy on the outside and soft in the middle with, again, a lemony twang. I guessed that lemon was a chief ingredient in Greek cooking. It certainly seemed to complement pretty much everything I had tasted so far since arriving in the country.

I took one last piece of bread to sop up the juices from the salad and a remaining dollop of yogurt sauce—*tzatziki*—before pushing aside my plate. "That was a treat. Thanks so much for bringing me here, and for the whole day. It has been a special adventure."

Matt smiled with pleasure as he finished his beer. "I'm glad you enjoyed yourself. I wanted to show you a little more of the mainland outside the center of Athens. A lot of visitors never set foot beyond the Plaka area, which is a shame considering how much more there is to see." He raised his hand and gestured at the waiter. "Tomorrow, I thought we'd stay a little closer to home. Give you a chance to explore the historical area of Athens."

"I really appreciate that, but don't you need time to do whatever it is you do every day? For work, I mean?"

He shook his head. "As I mentioned, my tour for tomorrow was canceled. I do have some work I need to take care of on my computer for a few hours, but after that, I'm free." The waiter arrived at the table and placed a small plate of fruit in front of each of us, along with a tiny glass of clear liquid. I pointed at the glass.

"Tsipouro?" I asked.

Matt shook his head. "*Mastiha*. It's sweeter and lighter." He pushed his glass in my direction. "I'll pass on it since I have to drive us home. It's yours if you want it."

I considered his offer but decided to stick with the fruit. The wine and food had made me a bit sleepy, and I didn't want to nod off in the car on the way back to Athens.

The drive home seemed to take less time than I anticipated, and before I knew it, we were pulling up in front of Matt's building. He stopped the car and handed me a set of keys. "I'm going to look for a parking space. Why don't you go on up, and I'll join you shortly?"

I accepted the keys and stepped out of the car, waiting for him to drive away before crossing the road. I inserted one of the keys in the lock on the front door and then climbed the stairs to the second floor. It was dark in the hallway, and I felt around on the wall before locating a light switch that allowed me to see well enough to unlock the door to his apartment. The inside of his apartment was dark except for the light that came through his uncovered windows, and I quickly flipped two more light switches. I paused and looked around, enjoying the simple and yet comfortable way in which Matt had decorated the place.

I made my way down the hall to the bedroom, tossing my bag on the bed before gathering my night clothes and heading for the bathroom. Even though I had rinsed off after our swim, the combination of the hike up to Sounion and the heat of the day had left me feeling sticky. I quickly turned on the shower, hoping to finish before Matt returned. It was a little difficult to share one bathroom, and I didn't want to inconvenience him any more than I already had by taking over his bedroom. I stepped under the shower spray, tensing as the cold water hit my skin. I had forgotten I was supposed to turn on the heater so that the water could warm up first! I quickly rinsed off and toweled dry as fast as I could.

When I emerged from the bathroom, Matt was in the hallway flipping a switch in a box on the wall. He looked at me with a grin.

"Enjoy your cold shower?"

"Brrr! I forgot you have to let the water get hot first. That was a shock."

"I'm sorry, I should have reminded you. Would you like a cup of something hot to warm you up?"

I considered his offer. "I'd love a cup of tea, but I can get it for myself if you'll show me where you keep the bags."

We entered his kitchen, where he pointed out the various things I would need to make tea.

"Can I make a cup for you, too?" I asked.

"That'd be great. I'm just going to wash up a bit first." He grabbed some clothes out of the closet in the front hall before heading to the bathroom.

I busied myself making the tea and then poured a cup before taking a seat at the dining room table. I pulled my cell phone from my pocket, where I had tucked it after the shower, and decided to check for messages. I had made a concerted effort to ignore my phone during most of our outing, choosing instead to allow myself to enjoy a tech-free day. I glanced at the screen and was surprised to see a text message from William Harris, the man I had met at the Acropolis Museum with Shelly.

"Huh. Wills Harris. I wonder what he's texting me about." I scrolled down the message, finishing just as Matt returned to the room. He picked up his cup from the kitchen counter and took a seat opposite me.

"Interesting message?" He nodded at my phone as he took a sip of tea.

I glanced up at his question and shrugged. "I'm not sure what to make of it. It's from a man I met when my new friend, Shelly, and I were having lunch at the Acropolis Museum. He wants to know if I would like to meet him for coffee tomorrow afternoon at some place called *The Green Park.*"

"I know it. It's a nice place with lots of outdoor seating under shade trees. Are you going?"

I put my phone down and picked up my cup of tea. "I'm not sure. I barely know the guy."

He studied me for a moment. "But you'd like to. Am I right?"

I rolled my eyes at him. "You're doing what you always did when we were kids. Trying to analyze my feelings."

He grinned at me. "I don't remember that."

"Well, it's true. I always thought you'd become a therapist when you grew up. Or a mechanic, at least. Something where you'd spend your time trying to figure out how things worked and how to fix them when they didn't. Anyway. I'm just wondering what this guy Wills wants. He seemed pretty self-assured when I met him, although we only spoke for a few moments. I honestly thought he was interested in Shelly and was just being nice to me because I was with her." I glanced back down at his text message. "Maybe I should just ignore his text."

Matt finished his tea and carried his cup to the kitchen. "Maybe. But maybe instead you should take your own advice."

"What are you talking about?"

"Like when you told me I should have been upfront with the girl at the restaurant the other night. If I had come right out and asked her what her feelings were and made mine clear, maybe I could have avoided hurting her, not to mention ruining my chances to eat at my favorite place. Maybe you should just meet him for coffee and then decide whether or not to let things go any further. In the meantime, how about you take this matter to the bedroom so I can get ready to go to sleep. I'm pretty tuckered out."

I hopped up from my chair. "Oh! I'm so sorry. I forgot that I've basically taken over your home."

"Don't worry about it. If I didn't want you here, I'd say so. But unless you want to listen to me snore, which is going to happen in about three minutes tops, I suggest you head down the hallway."

I stood on my tiptoes and gave him a quick kiss on the cheek. "Nighty, night."

"Sleep tight."

The next morning, I was awakened by what sounded like a loudspeaker calling out words in Greek. I couldn't make out what was being said, but the words seemed to repeat every minute or so.

I rubbed a hand over my face and yawned. After going to bed, I had responded to Wills' text with a simple 'Okay', expecting him to fill in the details of what he was suggesting. When I hadn't heard from him in several minutes, I decided to put my phone on *do not disturb* and *airplane* mode and go to sleep. Unfortunately, the knowledge that I wouldn't be able to hear a ding should he reply kept me from settling down for over an hour until I finally fell into a fitful doze.

I reached onto the bedside table where I had placed my phone, clicking the buttons to activate it again. Almost immediately, my phone started pinging. I studied the screen and saw that Wills had left me three text messages sometime after midnight. *Wow. He must really be a night owl,* I thought. I read through the messages and then laid the phone on the bed next to me. The first one had simply said, '*Great. I'll get back to you with the plan.*' Followed by, '*Would 11 a.m. work for you?*' And then, '*Or maybe we should say 3 and have a late lunch?*'

I wondered if he had stayed up all night waiting for my reply, which made me feel momentarily bad until I realized how crazy it was to expect anyone to answer a text after midnight. I picked up my phone again and typed a response, suggesting that 11 a.m. would work best for me. It was already 9 a.m., which meant I would have to hustle if I was going to get ready and find my way to the restaurant in time. But coffee felt like less of a commitment than lunch.

I got out of bed and headed to the bathroom, and then dug around in my clothes until I found an outfit that felt right: one that didn't scream *I'm interested,* but that I felt reasonably attractive in.

When I walked into the kitchen, Matt was already up, working on his laptop. He looked up with a grin as I entered. "Going somewhere?"

"Uh huh. I'm hoping you can tell me how to get to that Green Park place. I'm supposed to be there at 11 a.m."

"Good for you." He glanced at the time. "I'd offer to give you a ride, but I don't think I can get ready in time. Some work came through that I have to finish this morning. Why don't I call you a taxi? It's only about a ten-minute ride from here, so I can arrange for them to come at 10:45 a.m. That'll give you time for some breakfast first if you're hungry."

I considered his suggestion. For some reason, the idea of eating didn't interest me, but I decided I should at least have a bite of something before I left. "I'll just have a piece of fruit." I reached for a banana out of a bowl on the kitchen counter. "Say. What was that noise outside this morning? It sounded like someone was making an announcement."

"Gypsies. They drive around the neighborhood with a loud-speaker on their truck and ask for donations: furniture, clothes, and other household goods that people want to get rid of. Then they take them to one of the weekly farmers' markets held in different places around the city and sell them. At least that's what you heard this morning. At other times, they're announcing things they have for sale. Like fruit, vegetables, and eggs. They only do that in the neigh-borhoods where there isn't a weekly market. A lot of places have a market, or *laiki agora,* that takes place on the same day each week. They cover several blocks of a street with tables and tents selling everything you could imagine: fruits, vegetables, eggs, herbs, olives, nuts, clothes, and cleaning supplies. A lot of other stuff, too. It's pretty amazing. At the end of the sale time, everything goes for half price or more. That's when you see a lot of people hustling up with their rolling carts."

His description of a farmer's market in Greece was intriguing, and I immediately started conjuring up images of what it must be like. "That sounds interesting. I'd like to go to one of those some time."

"I can arrange that. There's not one in this neighborhood, but I know of a couple close by." He turned back to his laptop. "I need to get back to work now, but why don't I pick you up outside the Green Park at one o'clock? Unless you'd rather keep your options open." He grinned at me teasingly.

"I think that will be fine. As I said last night, I'm not sure what Wills has in mind, but my plan today is to just see how things go."

"Makes sense. I'll see you at one then. I'll pull up in the street just outside the door of the restaurant. If you change your mind, just text or call me."

---

I stepped out of the taxi a few minutes before 11 and spotted a sign for the restaurant just in front of where I stood. I glanced up and down the street, noticing that the restaurant appeared to be on the front edge of a park with both paved walking paths and green, grassy areas. *Hence the name*, I thought.

I headed to the front entrance of the restaurant. There was an enclosed area just to the right, but the majority of the dining area appeared to be outdoors, with seating that was spread out over a large area to the left side and rear of the indoor space. Many of the tables stood under the cover of large umbrellas or wooden pergolas, while others were out in the open. I felt a momentary sense of panic when I realized I might not recognize Wills, having seen him only once. But my worries were quickly erased when I spotted him waving in my direction. He stood as I approached and pulled out a chair for me to sit.

"Hello, Jesse. It's good to see you again."

"You too, Wills. How have you been?"

"Quite well, thank you. I've been getting things sorted out here in preparation for my uncle's return. I believe I mentioned to you that he has been on a dig on Santorini. He'll be returning tomorrow, and then I'll join him on his next venture."

The waitress brought menus to the table and asked about our drink orders. Both of us ordered coffee—a frappe for me and an Americano for Wills. I laid the menu aside.

"Where will you be going with your uncle?"

"To an island called Andros. It's the northernmost island in the Cycladic chain. We'll be leaving from the port of Rafina. The ferry ride from there is about two hours. Then there's another half hour or so to get to the village where we are scheduled to meet his team."

The waitress brought our coffee and asked if we would like to order anything to eat. Wills asked for a croissant, and I decided to join him.

"What sort of team are you referring to?" I asked.

"An archaeological group. There is a place called Strofilas on the island. Apparently, it's the site of the oldest city in Europe, dating back to 4500-3300 B.C. It was found almost entirely intact in early excavations and revealed a social structure that was amazing for the time, or actually most anytime."

What he was describing sounded vaguely familiar to some things I had studied in one of my college classes, but there was still a lot I was struggling to comprehend. "That sounds fascinating, but I'm afraid my understanding of archaeology and the historical roots associated with it is pretty limited. I hope to remedy that eventually, but for now, I'd appreciate a little more detail about what you're referring to."

"No problem. I'm happy to elaborate." He paused for a minute as he appeared deep in thought. "Imagine coming across the ruins of your hometown ... Nashville wasn't it? But many, many years earlier than it was actually built. Wouldn't it surprise you to find evidence of a well-planned city thousands of years before anyone knew they could even exist?"

I frowned as his description began to take shape in my mind. "Was Strofilas a very large place?"

He nodded emphatically. "Over 30 acres. The excavations showed evidence of large buildings with thick, quadrilateral walls. There have also been a number of artifacts like clay pots, stone tools, jewelry, statuettes, and bronze objects uncovered. Perhaps the most surprising findings were carvings on the rock walls of animals, fish, and over 60 ships that give even more information about life at that time. Overall, these things suggest that during this period an advanced culture took shape with large, organized, maritime societies. It's utterly fascinating!"

Although I still felt somewhat lacking in my ability to see the big picture of what he was describing, his enthusiasm was contagious, and I found myself getting excited about the implications. "And all of that was found on this island you mentioned. Andros?"

"Yes. Along the western coast of the island."

"And that's where your uncle has been working? Or, plans to go for work?"

"Not exactly. The archaeological findings at Strofilas are closed now, but there's another site nearby called Paleopolis, which translates to *old city*. Supposedly, it was the ancient capital of the island, and the only city during the Classical years. Part of the city was destroyed by an earthquake during the 4th century A.D., but it continued to be inhabited until the early Byzantine period. Recently, they found evidence of a basilica thought to have been destroyed by the earthquake, but that may have been replaced in later years. A few years ago, they uncovered a mosaic floor in the nave of the basilica. Excavations were halted in an effort to preserve the findings. My uncle and his team have been commissioned to revamp the work."

"Wow! That's pretty impressive. Although I took some classes on archaeology in college, I'm still constantly impressed by how much can be learned by simply digging around in the ground. I'm sorry. I guess that sounds pretty silly."

He shook his head with a slight smile. "Not at all. Most people have no idea what we can learn by, as you say, *digging around in the ground*. It's a lot to take in." He leaned back in his chair and lifted his cup, swallowing the remains of his coffee. "I've been selfishly yakking away while barely giving you a chance to tell me about your travels. What have you been up to since I saw you at the museum?"

I tore off a piece of the croissant and stuffed it in my mouth to buy time before answering. *What had I been doing that could possibly match the things he'd been talking about? Sightseeing? Shopping?* When I finished chewing, I looked at him with a shrug.

"Not much, I guess. I roamed around Plaka on my own after Shelly left. Then my cousin picked me up and took me to his apartment, and we went to dinner in an area called Fokionos Negri. Yesterday, we took a drive to a place called Sounion, where there's the Temple of Poseidon. It was really lovely."

He smiled and said, "Sounion is on my wish list. Although I'm afraid I've been under the cosh since arriving here. What with my uncle's plans and all. There always seem to be odds and sods for me to take care of."

*Did I hear him right? Under the cosh? Odds and sods?* "I'm sorry. What did you just say?"

He chuckled. "Forgive me. I guess I'm a bit tired. I was describing how I've been feeling under pressure, dealing with a lot of assorted things to attend to. The expressions I was using fall under the category of British slang, which I'm really not in the habit of using very often, although they tend to trickle out now and again."

I lifted a hand to wave off his apology. "I totally understand. We have a lot of slang expressions in the southern part of the States that I'm guilty of throwing out from time to time. Being a school teacher, I've tried to erase them from my vocabulary. But sometimes they just pop out."

He looked at me curiously. "Like what? I'd love to hear some *Southern slang*, as you called it."

I thought for a moment before answering. "Well, like, *if I had my druthers*, which means, if I had things my way. Or, *over yonder*, to indicate something at a distance. And one of my favorites, *all gussied up*. You use that one to mean someone is dressed very nicely. Nicer than usual, that is. Oh, and *preaching to the choir*. That one means someone is trying to convince you of something that you already agree with. There are a lot of others, too. Just like I bet there are other British slang expressions you know."

He laughed and nodded. "I'm absolutely *gobsmacked* by you, Miss Holloway. What a delight you are!"

I blushed at his compliment. Although I again found myself wondering exactly what he'd said, his general meaning was clear. I had to admit I was beginning to feel very positive about Wills, which was a feeling that came about somewhat unexpectedly, given our uncertain start.

Wills glanced around the restaurant as if noticing it for the first time. "Lovely place, this. I've walked past it a time or two on my way somewhere else, but I've never ventured inside until today." He looked directly into my eyes. "Thank you for joining me. I hope you'll allow me to call you sometime. Perhaps we can take in some of the sites together. There's still a lot of Athens I'm yet to explore, and it would be lovely to have your company."

I was pleased at his suggestion, although I wondered how we could fit in another outing given his plan to leave shortly with his uncle. "I'd like that. But it sounds like you'll be leaving Athens soon."

"Not for a few days at least. My uncle will need some time to sort things out before his next venture and have a bit of a rest, although that's rather rare for him. He's not one for lying about much."

Just hearing his description of his uncle made me feel tired, and I stifled a yawn as Wills flagged down the waiter. He asked for the bill before giving me an apologetic look.

"I'm sorry if I've been going on a bit too much about myself. I'd love to hear more about you. Your life. What your work entails, and what brings you to Greece."

I shook my head at his apology. "I've enjoyed hearing about your uncle and his explorations. I'm afraid my story would be pretty dull by comparison. I teach history at a high school in California, although I think of it as just a necessary break to allow me to get in better shape financially. I would really rather have continued on for my master's degree. I've thought about majoring in archaeology. Not that I know a lot about it at this time. But the few classes I've had were so fascinating that I've decided that might be what I want to do with my life. Like exploring ancient history. Unfortunately, I had to face the fact that it would be smarter for me to pay off at least part of my student loans first.

"As for being in Greece, I guess you could say I'm here because of a lucky break. A friend had booked a trip here, but when her plans fell through, she offered me the chance to take over her booking. I was hesitant at first, but when I mentioned it to my dad, he suggested it would be a good chance for me to reconnect with my cousin, Matt.

"Apparently, the trip was available through a special booking agency that offered a deep discount when ten or more people booked at the same time. My friend was told about the deal by a mutual friend, and she joined a group who were making the booking. Unfortunately, shortly after she committed to it, she found out she wouldn't be able to make the trip after all because of a family emergency. The flight was non-refundable, but it offered the possibility of transferring the ticket to someone else. So, I guess you could say her misfortune became my jackpot. I chose to venture out on my own after the flight was over rather than join the rest of the group. That's where visiting my cousin, Matt, comes in."

"That's remarkably good luck, as you said. So here you are in Greece. How has the trip been for you so far?"

"Good, overall. I'm still trying to adjust to the time zone difference, although my cousin has been very accommodating. He's pretty much turned over his bedroom to me and taken time off work to show me around."

Wills glanced at the bill that the waiter left and laid several euros on the table. "I believe you said he works in the tourism industry?"

"That's right. My understanding is that his job is mostly done by computer or phone, but he's talking about taking a trip soon to monitor one of their new tour guides. He mentioned Santorini and said he might be able to arrange for me to tag along."

"Really? How exciting. I'm sure you'd love it."

"It sounds like a wonderful place, although I'm worried I'd be intruding. I need to talk about it with him some more."

Wills stood and stepped around behind my chair, pulling it out slightly as I stood. *Must be a British thing*, I thought. Because I certainly wasn't used to such manners from any of the American men I spent time around.

We walked to the door of the restaurant and stepped out onto the street. I glanced at my watch.

"I hope I haven't kept you too long?" Wills asked.

I looked up and saw he had been watching me. "No, no. Matt said he'd pick me up at 1 p.m. I was checking the time and saw that I still have about twenty minutes before he's supposed to be here."

Wills smiled happily. "Grand! Fancy a short stroll through the park then?" He held a crooked arm in my direction.

I laughed and looped my arm through his. "Lead the way!"

By the time Matt arrived to pick me up, Wills and I had walked through enough of the park for me to get a good idea of how large it was. There were paved or dirt-covered walkways that wound through tree-lined paths everywhere, with occasional green spaces occupied by people letting their dogs run free or children playing. I spotted a sign for an open-air theater at one point, and a small building that appeared to be selling a variety of drinks and snacks in another area.

When I said goodbye to Wills, we agreed to talk later in the evening to see if we could come up with a plan for exploring another part of Athens the next day. As I slid into the front seat of Matt's car, he looked at me with raised eyebrows.

"If the look on your face is any indication, it seems that went well."

I made a point of studiously fastening my seatbelt to buy

myself some time before responding to him. "Yes. It was nice. Better than I expected."

"Glad to hear it. Do you plan to see him again while you're here?"

I nodded. "I think so. At least we talked about it. His uncle is arriving from Santorini tomorrow. We said we'd talk later and see if we can come up with a plan."

He pulled out onto the road. "Speaking of Santorini, I checked with my office, and it looks like there won't be any problem including you on my trip there in a few days. That is, if you'd still be interested in joining me."

I thought back to my conversation with Wills. I would *love* to visit one of the Greek islands. Especially Santorini, which had captured my attention even before I arrived in Athens. But I was also intrigued about the other island Wills had mentioned.

"Have you even been to an island called Andros?"

He shook his head. "No, but I've passed by it. It's one of the other Cycladic islands. When you leave Athens from the port of Rafina, Andros is the first ferry stop. After that, you have several more, including Tinos, Syros, Mykonos, Paros, Naxos, Ios, and several others, before you come to Santorini. Since Santorini is such a long ferry ride, many people choose to fly there instead."

His description suggested that Andros was quite a distance from Santorini, which meant there was little chance I could see both during the same trip. "Do you have any interest in going there? To Andros, I mean?"

He glanced at me curiously. "Possibly. Why do you ask?"

I tried to appear nonchalant. "Wills mentioned it. He said there's a large archaeological site on the island. It sounded interesting."

"I see. Did he mention going there anytime soon?"

"Maybe. I got the impression it's one of the next stops on his uncle's agenda."

He was silent for a moment. "It's possible we could include a visit there at the end of our trip to Santorini. Or, if I'm not able to join you, I could make arrangements for you to go there by yourself."

I could feel my heartbeat increase at his suggestion. *Is that what I wanted? Really?* I had only spent a small amount of time around Wills, so why would I even consider planning an excursion to an unknown island just in the off-chance he would be there? And did I even *want* to see him again? As soon as I had that last thought, I knew the answer. Crazy as it seemed, yes, I did want to see Wills again. And more to the point, I was intrigued by the archaeological dig site he had described.

"Do you really think that would be possible? I wouldn't want to cause you any unnecessary trouble."

He chuckled. "I can't promise anything until I check a few things. But I can certainly see what I can arrange. Now. Why don't we put that issue on the back burner and turn our attention to what I have planned for the rest of *this* day?"

I felt embarrassed as soon as he reminded me we were supposed to be off on an adventure of our own. "I'm so sorry! I promise you have my full attention now. That is, if you'll tell me what we're going to do."

I had barely noticed the route we had been traveling since he picked me up, so I was surprised when he pulled into a narrow street and pointed to the right. "There. Do you see that tall hill over there? It's called Lycabettus. It's the highest point in Central Athens. I thought we could head to the top and take in the view. If we walk up, there's a nice café along the way where we can stop and have a bite to eat. If you're hungry, that is."

When he mentioned eating, I realized I barely had any breakfast and nothing except coffee and a croissant since then. "I actually am hungry. But are you saying we're going to *walk* all the way to the top? That looks like an awfully long way."

He laughed. "It's not as long as it appears. We'll park just below where you see that ring of pine trees and then take a path that winds its way up to the top. If that doesn't appeal to you, there's also a cable car we can ride to the top."

I looked down at my feet. "Walking will be fine. I'm just glad I put on my sneakers this morning."

"Well, I did warn you to prepare for some walking today. I promise you the view will be worth the effort.

We drove a little farther before Matt pulled into an open parking space on a street before the pine forest he had mentioned. He lifted a small backpack from the backseat, from which he pulled out a baseball cap.

"I thought you might need this. The sun can get pretty intense this time of day."

I glanced at the cap curiously. I hadn't seen anyone except tourists wearing one since I'd been in Greece, although fedoras like the one I had purchased seemed quite popular. Not that it would do me any good today, since I had left it back at Matt's apartment. I noticed the cap had an image of an eagle on the front. "What's with the eagle?" I held it up for his inspection.

"The Boston College Eagles. That was the team I used to play for. I just wanted to make sure you didn't get sunburned."

"That was thoughtful of you. Thanks." I pulled it snugly onto my head as we made our way up the sidewalk to a dirt path strewn with rocks.

"This is the only part of the route up that isn't paved. It gets better once we walk a bit farther."

In another five minutes or so, we reached the promised paved part of the path and began our trek up the hillside. We were passed along the way by a few other hikers, some of whom I was surprised to see wore sandals, and one hearty soul—or perhaps, *crazy* soul, I should say—wore flip flops. Eventually, we approached what appeared to be a café on the left side of the pathway. A sign over the entrance showed the name *Prasini Tenta.* Matt gestured to it with his left hand.

"This is the restaurant I mentioned. We can stop now, or wait until we're on our way back down. Whichever you'd prefer."

I glanced at the two-level terraced layout with views over the city, the Acropolis, and the distant sea. It was beautiful, and a lovely spot to have a bite to eat and take in the scenery.

"Maybe we should go to the top first. I'm afraid that if I stop here now, I'll never want to finish the hike up."

"Good idea. There's also a café at the top if you'd prefer to eat there. We can decide later."

We set out again, winding our way up the paved path, stopping on occasion to allow ourselves to enjoy the scenery. The

360-degree view over Athens was magnificent and gave me a totally different perspective of the city.

"It's really big, isn't it?"

Matt held out a bottle of water, which I gladly accepted. "Yes, it is. It's hard to realize just how big unless you get up above it like this." He pointed to his left. "Over there is the Panathenaic Stadium, where the first modern Olympic Games were played in 1896. Further to the right is the Acropolis, of course. And beyond that is the port of Piraeus."

I took in the sights he was describing, marveling at the beauty and scope of the surroundings. "It's unlike anything I've ever seen before." I took out my phone and shot a few photos before turning to follow Matt as we continued walking. When we finally reached the top, I was surprised to see a large white-washed church.

"That's the church of Agios Georgios. St. George. You might like to step inside to see what a Greek church looks like, and then there's a platform just in front that gives a great view over the sprawl of Athens."

I took his advice, stepping inside the dimly lit and cool interior of the church for a few moments before walking onto the sunlit platform. Matt walked up beside me and held out a second bottle of water. I hesitated before accepting it. "I don't suppose they have a bathroom up here?" I asked.

He laughed. "Yes, they do. It's just down those steps over there. I'll wait here if you want to go down." I scurried off in the direction he indicated, returning to find him sitting on a stone bench to one side of the church. I took a seat beside him and picked up the water bottle he had offered before.

"The other café I mentioned is over there, and beyond it is an outdoor theater that just recently reopened. There's also a restaurant, but it's only open for dinner." We sat for a while in silence, taking in the sights and sipping from our bottles. Finally, Matt stood up. "My turn to visit the toilet. I'll take your empty bottle and toss it on my way. While I'm gone, why don't you take a look at the café I mentioned and decide whether you'd like to eat there or walk back down to the one we passed."

I hopped up to walk to where the café was located. It seemed okay. The food certainly smelled good, but the view was nothing compared to the one lower down. I returned to the bench just as Matt was walking up. "What do you think?" He asked.

"I think I'd like to go to the one we saw earlier."

"Great. That would be my choice, too."

We headed back down the way we had come, arriving at the *Prasini Tenta* a short time later. Matt led us to a small table for two at the front of the lower level, which gave us a splendid view over the city. The table was shaded by a green umbrella, which provided a welcome respite from the intense sunlight overhead. I took off my baseball cap and hung it over the chair arm. "I'm glad they have these umbrellas. It cools things down quite a lot."

He glanced overhead and nodded. "The name of this place translates to *Green Tent*. I'm not sure which came first: the name or the umbrellas, but either way, it fits the space."

A waiter arrived with two menus and asked if we would like anything to drink.

Matt raised his eyebrows at me. "Coffee or beer? Or maybe an ouzo."

I looked at the walkway leading down the hillside. "I think I'd like some juice. Maybe orange if it's fresh. And some ice water."

He ordered a fresh orange juice, *freskos heemos portakali*, for me and a Mythos beer for himself.

"Would you like a snack or something more substantial?" Matt opened his menu and studied it.

I glanced at my copy before deciding on what the Greeks call toast, or *tost*, which I now knew meant cheese melted between toasted bread. In this case, the toast on the menu contained Gouda cheese and turkey pastrami with tomatoes, mayo, and chips on the side. Matt ordered spanakopita—spinach and feta cheese cooked inside phyllo dough—and a small Greek salad for himself and then handed the menus to the waiter.

I glanced across the view that spread out below us and sighed. "It's magnificent. It really gives a different perspective of Athens than what you get from just walking around the city."

The waiter brought our drinks, and Matt took a sip of his beer. "The first time I came up here, I couldn't believe it. I had seen the Acropolis from a rooftop restaurant down in Plaka. But this shows so much more of the city and the surrounding area. It made me want to just sit for hours taking it all in."

I took a drink of my orange juice. "Umm. This is really good. And fresh!" I took another sip before setting the glass down. "Moving here must have been a real culture shock for you. Did it take you very long to adjust?"

He smiled. "Who says I've adjusted? Actually, I couldn't sleep for most of the first week, what with the jetlag, which was to be expected. But also, the city was so vibrant with sounds and sights and smells. I found it hard to relax. Eventually, I got used to it, for the most part. Although I still find it so different from what I was used to in the States. Better, in some ways. But definitely different." He took another swallow of beer and looked across at me. "How about you? What do you think of life in Greece?"

I twirled the straw in my glass as I considered his question. "I haven't been here as long as you. Obviously. But it's definitely different, as you said. Much busier than any place I've ever lived. Beautiful, overall. But more than a little overwhelming, too."

The waiter brought our food, and we busied ourselves sampling what we'd ordered. My sandwich was delicious: crispy on the outside and soft and gooey in the middle. Matt took a big bite of his spanakopita and then offered a piece to me. I accepted it and, in turn, offered him some of my chips, which he laid on his plate. I pointed at the table.

"The food in Greece is something I could get used to on a regular basis. Everything I've tried has been so good."

He nodded as he speared a tomato and chunk of cucumber before dipping it in the oil in the bottom of his salad bowl. "I agree. Before I came here, I'd never eaten a salad that wasn't floating in ranch dressing. The idea that you could just pour on a little olive oil and create something so good was a shock, and definitely a healthy change, for me."

I looked over at the man sitting across the table from me. It was a little difficult to reconcile the image of the boy I remembered with the man he had become. He seemed the same, in some ways. Confident and thoughtful. But at the same time, I could detect a level of tension in his demeanor that was new.

I looked at him curiously. "Do you think you'll stay in Greece a long time? You haven't said what your long-term plans are."

"Huh. That's because I'm not sure what they are. Most of the time, I feel like this is just a temporary stop as I prepare for my next move. But other times, I can imagine myself settling down here. At least for a good amount of time. I guess part of my uncertainty has to do with the fact that I have no family or close ties here. I mean, I have a few friends I hang out with sometimes. But no one special."

I remembered the young woman at the restaurant we went to on our first night together. "But you gave me the impression you were avoiding getting too involved with anyone. At least, with the girl at the taverna where we went the other night. Was that just because you weren't that interested in her, or is it something more?"

He looked thoughtful for a moment as he stared across the view below us. "I'm not sure. There's a part of me that would love to have someone special in my life. Someone to share things with. But I also feel myself pulling back whenever anyone acts like they're getting too attached to me." He shook his head and shrugged. "I'm kind of a mess, I guess. It's been this way ever since my parents split up."

My head shot up in shock. "They what? I had no idea your parents got divorced. When did that happen?" It's true, it had been several years since I'd seen his parents, but no one in the family had mentioned anything about them no longer being together.

"A few months ago. But, apparently, they hadn't been happy together for some time before that. At least, that's what my mom told my sister and me after they split up. She said they had been holding on until both of us left home and seemed somewhat settled in our own lives before they threw in the towel. It was a real shock, I can tell you. They haven't officially divorced yet, but it's just a matter of time before they do.

"Maybe that's why you haven't heard about it. I think some of the family are holding out hope that they'll reconcile, but I get the impression that's not in the cards for them. I feel bad that I hadn't noticed how unhappy they must have been. It's hard to imagine that two people who seemed so right for each other could have actually been so miserable."

I was in shock by what I'd heard. To my knowledge, no one in our family had ever gotten divorced, and I found it hard to imagine what it must feel like for Matt to be going through this with his parents. "I'm so sorry. I can see how that might make you question your own choices. Have you ever been in what you would call a serious relationship?"

He shook his head as he finished the last bite of salad. "Not really. There was someone while I was in college. But after my baseball career blew up, I realized she was just enamored by the person she imagined I would become, rather than who I really am. I guess she thought life with a baseball star who had the chance to travel a lot would be more exciting than being with a guy who spends his days arranging fun trips for other people. Since then, there hasn't really been anyone special." He set down his fork and looked directly at me. "What about you? Is there anyone special in your life?"

I shifted in my chair. There *had* been someone. But I was reluctant to tell him about it. At the same time, I'd been enjoying the level of honesty we had reached with each other, and I didn't want to pull back from that. I decided to trust my instincts and share with him as he had been doing with me.

"You remember Tom Trahorn? He was our classmate in grade school. We ran into each other again in the 11<sup>th</sup> grade and started going out some. In fact, for a while, I thought he was my forever love. That was until I found out he was also dating another girl who went to one of the public schools in Nashville. Since we didn't run in the same circles, we never crossed paths. I only found out about her because one of my best friends went to a dance with a boy who went to the same school, and she saw Tom there with this girl. When I confronted him about it, he just said it was no big deal, and that he was only seeing her because she wasn't as hung up on wanting to wait to have sex as I was." I sighed and leaned back in my chair. "I was shocked, to say the least. It made me feel like some kind of prude, when really all I was trying to do was take things slow until I knew how I really felt about him. I thought we were on the same page, but obviously, he was in a whole different chapter."

Matt frowned and looked uncomfortable. "I remember him. He was always hooking up with one girl or another, even when we were in the eighth grade. I remember him saying once that the only kind of girl he was interested in was one who looked good and felt better. I thought he was pretty crass saying something like that, but, truthfully, I was also a little envious of him." He shifted in his chair and glanced at me out of the sides of his eyes. "I'm sorry you went through that. Guys can be real jerks sometimes."

I wagged my head from side to side. "SOME guys. I'm still hoping to find one who can redeem my faith in relationships."

I tossed my napkin on the table and reached for the bill. "That was nice, Matt. But you have to let me treat you. After all, I've basically turned you out of your bedroom and taken all of your time since I arrived."

He smiled. "Not true. But I'll let you pay this time. That way, you won't be able to argue when I tell you what I have in mind next."

I raised my eyebrows and looked at him askance. "Next? Don't tell me you have another hike in mind. I'm afraid that getting back down this hill and into your car is all I have left in me."

He chuckled and stood up. "Don't worry. I promise our next adventure will be a piece of cake. Literally. We're going to stop on the way home and pick up some sweets from a bakery I discovered. They have the best carrot cake I've ever tasted and, if I remember correctly, that's your favorite."

I was surprised he remembered such a small detail about me. "I can't believe you remembered that!"

He picked up his backpack and swung it over his arm before turning to head back toward the path that led down the hillside. "Don't you remember how our parents used to have those card parties during the summers we were in grade school together? They used to put out a spread of food to snack on, and I remember we used to sneak in and grab some when they weren't paying attention. You always went right for the carrot cake."

"And you always loaded up on potato chips and those miniature hot dogs in barbecue sauce. I also remember the time your dad walked into the kitchen while we were sneaking sips from that pitcher of sangria they always made. I was scared to death he saw us until I noticed he seemed to have already imbibed a few himself. He was so intent on refilling his glass, he didn't even notice we were there!" We laughed heartily as we made our way down the path.

*nine*

I slept in later than usual the next day. Whether it was my lingering jet lag, the hike we took the day before, or the assorted activities I'd been involved with since arriving, I clung to the bed long past my usual waking time. When I finally opened my eyes and glanced at the clock on the bedside table, I was surprised to find it was nearly 10 a.m. The bedroom was still reasonably dark thanks to the heavy, blackout shades that were rolled down to cover the windows each night.

I swung my legs over the side of the bed and stretched my arms overhead before sliding on the flip-flops I used for slippers. When I emerged from the bathroom, I walked down the short hallway to the kitchen and quietly opened the door. Matt was nowhere in sight, but I noticed a folded piece of paper propped up against the side of a coffee mug on the counter. I picked it up and smiled to myself as I read his message.

*Good morning, sleepyhead!*

*I hope you had a good night. I've gone into the office for a couple of meetings. There's some fresh spanakopita and tiropita on the counter that I picked up from the corner bakery after my run this morning, and the coffee pot is still half full. Enjoy your morning (or what's left of it 😊) and I'll talk to you later.*

*Matt*

I laid the note on the counter and picked up the mug, filling it with coffee from the pot before opening the fridge to add a splash of milk. I lifted the edge of a foil-covered plate and found the promised pita treats. I took a plate from the cabinet and slid out a wedge of spanakopita before carrying it and my mug of coffee to the sofa.

The shutters in the living area were open, allowing bright sunlight to fill the room. I could see a neighbor across the way leaning over her balcony railing as she peered down into the street below. A cat wove its way between her legs until she picked it up and caressed it as she headed back inside.

I lifted my mug of coffee and took a cautious sip in case it was too hot, and then a deeper one before setting it down so I could sample the spinach and cheese pie Matt had thoughtfully left for me. It was crispy on the outside, warm and salty on the inside, and I moaned in delight as I munched away. Since I had been in Greece, I had become aware of the presence of little bakeries, or *fournos* as they were called here, in practically every neighborhood I had visited. The scent of freshly baked sweet and savory treats tended to waft out their open doors as I wandered by, causing my mouth to water in anticipation. I had allowed myself to sample a few of the daily offerings from different places, and was surprised to find that even if I ordered the same thing, it usually tasted slightly different from one bakery to another. Spanakopita had become one of my favorite choices, but the tiropita filled with feta and other types of cheese was a close second.

I placed my now half-empty plate on the cocktail table in front of the sofa before lifting my mug of coffee again, taking a generous sip to wash down the remnants of the pita. I glanced around the room, noticing the pile of bed covers neatly folded at one end of the sofa. That was one thing my cousin and I didn't share in common. I had to remind myself to even make the bed, whereas he was much more of a neat-freak than me. That had been a trait I remembered even when we were children. Matt always looked neat and clean, even when we'd been outside playing, whereas I managed to collect a variety of dirt smudges within the first few minutes of leaving the house.

I stood up from the sofa, checking to make sure I didn't leave behind any crumbs before carrying my things into the kitchen. I decided to change my pattern by washing, drying, and putting away my coffee mug and plate, and then wiping down the countertop, making sure to also turn off the coffeepot. I glanced around the room, feeling satisfied with my efforts, and then returned to the bedroom where I set about restoring order to the mess I had made there. I had just finished making the bed when I heard my cellphone ringing in the kitchen, where I had left it. I hurried to pick it up.

"Hello?"

"Good morning, Jesse. Wills here. How are you this morning?"

I carried the phone over to the sofa and sat down again. "I'm good. How are you?"

"Excellent! I wondered if you fancied a midday stroll? Or perhaps a little lunch somewhere?"

I considered his suggestions. "Maybe. I'm afraid I slept in a bit later than usual today, and I've just finished breakfast. What time did you have in mind?"

There was a pause on the line before he answered. "How does a walk in the park followed by a late lunch sound? I could swing by your place to pick you up at say … noon?"

I glanced at the clock. Noon meant I had about 45 minutes before he would arrive. Since I had pretty much finished everything I needed to take care of, except for taking a shower and getting dressed, I decided that would work. I gave him Matt's address, and we agreed he would text me when he was a few minutes away. I walked back into the bedroom and studied the clothes hanging in the closet, finally selecting a pair of jeans and a blue and white striped, long-sleeve button-up shirt. I added a sleeveless red top to wear under the shirt in case it was too warm to keep the shirt on while we walked. I was just tying the laces on my sneakers when I heard a ding on my phone. I glanced at it to confirm that Wills was nearby before heading out the door.

A black BMW was pulling up in front of Matt's building when I stepped outside. The passenger window rolled down to reveal Wills waving at me as I approached the car. I strapped on the seatbelt as we continued up the street.

"Good morning, Wills. Or I guess I should say good afternoon by now." I smiled as I glanced in his direction. He was wearing a white button-down shirt with the sleeves rolled up partway and a pair of denim jeans. His light brown hair was slicked back from his forehead, and a pair of sunglasses hung from the neck of his shirt. I had to admit he was easy on the eyes, and I smiled to myself in appreciation.

He glanced at me quickly before pausing at the next intersection, looking both ways before turning onto a road made even more narrow by the fact that both sides were filled with parked cars. "You could say it's *after* noon. By a few minutes, to be precise. In Greece, they consider afternoon to occur between noon and around 6 p.m., although lunch, which is typically their biggest meal of the day, is eaten sometime around 2 or 3 p.m."

I considered what he was saying. "That's been hard for me to adjust to. Eating a big meal at that time of day. At home, I'm used to eating a decent-sized breakfast, a light lunch, and then having my biggest meal at dinner. Since I've been in Greece, I don't think I've actually ever had dinner, at least not the type of dinner I'm used to. If I eat anything at all late in the day, it has been something light. Like a snack."

"Right. Greeks typically have dinner around 9 p.m., which can include anything from a light meal to a multi-course feast. I remember the first time I was invited to someone's house for dinner here. I was certain we had finished after the first four courses, but then at least four more were brought on. By the time I left, it was well after midnight, and I was stuffed to the gills."

He paused at the next intersection and then made a rapid turn into a busy street with two lanes of traffic moving in each direction. We drove in silence for a few minutes until he pulled into a parking space beside the road. He shifted the car into park and turned off the ignition.

"Here we are. We're lucky to have found this parking spot. I thought I might have to drive around a while before finding something." He nodded out the window. "As you can see, we're back at the park where we walked the other day. Since we didn't have much time then, I thought you might fancy a longer exploration." He stepped out of the car and came around to open my door, a gesture that still took me by such surprise that I was halfway out before I realized what he was doing.

"Oh! Thank you. I'm not used to such chivalry."

"My pleasure." He held out a crooked arm. "Shall we?"

That was another trait of his that I was fast getting used to. I only hesitated a moment before I hooked my arm through his. We strolled up the sidewalk alongside the park, turning eventually at an entrance that led to a wide, double-sided walkway with a large bronze statue of a soldier on a horse in the center. We stopped to read the inscription.

"*Konstantinos Basileyee Ton Ellinon.* King Constantine the First." Wills said out loud.

"Huh. He must have been someone important".

"He was the King of Greece in the early to mid-1900s. As I understand it, he had a rather tumultuous reign on the throne."

"In what way?" I asked.

"From what I have read, he was in and out of command for several years with some rather unpleasant results. For example, he was king when the Greeks lost the war to the Turks, and later his reign resulted in a national split between the north and south sides of Greece."

As we continued our stroll through the park, I noticed several other statues scattered amongst the various walkways and grassy areas. "Has this park been here a long time? There seem to be a lot of old statues here."

"It was designed in 1934 and called *Pedion tou Areos*. That means Field of Ares, who was the God of War, according to Greek mythology. It's one of the oldest and largest parks in the city of Athens. The reason there are so many statues is that it was designed to pay tribute to the heroes of the Greek War of Independence of 1821."

His explanation was interesting, but I was far more impressed by the appearance of the grounds. "It's very clean."

He smiled. "Perhaps now. When it was first built, they ran short of funds to complete it the way they had planned, but it underwent a complete renovation in 2010. Before that, I'm afraid it was a bit seedy. Lots of questionable people. Drug transactions. Garbage everywhere. It's a rather lovely spot now."

I glanced around appreciatively. "Yes, it is." I wondered how he knew so much about the park and Athens, in general. "Have you been here many times before? To Athens, I mean."

He stopped beside a wooden bench with stone arm supports. "A few times. This is a good stopping off point for my uncle's work travels. I've been accompanying him more often recently. I can't say he's exactly slowed down, but there has been a difference in his demeanor over the past six years or so." He gestured to the bench questioningly, and I sat down. "Truth is, he's a bit off his kilter these days, although most people wouldn't notice. I just feel better keeping close by." He took a seat next to me.

"That's nice. For him, certainly. But I'll bet it's also pretty exciting to see his work close up. As I mentioned, I have a degree in history from UC Berkeley. I plan to eventually get my master's and maybe even a doctorate in archaeology, but I had to take a break in order to put aside some money to continue my studies. That's why I've been teaching high school in California for the past two years." I shifted in my seat. "It's not bad, but it's not what I really want to be doing either. At least, not long-term."

He looked thoughtful for a moment. "My uncle mentioned he's looking for an assistant. The one who was working with him took a fall on site and had to head back to England. Perhaps you would be interested in talking with him? Or maybe I'm overstepping." He turned sideways on the bench and looked at me directly, which made me feel more than a little uncomfortable. When he looked at me that way, it felt as though he was seeing inside my mind. And since I wasn't at all certain what was in there, I wasn't sure I wanted him to look.

"I don't know. I don't see how I could possibly even consider changing jobs right now. At least, not until I have saved more money." *But maybe it would be a temporary solution?* I had planned to return to California and work part-time at a job I had lined up for the remainder of the summer. Maybe what he was suggesting could provide an alternative.

He nodded. "I understand. But perhaps it wouldn't hurt to chat with him? He might have some useful insights on your potential career."

I crossed my right leg over the left and shook my foot up and down—a gesture I was prone to when I was mulling over a decision. It occurred to me that it was also a mannerism I seemed to share with Matt. "Okay. I guess it wouldn't hurt to talk to him."

He clapped his hands together. "Grand! He's arriving later today. I'll see if I can set something up for tomorrow. Is there a time that would work best for you?"

Hearing that he would arrange something so soon was a little scary, and I froze for a moment before answering. It was true I didn't have any plans for the next day, but was I ready to meet his uncle and talk about something that might turn my plans for the rest of the summer upside down? On the other hand, it could be just the opportunity I'd been hoping for. "I don't think I have anything planned. Why don't you just check with him, and I'll try to make myself available at his convenience."

"Right-O. I'll ring you when I find out. In the meantime, how about that lunch? I'm famished, and I fancy one of those pita things I saw at the *fournos* across from the park. The one we passed while driving here. I believe it's just a short walk away." We stood and headed in the direction of the park entrance. My mind was spinning with *what ifs* and *shoulds* or *shouldn'ts*. I wasn't sure I had any appetite for lunch, but I decided it would be a good distraction from our conversation.

# ten

The next day arrived too soon for my comfort. I had spent the previous evening with Matt, watching old movies on TV and talking about the past. It had been fun and a welcome distraction from waiting for a phone call from Wills. So far, I hadn't heard anything from him since we parted ways after lunch the previous day, and I was beginning to regret agreeing to meet his uncle. Maybe he'd had second thoughts about recommending me for the job. Or maybe his uncle had already found someone else to fill the position.

I busied myself around the apartment. The coffee maker was filled and starting to perk. My bed had been made, and the room was tidied up. Matt had left early for an appointment, and I had the apartment to myself, which, under normal circumstances, I would be grateful for. But on this particular morning, I would have welcomed the distraction of someone else's presence.

I walked over to the sofa and clicked on the TV remote, scrolling through the channels in an effort to find one with

English, or at least English subtitles. I finally settled on a cooking show. The dialogue was in Greek, but it was still fun to watch how the male chef mixed up the various ingredients for the dishes he was preparing.

My mouth started to salivate in response to the delicious-looking food, and I made my way to the fridge to scan the contents. There was some leftover souvlaki from the night before and another container of cut-up tomatoes and cucumbers. Neither appealed to me, so I took out a container of jam and a package of cheese, intending to layer them on top of a couple of crispy rusks from a package on the counter. That was what I had learned the little bread-shaped cracker-like things were called. I took out a plate and arranged the food before carrying it to the dining room table, refilling my mug with coffee on the way. I had just filled my mouth with a generous portion of cheese and jam-topped rusk when my cell phone rang. I chewed vigorously in an effort to free my mouth to speak, finally managing to get out a muffled *Hello.*

"Jesse? Did I wake you?"

I swallowed the mouthful of food before answering. "No. I was just having a little breakfast."

"Ah. Well, I have some good news for you. Or at least I hope you'll feel it's good news. My uncle is interested in meeting you. He said that from what I've told him, you might be a perfect fit for the job as his assistant."

"Really? I'm surprised. I mean, that's great, but he hasn't even met me yet."

He chuckled. "Of course, you'll have to pass inspection. But I've put in a good word for you."

I shifted in my chair. The news was great. *Wasn't it?* Everything was moving so fast that I couldn't decide if I was thrilled or scared to death. A little of both, I guess. "Thank you, Wills. When does he want to meet with me?" I was hoping he'd give me a little time for the news to digest, not to mention the food I had choked down, which was currently threatening to come back up.

"This afternoon, if you're available. He has to wrap things up fairly quickly since he'll be leaving again in a couple of days. He asked if you'd be able to come to a hotel near his apartment around 4 p.m.? It's called the Radisson Blu. It's just next to the park where we walked yesterday. He's meeting a colleague there for a late lunch, and thought he'd combine a chat with you afterward in the lobby. I could stop round and fetch you."

I glanced at the clock on the wall. It wasn't even noon yet, so meeting him around 4 p.m. shouldn't be a problem. "That time should work, but you don't need to pick me up. I can take a taxi."

"Certainly, you COULD. But it will be much easier for me to come by since I thought I could join you. At least for the beginning of your meeting. That way, I can properly introduce you."

I thought about what he said. Sure. It made sense for me to ride with Wills since he was going to be there anyway. I was just a little hesitant to give him the impression we were becoming a THING, whatever that was. "If you're sure it won't be a bother, then, yes, I'd like you to pick me up."

I reminded him of Matt's address, and we agreed on a meeting time. After I hung up, I leaned back against the dining room chair and took a deep breath, releasing it slowly as I tried to calm my nerves. *What was I thinking!?* It's true I was on a break from teaching for the summer, but I had every intention of returning to California after my vacation in Greece. I had lined up a part-time job for the rest of the summer at a local art gallery near where I lived to add to my meager savings. There was no way I could accept a job with Wills' uncle without throwing a major wrench into those plans. Plus, I only had a small suitcase of clothes with me, which would just barely be enough to carry me through the rest of my vacation.

Thinking about clothes sent my heart racing again. *What did I have to wear that could possibly be acceptable for a business meeting?* I stood and hurried into the bedroom, pulling clothes out of the closet and tossing them in a heap on the bed as I rejected one after the other, finally settling on a pair of black slacks and a turquoise button-up shirt. It wasn't very fancy, but it would have to do. Luckily, I had packed a pair of black flats at the last minute, which would keep me from having to show up in my well-worn sneakers.

I checked the clock again and decided to head to the shower. What was supposed to be a relaxing and possibly boring day was quickly turning into a major ordeal!

---

Wills picked me up shortly before 4 p.m., and we drove the short distance from Matt's apartment in Kypseli to the hotel on Alexandras Avenue. He pulled up in front of the hotel, and a valet rushed out and opened the car doors for us to exit before hopping in and speeding away. Wills gestured for me to walk ahead of him through the automatic doors that led into the hotel lobby. We paused just inside as Wills looked around until he spotted his uncle in a far corner of the room. He placed one hand on my elbow and steered me in that direction. I was embarrassed to find that my feet had suddenly become as heavy as concrete and my mouth was so dry I was afraid I wouldn't be able to speak. We stopped in front of a man who smiled up at Wills and stood in greeting.

"Jesse Holloway, this is my uncle, Simon Harris." His uncle had dark brown hair that was thinning on top with streaks of silver along the sides, and a ruddy complexion that spoke of the hours he spent outdoors. I guessed him to be in his late 40s or early 50s since Wills had indicated he was his father's younger brother, but by appearance alone, it was hard to guess. He held out a hand in my direction.

"Miss Holloway. It is a pleasure to meet you. My nephew speaks highly of you."

I extended my hand, which he gripped firmly, causing me to wince in response. He must have noticed my reaction because he smiled and softened his grip. "Forgive me. I'm afraid my years of manual labor have left me with a rather rough grasp." He released my hand and gestured to the sofa behind him. "Won't you sit down and join me?"

I settled into the seat, smoothing my blouse in an attempt to straighten out any wrinkles.

He gestured at a passing waiter. "Three coffees, *parakalo*. Or, perhaps you'd like something cold to drink instead?" He looked at me questioningly.

"Coffee is fine, thank you." I noticed that Wills was still standing in front of where we sat.

"I thought I'd leave you two to get acquainted." Wills turned to the waiter. "I'll have my coffee over there." He pointed to a table and chair next to a window that looked out on the street in front of the hotel.

Mr. Harris shifted so he could face me. "Wills tells me you have a degree in history from the University of California at Berkeley, and that you're teaching high school now."

I nodded. "That's correct. I plan to continue my studies eventually, but I have to work out the finances first. I would love to get a master's in archaeology and possibly a doctorate. Unfortunately, graduate school at UCB is pretty expensive, and I still have student loans to pay off." The waiter returned with our coffees and two glasses of water. I reached for the water and took a long swallow, grateful for something to quench my thirst.

Mr. Harris picked up a packet of sugar and added it to his cup, followed by a small amount of cream. "I remember those days. It can be very frustrating when all you want to do is follow your passion, but practicality gets in the way. I was lucky to get a scholarship at the undergraduate level, and then a chance meeting with a professor from Oxford who specialized in my area opened the door to my graduate studies. "He took a sip from his cup before placing it back on the saucer. "I understand Wills has told you about our excavations on the island of Andros?"

"Yes. And in Santorini before that. It sounds very exciting."

He smiled and nodded. "Exciting and exhausting. I'm lucky to have a very diligent team. Nonetheless, the days can be quite long. I'm not involved as much in the actual physical work anymore. My job is more about researching the finds, cataloguing them, and communicating our progress with our benefactors. Unfortunately, my assistant, who was responsible for helping me with all of that, tripped on a shovel and fell into an open site, causing her to suffer a broken ankle. She had to be flown back to England, where she'll spend several weeks recovering before she can rejoin us." He shifted in his seat and crossed his arms. "That's what brings me to our meeting. Wills seems to think you would be a valuable addition to our team."

I lifted my cup of coffee and took a sip in an effort to collect myself. I didn't know why I felt so flustered meeting Simon Harris, but I felt like a child meeting one of my friends' parents. "I'm flattered, but I honestly don't know if that's true. I've only been on a few digs, and then it was just to observe how things are done for a class I was taking. I've always dreamed of being more directly involved, but I imagined that would have to wait until I finished my graduate work. Or, at least until I was well into the process."

He squinted at me as if he were peering into my mind. "What is your dream, Miss Holloway? If you could conjure up the ideal scenario, what would it look like to you?"

That was a good question. What *would* it look like? I thought about my answer for a few moments before responding. "I like the idea of being somewhere uncovering hidden secrets from ancient times. I mean, I know that's basically what archaeology is all about. But I want to be directly involved in the process. Everything from getting my hands dirty to writing up my findings and then presenting them. Not all of that right away, of course. I imagine my involvement would have to start at the grassroots, if you'll excuse the pun. I think it would be fascinating to just be able to play a role in uncovering something amazing and helping people be aware of it. I always thought Greece would be the ideal place for that to happen since its history is so deep. That's one of the main reasons I chose to take a vacation here. I wanted to get a feel for the country. To absorb a bit of the vibe of the place. From what I've seen so far, it's absolutely fascinating."

As I was talking, I noticed a glint in his eyes that widened into a smile as I finished. "Yes, it is. And the more we can uncover its past, the more fascinating it becomes." He took out his phone and touched the screen. "We'll be leaving Athens by ferry on Wednesday to head back to Andros. Can you be ready to join us by then?"

His words took me by surprise. "Really? Are you asking me to be your assistant?"

He smiled. "Not right away. To start, I thought you could tag along and get a better feel for what you would be asked to do. After that, we'll see whether or not it would be a good fit for us and for you."

Wednesday was only three days away. Leaving Athens then meant I would have to cut my visit with Matt short. But it also meant I would be given the chance to see first-hand the inside workings of an archaeological dig. And one in Greece at that! It was a scary prospect, but it also felt like an opportunity I just couldn't pass up. "I'll need to talk with my cousin. He was in the process of arranging for me to join him on a tour of Santorini. I just need to make sure I won't be messing up any plans he's already made if I bow out of that."

He looked thoughtful. "Santorini? When was that visit supposed to occur?"

"I'm not certain. My plan is to be in Greece until the end of the month before heading back to California. I suspect he was trying to arrange a visit there sometime in the next week or so."

He tapped one finger against his phone. "Part of my team is on Santorini as we speak, finishing up some things we've been working on for the past several weeks. The rest of us were planning to head there immediately after we checked on things on Andros. You could go with us to Andros and then, regardless of whether or not we decide to move forward with employing you, you'd be able to join your cousin on Santorini. I'd hate to cause you to lose time with your family member. I know how important those connections are."

What he was describing sounded perfect beyond belief, and I was grateful to Wills for recommending me to his uncle. "Could I get back to you after I talk with my cousin? That way, I'll have a better idea what his plans are."

He nodded and waved a finger at the waiter. "Certainly." He reached into his coat pocket and pulled out a card, extending it to me. "Here is my number. Just text or call me with your decision." He laid a ten euro note on the tray the waiter presented and stood up. "Now, if you'll forgive me, I need to return to my apartment. I'm afraid my recent travels have taken their toll on me, and I need a bit of rest before continuing my work."

I stood, as well, as I said goodbye and promised to get in touch with him soon. As I watched him leave, I became aware of Wills walking rapidly in my direction.

"I trust that went well? My uncle seemed quite taken with you."

I raised my shoulders uncertainly. "Oh, I don't know about that. But he invited me to join him when he travels to Andros in a few days. The way we left things is that I will get in touch with him after I speak to Matt. We had tentatively planned for me to join him on Santorini, and I want to see when that's supposed to happen. Your uncle said it would be possible to combine the two trips regardless of whether or not I decide, and he decides, if I will become his temporary assistant."

"That sounds grand! Now, if you fancy taking a walk, there's a café not far from here on the grounds of the National Archaeological Museum. We could leave the car here, so there's no need to find a parking spot."

I pulled out my phone and glanced at the time. "Let me just check with Matt first. I haven't seen him yet today, and I don't know if he had anything planned for us."

After speaking with Matt, we agreed he would meet Wills and me at the café near the museum. That way, I'd be able to discuss what he had worked out for the trip to Santorini and, hopefully, figure out if it would be possible to combine it with a visit to Andros with Wills and his uncle.

Wills had mentioned he would be coming to Andros, as well, in order to assist his uncle with the logistics, and I found the prospect of spending more time with him to be oddly exciting. Odd, because I wasn't used to warming up to someone so quickly. Especially after my recent dating experiences. I thought of Shelly and wondered how her visit to Rome was going, promising myself to ring her up as soon as I had some time to myself. She might have some helpful insights about Wills since they were from the same general area of England. Not that she knew him at all. But it couldn't hurt to run some thoughts by her.

# eleven

That evening, I was settled on Matt's sofa with a glass of wine, trying to sort through the things that had been discussed earlier in the day. Matt had joined Wills and me at the café near the museum, which was called *Kipos tou Mousiou,* which Matt told me meant *garden of the museum.* The place looked inviting with open-air seating spread out over a large area of lawn in front of the museum. Unfortunately, I had the most disappointing food I'd eaten so far in Athens. To be fair, that may have been due to what I chose off the menu. Their listing of milkshakes had drawn my attention, but what they brought was a far cry from the thick, creamy, delicious drink I was used to. Instead, it was more like a glass of milk that had a little ice cream—and I do mean LITTLE ice cream—stirred into it.

The guys did much better. They each ordered chicken souvlaki, which was accompanied by a generous portion of French fries. The few fries I managed to steal off Matt's plate were delicious, and more than once I found myself wishing I had ordered some for myself. The only thing that held me back from doing so was the lump in my throat that hadn't dissipated since I met with Simon Harris. I had hoped the milkshake might force it down. But all it did was make it more noticeable.

Matt and Wills had gotten along very well over lunch, which was a big plus in my book. After discussing the various possibilities for my potential travels to Andros and Santorini, we decided I would leave for Andros with Wills and his uncle on Wednesday and then continue on by ferry to Santorini a few days later—either alone or with Simon and Wills—to meet up with Matt.

As Matt described it, the ferry ride between Andros and Santorini was quite long, typically taking at least six-and-a-half hours due to the multiple island stops. Luckily, there was a fast ferry that reduced the time by at least an hour and a half. That was still a long time to spend on a boat. But I was looking forward to catching a glimpse of the other islands where we would briefly dock in order to allow passengers to exit and enter.

I was excited beyond words at the prospect of seeing one of my "wish list" islands during the next week, and visiting a new one that sounded extremely interesting. I decided it would be a good idea to jot down a list of things I needed to try and pick up to add to my packed items before the trip. Sunscreen was tops on my list. I had brought a small tube with me from California, but I was already halfway through it. Below that, I wrote *two more sleeveless tops, a hoodie,* and then added *a dress* to the list. The latter was an afterthought. I wasn't sure it would be needed, but I didn't want to be caught unprepared should I need something a little nicer to wear than shorts and slacks.

I stood up and walked to where Matt sat at his desk in front of his open laptop, pausing to wait for him to notice me rather than interrupt his work. After waiting a few moments, I cleared my throat, causing him to glance up.

"Oh, hi! I'm sorry. I guess I was absorbed in what I was doing. What's up?"

"I need your help. Can you tell me where I can find these things?" I held out my list for him to read.

He took it from me and frowned slightly. "The first one is easy. You can find sunscreen in any supermarket. Pharmacies, too, but it tends to cost more there. The other things I'm not sure about. I honestly haven't been clothes shopping since I've been in Athens, although I did overhear two women on one of our recent tours talking about some discount stores they'd discovered. Apparently, they're similar to thrift stores in the States, although they pass themselves off as fancier. I heard them talk about prices under five euros for everything sold in the store." He leaned toward his laptop and typed for a moment. "Here we go. They're called *Italy Outlet*. Apparently, there are several in the area. The closest one seems to be on a street called 28 Octovriou 55. It's a short walk from here. There are others, too, if that one doesn't pan out."

"So, the clothes are from Italy? That doesn't sound like it will be very cheap."

He read the description further and laughed. "I don't think there's anything Italian about most of the things you'll find there. My impression is that they import the clothes from places like China and Pakistan. You might find a few items from Italy, but mainly they're just discount clothes from all over the world. Probably secondhand, too. At least some of them.”

I shrugged at his description. “Oh well, it might be worth a look. Can you write down the address for me? Or better yet, the directions for how to get there?”

He tore a scrap of paper from a notepad and scribbled on it before handing it to me. “The one I read about opens at 9:30 tomorrow morning. It’s about a twenty-minute walk from here. Maybe less.”

I glanced at what he wrote. The directions seemed pretty straightforward. “Thanks. I’ll check it out.” I reached for my glass of wine, which I had set on the counter, and jiggled it in front of him. “Can I get you one?”

He sighed. “I wish. I need to finish what I’m working on first, and I’d better keep a clear head while I do it. It shouldn’t take me more than half an hour. If you’re hungry, you can phone that pizza place on the brochure over there.” He gestured to a flyer that lay on the side of his desk. “They understand English, so you shouldn’t have a problem.”

I picked up the flyer and studied it. “Ham, bell pepper, and mushrooms?”

He smiled and turned back to his computer. “Perfect.”

---

The next day, I woke fairly early and decided to check out the clothing store Matt had mentioned. I studied the piece of paper where he had written the directions and set out. To my surprise, I arrived in front of the store in less than twenty minutes, despite the fact that I had stopped along the way to purchase a kotopita from a fournos in the neighborhood. Kotopita was a chicken and cheese pita with slivers of tomato and bell pepper. I had been wanting to try one since arriving in Greece, and I was not disappointed. It was a little chewier than spanakopita, with chunks of chicken in a creamy filling.

I stopped outside the clothing store and studied the windows. A sign read *όλα τα ρούχα 1 ευρώ*. I knew the last part meant one euro, but I wasn't sure what the rest meant. A young woman was walking her dog down the sidewalk toward me, and I decided to take a chance and speak to her.

"Excuse me. Do you speak English?"

She smiled slightly and nodded. "Yes. Can I help you?"

"What does that sign say?" I pointed to the front of the store.

"All clothes cost only one euro." She glanced in my direction with a smirk. "You may find something worth that much. Or maybe not."

I was confused by her skepticism, but decided not to comment. "Thanks. I think I'll check it out." She continued on her way as I headed into the store.

The inside was larger than I guessed. There was a main floor, as well as a second level accessible by a set of stairs to one side. Each level was filled with numerous racks of both men's and women's clothing. I headed to the women's area and leafed through the blouses, pulling out four that seemed interesting. On another rack, I found a zip-up, fleece jacket with a hood. I looked around and spotted two dressing rooms at the back and headed in that direction, grabbing a couple of sundresses along the way. After trying everything on, I decided that three of the blouses, the jacket, and one sundress would work. As I carried them to the check-out counter, I spied a pair of black crop pants that caught my attention, adding them to my pile. I decided to take a chance that they would fit without trying them on. *After all,* I thought, *what harm would it do if I threw away one euro?* I scoffed at myself for thinking that way, since my whole reason for buying anything in this store at all was to save money.

The woman at the check-out counter folded my purchases and placed them in a plastic bag while I pulled out six euros and laid them on the counter. I half expected her to tell me it wasn't enough, but she simply picked up the money and placed it in the cash register drawer without a second look.

Once outside, I headed in the direction I had come, stopping along the way at a supermarket to search for the sunscreen that completed my shopping list. It was reasonably priced, so I bought two tubes. When I stepped back onto the sidewalk, there was a spring in my step as I smiled with pride at my successful, solitary shopping venture. *I can do this!* I thought. I no longer felt so *lost in translation.* In fact, I didn't feel lost at all. I was beginning to recognize the businesses I was passing, even going so far as to veer off onto a side street in search of a new discovery. As I did so, I came across what must have been one of the farmer's markets Matt had mentioned. I walked along in awe of the variety of fruits and vegetables that were on display, in addition to fresh eggs, olives, nuts, household goods, and even clothes. I decided to buy a few tomatoes and cucumbers to replace what Matt and I had eaten, and then added a few peaches and some tasty-looking plums.

The market seemed to go on for several blocks, ending with several tables of clothes. I browsed through the piles for a few minutes before deciding that what I had bought at the Italy Outlet store seemed much better in both quality and price. When I came to the end of the market, I looked up and realized I had no idea where I was! The street name was unfamiliar, and I didn't recognize anything I saw. I was about to backtrack to where I started when an elderly woman stopped in front of me and asked, in English, if she could help me.

"Oh! You speak English. Yes. I'm afraid I wandered too far from my destination and now I'm lost." I gave her Matt's address. "Do you know where that is?"

"Of course. You turn here and walk past four more corners before you come to a street called Skopelou. Go to the right, and that will take you directly to your destination."

"Thank you so much. I really appreciate your help."

She nodded with a pleased look and turned to walk away. I followed her directions and was relieved to eventually find myself in front of Matt's building. I entered the front door and made my way up the steps to his apartment. I called out his name as I walked in, but there was no reply. "I guess he's at work," I spoke out loud to myself. I laid the things I had bought at the market on the kitchen counter and then proceeded to the bedroom, removing the clothes from the bag so I could hang them in the closet. I glanced over my purchases with a satisfied smile. "You did good, Jesse." I felt a little more confident now that I had a few more items to select from during my trip.

I walked back into the kitchen and removed the fruit and vegetables from the bags, rinsing them under the kitchen faucet before placing them in two bowls I found in one of the cabinets. At that moment, my phone rang, and I hurried to pick it up from where I had left it on the bed. To my delight, the screen showed Shelly's name.

"Hello! I can't believe it's you! I was just thinking yesterday that I wanted to call you. How are things going?" I plopped down on the bed with a smile.

"Just grand! I've been having the best time in Rome with my friend, Barbara. We've just come from a lovely spot near the Pantheon, and it made me think of you. It reminded me so much of some of the places we saw near Plaka. How have things been for you in Athens since I left?"

I turned onto my side, propping my head up with one hand while holding the cell phone in the other. "I've been staying with my cousin, Matt, since I checked out of the hotel. He has an apartment in a lovely area called Kypseli, and he's taken me around to some other parts of Athens, too. Did you know that Greece has a waterfront they call the Riviera?"

"Yes, I've heard of that. There's a place there called Sounion, I believe, that's supposed to have wonderful sunsets."

"Exactly! We went there one evening. Oh! And guess who else I heard from? Wills. You know, the guy you introduced me to at the Acropolis Museum. He rang me one day, and we met for coffee near a park. Then he invited me on a walk in the same park another day, followed by lunch. And then ... get this ... he introduced me to his uncle, who's an archaeologist. As it turns out, he's invited me to accompany them to an island called Andros in a few days to see a dig there. It's sort of a *feel things out* trip because the uncle is looking for someone to replace his assistant, who had an accident. Wills suggested to him I might be that person."

"My goodness! What wonderful news, and such a surprise, I must say. I had the impression you weren't at all keen on Wills the day we met him. Something must have changed your mind."

I frowned as I remembered my first reaction to meeting Wills. It wasn't negative, exactly. But I definitely had my guard up. "I really don't know how I feel about him. At this point, I'm just excited about the possibilities he has opened up for me. The idea that I might have the chance to participate in an actual archaeological dig on a Greek island is incredible. And even if that doesn't happen, just going to a couple of islands with such rich histories is a dream come true. Wills has been such a huge help. Matt, too, by the way. I had no idea how it would work out for me to visit him after all this time. We haven't actually seen each other since we were kids. And since we're a few years apart in age, I didn't really run in the same crowd as him most of the time. But he's been nothing but gracious and welcoming."

"I'm so glad for you. By the way. I rang to let you know I'll be stopping off in Athens again before heading back to England. But it sounds as though you won't be there anytime soon."

"When were you thinking of coming?"

She paused. "I'm not certain, but probably toward the end of next week. I don't have to be back at work for another two weeks, so I've plenty of time for a side venture."

I considered what she was saying. "I wonder if there's a flight between Rome and Santorini? I'll probably be there with Matt around the time you're considering coming to Athens. What do you think of visiting Santorini instead?"

There was silence on the line aside from what sounded like faint typing. "Shelly? Are you still there?"

"Oh, sorry. I was just checking my laptop to see if there is a reasonable way to get from Rome to Santorini. To my delight, Aegean Air has several flights a day between the two, and the fare seems quite reasonable. Why don't you check with your cousin and try and nail down the dates you'll be on the island? Then I can book a flight on my end."

"That would be wonderful! I can't believe we might actually see each other again. And on a Greek island, at that!"

She laughed. "Yes, that would be quite a treat. Well, I'll be off. Barbara and I are heading out for a late lunch. I'll look forward to hearing back from you. Ta, for now!"

"Bye, Bye."

After we hung up, I inhaled deeply, letting the air out of my lungs in a slow whoosh. I couldn't believe how everything was lining up so perfectly. If all went well, it looked like I was going to have the chance to visit a real bona fide Greek archaeological dig first hand, possibly working as a member of the team, visit a second Greek island that had long been on my bucket list, AND combine it all with the opportunity to spend more time around Wills, Matt, and Shelly. *Could things get any better?*

When that last thought came into my mind, I shook my head and scolded myself for getting ahead of myself. Sure, things could get better. But they could get a lot worse, too.

I sat up abruptly and scooted to the edge of the bed. The best thing for me to do at this point was to check with Matt on the Santorini schedule, get back to Shelly with the details, and start packing for my trip. Everything else would have to sort itself out with time. Time and a lot of luck, which wasn't something I had been privy to much of lately. But maybe the tide was turning for me. At least, I chose to believe that was what was happening. I remembered a poem I once read: *Ebb and flow, to and fro, come what may, luck make it so.* I never understood quite what the ending meant, but at this point, I chose to believe that it was a wish for all to work out for the best.

# twelve

By the time Wednesday rolled around, I had been able to lock down the date I would meet Matt on Santorini. The plan was for me to take a ferry there on the Sunday after I arrived on Andros. That would allow me enough time to check things out at the dig with Simon Harris, and see what could or could not work out as far as his assistant position went. If things went well in that regard, I could spend a few days touring Santorini with Matt and Shelly before returning to Andros to join the team.

I had contacted Shelly right away with the plan, and she'd been able to book a flight from Rome to Santorini to arrive the morning after I arrived. The timing would allow me to sort out the living arrangements while we were there, and rest a bit before her arrival.

Since I didn't know how long I would be away from Athens, I decided to pretty much pack everything I brought with me from the States, plus the items I had purchased since my arrival. It was a struggle to fit everything into my backpack and roller bag. Luckily, the bag had a side zipper that allowed me to add a couple of inches of space to the main compartment. I lifted it to test the weight. Ugh! It was quite heavy, but just manageable as long as I didn't have to lift it overhead. Matt told me I would be able to leave my suitcase in the car on the ship, but I planned to carry my essentials with me in my backpack, which I would take up to the passenger deck.

On the morning we were to leave, Wills picked me up two hours before our departure time in order to allow for the one-hour drive across the city. The day was supposed to be hot, but I decided to tuck my new jacket into the top of my backpack in case the boat was chilly. That, plus a large bottle of water, filled every remaining inch of space in the pack.

There was already a line of cars waiting to board the ship when we arrived, as well as a queue of passengers. The ship wasn't due for another 30 minutes, so Wills pulled to the end of the line and parked, suggesting we should get out and stretch our legs. His uncle, Simon, wasn't traveling with us. He would join us on the ferry, but he decided to arrive by taxi with another member of his team who had also spent the last few days in Athens. Fitting all of us and our luggage into Wills' car when we arrived on Andros would be a challenge, but Wills assured me he would make it work.

Once we were safely parked on the ship, I followed Wills up two sets of stairs to the main deck. I expected him to stop there, but he continued walking past the seating area to another set of stairs ending in an area marked "First Class." He turned to look at me with a smile.

"Uncle Simon arranged for seats up here for all of us. It's a bit more comfortable than the standard seating area, and far less crowded." He showed our tickets to an official-looking man, who gestured to the area on the far left of the ship. I followed Wills in that general direction, spotting Simon seated at a table just ahead. "There they are." He walked to the table and pulled out a chair, indicating I should take a seat. I placed my backpack on the chair next to me before sitting down. His uncle looked up when he saw us.

"Good morning, Jesse. Wills. Let me introduce you to another member of our team, James Branson. James, this is Jesse Holloway, and of course, you remember my nephew, Wills."

James appeared to be around my age. He looked American, although his accent suggested otherwise.

Wills leaned across the table and held out his hand to James. "Nice to see you again, James. Did you have a good trip over?"

James shook his hand and nodded. "Aye. Though there was a blether seated next to me most of the way. I wanted tae tell him tae shut yer geggie, but I din't. Made me feel a bit crabbit by the time we arrived."

I turned to Simon with a wide-eyed expression, which he responded to with a smile and a nod. "James is from Scotland. He arrived in Athens by plane a couple of nights ago. He'll be working with us the rest of the summer until he has to go back to Uni."

I smiled at James. "Welcome, James. I'm from the States. California, most recently."

Simon turned to me. "James is in a master's program in archaeology at the University of Edinburgh. He has worked on my team for the past two summers, and I'm hoping he'll join us permanently at the end of the year." He held up a hand at a passing waiter who stopped next to our table. "Four club sand-wiches with chips." He looked around the table. "I assume everyone is hungry. What would you like to drink?"

James asked for an orange Fanta drink.

Wills raised his eyebrows at me. "Beer? Frappe?" I asked for a frappe, and Wills held up two fingers. Simon ordered a *kafe Americanos* and a large bottle of water for the table. The waiter nodded and walked away.

We spent the rest of the trip chatting about various things. Mostly, Simon was catching James up on what had been happening with the digs on Santorini and Andros, which I listened to eagerly. After we had finished our food and drinks, Wills asked if I wanted to accompany him to the outer deck for some fresh air. When we stepped outside, I was surprised by how windy it was. I struggled to keep my footing, causing Wills to grab my arm to steady me, a gesture that caused me to blush at him in appreciation.

"The wind here is called *meltemi*. It occurs annually from June until September or longer, but the strongest winds are typically in July and August. The wind blows from the north and usually brings with it dry and warm temperatures, although at night it can become a bit cool. Andros is one of the Greek islands known for its strong winds." He pointed to an open area of sea between two strips of land. "We're traveling across what is called the *cavo doro,* where the winds pick up more forcefully due to the lack of land blocking them. In years past, it often became necessary for ferry lines to suspend service until the winds died down. Now, with larger ships, that happens much less frequently."

We stood looking at the view a few minutes longer until Wills suggested we go back inside. I made my way to the restroom so

I could try and bring my wind-blown hair into some sort of order, finally resorting to tying a bandana around my head.

When I returned to the table, the men appeared to be in deep discussion. As I sat down, I heard Simon mention *Paleopolis*.

I leaned forward eagerly. "Paleopolis. That means old city, doesn't it?"

Simon nodded and smiled. "Correct. Paleopolis was the ancient capital of Andros. It was destroyed by an earthquake in the 4th century A.D., but excavations since then have been able to tell us a great deal about the city and its inhabitants. For example, it's apparent that the people knew quite a lot about metalworking, and that the village had a thriving marketplace, a theatre, and some temples. In the modern village that exists there today, there is a small museum that houses numerous artifacts from the excavations. We will be stopping there en route to our lodgings in order to speak to the museum director. Part of our team has been onsite for the past few weeks in order to continue a dig that was started some time ago but never quite completed."

My stomach fluttered with excitement. "Will we be participating in the excavations while we're here on Andros?"

Simon nodded. "Some of us will be actively participating. James, for example. The rest of us will be cataloging the finds and determining how much further the excavations should go." He paused and looked directly at me. "I'm hoping to get your impressions once we are on site."

*Me?* I as flattered by his suggestion that I might have anything of value to contribute, but also fearful of the prospect that I would fall far short of his expectations. Luckily, Wills spoke up, preventing me from having to reply.

"Previous excavations uncovered a mosaic floor in the nave of a basilica there. It appears that the original church was destroyed by the earthquake my uncle mentioned, but a smaller one was rebuilt and is preserved in fairly good condition. Paleopolis is considered by many to be one of the most important archaeological sites on Andros, if not the MOST important one."

An announcement came over the loudspeaker, first in Greek and then English, informing us that the ship would be docking in approximately 15 minutes, and that persons having vehicles in the hold should proceed there immediately.

Wills stood up. "That's my cue. Jesse and I will go below and meet the two of you outside."

We joined the line of passengers heading down the stairs. The scene felt a little frantic as everyone scrambled to locate their car and climb inside. The noise and confusion were nerve-racking, and I was anxious to get out of the ship as soon as possible. At one point, Wills grabbed my hand and pulled me after him and into the safety of our car. The noise quickly subsided, and I took a long, slow breath.

"Getting on and off these things is the worst part. It will take some time for all of us to disembark."

I nodded, still trying to calm my racing heart. Wills reached into his backpack and removed a bottle of water. "Here. Have some of this."

I accepted the bottle gratefully since I had already finished mine. I took a few sips before handing it back to him. "Thanks. That helps."

He waved off my offer. "Keep it. I always carry two." He looked around at the cars on either side of us. "Truthfully, I don't fancy this part of ferry travel one bit. I'd much rather take a taxi to and fro, rather than fight this crowd. Unfortunately, that wasn't possible this go around." We heard a loud sound of something like metal creaking. "They must be docking now. We'll get underway soon."

True to his prediction, within minutes the line of cars began to creep forward, eventually spilling us out onto a metal ramp that I guessed had been the source of the noise we heard. Wills pulled away from the ship and parked off to the far right side to wait for Simon and James to appear. The scene around us was a frantic mess of departing cars, taxi drivers signaling to their pre-arranged pick-ups, and passengers spilling out onto the pavement. Finally, Wills looked out his side window and announced, "Here they are." He popped open the trunk, allowing Simon and James to place their baggage inside, and waited for the two of them to be seated before pulling out into the line of exiting vehicles.

We wound our way out of the port of Gavrio and up narrow streets until we reached a wider, two-lane road. I looked out the window at the sea on my right and the buildings along either side. It was beautiful! The sea was a deep turquoise color with glimmers of the midday sun shining across its wide expanse. The buildings were mostly whitewashed with burgundy shutters and doors and flat roofs, changing to peaked, red-tiled roofs the farther we drove.

Simon spoke up from the back seat. "This area is called Batsi. Many people feel it is the most desirable place on the island, although, in my opinion, it has become too intent on attracting tourists, and less committed to preserving the charm of what was once a beautiful fishing port."

I studied the village from the car window. It appeared to be filled with many restaurants, cafés, shops, hotels, and other accommodations spread along a large area of land on both upper and lower levels adjacent to the sea. Most of the establishments seemed to benefit from the stunning views across the bay, and there was a lovely beachfront that stretched along its expanse. Everywhere I looked, a large number of people appeared to be taking advantage of the various offerings.

"It certainly looks popular," I said.

Wills looked out the window and nodded. "Especially with young people. It has quite a vibrant nightlife. At least, that's what I've been told." He glanced at me with a grin. "Uncle Simon doesn't usually allow enough time for exploring places, other than the ones associated with whatever excavation he's intent on uncovering."

We drove on for another 20 minutes or so until I noticed a small sign that read *Paleopolis* with an arrow pointing down the hillside to our right. Wills turned in the direction indicated, and we slowly made our way down. The area to either side looked arid, with dark green shrubs poking up throughout the grounds. I could spot the rooftops of houses scattered haphazardly around, as well as church steeples and piles of rocks that marked the ruins of ancient dwellings or walls that lined rock-strewn paths.

Simon leaned forward and pointed out the front window. "Can you spot those hikers? This area has a very popular hiking route that follows the road we're on. It makes a loop from the top to the bottom and back again, requiring a couple of hours to complete." He leaned back in his seat. "I'm proud to say I've made that trek a time or two, although I prefer our current mode of transportation these days."

James had been strangely silent for most of the drive, but he spoke up at Simon's comment. "I've biked the path as well. It's a breeze going down. Literally. But quite a challenge coming up again."

"I can imagine," I replied. James was an odd one, from what I had observed so far. Seemingly full of himself at times and then remote at others. But then again, wasn't that what made for a good archaeologist? In my limited experience, it certainly seemed to be.

The most consistent factor along our descent was the multi-toned blue sea that lay in front of us, with what appeared to be mountains rising out of its distant depths that, Wills explained, were actually islands. Eventually, we reached a spot where it was possible to view the beach below us with the sunken remains of the ancient port and agora, or meeting place, poking out of the waters, or along the shore. Wills turned the car to our left and made his way to the modern village of Paliopolis, which sat on the slopes of Mount Petalo. We pulled into a parking lot where there was a two-level, white stone-washed building with a sign identifying it as an archaeological museum. He pulled into the parking lot and stopped.

Simon unhooked his seat belt and opened the car door. "The rest of our team is waiting for us inside." He stepped out onto the pavement.

Everyone else began to get out of the car, and I hurried to follow. Simon led the way inside, pausing to speak with a young woman at the door who seemed to have some official role at the museum. We entered a back room where several people were seated around a large table, with others standing around the room talking on cell phones.

Simon stopped just inside the door. "Hello everyone. I trust you've been getting on well. Wills and I have just returned from Athens, where we picked up James here. Some of you may remember him from last summer. This other young lady is Jesse Holloway. She's from the States, where she studied at the University of Berkeley in California. She's presently on sabbatical from her studies while she teaches school. She's here to see what we've been up to." He gave no indication that I was being considered for the assistant position, and I briefly wondered why.

I nodded at the group and muttered hello.

Simon took a seat at the head of the table, and everyone else who wasn't already seated hustled to claim a chair. I chose a spot toward the far end, and Wills pulled out a chair next to mine. Simon flipped open a notepad and cleared his throat.

"I've been looking over the notes that Margaret and Brian gave me, detailing the findings you have all produced. It's quite impressive, I must say. Margaret also informed me that she has spoken with the museum director, who is anxious to include several of the artifacts in the collection here. Margaret, why don't you fill in any details I've omitted?" He looked across the table at a woman who appeared several years older than most of those gathered, except for the man sitting next to her, whom I assumed was the person Simon had referred to as Brian. She removed a broad-brimmed hat, placing it on the table in front of her before leaning forward.

"Thank you, Simon. As you indicated, our digs have garnered quite a bit of local interest. Apparently, it was presumed that anything worth finding had been uncovered some time ago. So, the idea that there was more came as a surprise to the museum director, Eleni, and her staff. She has indicated she would like to hold a special showing of our findings once we are ready to release them. It's my impression that many of the dignitaries from Andros, as well as the mainland, will plan to attend." She leaned back against her chair. "That should gain us substantial attention and, I hope, help produce the funds to carry on here for some time. On the island at large, I mean. Brian and I feel we have pretty much exhausted our work here at Paleopolis."

Brian nodded his agreement. "Quite right. Margaret and I both feel our efforts would be better directed at another site from this point forward. Perhaps have a look at the Bistis Tower in Steinies. It has pretty much been neglected in recent years, so there's no telling what remains to be discovered there. Of course, we still believe Santorini has more to offer, as well."

Simon spoke up. "Fine suggestions, both of you. We plan to pop over to Santorini in a few days to check in with our team there. In the meantime, let's look in on the Bistis Tower and see what's happening there. Wills, why don't you take Jesse on a tour of the museum, and then we'll head on toward Hora. I've arranged for a stopover tonight between here and there. James, you can ride with some of the crew here and get yourself settled into the local hotel. As for the rest of you, good work! Once things are wrapped up in Paleopolis, we'll plan a celebration to reward you for your efforts."

The group began to disperse at that point. Wills stood and walked to where Simon sat, leaning over to chat in his ear before returning to join me. "Let's have a look around here, and then we'll meet Simon at the car," he said. I followed him to the front entrance of the museum, where I spotted the same woman who had first greeted us upon our arrival. Wills stopped in front of her.

"Eleni, allow me to introduce Jesse Holloway. Jesse, Eleni Papadapoulis, the museum director."

Eleni offered her hand to me. "It's a pleasure to meet you, Jesse. Would you like a tour of the museum?" she asked.

I was temporarily distracted by her English, which was flawless and with barely a detectable accent. "Yes. Yes, I would. Thank you."

"Let me start by giving you a little of the history of the archaeological site in general. Wills, I apologize for making you listen to what you already know quite well."

He waved his hand in dismissal. "No need to apologize. I can always learn something new from you, Eleni."

"Thank you." She turned her gaze to me. "The religious and public buildings at the Sanctuary area of the old town are mainly the ones preserved in the ruins you can see today. The first excavations in that area date from 1863. Among the significant finds are the Palace with the sacred house Arsinoio, a temple, a theatre, an altar, the house of Tributes, the Stoa, the Fountain of Niki, a cemetery, and the buildings of Kings Phillip III, Alexander IV, and Propylon Ptolemy II." She walked to where a framed map hung on the wall. She pointed to the image of a large building. "When you first enter the area, you see the Palace, which is this rectangular building. That's where the first state of initiation took place into what are called the Kaviria Mysteries. Just behind the Palace was a sacred house where those who participated in the ceremony gathered.

"In the sanctuary of that house, which was constructed between 325 B.C. and 150 B.C., the most important part of the ceremony, called the Supervision, took place. This museum was inaugurated in 2003 and was dedicated to the antiquities of the old town of Paleopolis, which was the capital of Andros Island for twelve centuries. Within the museum, the exhibits are grouped into five sections: pottery, tools, figurines, jewelry, and coins."

We followed her down a hallway that led to several rooms containing displays of the aforementioned items. I was particularly struck by a statue of the mythical winged horse Pegasus, a life-size marble lion found in a cemetery in ancient Andros, and a statuette of Artemis. The rest of the items contained in the museum were tastefully displayed on marble stands or mounted on walls painted a subtle blue, which allowed a pleasant contrast to the mostly beige and cream tones of the artifacts. Overall, the contents of the museum were impressive, but I found myself distracted by something Eleni had mentioned at the beginning of our tour.

"Can you tell me more about the mysteries you mentioned? I believe you called them the Kaviria Mysteries."

She smiled. "Yes. It is quite an interesting story. In ancient times, mystical ceremonies, or rituals, were believed to have taken place to honor fertility and the rebirth of nature. According to legend, those who participated in the ritual were women who could not conceive, but after the secret ceremonies, they were able to bear children. That is what is referred to as the mystery.

"Although there are different legends to explain their origin, the Kaviria rituals are believed to have honored the sons of the god Hephaestus, who were worshipped as gods of the sea, the vineyards, and fertility. The worship services were conducted at a certain period every year and lasted nine days. In essence, they celebrated birth. Initially, the worshipers of this mystery cult were located on Samothraki and Lemnos. Later, their practices spread throughout Greece, including here on Andros."

Her explanation was fascinating, but it left me wanting to know more. Unfortunately, we had reached the end of our tour, and Wills stepped forward.

"Our thanks for your time, Eleni. We must be joining my uncle now, but I'm sure we'll be seeing you again soon." Eleni nodded her goodbye, and we stepped outside the entrance to the museum. The sun was beginning to diminish, as clouds moved in to occlude the light. A slight breeze had begun to stir, and I could hear the sound of the waves as they gently lapped against the shoreline below where we stood. The front of the museum sat flush with a road that passed in front, and just across was a small parking area where I could see Simon waiting with James. They turned in our direction as we approached.

"There you are. James here has just been regaling me with tales of his recent adventures. Quite fascinating, but I'm afraid we must be off if we are to reach our next destination before nightfall."

James nodded before walking off toward a car where a few other members of the team were waiting. Simon stepped into the front passenger seat, and Wills opened the door to the back for me before climbing once again behind the wheel. He pulled out in the opposite direction from where we had come before turning right again onto the main road.

He looked at me with a curious expression. "How are you? You seem a bit distracted."

"It was an interesting day. I guess my mind is just full of things to process." I leaned back against the seat and closed my eyes, hoping that Wills would take the hint and allow me to ride the rest of the way in silence.

# thirteen

I was jarred awake sometime later when the car came to a stop. I opened my eyes and looked out the front window. I wasn't sure how long I had been asleep, but my mind felt fuzzy in the aftermath. Jetlag was still affecting my sleep, causing me to tend to doze off at unexpected times. I rubbed my eyes and yawned.

"Where are we?" I asked.

"A place called *Ktima Lemonies*. It's in the village of Lamyra, a short distance from the main village of Hora. Uncle Simon always likes to stay here when we're on this part of the island. The name means *Lemon Estate*. You'll see why in a few minutes." He pulled up the parking brake and climbed out of the car.

I unhooked my seatbelt and stepped out as well. Wills opened the trunk and removed our bags, which he placed on the ground behind the car. "Don't worry about these. Someone will come fetch them momentarily."

The three of us set out from the parking area, winding our way through vegetable gardens exploding with eggplants, squash, and tomatoes, a small vineyard, and an orchard bearing fruit of every imaginable variety. I could spot the lemons for which I assumed the estate got its name, as well as oranges, pomegranates, apricots, and some others I couldn't recognize.

After a short walk, we arrived at the main estate house that was built on the slope of a valley in a forest of eucalyptus, cypress, and olive trees. I stopped on the terrace and took a slow, deep breath, my nostrils filling with the delicious scent of citrus, jasmine, and herbs. I gazed across the valley at the distant sea and what I presumed was a nearby village. It was beautiful, and so peaceful. Wills and Simon walked up next to me.

"Lovely, isn't it?" Simon asked.

"It's beautiful. And it smells so good!" I exclaimed.

They both chuckled. "Wait until you see the inside," Wills said.

We entered the main house, where we were greeted by the owners, Helene and Mihalis Kargaris. Helene was a picture of grace and understated elegance, while Michaeli's rugged and tanned appearance gave the impression of someone who spent a lot of time outdoors.

Helene stepped forward and leaned in to kiss Simon and Wills on each cheek, while Mihalis extended a hand to shake. "Welcome back. I hope you had an easy drive here." Helene said.

Both men returned their greetings, and Simon gestured to where I was standing.

"Helene, Mihalis, allow me to introduce you to Jesse Holloway.

She's visiting from the States with a keen interest in archaeology. She's come to see what we're about here on Andros."

Helene looked at me with a smile. "It's a pleasure to meet you, Jesse. I hope you enjoy your time on our island." She stepped back and gestured to the front door. "Let me show you to your accommodations."

We followed her back outside and around the corner of the main house, where there were four separate small buildings. We stopped in front of the first one.

"Jesse, you'll be staying here." She opened the door, and I stepped inside to find a comfortable-looking bedroom with a small sitting area and a bathroom off to one side. The rooms were simply yet tastefully decorated in soft colors with a smooth, brick floor that reflected the cool from an air conditioning unit located at the top of one wall. I walked to a window and peered out. I could just see across the top of what appeared to be a swimming pool shaded by olive trees at one end, with a sunny terrace at the other. I noticed my suitcase and backpack sitting next to the bed as Helene stepped in behind me.

"I hope you will be comfortable here. We'll have drinks and appetizers beside the pool shortly, and in the morning, we serve a full breakfast at 8 a.m. in the main house. We don't usually provide dinner since most of our guests choose to go out to a restaurant, but I believe you'll find that the Greek idea of appetizers is quite filling." She smiled at me warmly.

"The room is lovely, and the view is amazing. Thank you."

She nodded. "I'll leave you now to get settled. Come down to the pool when you're ready."

She left with Wills and Simon close behind. Wills turned around and gave me a slight wave and a smile before disappearing inside another cottage.

I walked to the bed and sat down. The mattress was perfect: not too soft, and not too hard. I was reminded of the story about a momma, papa, and baby bear who found their beds in turn too hard, too soft, and finally just right. I chuckled to myself. *Get a grip on it, Jesse. These people probably wouldn't appreciate being compared to a nursery rhyme!*

That night, I probably had the best sleep I'd experienced the entire time I had been in Greece. Or possibly even before that! We had been treated to a relaxing time by the pool, where Mihalis had kept our glasses filled with Moscato from their vineyard. There had been a generous assortment of snacks ranging from chunks of feta drizzled with olive oil and oregano, warm, crunchy homemade bread, vine leaves wrapped around a mixture of ground meat, rice and herbs, crispy pitas filled with chicken, mushrooms, and cheese, and skewers of savory beef chunks with tzatziki dipping sauce. A selection of fresh fruit and cookies topped off the night, and when I finally climbed into bed, I pulled the sheet over my shoulders with a smile and sank into a deep, dreamless sleep.

The next morning, I rose early and opened the curtains to witness the sunrise, which featured an orange orb enclosed in deep rose and purple tones. I headed down to the main house just after eight to find the others already filling their plates from an impressive buffet.

"Good morning, everyone," I said, before picking up a plate and making my way to the start of the buffet.

"Good morning, Jesse. Did you sleep well?"

I turned around to find Helene standing just behind me.

"Wonderfully! The bed was so comfortable!"

She smiled. "I'm so pleased. It's very important to sleep well. It's the key to good health and long life." She gestured to the food offerings. "Please help yourself. Mihalis will bring you some coffee once you're seated on the terrace."

I turned back to the buffet and scanned the dishes. There was an impressive selection of breads, cakes, cheese, fruit, sliced meats, and both scrambled and boiled eggs, along with black and green olives, fresh preserves, and honey.

"Everything they serve is either grown here on the estate or locally sourced from elsewhere on Andros." Wills appeared at my side.

"Oh! Good morning."

"Good morning to you. Did you sleep well?"

"Perfectly. Better than I have this entire trip." I began to help myself to the food offerings before making my way outside to the terrace. The sun was well up by that time, but the nearby trees cast a welcome shade across the seating area. Mihalis appeared with a pot of coffee.

"May I fill your cup?" he asked.

"Yes, please." I was happy to find he was pouring regular coffee, or coffee *Americano*, instead of the little cups of Greek coffee I was still struggling to get used to. I added a generous amount of cream and sugar to my cup and took a sip. *Ummm.* It was just right: not too sweet, and not too bitter. *The three bears again!* I chuckled to myself.

Wills pulled out the chair on my right and sat down. "I noticed you didn't have any of this." He scooped a spoonful of what appeared to be lumpy pudding onto my plate. "Try it. It's homemade."

I took a small amount and placed it in my mouth. Groaning with pleasure. "What is it?"

"Rice pudding. It's especially good if you top it with some of the fresh fruit."

I took his suggestion and nodded my agreement. "It's all so delicious."

He took a bite of toast spread thickly with apricot preserves and nodded. "Staying here is one of the perks of visiting Andros. Helene and Mihalis are always such gracious hosts, and the combination of fresh air and local food can't be beat." We continued to eat in silence for a few minutes before I laid down my fork and picked up my cup of coffee.

"What are the plans for today?" I asked.

"After a while, we'll drive on to Hora to pick up a few supplies for Helene and Mihalis, and then continue on to a village called Stenies. That's where the Tower of Bistis is located. We'll take a look around the tower. Shoot some photos and examine the surroundings, and then return here in the early evening after a stop for lunch. There's a nice restaurant in Stenies that's one of Uncle Simon's favorites." He took another bite of his eggs. "Is there anything in particular you'd like to do while we're here?"

I thought for a moment. "I need to talk with Matt and firm up when I'll be meeting him on Santorini. Do you know when Simon plans for us to head there? My friend, Shelly, who you met at the Acropolis Museum, plans to meet us there, too, and I need to let her know the timing so she can book a flight."

"Yes, I remember her. How grand the two of you can see each other again while you're both still in Greece. I believe Uncle Simon mentioned he intends for us to stay on Andros another two nights and then make our way by ferry to Santorini. Most likely, we would arrive there sometime late in the day on Saturday. It might be wise if you advise Shelly to delay her arrival until Sunday, so there's time to settle into the accommodations there. I suppose you'll want her to stay with you?"

"Yes. If that won't be a problem."

"I'll make a call to the owners. I'm sure they can arrange it so your room is equipped with an extra bed, or at least a cot." He folded his napkin and laid it on the table. "In fact, I'll look into that right away." He glanced at his watch before standing up. "We plan to head out for Stenies by 9:30 a.m. We'll meet you on the terrace."

I ate my last few bites of breakfast and walked to my room in order to phone Shelly in privacy before we left. She answered on the second ring. We discussed the details of my arrival on Santorini, and she managed to book a flight while we spoke. Everything was falling into place. Everything, that is, but the outcome of the assistant position with Simon. He hadn't mentioned it to me once since we left Athens, and I was beginning to wonder if he was having second thoughts. I decided to put that possibility out of my mind as best I could and turned my attention to getting myself ready for the day's outing.

The sun had seemed hotter than usual in the morning, and I carefully slathered on sunscreen before layering a light blue, button-up cotton shirt over the dark blue camisole I was wearing, deciding it would match well with my khaki shorts. I decided to forego my usual sneakers, instead pulling on a pair of leather sandals that fit my feet snugly enough to allow me to walk comfortably, even on the rough terrain I had grown used to since arriving on Andros.

The drive to Hora from *Ktima Lemonies* only took us about fifteen minutes. The terrain had changed dramatically since we'd left the west side of the island, where the port of Gavrio, Batsi, and Paleopolis was located. The east side, which included the lemon estate and the town of Hora, was fertile and green with massive forests of pine and cypress trees, and fresh water springs that flowed down the hills to pebbled beaches with azure water. In several spots, I had noticed the same water flowing out of the marbled heads of lions where it dropped into a trough. Once, we had stopped next to one of those spots in order to fill our bottles with the cool, clear liquid.

As we pulled into town, I spotted a wooden sign with the name Chora carved on the front. "Chora. I thought you said the name of the town was Hora?"

"It is. But the C is silent when you pronounce it. The correct spelling is as you see it there."

We wove our way slowly through the narrow streets that were barely wide enough to accommodate one car, much less two. The fact that parking was scarce, causing cars to be crammed along the streets in every conceivable spot, made passing even more difficult. I was glad I wasn't driving, and I glanced appreciatively at Wills, who seemed to be taking the challenging conditions in stride.

At one point, we turned left down a winding road, stopping in a parking lot next to a supermarket. I noticed several stray cats hunkered under the shade of parked cars, and I wondered if it was common for shoppers to toss scraps of food their way.

Wills stepped out of the car and leaned down to speak to me. "I'll just be a few minutes. You're welcome to wait here unless you'd like to come inside."

I considered the choice of sitting in a hot car watching hungry cats, or joining him to explore an air-conditioned store. "I'll come with you." I quickly stepped outside, noticing that Simon had rolled down the window on his side and seemed to be absorbed with texting someone on his phone.

The supermarket was smaller than the one Matt and I visited in Athens, but larger than I expected to find on a Greek island. Display cases containing a variety of fresh meats and cheeses lined the back of the store to the right, just behind an area with fruits and vegetables. Other aisles were replete with an assortment of boxed or canned goods, wine, liquor, and beer, breads and crackers, dried pasta and rice, nuts, and olives. The left side of the store was mostly dominated by cleaning supplies and paper products. It was not as plentiful as the markets I had visited in Athens, and certainly nothing compared to the huge stores in the States, but it had a good selection of most things one could want.

I followed behind Wills as he grabbed a basket to which he added coffee, dried beans, several types of pasta, and a package of paper towels. He headed to a check-out aisle, pausing to add a large bag of mints to the basket.

"These are Uncle Simon's favorites. I try to remember to buy them whenever I can."

I nodded, leaning to grab a tray of cooked meatballs from a case near the door. "For the cats," I explained.

"That's thoughtful." He smiled at me warmly.

Once outside, I opened the container of meatballs, carrying them to the far side of the driveway and calling to the cats. The smell must have drawn their attention, because they immediately began scurrying in my direction, each grabbing a round morsel out of the container before trotting off to eat it in safety. In less than a minute, the food was gone, and the cats stood licking their lips while looking at me with an expression that seemed to say, *Where's the rest?* Wills placed the other items in the trunk of the car and glanced over his shoulder at me with a laugh.

I shrugged. "Maybe I should have bought more."

He walked over to where I stood. "If you had, I'm afraid we'd have a posse of cats blocking our way from leaving. I'm sure that's more than they usually have in a day."

I looked at him askance. "Really? That's sad."

He frowned. "Greece has a problem with stray cats. There are far too many of them, and I'm afraid they often die of hunger or disease." When he saw my expression of dismay, he tried to deflect the topic. "Come on. We're supposed to be in Stenies in ten minutes. It will take us at least that long to get out of Hora." Simon looked up from his phone when we climbed into the car.

"I've just heard from Miriam at the Tower. Apparently, they've been uncovering some interesting artifacts there. She'll fill us in when we arrive."

We drove on for a while across the main part of the village. The view along the way was a mixture of white-washed and pale-colored buildings with bright blue or red shutters, green trees and shrubs, and the sparkling turquoise water. At one point, I could see what appeared to be a small peninsula that jutted out into the sea. A church and lighthouse were visible on its north side, with a sandy beach that stretched the length of the shore just below the road we were on. I looked more intently at the lighthouse, noticing what appeared to be a series of stone steps that wound around the main body up to the door of the tower. It was a mystical-looking structure, and I wondered if it was still functional. I pointed out the window.

"What's that lighthouse called?"

"Tourlitis. The original one was built in the late 1800s, but it was destroyed in World War II. It was rebuilt in the early 1990s by an oil tycoon. Luckily, he saw fit to make sure it is fully auto-mated, eliminating the need for a lighthouse keeper. Now, it's mostly revered as a tourist attraction.

"The beach just below us is called Nimporio. There's another beach on the other side of the village, but it's not considered as desirable as this one." He pointed out the front of the car wind-shield across the expanse of water to what appeared to be a two-story, open-air building with a long terrace jutting out from one side. "That's the Nautical Club of Andros, or *Omilos* as the locals call it. Membership is a bit pricey, but it's a lovely spot to have a coffee or something to eat after a swim in the sea. They also have sailing lessons every summer for children, and a yacht race in August."

I looked across the water at the building to which he was referring, admiring the shaded exterior that jutted out across the water, and taking note of the metal ladders that provided easy access for a swim.

"It looks lovely and inviting. Especially on a hot day like this."

Simon had been unusually quiet during our drive so far, but he leaned forward at that moment to gaze out the window. "Yes. It's a lovely spot to spend an hour or two on a hot day. We can arrange to go there if you'd like. Perhaps tomorrow, if there's time. Helene and Mihalis have a membership."

Wills headed up a winding road, eventually turning to the right before continuing down the same hill on the opposite side. Eventually, he parked the car just below a visible stone pathway.

Simon stepped out of the car first and stood staring up at the hillside.

"Ah, now we will see the famous Tower of Bistis. It's the oldest one on the island, having been built in the 17th century by Stametelos Bistis. He was often called by his nickname, Mouvelas, which means representative of the Turkish Kadi. That is why the tower is often referred to as Bistis-Mouvelas."

We began to make our way up the path with Simon leading the way. "The house was originally built over an older, medieval tower from the 13th century. In the 19th century, two walls were added to provide support to the building. Unfortunately, since 2006, it has belonged to the Municipality of Andros but has been totally neglected. At present, its condition is considered beyond repair."

His description made me wonder why we were bothering to visit a site that could not be restored. "Is it still considered a valuable archaeological site?" I asked.

He chuckled. "By those of us who are inclined to think that way. Others would just as soon allow it to crumble into dust. As you will soon see, it is not far from that state now."

We stopped just below the tower and stood looking up at it. It was certainly in bad shape, as Simon had stated. But there was still a certain intrigue about it. Simon pointed to the top of the three-story structure.

"The building went through three phases of reconstruction. The first, which started in the 13$^{th}$ century, was built on the ruins of a square tower. Its entrance was from the door of the catwalk. The windows were small, each with its own heater for protection."

I looked at him for clarification. "Are you saying they had heating units at that time?"

He smiled. "Not exactly. The so-called "heater" was manually controlled to pour hot oil or water on attackers to delay them from further advancement." He pointed to either side. "There were two side walls here and here for support, which extended the area of the tower. There was also an auxiliary building on the roof that was later converted into a dovecote."

I tried to imagine the original structure as he described it, struggling to do so as I viewed the current ruins. "It sounds pretty impressive. Why has the Municipality of the island chosen to abandon it?"

He shrugged. "Money. Like most things, if it is deemed to be too expensive, it is decided to allow it to crumble to rubbish rather than attempt a repair." He began to walk around the side of the building. "Our interest is in seeing what may be uncovered from the remains. There will likely be quite a lot of artifacts that will turn up once the walls come down."

"So, there's no hope of restoring the tower? That seems to be a waste." I said.

"There's a slim possibility. The inhabitants of Andros are quite incensed about the town's abandonment of the tower, and there's talk of a private benefactor who may step up and resume the restoration plans. Whichever way it goes, there will be much for us to find."

Wills had disappeared while we were talking, and we turned as he walked up from the rear of the building. "There's a sign back there that I believe says the building is considered dangerous and has been condemned. I took a photo of it." He held out his phone, and we peered at the image.

Simon nodded. "Yes, you are correct. Please send that to me. I'll have one of our lawyers take a look at it."

A woman appeared from around the side of the tower. "Hello, Simon! Wills. I'm glad you made it back in time to see what we've uncovered." She turned and began to walk back in the direction she had come from. Simon headed after her as Wills and I scurried to catch up.

Wills turned to speak to me. "That's Miriam. She's the chief archaeologist on our team here and has quite an impressive background. She's been working with us for several years, both before and after she completed her studies. I guess you could say she's Uncle Simon's right-hand man. Or woman, to be precise. You should get to know her."

I nodded as we stopped next to where Simon and Miriam stood looking at a pile of debris on the ground. I couldn't hear what they were saying, but Simon was nodding fervently. I leaned forward to get a better look, noticing what appeared to be fragments of clay pots and implements mixed in amongst the dirt and rocks. Simon turned to us with a smile. "There appear to be several artifacts that are likely traceable to the Byzantine period, and others that are more recent. If that turns out to be true, it could help us make a case for halting any further destruction of the Tower until we can do a more thorough exploration."

The woman Wills had identified as Miriam stepped forward and offered me her hand. "Hello. I'm Miriam."

I accepted her hand to shake. "Jesse. It sounds like you've made some impressive discoveries."

She pushed her shoulder-length hair back, wrapping it in a braid before replacing her cap. "I believe so, but we need a little more time to see exactly what we're dealing with." She glanced to my right. "Hello, Wills."

He nodded in her direction. "Miriam."

I briefly wondered why he seemed so reserved in greeting her, but my curiosity was interrupted by Simon.

"Well, enough of that for now. I believe it's time for lunch. Miriam, give a call to the mayor. See if he's available to stop by the site later today or tomorrow. In the meantime, instruct the team to keep any tourists away from the premises. Tell them to put up some hazard cones if necessary." He turned to walk back down the path toward where we had left the car.

Wills smiled at me as we turned to follow him. "I told you he has a favorite restaurant in the village here. Most of the time, Uncle Simon is all business. But when it comes to food, he is quite capable of changing course."

We piled into the car and reversed our route down the hillside, turning onto another narrow road that led to the seashore. There were already several cars parked along the road, leaving no space for us to squeeze in. Wills pulled to a stop. "I'll let the two of you out here. There's probably some place to park a little farther away."

Simon and I stepped out in front of an open-sided restaurant with a sign that read *Εστιατόριο Γυάλια* Snack Bar. We were greeted immediately by a young waitress who seated us at the front, just behind a row of white plant holders that created a border between the dining area and the road. My eyes were immediately drawn to the turquoise blue water that stretched across the expanse of sea on the other side of the road. It was bordered by a beach that appeared to be both sandy and rock-strewn. A row of thatched-roof umbrellas with a couple of lounge chairs under each was lined up along the beach. Tall, rocky hills rose from the right side of the water, and I could make out a few bold figures scrambling up to the top before diving off into the sea.

The waitress returned with a paper table cover, which she placed over the top after fastening clips along the edges to keep it from blowing away in the sea breeze. I picked up a menu to scan the contents and was pleased to find it was written in both Greek and English. Wills arrived and took a seat across from me as Simon excused himself to head to the restroom.

"I was lucky. Some bloke pulled out of a parking spot just as I drove up." He picked up a menu and glanced at it briefly before setting it down again.

I pointed to the cover where the restaurant name was printed. "What does this mean?"

"*Gialia*. It's the name of this beach." He nodded across the road. "I believe it is literally translated as *glasses,* which may refer to the glass-like surface of the water here." He turned around to his left and gestured down the road. "If you go down a way, there's another beach called *Piso Gialia*, which means back of Gialia. It is usually much more crowded than Gialia because there's a beach bar with lively music that serves food and drinks all day. At this beach, you have to flag down one of the restaurant waiters if you want something, or walk around the corner to the lower level to place your order. It's not as convenient in that respect, but it's easier to get to the water from here because you have to climb up and down a long set of stairs to access Piso Gialia."

The waitress approached our table and asked in English if we would like to order. Simon had returned by that time and began rattling off a list of items in Greek before turning to me. "Is there anything special you would like, Jesse?" I looked at him askance before shaking my head.

Wills laughed at my confusion. "I usually just let Uncle Simon order for us. He is quite familiar with the food here, and everything I've ever tasted has been delicious."

I nodded. "That's fine with me, too."

The waitress left, returning shortly with a large, plastic bottle of water and three glasses, followed by a small pitcher of white wine and three little glasses. Simon reached for the pitcher and filled each of our glasses, lifting one in a toast. "*Stin uyeia mas!*"

Wills and I reiterated his toast, which I now recognized was the traditional Greek way of saying *cheers!* and the literal equivalent of wishing everyone good health. I took a sip of the wine, finding it crisp and refreshing. I looked around the restaurant. There were several tables filled with people dressed in variations of swimwear. A few stray cats were wandering beneath the tables, sniffing for scraps of food. The waitstaff, which consisted of two young women and a man, were hustling about carrying plates of food balanced on their arms. All in all, the atmosphere was relaxed, except for the busy staff, and I felt lucky we had been able to grab a table in the front, overlooking the sea. I commented on our good fortune to Simon, who smiled and patted my hand.

"I am good friends with the owner. Whenever I am on Andros, I make it a point to come here at least once. As a result, all I have to do is call ahead and let them know when to expect me, and they save my favorite table. It is one of the advantages of being a loyal customer."

The waitress and waiter arrived with several plates loaded with food, which they placed on the table in front of us. "That, and the food. Which is some of the best I've ever had in Greece." He speared a round, fried piece and placed it on my plate. "Try this. It's called *kolokokefthedes,* fried zucchini fritters." He spooned a scoop of white dip and laid it beside the zucchini. "It's best with this *tzatziki.*"

I followed his direction and cut off a piece of the fritter before dipping it in the yogurt sauce, which I recognized from previous meals. The fritter was light and fluffy on the inside with a crisp outer covering, and the yogurt sauce provided just the right amount of creamy zing. "Mmm. Delicious!" I smiled in appreciation.

Simon nodded as he proceeded to serve me from the other dishes."Horta or wild greens, fried calamari, *moussaka*, or eggplant and ground beef casserole, beet cake topped with creamy cheese, and grilled anchovies. Enjoy!"

The three of us proceeded to sample the various dishes, groaning in delight as we chewed enthusiastically. While we ate, Simon and Wills discussed the possibilities of work at the Bistis Tower. From what I could gather, they were a bit skeptical whether the private funding would come through for the restoration, but still felt there would be opportunities for excavating the ruins either way. I tried to pay attention to what they were saying, but I was distracted by the gorgeous view in front of me, and I felt my mind constantly wandering. That may also have been partly due to the second pitcher of wine that the waitress brought halfway through the meal. In general, I wasn't much of a white wine drinker. At least not while I was in the States. But there was something about the quality of the air and sun in Greece that made it more appealing.

After a while, I pushed back from the table, intent on stopping myself from licking every last morsel of food from my plate. The food had been delicious, and I was once again struck by how such seemingly simple fare could taste so good.

Wills looked at me curiously. "Did you enjoy your meal, Jesse?"

"Absolutely. Everything was so good."

Simon looked pleased. "What was your favorite?" he asked.

I thought for a moment. "It was a close tie between the zucchini fritters and the calamari. Although the moussaka was fantastic, too. And I don't believe I've ever tasted such fresh beets. And the addition of the creamy cheese on it was just the right touch!" I cautiously omitted mentioning the grilled anchovies, which I had only been able to take one bite of before realizing they were just too fishy for my taste.

They both laughed at my answer. "In other words, you found it acceptable," Simon said with a smile.

"Oh, much more than that," I replied, and then blushed when I realized he was teasing. Luckily, I was saved from having to stumble over my reply any further by the waitress returning with a generous plate of bright red watermelon.

Wills speared a large chunk. "One of my favorite customs here is their complimentary *karpouzi* at the end of a meal in the summer. It's light enough not to feel oppressive, but bursting with sweetness."

*Bursting* was precisely the correct term, I thought, as the watermelon juices threatened to drip from my mouth to my chin.

When we had finished our dessert, the waitress appeared with the bill, followed by an older woman dressed in a colorful smock. She clasped one hand on Simon's shoulder, and he stood to give her a kiss on each cheek. "Maria. You remember my nephew Wills, and this is Jesse Holloway from the United States." He turned to us. "Maria and her husband Nikos own this restaurant, and she is responsible for most of the delicious recipes it offers."

Maria greeted us by saying *Welcome* to me and *einai hara mas na sou doume* to Wills. Wills responded with *kai ego*. I restrained myself from asking him to translate for me. Instead, I smiled and said *thank you* before telling her how delicious her food was.

"I am pleased you liked it," she replied. "Simon is one of our favorite customers, although he is more like family."

"At least she doesn't expect me to wash the dishes," he said with a smile, causing the rest of us to chuckle.

After leaving the restaurant, we decided to stroll along the road fronting the water for a while to allow our food to settle. I noticed a dirt path off to the right side that went up a rather steep hill and asked Wills about it.

"That's one of the hiking paths Andros is known for. They're actually called *Andros Routes*. Their popularity brings tourists from all over the world to hike the paths, many of which are quite steep and challenging. This one passes by a small church on the crest of the hill before continuing down to the main village of Hora."

I looked up the path with interest. "Have you done much hiking here? On Andros, I mean."

"Unfortunately, not as much as I would have liked. Work keeps me far too busy."

We strolled on in the opposite direction, passing a few private residences on the left, followed by an outdoor café and a garden area with several small buildings, which Simon identified as a recently opened Airbnb. A little beyond that, on the right side of the road, there was an iron gate with a set of stone steps leading up to a small church. Wills pointed to it and explained that the stairs continued down the other side, ending at the beach he had referred to as *Piso Gialia*. His earlier description of the area had piqued my interest in seeing it, but my fullness kept me from suggesting that we attempt the up-and-down trek. Instead, we turned back down the road until we arrived at the car.

We climbed in, and Wills turned to us. "I'm just going to take a short detour before we head back. Mihalis reminded me of a small village just above here called Apoikia that is known for its fresh water. I brought several jugs to fill up for the Estate."

He pulled onto the road and wound his way back up the way we had come down until we reached a larger road. I spotted the small church he had mentioned perched on a hill to our left while he turned to the right. We drove for another several minutes. The view along the way was breathtaking. The sea was to our backs. On the left was a line of hills lined with rock walls and an occasional tree. To the right were more tree-covered hills that were dotted by houses that spanned an area both far below and high above where we were driving. The drop off on that side was daunting, protected by only a row of azalea bushes that were unlikely to stop anything from falling over the edge.

Simon leaned over the front seat and pointed to my right. "Just below is Stenies. If you look carefully, you can see the Bistis Tower just over there. Above is the village of Apoikia, known for its healing waters from Sariza. The water flows freely from several spots in the village. There is also a factory there that bottles the water from Sariza to sell across Europe." He leaned further forward and pointed high up the mountain where I could see several more houses. "That's the village of Katakalaioi. There isn't much there, but they have a lovely view."

I noticed signs for a monastery along the route we were driving, eventually spotting one tucked into the hillside to our left. Other signs along the way mentioned a waterfall and another monastery farther up the road. Wills stopped the car next to a set of marble stairs. A sign at the bottom of the stairs read *Sariza Springs* and a hotel called *Pighi Sariza*, which was visible halfway up the steps on the right side.

"This is what the village of Apoikia is famous for. Natural spring water that flows out of a marble lion's mouth just across from the hotel entrance. I'm going up there to fill the water jugs. Perhaps you'd like to join me?"

I unclipped my seat belt and followed him outside and up the steps until we stopped in front of a small white building with a stone archway on the front and right side. Inside the room, I could see a large, marble piece with a lion's mouth out of which water flowed into a drainage bowl just below. A sign marking the hotel entrance was just to the right of the spring.

I stepped across to the hotel entrance while Wills was filling the water jugs, noticing that the steps we had taken continued upward for some distance beyond where we had stopped. I peeked into the door of the hotel. I could see a courtyard just inside with some tables and chairs scattered around. The main entrance to the hotel appeared to be to the right of that space. I walked back to where Wills was just finishing filling the jugs.

"The hotel sign says it has a pool, restaurant, café and bar, and sauna. That sounds pretty fancy for such a small village."

He grimaced. "Maybe it was at one time. But the last time I looked, the entire place was in much need of TLC. It's a shame, really, since it's the only nearby hotel. And aside from the complimentary breakfast they serve to guests, you can only purchase drinks and a bag of crisps during the rest of the day. There is one taverna on the main road just across from where we parked, but that's all you'll find here now, I'm afraid."

I looked back at the door to the hotel and sighed. "I suppose they just don't get enough visitors to make it worthwhile to renovate."

"True. Aside from the hikers who trek up here to fill their bottles from the spring. The legend has it that the spring was named after Pasa San Riza, a Turkish man who lived in Evia. Apparently, his hat fell into a stream here and was washed away in one of the springs.

"The dates are unclear, but the creation of the marble font of the spring occurred sometime in the 1700s by Makarios Polemos, who funded the entire project. The water was mainly used for drinking, washing clothes, and other household uses. Around 1929, I believe, a factory was built to bottle the water and export it throughout Europe. It still stands just up the road a ways, although its use has diminished in recent years. The water has long been believed to have healing properties. In fact, in 1932, a royal charter decreed that it had the ability to cure kidney disease."

I looked down at the water flowing from the lion's mouth and decided to fill the small bottle I carried in my backpack, taking a generous swig of the contents before refilling it and returning it to my bag. I looked up at Wills' amused expression. "What? It can't hurt, can it?"

We collected the water jugs and carried them back down the steps to the car. I glanced over at the taverna Wills had mentioned. It had a covered, outdoor dining area where I could see that there were a few tables occupied. Unfortunately, the view, except from the far left corner, was of the street and nearby houses, which made me wonder why they hadn't positioned it to take advantage of the scenery on the other side.

Simon was sitting on a nearby bench and stood as he saw us approach. "We'd best get a move on. I've just been texting Margaret to set up a phone call with her and Brian in a little while."

The drive back felt very quick, which was likely due to the fact that I dozed off shortly after we left, waking only when we pulled to a stop below the Lemon Estate. That seemed to be a common habit of mine since arriving in Greece, and I glanced at Wills and Simon in embarrassment until I noticed that Simon also appeared to be just waking up from a nap.

Wills walked to the rear of the car and began removing the water jugs and the things we had purchased earlier in the day. "I'll just take these to Helene and Mihalis. Why don't you go on ahead and relax a while? I don't imagine any of us will be very interested in the snacks they'll put out later, but in case you are, they'll be set up by the pool at half past eight."

"Thanks. I think I'll take a walk, and then get cleaned up." I stopped by my room first to put down my bag and change into my sneakers, and then headed back out to explore the Estate.

---

That evening, while we were relaxing by the pool, I learned that Simon had arranged for a team to meet us back at the Bistis Tower the next afternoon to assess the potential for excavating the entire ruins. Wills seemed skeptical about the whole endeavor, given the condition of the building and the town's reluctance to pursue any sort of renovation. But Simon remained steadfast in his belief that something of value could come from devoting time and effort to the site. Miriam had been unsuccessful so far in convincing the mayor to visit the tower in order to view the artifacts uncovered thus far, but she promised to continue her efforts.

When I stood up to take my leave for the night, Simon called me aside and asked me how I was feeling about the assistant position we had first discussed. His question took me by surprise, and I stumbled over my answer.

"I ... I wasn't sure you were still interested in that. I would be thrilled to join you. That is, if you're sure."

He narrowed his eyes at me and pursed his lips. "My dear girl, you must learn one thing if you are to have any success in life: digging around in ruins is only one way to uncover the truth. One must also find his or her own hidden treasures that may be buried deep inside the heart. I predict that once you are successful at that endeavor, you will be unstoppable."

His words were both puzzling and flattering, but it was clear he was telling me to buck up and stop being such an insecure nincompoop. I nodded my agreement. "Thank you, Simon. I would be very pleased to join your team as your assistant. When would you like me to start?"

He smiled. "That's more like it. Tomorrow we'll sit down and chat about the details. In the meantime, I've asked Wills to fill you in on our plans for the next several weeks. We'll get things in motion here and then travel on to Santorini to check on the progress of our work there. Beyond that, we'll have to wait and see. There are several things up in the air now that I need to sort out." He turned to Wills. "I'll leave you to it, then. Let's plan to meet back here at seven in the morning. I want to make sure we're all on the same page before we meet the team tomorrow." He began walking in the direction of his room.

Wills looked at me with a slight grin. "You seemed a bit thrown by his question. Are you having second thoughts?"

"No. It's just that he hasn't mentioned it since we arrived on Andros. I had the impression he'd changed his mind."

"Far from it. That's just the way he works: he lets things simmer for a while, and then turns up the heat when he feels the time is right. Obviously, in your case, he feels it's right." He gestured to a table and two chairs that were sitting to the far side of the pool patio. "Why don't we go over there and talk in private. I'll bring you up to date on things."

We spent most of the next hour discussing the plans for the remaining work at Paleopolis, the potential they saw for the Bistis Tower, and the dig that was nearing completion on Santorini. As he spoke, I became increasingly excited and found myself looking forward to my involvement. What he was describing was the fulfillment of a dream. It was not only exciting for my present, but it could pave the path for unlimited opportunities in the future.

Wills regarded me with a smug expression, "I take it you've grown used to the idea of staying around for a while. I can't say I'm at all unhappy about that." He stood and pulled me up beside him. "In fact, I couldn't be happier." He leaned forward and kissed me gently on the lips before stepping back again." I'd best go now. See you in the morning." He turned to walk away, leaving me standing there with a silly grin on my face.

My mind was drawn back to the fortune-telling/coffee grounds reading I had experienced at the hotel in Athens. *Was this the adventure she was referring to? And, if so, how did Wills figure into that scenario?*

Since I had no answers for either question, I decided to sleep on it. Not that there was likely to be much sleep that night.

# fourteen

Two days later, we were back on the ferry heading for Santorini. The sea, which I had been told was normally rough at this time of the year, was as still as glass. Or, as I had been told the Greeks would say, *ei Thallassa eine san lathi,* an expression that meant *the sea is like oil.*

I was glad for the peaceful journey. It gave me a chance to wander up to the outer deck by myself in order to contemplate the events that had occurred over the past few days and consider what lay ahead for me.

Shelly and I had communicated again since I first informed her of my arrival plans for Santorini; and Wills had arranged for a taxi to collect her the next morning after her plane arrived on the island. I was excited to see her again. We had only known each other a few days before she left for Rome, but we had spent so many hours together in such a short time that I felt I had known her much longer. I was also looking forward to having another woman to talk things over with. Being around Wills and Simon was interesting, but there was just nothing like having another female to bounce things off of.

I had also managed to speak to Matt, who was presently on Santorini helping to conduct a guided tour. He indicated he would be pretty busy with work there for the next couple of days, so we made plans to talk again after that. That worked out fine with me since I was also going to have my hands full hosting Shelly and visiting the excavations with Simon and Wills. By Wednesday, which is when Matt had indicated he would be free, things should have settled down enough for me to be able to better plan my time.

The ferry ride to Santorini was long: nearly five and a half hours after leaving the port in Andros. I alternated the time between sitting on the deck looking at the sea, watching the television that hung on the wall in front of the cabin, reading, and snacking on tiropita, chips, and coffee. I even snoozed a little while we were cruising, helped along by a Mythos beer that Wills insisted on sharing with me.

As we were nearing the end of the journey, an announcement came over the loudspeaker directing drivers to return to their vehicles in the belly of the ship. Wills left to ready the car for our departure, while Simon and I took our places in the queue of passengers waiting to exit the ship. There was an air of excitement around us as the other passengers jostled one another in an effort to be among the first to get off.

Simon looked at me and rolled his eyes. "I don't know why everyone has to be in such a state. We'll all be getting off at the same locale." I bent down to see if I could get a view of our docking area. The water was the same amazing, deep, turquoise blue I had grown used to over the past few days, although it still took my breath away every time I viewed it.

"We're arriving on the southwest side of the island at the port of Athinios. The locals call it 'new port' because there is one additional, smaller port for cruise ships elsewhere on the island. Athinios is also known as 'Thira port' because we will be docking just below where the main town of Thira, or Fira as it is more commonly called, is located. Be sure you stay close to me when we get off. The port can get very crowded, and it's easy to get separated."

I nodded and shifted my backpack on my shoulders into a more comfortable position. Soon, the crowd of people surrounding us began to shuffle toward the exit stairs. I gripped the railing with one hand, worried that the press of bodies against me could cause me to lose my balance. It seemed to take forever for us to reach the bottom of the stairs, and I was relieved when I finally stepped out onto the metal ramp leading to the port.

Simon grabbed my arm and pulled me to the right side of the parking area, where a line of taxi drivers stood waiting with signs to indicate the names of their reserved fares. Cars were pouring out of the ferry on the same side, and the general state of the arrivals could only be described as hectic! I was glad for Simon's presence, and I stepped back out of the way of traffic to wait for Wills.

"There. He's coming now." Simon pointed toward the line of exiting cars. Wills pulled up next to where we stood, and we quickly tossed our things in the trunk and climbed inside.

I took a deep breath and exhaled loudly. "Wow! That was crazy!"

Wills smiled as he joined the line of cars and taxis making their way out of the port to a street that led up the adjacent hillside.

"It was even crazier down below. I thought I was going to have a fistfight with two blokes who were trying to squeeze past me in line. Luckily, one of the ship's mates came by and waved them back."

As we drove up the hillside, I glanced out the window. The top of the hill was covered with whitewashed, rectangular buildings with bright blue trim surrounding the doors and windows. To the far left, I spotted a line of donkeys carrying passengers up the same hill. I felt sorry for the donkeys as they trudged wearily up the steep incline, and wondered why anyone would want to choose that form of transportation. Especially since there was also a string of cable cars available just behind where the donkeys were plodding along.

Simon bent down and followed my gaze. "There has been more than one incident when a passenger slipped off the donkey it was riding and landed on the ground. Most of the time, it involved too much alcohol on the ferry ride over. It's hard to imagine why anyone would want to put themselves in that precarious position. But I guess the glamour of a donkey ride on a Greek island is just too much for some people to ignore."

He leaned back in his seat and pulled out a map, scanning it for a few moments before addressing Wills. "We'll be staying at the *Canaves Ena* hotel. It's just a few miles up this road and then to the left. The hotel overlooks the caldera, and is nicely situated between Fira and the road to Akrotiri, where our excavations have been taking place."

We continued to drive for several more minutes before Wills pulled into a short road marked by a sign for the hotel Simon had mentioned. As he pulled into a parking spot, I noticed the view of what Simon had referred to as the caldera over the edge of the cliff, filled with the rich, blue waters of the

Mediterranean. A hotel employee met us as we exited the car, informing us that someone would bring our bags to our rooms once we had checked in. We strode up a set of stone steps past a delightful-looking pool affording the same view I had first spotted when we pulled up. The pool was surrounded by lounge chairs with a shaded snack bar across the back side.

When we entered the hotel lobby, Wills and I stood to one side as Simon stepped up to the desk, returning to hand us each a key card. "Your accommodations are next to each other, just down those steps there. Someone will bring your things to you shortly. My room is a little farther away on the same side. Suite 101. I'm just going to check in with the manager first." He glanced at his watch. "I suspect you could each use a little time to get settled. Why don't we plan to meet in my room in an hour? I've arranged for a little dinner to be served to us there."

His announcement that we would eat dinner in his room surprised me. I was used to Simon's preferences for comfort at every opportunity, and the idea of eating in a hotel room didn't sound as if it would fit that category. I mentally shrugged to myself as I followed Wills in the direction of our rooms, pausing at every corner to gaze in awe at the beauty below and surrounding the hotel grounds. The buildings that housed the hotel rooms were dug into the hillside, like many other properties I had spotted on our way up from the ferry port. The view across the caldera with the deep, blue sea and distant hills was drop-dead gorgeous. I couldn't believe how lucky I was to stay in such a place, and in the company of a man like Wills. I looked at him appreciatively as he stopped outside the door marked 110 and handed me a key card.

"This is for you. I'm just next door, as Uncle Simon mentioned.

Why don't I stop by in an hour, and we can walk to dinner together?"

"Sounds good." I held my key card in front of the door, turning the knob as a green light flashed. I came to an abrupt halt when I stepped inside. *This was a hotel room?!* It was nothing like any hotel I had ever stayed in, not that there had been that many. But this was enormous and beautiful beyond description!

I closed the door behind me and walked farther inside. There was a living area in the front with comfy-looking sofas and chairs facing a stone fireplace, with a large flat screen TV attached to the wall overhead. A wood and granite bar stretched across one wall with four chairs in front of it. There was a counter behind the bar that held a microwave with a small refrigerator below. The bar was also equipped with an assortment of alcoholic beverages and glassware, and a basket holding a variety of packaged snacks.

The bedroom was set off to one side of the living room with two double beds, two recliners, and a dressing table and chair. Just beyond the bedroom was a door leading to the bath, which was almost as large as the bedroom. I stepped inside, noting the gleaming, marble-topped vanity featuring an assortment of toiletries, and a large shower area with a sign that read *Rain shower. Huh.* I thought. *I wonder if that means it uses water collected when it rains?* Just then, my cell phone rang, and I hurried to collect it from my backpack, which I had tossed onto one of the sofas. The face showed Shelly's name, and I answered it with a smile.

"Hey, you! How's it going?" I said.

"Wonderfully. I've just finished packing and thought I'd buzz you and see if everything is set. How are the accommodations on Santorini?"

"Unbelievable." I walked to the window in the living area and gazed out, again struck by how beautiful it was. "The so-called hotel room is more like an apartment. It's large and equipped with pretty much everything. Say. Do you know what a rain shower is? There's a sign in the bathroom on the wall next to the shower that says that's what it's called."

She laughed. "That means you're in a luxury hotel. A rain shower has a nozzle that cascades down like you're standing under a gentle rain. It's deliciously refreshing!"

"Good to hear. And, yes, this is definitely what I would call luxury. So, when are you arriving tomorrow morning? I know Wills arranged for a taxi service, but I never heard what time that would be."

"I should be there by 10 a.m. How far are you from the airport?"

I realized I had no idea where things were on the island in rela-tion to our hotel. "I honestly haven't a clue, but I'm sure Simon took all of that into consideration when he chose our location. The man is on top of everything. Gosh. I can't wait to see you!"

"Me, too. You'll have to tell me all about your adventures. Including your time with Wills."

I squirmed at her implication that there was anything to tell about my relationship with Wills. "Not much to tell there." A knock on the door startled me. "Oh! That must be the bellman with my luggage. I guess I'd better go now. I have to meet Wills and Simon soon, and I really need a shower first."

She chuckled. "Wear something pretty. See you tomorrow."

"See you." I hung up and hurried to the door.

The bellman placed my luggage inside and stood back. "Do you need anything else?"

I suddenly realized he was probably expecting a tip, and I grabbed my backpack to dig out my wallet. The bellman spotted my efforts and held up his hand. "Please. It is not customary to tip in Greece. Especially not at the *Canaves*. If I can do anything else for you, please let me know."

I thanked him and closed the door.

Later, after I had put my things away, I decided to check out the rain shower, which proved to be as heavenly as Shelly had said it would be. I wrapped myself in the plush robe I had found hanging behind the bathroom door and strode over to the closet to choose something to wear for dinner. The property certainly screamed *fancy,* but then again, having dinner in Simon's suite felt like something more casual was called for.

I flipped through my possible choices before finally deciding on a simple sundress with a matching cardigan. I had just finished dressing and applying a little light makeup to my face when I heard a knock on the door. I slipped on my sandals and hurried to open it. Wills appeared on the other side, holding a small bag in his hand.

"I thought you might like these. I've never fancied chocolates myself." He held out the bag to me.

I glanced at the bag in his hand, struggling to focus on what he'd said. *Chocolates?* Well, that sounded delicious. But not as delicious as the sight that stood before me. His hair was still damp from his shower, I presumed, and was slicked back from his face. He was wearing a pale blue linen shirt untucked at the waist, with the sleeves rolled halfway up to reveal his tightly muscled forearms, and a pair of white trousers and flip flops. He reminded me of a beach boy from California, which caused me to smile.

He pulled his extended hand back with a puzzled expression. "I'm sorry. Perhaps I shouldn't have assumed you'd want these."

"No, no! I love chocolate!" I reached for the bag. "Thank you."

He looked relieved, and then I noticed his eyes scan down the length of my dress. "Wow. You look lovely!"

I blushed as I turned to place the bag of chocolates on the kitchen counter next to a similar bag sitting next to the coffee pot. "I didn't even notice these before." I peeked inside the bag. "Shelly will love some of these."

"Oh, I almost forgot. The taxi driver will meet her plane at 10 a.m. tomorrow and bring her here. It's supposed to be about a 30-minute drive, so she should be here around 10:30 or 10:45." He glanced around the room. "Is there enough space for her to stay? My room has a king-sized bed, and I didn't think to ask if yours was the same."

"Luckily, I have two doubles. I suspect Simon made sure of that. He always seems to think of everything."

"Speaking of Simon, we'd best be going. We wouldn't want to keep him waiting."

Simon's *room* turned out to be what the hotel called one of their *superior suites*. It was very large. At least twice the size of mine with an open plan living and dining area, a separate bedroom, and a private veranda with a plunge pool, Jacuzzi, and space for outdoor dining. The table had been set for three, and two waiters, resplendent in white shirts and black slacks, stood nearby waiting to serve us.

I looked around the space and the consistently breathtaking views of the caldera and the sea, and breathed a deep sigh of contentment. "Simon, this place is wonderful. I feel so honored to be part of your team."

He walked behind my chair, pulling it out slightly and indicating I should take a seat. "It is my pleasure, Jesse. I predict it will be a rewarding situation for all of us."

As soon as we were seated, one of the waiters poured a generous glass of white wine for each of us before setting the remainder of the bottle on the table. The other waiter then placed a plate with calamari in a walnut pesto sauce in front of each of us. The calamari was lightly grilled rather than fried as I had previously experienced in Greece, and it was nicely complemented by the sauce, which had a tangy sweetness.

The rest of the meal consisted of a ribeye steak in a shallot sauce with truffle puree and roasted asparagus, accompanied by a nice red wine, followed by cheesecake with a coconut pineapple compote and mango sorbet. Thankfully, a card in front of my plate gave a description of each course, which kept me from having to ask what I was eating. But even if I hadn't known the names of the various foods, I would have still been able to describe them with one word: Delicious!

While we ate, Simon described what we would be encountering when we visited the excavation site the next afternoon. Apparently, excavations at the prehistoric site of Akrotiri had begun as far back as 1870 by a French geologist, but became more prominent during the late '60s and '70s, thanks to the work of two Greek archaeologists.

Simon pushed back his chair and signaled to one of the waiters, who brought a pot of coffee to the table. I waited patiently for him to fill Wills and Simon's cups before declining some of my own.

Simon took a sip before continuing his description of Akrotiri. "Evidence of human habitation at Akrotiri dates back as far as 4500 B.C., during what is now referred to as the Neolithic Age. Based upon some of the artifacts uncovered there, it seems that the village grew from what had been a small farming and fishing community to become an important part of the trading business in the Aegean. A lot of copper and pottery artifacts have been found that suggest the residents of Akrotiri had trading relations with Crete, the Dodecanese, the mainland of Greece, Cyprus, and possibly Egypt and Syria.

"All of the trading activities allowed the civilization at Akrotiri to flourish, not only in the areas of architecture, agriculture, animal husbandry, and construction, but also in the arts. A large variety of vessels have been found in many different shapes, sizes, and colors, as well as large murals that depict the way of life back then."

What he was describing sounded like a very advanced form of civilization at any time in history, but especially at such a long time ago. That was one of the key things that fascinated me about archaeology: the ability to tell a story about the lives of those who lived in the distant past. "How long did that civilization flourish here on Santorini?" I asked.

"That's where things take a downward turn. Around 1613 B.C., a powerful volcano erupted simultaneously with an earthquake, causing most of the town of Akrotiri to be buried. It seems that the inhabitants were able to survive because the earthquakes that occurred before the volcanic eruption forced them to leave. There were no human remains uncovered by the excavations, but there have been quite a few artifacts unearthed that help tell the story of the lives of the inhabitants prior to the destruction. Some of the most significant objects are on exhibit here at the Museum of Prehistoric Thera. Others, including some of the wall murals I mentioned, can be seen at the National Archaeological Museum in Athens."

Something nagged at my memory. "Does this have anything to do with the myth of the Lost City of Atlantis? I seem to recall there was a connection between that story and Santorini."

Simon nodded. "You're absolutely RIGHT. Although there are a lot of facts that remain unclear about the story, which is why it is referred to as a myth. The first written source for the myth of Atlantis originated with Plato, who wrote about a civilization that lived on a prosperous island beyond the pillars of Hercules, which is now known as the narrow straits of Gibraltar. It was believed that Atlantis was probably located somewhere between Europe and America.

"Aside from Plato's writings on Atlantis, the story was conveyed by Egyptian priests who reported that the Atlantians originally had magical powers that were gradually lost. When they were left with only human powers, they decided to battle against other prosperous islands, which they continued until they were defeated by the Athenians. The myth of Atlantis states that the gods became angry at the arrogance of the Atlantians, which led to the volcanic eruption that obliterated their city in a single night.

"While the connection between the myth of Atlantis and the Minoan settlement of Akrotiri is unknown, there are many common points between the two stories that have led historians to wonder if they were, indeed, the same. To date, the mystery of Atlantis is still considered a myth with countless unanswerable questions. Of course, as archaeologists, it is our desire to uncover facts from the past to help the truth unfold. But it is unlikely that the truth of Atlantis, if there is one, will ever be known."

A waiter arrived at the table and paused to wait for a lull in the conversation before asking if he could bring us anything else. Wills asked for a small glass of Metaxa brandy, which was seconded by Simon, but I just shook my head. The story Simon told had filled my head with such wonder and awe that I wasn't sure I would be able to relax enough to get any sleep that night. The addition of caffeine or more alcohol on top of what I'd already consumed did not seem like a good idea, although I supposed the effects of one would likely cancel out the impact of the other.

While I was waiting for the men to finish their drinks, I wandered to the edge of the terrace and looked down at the dark waters below. It was hard to imagine that the still expanse of sea I was looking at had once harbored a volcanic eruption, and the thought of it made me shiver. Was it possible that the bowl of water I was looking down on, the *caldera,* could have been the burial spot for the lost city of Atlantis? I pulled my cell phone out of my pocket to search for a more precise meaning of the word caldera, reading that the definition was a "large depression formed when a volcano erupts and collapses." *Huh,* I thought. *There absolutely could be a connection with Atlantis.*

The next morning arrived sunny and bright after a night filled with fitful dreams of turmoil and drownings at sea. My eyes felt red and swollen, and I climbed out of bed to splash water on my face before padding over to the kitchen to start a pot of coffee. The clock on the wall read 8:30 a.m. That meant breakfast was probably being served somewhere within the hotel compound. I remembered Wills had mentioned something about it the night before, but I had been too distracted by Simon's discussion of Atlantis to focus on what he was saying.

I walked over to where a coffee pot sat on the kitchenette counter and filled it with water, inserting a paper filter with ground coffee before flipping on the switch. I removed a mug from the cabinet, adding a spoonful of sugar and a couple of splashes of milk before placing it on the counter beside the bubbling pot. I walked into the bedroom and pulled on a robe over my night clothes, and then sat down on the sofa while I was waiting for it to perk.

The view out the window was peaceful, filled with a blue, cloudless sky. I yawned deeply before raising my arms overhead in a stretch, twisting my body side to side in an attempt to relax my stiff muscles. I was used to getting quite a bit of exercise. Mostly walking around my neighborhood as I ran errands or made my way to and from work. But the countless steps up and down steep hills I had been encountering since arriving in Greece were no comparison with the only slightly hilly terrain in California.

When I heard the gurgle of the coffee indicating the end of the brewing cycle, I got up to fill my mug and then stepped out onto the patio outside my room. There was a slight chill in the air, which surprised me given that it was the peak of summer on the island. I took a sip of coffee and then a deeper one as I realized the liquid had cooled slightly from the chill in the air and the added milk. I walked over to one of the metal chairs that sat nearby and curled my legs under me as I sat. I glanced at my watch and saw that there was a little less than two hours before Shelly would arrive. I shifted in my seat and considered my options. I could go search for the breakfast buffet or dig around in the kitchen for a few snacks. There was also the option of taking a swim in the hotel pool, which would likely help me shake off my weariness. Or, I could just crawl back into bed with my coffee and a book and relax until it was time for her to arrive. I was finding it difficult to decide what I wanted to do when I heard a sound.

"There you are. I thought I'd check and see if you wanted to join me for breakfast. I'm headed there now."

I turned to spot Wills as he walked around the edge of the patio and gave him what I hoped was a friendly wave. "Good morning. I'm just having some coffee. I didn't sleep very well last night."

He pulled up a second chair near mine and sat down. "Too many ghost stories, I imagine. Uncle Simon revels in pulling those out whenever he can. Finds them fascinating, you know. Although they're a bit too steeped in mystery for my taste. I prefer the known facts that can be dug out of the ruins." He looked at me closely. "You look a bit knackered. Perhaps you'd like to go back to sleep for a while? I can bring you something to eat a little later."

I considered his suggestion. "I'm not sure I could sleep right now, but thank you. I was actually thinking about taking a little swim in the pool. I thought the cool water might invigorate me."

He nodded and stood. "Great idea. I'll head on down to the buffet then. I'll stop back after I finish and leave you some snacks. I'm sure Shelly will be hungry when she arrives, so I'll make certain to include enough for her."

I thanked him and watched him walk off. *What a sweet man*, I thought.

---

After a chilly swim followed by a warm shower, I felt both calmed and re-energized enough to be somewhat in balance. Shelly had phoned from the taxi to give me an idea of exactly when she would arrive, and I was waiting anxiously in the front lobby when she finally pulled up. I jogged to the side of the cab, pulling open her door and grabbing her in a hug when she stood up.

"I can't believe you're here!" I said.

"I know. Seeing you again on a gorgeous Greek island is an answer to a dream. More than one, actually."

The driver deposited her bags on the ground and waved off her offer to pay. "Is done. Man pay over phone."

She looked at me for confirmation, and I could only shrug, assuming that Wills had handled the payment when he booked the taxi. I lifted one of her bags over my shoulder. "Come on. Let me show you where we're staying." We walked across the lobby area and out a side door leading to steps that took us to the door of my suite. I opened it with a flourish and moved aside so she could enter. She took one step inside the doorway and dropped the bags she was carrying.

"Good grief! You said it was nice, but you never said it was so ... impressive!"

I laughed at her reaction and followed her inside. "Wait until you see Simon's suite. It makes this one look like a slum." I led her into the bedroom, showing her where she could hang her clothes before giving her a tour around the rest of the rooms, ending on the outside patio. She walked to the wall over-looking the caldera and stood staring at the scene below. I walked up beside her. "Nice, huh?"

She turned to me with a look of awe on her face. "Nice does not even begin to describe it. This is heaven!" She pulled me into an embrace. "Thank you so much for sharing this with me."

I returned her hug. "I'm so happy you're here. Now let's get you settled. Simon said we'll be heading to Akrotiri in about an hour. That's where the archaeological site is located. Are you hungry? We can get something to eat before then if you'd like.

Wills brought back some things from the breakfast buffet. I didn't go down with him this morning, so he thought we might like to have some things to munch on later."

"I wouldn't mind a bit of nosh."

Luckily, I had heard that expression from Wills and knew it meant food, or something to eat. "Great. Why don't I dig out the things he brought while you get settled? Would you feel like joining us when we go to Akrotiri, or would you rather stay around here? There's a nice pool on the grounds. I had a swim this morning, and it was wonderful."

"A swim sounds grand, but I think I'd like to see the place you mentioned. Perhaps we could take a dip later when we return. I suspect it will have warmed up quite a bit by then."

After we had something to eat, we made our way down to the hotel lobby to wait for Simon and Wills. Simon arrived first, prompt as ever. He spotted us and strode purposefully to where we were seated, stopping in front of Shelly.

"You must be Shelly. I'm Simon Harris. I hope the flight from Rome wasn't too much of a bother?"

Shelly looked up at him with a smile. "Not a tad. It was quite easy, to tell the truth."

"Grand." He looked over his shoulder. "Wills should be along in a moment. Why don't we collect some bottled water from the front desk, and then we'll be off."

When Wills arrived, he and Shelly exchanged warm greetings, and then we all marched off to the car. The two men sat in the front, leaving the back seat for Shelly and me. The drive from the hotel took us past the town of Fira, and then down the hill on the back side of the island.

We arrived in the modern village of Akrotiri about 30 minutes after leaving the hotel. It sat on the southwest side of Santorini, facing the Aegean Sea. The village was small, consisting of narrow stone-paved streets with simple houses and a handful of restaurants and hotels. The main draw of the village was the ancient remains of the city, which were evident all around us. We pulled to a stop in a public parking place and walked through a gate leading to the archaeological remains. The site was covered by a roof that, in archaeological terms, was considered bioclimatic. That meant it was designed with the local climate in mind, but also with the aim of blending in with the natural surroundings. Throughout the site, walkways had been suspended above the remains, and I noticed that in certain areas the paths were laid out in a way that would allow visitors to walk down among the excavated ruins. Overall, the area looked well designed to allow for ample preservation of the site while still allowing visitors to get a true look at how life may have taken place in the ancient town.

As I gazed down into the ruins, I was struck by how carefully everything had been placed. Piles of stones had been laid along the sides of the walkways or stacked to create walls in the excavated buildings. Large pieces of pottery, some still completely intact, sat on the floor of what appeared to have been rooms of the original buildings. Overall, it looked as though the excavations had been well thought out and carefully conducted. I wondered how much of a part Simon and his team had played in the excavations thus far, and to what extent they would still be involved.

Wills walked up behind where Shelly and I stood. "Impressive, isn't it? Our teams have been able to uncover evidence that the original town had an intricate drainage system, paved roads and alleys, two and three-story buildings with stone walls, heating, running water, balconies, intact doors, and windows. There is also ample indication that the civilization was rather advanced, with a complex economy based on working the land, cultivating grains, grapes, saffron, and olives, as well as beekeeping, fishery, and sea trade. That's much more than one would expect from a more recent civilization, not to mention one that existed so long ago.

"A lot of the ceramic jars, vases, and vessels you can see were believed to have been used to transport goods and preserve and store food, grain, and oil. Some of the smaller ones were likely used for cooking and eating. These are just educated guesses based on the excavated findings, but there is more confirmed evidence of their lifestyle on the frescoes and murals that have been restored and that hang in museums here and in Athens."

"It's quite impressive," Shelly said. "But can you explain the difference to me between a fresco and a mural?"

"Certainly. A mural is a picture painted directly onto a wall surface, while a fresco has been bound to the wall by applying pigments."

"How much of the current excavations were carried out by Simon's team?" I asked.

"The dig has been going on for quite some time. Simon and his team only became involved during the past few years. There's still a bit left to accomplish, but my understanding is that only a small crew will remain here to work from this point forward. The rest will be transported back to Andros to help with the excavations at the Bistis tower. That's considered more of a priority at this time, given the precarious status of the tower." We turned at the sound of Simon's voice.

"That's correct. We'll leave a skeleton crew here, and the rest of us will return together to Andros. Jesse, I wanted to speak to you about that. Wills mentioned you are planning to meet up with your cousin while you are on Santorini. He's a tour guide, I believe Wills said. Given those circumstances, I am wondering if you would be willing to stay here for a few extra days to record an update on our most recent excavations? I'll give you details on how that should be done. We could plan to meet you back on Andros toward the end of the week."

His question made me smile. "That would work out perfectly for me. It will give me time to visit with Shelly, and hopefully have my cousin, Matt, show us a bit more of the island."

Simon nodded and turned to Wills. "I need to check in with our team now. Why don't you join me so we can sort out the details of our next move? I'll count on you to stay behind with Jesse to assist her after I leave."

Wills glanced at me quickly with a slight smile. I couldn't read his expression, but if he was thinking anything close to what I was, it meant he was pleased we would have more time around each other. He nodded at his uncle.

"That's settled then. Wills, let's be off. Jesse, why don't you and your friend have a closer look around, and we'll plan to meet back here at ..." He glanced at his watch. "...half past one?" He turned to leave without waiting for anyone to respond, which was a characteristic I had come to expect from him. I remembered Wills saying something to the effect that his uncle had seemed to slow down some in recent years, but I had to say I couldn't find any evidence to confirm that description. Of course, I hadn't known him before that time. If the Simon I saw now was a slowed-down version of who he had been, I could only imagine what he must have been like!

After Wills and Simon left, Shelly and I spent another half hour or so roaming amongst the ruins of Akrotiri before my cell phone rang. I was happy to see Matt's name on the screen, and I hurried to answer.

"Hello! Are you here on Santorini?" I asked.

"Yes. We've just disembarked from the ferry and are driving up the hill toward our hotel. We're staying in a village called Imerovigli. Have you heard of it?"

"No, I haven't. Is it close to Fira?"

"A few kilometers. It's at the highest point of the caldera cliffs on the north part of the island. We're staying at a place called Afroessa. I've stayed there before. It's very nice and has wonderful sunset views over the caldera. It's not as far away as Oia, which is where most of the tourists go for sunsets, but Imerovigli is more conveniently situated, in my opinion."

I chuckled. "If that's your opinion, then I'm sure it's correct. Shelly and I are down at ancient Akrotiri now. The good news is that Simon asked if I could stay on here for an extra few days after he and his team leave for Andros. The plan is for me to meet them there by the end of the week."

"That's great! I'll be helping with the tour here until sometime Wednesday, and then I arranged for an assistant to take everyone back to the mainland by herself, which will free me up until sometime after the weekend. I could give you and Shelly a mini-tour of Santorini on Thursday, and then we could leave for Andros together on Saturday or Sunday. How does that sound?"

Since I had my phone on speaker mode, Shelly had been listening in and nodded enthusiastically at his suggestion. "Great! We'd love that. Oh, and Wills will be joining us, too. Simon, his uncle and the head of the excavation team, told him to stick with me until we return to Andros."

"Huh. Pretty convenient, I'd say." He laughed. "Okay then, it's settled. Text me the address where you're staying. I can arrange to keep a couple of bookings at the Afroessa so the three of you can join me. They'll give me a generous discount since we always bring tourists to stay with them."

"That sounds good. I didn't ask Simon if we were supposed to stay here. But given the looks of the place, I suspect it would be too expensive to extend our visit."

We said our goodbyes and hung up. Shelly looked at me with a grin. "Well, won't that be convenient? Staying in the same place as Wills without his uncle looking over your shoulder!"

I punched her lightly on the arm. "Oh, stop! As I told you, nothing is going on with me and Wills. He's just a friend."

"Huh. We'll see how long that lasts!"

# sixteen

Two days later, Wills, Shelly, and I were pulling up to the back gate of the property known as Afroessa. A young man came running in our direction and opened the gate, waving us into the parking area. We pulled to a stop and piled out, pausing to gaze in awe at the view below. The buildings of the hotel were set into the hillside on five levels, each with an arch-fronted patio facing the water.

"Welcome to the Afroessa. I will help you check into your rooms and then acquaint you with our amenities." A name badge clipped to his shirt identified him as Yanni. He smiled at us pleasantly as he stacked our luggage on a rolling cart. As we followed Yanni in the direction of the reception, I spotted a pool and poolside bar a couple of levels below us, with a few people lounging nearby on sun beds or perched on barstools. He glanced in the direction I was looking. "The Afroessa is for adults only. As a result, it is always quiet and uncrowded. Except for those times when we host a pool party. Then, it can become energetic." He flashed us a big grin.

I had phoned Matt as we were approaching the property, and he appeared on the terrace in front of the reception lobby as we walked up. "You made it! Welcome, everyone." He strode over to shake Wills' hand and introduced himself to Shelly after hugging me. "I've already checked you in. Jesse, you and Shelly will share one of the larger suites. I think you'll find it quite comfortable for the two of you. Wills, we each have our own suite. They're not as grand as the one the girls will have, but every rental at the Afroessa is special."

He gave our key card to Yanni, who wheeled our luggage in the direction of a suite on the upper level. I was impressed by how easily he seemed to maneuver the cart given the steepness of the incline, but I supposed it was something that came with practice. Matt and Wills turned to leave, indicating we should meet them by the pool in an hour. We said goodbye and stood aside as Yanni waved our key card in front of the door to our suite, allowing us to enter first before walking past us to set our bags on the floor.

"This is the living area, and outside these doors is a veranda with a wonderful view of the caldera. Perhaps the best view of the entire property." He walked through the living area into a second room. "Here you have the bedroom. I'm afraid there is only one bed, but the sofa bed is almost as comfortable. The bathroom is through this door, and there is a small *kouzina*, kitchen, to the back of the living area."

I walked slowly through the various rooms, taking note of the fireplace in the living room, and two sets of bathrobes and slippers folded neatly at the end of the bed. There was a bottle of wine and a fruit basket on the kitchen counter, and a plate of what appeared to be pastries next to the coffee pot. The décor was a mixture of modern convenience, combined with an intentionally rustic element that included areas of exposed stone walls and pottery pieces in the bathroom and kitchen. It wasn't nearly as luxurious as the Canaves, but in some ways I found it more appealing.

"Jesse, look over here." I walked to where Shelly stood on the outside veranda.

Yanni followed behind me and nodded at the view below. "The sunset over the water and the distant hills is stunning. Many of our guests like to enjoy a glass of wine and a few snacks while they take in the view. In the morning, breakfast is included in the price of your suite. There is a menu of offerings on the kitchen counter. Just call the reception the night before to arrange a time for delivery. Or, you can even wait until you wake up and make your selection. That might take a little more time, but since we are not fully booked right now, it shouldn't be too long a wait. There is also a restaurant on site that serves lunch from 14:00 to 18:00. In addition, there are many restaurants nearby that offer meals later in the day."

"Your English is very good, Yanni. Where did you learn to speak so well?" I asked.

"It was required that we study English all through primary and secondary school. I'm attending University now in London, so being able to communicate in English has helped very much."

Shelly looked up with interest. "Where are you studying in London?"

"King's College. My major is physiotherapy."

"Impressive. That college has an excellent reputation."

He nodded with a smile. "I am fortunate to have been accepted there. It's an excellent school, and I have met many students from other countries. Even a few from Greece."

Shelly shook her head. "Yes. One of the things it is known for is its diverse student population. Do you hope to work in London once you finish your studies?"

He shrugged. "I'm not sure. Right now, I'm just trying to earn enough money to be able to return there. I wasn't able to get a scholarship, so I have to work on the weekends and throughout the summer to afford it. The classes are excellent, however. Which makes it worth all the effort." He glanced over his shoulder as if he suddenly realized where he was. "I'll leave you to get settled. Please let me know if there is anything else I can do for you."

As we watched him leave, Shelly sighed. "What a nice young man. It's a pity he has to work so hard in order to study at Uni." She sighed as she opened her suitcase and began setting her things on the sofa bed. "I'll sleep here. I tend to wake at odd hours, so it will be easier this way."

Okay, if you're sure." I lifted my bag onto the bed and unzipped the sides. "Why don't we get unpacked and go check out that pool?"

"Sounds like a grand idea."

We spent the rest of the afternoon relaxing with Wills and Matt, taking an occasional swim in the pool, or just lounging on the sun beds with a cold drink nearby. Subtle Greek music was wafting from speakers positioned on either end of the pool bar, and a waiter passed by frequently to check to see if we needed anything. The guys ordered Mythos beer, which came accompanied by frosty mugs, while Shelly and I opted for a couple of piña coladas. I was surprised when I saw them listed on the bar menu, and I took a cautious sip, half expecting to find something quite different from what I was used to. Fortunately, the drink was delicious, with just the right amount of sweetness, and frothed to a creamy consistency.

I stirred my straw in the mixture. "Um. This is really good."

Wills leaned over to look in my glass. "Looks like a milkshake."

"You're not far wrong. But it's a milkshake with rum and coconut cream instead of ice cream. Want a sip?" I lifted my drink in his direction.

He hesitated for a moment before leaning over to take a sip, puckering up his mouth as he tasted it. "Ugh. So sweet! Or maybe it's just the contrast with this beer." He shook his head. "I don't recommend mixing them."

I laughed. "No. I don't think I'd enjoy that either."

The four of us relaxed for the next half hour, luxuriating in the sunlight and quiet as we sipped our drinks and chatted about everything and nothing. Eventually, Wills sat up and stretched before turning to me. "Feel like a walk? I'm going to fall asleep if I lie about much longer."

I considered his question. Taking a nap didn't sound like such a bad idea. On the other hand, I was on an incredible Greek island, and there was still a lot of it I had yet to see. Matt had promised us a tour, but the four of us had decided to postpone that until the next day.

"Sure. I'm up for a walk. Just let me pop up to our suite so I can change clothes and put on my sneakers."

"I'll do the same and meet you outside Reception."

We checked with Matt and Shelly, both of whom seemed quite content to stay where they were.

Wills and I headed up the steps leading out of the Afroessa before turning left to walk along a stone path high above the sea. The views were incredible, whether we were looking at the caldera, Imerovigli, or the village of Oia, which was on the far end of the hillside that stretched out to our left. I was charmed by Imerovigli with its whitewashed properties, flowers, and cobblestoned pathways. It was peaceful. Much quieter than Fira, which drew much of the tourist trade. Although I did notice quite a few tavernas, restaurants, and cafés tucked into the hillside along our walking route, it still had a calm atmosphere.

At one point, we stopped at an overlook, and Wills pointed to an immense rock that rose out of the depths of the sea to the far left of where we stood. "That rock is called Skaros. It was one of the original fortresses of Santorini, and is considered the most important one because it served as an observation post to protect against invading pirates. These days, it's mostly used as a lookout point for hikers."

I looked at the tall rock and noticed the faint images of people making their way up the sides. "Have you hiked up it?"

"A couple of times. It's not too bad. Although the amount of foot traffic it attracts at certain times of the year makes it a bit too crowded for my taste. Can you see that small church on one side of Skaros? That's the chapel of Panagia Theoskepasti. There's a wonderful, panoramic view of the entire caldera from there."

At that moment, church bells began ringing somewhere nearby. "Are those bells coming from the church you mentioned?"

He squinted his eyes before shaking his head. "No. They're farther away. Most likely, they are coming from the chapel of Saint Mark. It's a small church, a little farther up this path we are on. We can have a look at it when we pass by."

We continued on for a while until Wills suggested we take a turn to the right along a small trail that took us to an area just above a small, whitewashed church. He paused on a large rock overlooking the church. "That's Saint Mark's. It's a popular spot for weddings, most likely because it is fairly easy to get to, and has a nice view."

I was puzzled by what he said. "Easy to get to? You mean the wedding party hikes up here?"

He chuckled. "No. There's actually a road just on the other side of the church. You can drive almost right up to the door."

"Ah. That makes more sense." I looked over the grounds of the church. There was a small, cobblestoned courtyard outside the door that provided some shade and seating areas on stone benches. The church had a small bell tower and a domed roof. Several nicely dressed people were milling about the grounds, and one tuxedo-clad man was even standing on the top of the roof. Suddenly, the bells began ringing loudly, causing me to almost drop the bottle of water I was holding. "Wow! That's loud! Why are they ringing now?"

Wills looked across at the church. "It could be a wedding. Or perhaps just a church service of some sort. Church bells in Greece are a way to communicate with the locals. The bells begin ringing long before the actual service starts to warn people that the priest has arrived and to start getting ready. As the time for the service gets closer, the bells ring more rapidly and frequently. It's a way of saying 'You'd better hurry up and get here!' And then when the service is about to end, the bells ring less frequently and slowly until they stop. That's what you are hearing now.

"There are other bell sounds, as well, that are used to indicate a funeral or memorial service, or a baptism or wedding. The bells may also be rung very fast and loudly to alert everyone of an emergency, such as a fire. It's a call for help."

His description of how the bells were used reminded me of my conversation with Matt about the same thing. I found it fascinating to try and imagine living in a place where a significant part of the local communication was controlled by the ringing of church bells. We watched as a few more people stepped inside the front door of the church, although far more remained outside in the courtyard.

"Matt told me it's fairly common for some people to remain outside the church instead of going in. Now I see what he meant."

Wills nodded. "Yes. This is especially true when there's a service at one of the smaller Greek churches, like this one. It's not only that there isn't enough space for everyone to fit inside, but I suppose some people would just rather bide their time until the after party, so to speak."

We stood watching the people milling about for a while longer until those who had been inside began stepping out into the courtyard. Several women quickly brought out trays filled with small cups or bite-sized snacks. A couple of men produced bottles of some type of clear liquid that I assumed was ouzo, or perhaps tsipouro, which they poured into the cups that were passed around to the attendees. The noise level became considerably louder as everyone began greeting one another. Eventually, the bride and groom emerged from inside to a burst of applause, a shower of rice, and calls of *na zisete!* I looked up at Wills for an explanation.

"The phrase they are saying is literally translated as 'may you live,' but what they are wishing them is a long life together full of health and prosperity." We watched for another couple of minutes before stepping back onto the walking path. Wills pointed to the left. "At the very end of that long strip of hills is the village of Oia. It is considered one of the best spots on the island to watch the sunset. There are also a lot of tavernas that serve delicious food."

My stomach was beginning to rumble, and I considered suggesting we head there for a bite. However, I estimated it was at least a couple of miles away, over what appeared to be a narrow, rocky path. I was torn between wanting to see this special place and wanting to take things a little easier for the rest of the day.

Wills turned around to look at me. "You've grown quiet. Is everything all right?"

"I was trying to calculate how far away we are from Oia. My stomach has been complaining for the past half hour or so."

"I'm afraid it's still quite far by foot." He slid off his backpack and unzipped the top, rummaging inside before pulling out two plastic-wrapped bars. "Here. Perhaps this will tide you over until we can get something more substantial."

I accepted the bar and tore open the top before taking a bite. It was chewy and chocolatey with a nutty consistency. "It's good. Thanks."

Wills tore into his and bit off a large chunk. "We can walk on to Oia if you'd like, although I'm afraid it's farther than it appears. Perhaps you'd like to return to the hotel? We can clean up and try one of the local tavernas or order something from the on-site restaurant and watch the sunset from one of the terraces. I don't know what Shelly and Matt have gotten up to, but perhaps they'd like to join us."

I considered the options. "I think I'd like to stay at Afroessa tonight. I'm a bit tired, and the idea of relaxing with a sunset view sounds wonderful."

We finished the snack bars and tossed the wrappers into Wills' pack before reversing our direction and walking back the way we had come.

When we entered the gate to the property, Wills suggested we stop by Reception to see about the possibility of ordering some food for a little later. Luckily, the serving hours were not quite over, and we were able to pre-order some food to be delivered to the suite that Shelly and I shared, where we could pack it away in the fridge until we were ready to eat. Wills and I said goodbye before heading to our separate units.

When I stepped inside our suite, Shelly was lounging on the sofa watching the TV.

She sat up and smiled when I entered. "There you are! I was beginning to wonder if I was going to have to send out a posse to fetch you."

I took off my shoes and laid my backpack on the floor before taking a seat on the chair next to the sofa. "Wills and I had a really nice hike along a path above Imerovigli that eventually goes all the way to Oia. We were considering walking all the way there until my stomach complained rather noisily. We stopped by reception just now and ordered some food to be delivered here in a little while. I hope that works with any plans you and Matt may have made?"

"Perfectly. We had a lovely time just relaxing by the pool and chatting about all sorts of bits 'n bobs. He's quite an interesting person, I must say. Clever and funny, as well."

I couldn't help but smile at the news that she and Matt were getting along. "I'm glad to hear the two of you enjoyed each other's company. He's a great guy." I stood up, collecting my backpack and shoes from the floor. "I think I'll freshen up before the guys get here. If the food arrives, why don't you put anything you think should be kept cold in the refrigerator? We can heat things up later."

"Will do."

I headed into the bedroom, closing the door behind me in case the men arrived before I had finished cleaning up. I pulled off my sweaty clothes, tossing them into a basket in the bathroom that seemed designed for that purpose, and then turned on the shower. I stepped under the spray and sighed with delight. The water was both soothing and refreshing, and I generously soaped my body and shampooed my hair.

By the time I finished, I could hear the sound of laughter coming from the living area. I quickly dried off and ran a brush through my hair before slipping on a pair of white shorts and a pink shirt. I looked around for my shoes and then spotted the slippers that still lay at the end of the bed. I considered them for a moment before grabbing them and sliding my feet inside. *Why not?* I thought.

The next morning arrived too early for my taste. The four of us had spent the previous night regaling one another with amusing anecdotes from our recent travels and helping ourselves to a generous amount of wine and food that had been delivered by the hotel restaurant. I couldn't remember when I had laughed so much and so freely, and I was grateful for the ease with which we had all become comfortable with one another in such a short period of time.

My attraction for Wills had been growing steadily since we'd first met, and I was more than a little bit smitten, as Shelly would call it. At least, that's how she referred to the interaction she'd observed between Wills and me after the guys had left the night before.

"Fancy him then, don't you?" She had asked.

Her question made me pause before replying. *Did I? Is that how I would define what I was feeling?* I really wasn't sure, but I knew the idea of seeing him again made me smile both inside and out.

"I guess so. And while we're on the subject, did I detect a spark between you and my cousin last night?"

She looked at me with a grin and raised eyebrows. "He's lovely, isn't he? And such a nice fellow. A girl would be lucky to catch his fancy." She took a sip of the cup of tea she was holding before setting it aside to regard me more seriously. "I suppose you and Wills will be seeing a lot of each other since you'll be working with his uncle as his assistant. At least, I assume you've decided that's what you'll do."

I cupped my chin with my hand as I considered her comment. "Yes, that's my plan. Although now you have me wondering if that's such a good idea. I mean, it could complicate things if Wills and I were to take our attraction any further. Simon might consider that a conflict of interest."

She wagged her head from side to side. "Why don't you talk it over with Wills? That is, if you think he has a similar interest in you. From what I can tell, you're both quite smitten with each other."

I rolled my eyes at her. "We haven't talked about it. But if I had to guess, I'd say we're very definitely on the same page. There's an undeniable spark between us, although I'm hesitant to put a label on it just yet."

Shelly clapped her hands together and got up from her chair. "Glorious. Now that's enough about that. At least until you've had a chance to mull it over with Wills." She carried her cup over to the kitchen counter and set it in the sink. "What time did Matt say we are heading out for our tour today? I'd like to pop in the shower before we leave."

I glanced at my watch. "In about half an hour. Did you have something to eat this morning, or do you want me to order something from reception?"

She waved one hand. "I had one of those cakes from the basket next to the coffee pot. Quite good, actually. I'll just get ready now." She pulled some toiletries from her bag and headed to the bathroom.

While she was gone, I tidied up the suite a little: putting away dishes from last night's dinner and pushing the furniture back in order. *More of Matt's influence rubbing off on me*, I thought with a chuckle. I had just helped myself to one of the pastries Shelly had mentioned when she walked back into the living area clad in one of the robes provided by the hotel.

"I wasn't sure what to wear. Do you imagine we'll be doing a lot of walking, or is this more of an auto tour?"

I considered her question. "Matt said he'd show us around the island. I suspect that means we'll be in the car most of the time, but I wouldn't be surprised if he included a stop at one of the beaches at some point. Why don't you pack some swimming things just in case?"

"Right-O." She began laying out some clothes on the sofa bed while I headed to the bedroom to get ready.

———

As Matt had promised, we spent the rest of the day taking in the key sights on Santorini, starting with the village of Messaria, which lay almost at the center of the island. It was an easy drive from Imerovigli, and its location made it convenient to access the airport, as well as other nearby villages and beaches. What struck me most about Messaria was that it was surrounded by vineyards and olive groves and provided an amazing view of the caldera and Aegean Sea.

Matt looked over his shoulder at Wills and me in the back seat. "If it wasn't so early in the day, I would recommend we stop at the ouzo distillery. We always include it as part of our tours. I believe Jesse has developed a fondness for ouzo since she's been in Greece." He caught my eye in the rear-view mirror.

"Oh, I don't know about that. I've had a sip or two since I've been in Greece. Or maybe it was something called tsipouro. I still get the two confused. Didn't you and I have some ouzo that first night we ate out in Fokionos Negri?"

"No. That night we were drinking white wine." He turned to look at Shelly, who was seated in the passenger seat next to him. "Do you like ouzo, Shelly?"

"I do enjoy it. Especially with some of those Meze the Greeks are so fond of serving it with." She replied.

Wills leaned forward to address Matt. "Let's stop at the distillery, Matt. It's not THAT early, is it then?"

We all readily agreed, and Matt drove a little farther until he pulled up in front of a sign that read *Canava Santorini Ouzo Distillery*. The four of us hopped out of the car eagerly and headed inside, where we were greeted by a young woman who spent the next hour guiding us on a tour of the distillery and the museum, before leading us into an area containing a long bar facing a row of windows that looked out over a vineyard. She indicated that we should seat ourselves behind the bar and then proceeded to pour a small amount of ouzo into four glasses, which she placed in front of us.

"Please enjoy this sample of our best ouzo while enjoying some local treats." She gestured at the bar.

Wills pulled out a barstool for me and then climbed up beside me. Shelly took the seat on my other side, followed by Matt. "Wow. That's quite a spread!" I gestured at the platters of food that were laid along the length of the bar.

"It certainly is." Shelly lifted her glass of ouzo and took a sip. "Oh my. It's delicious! Much better than any I've tasted before."

Our tour guide nodded with a smile. "I'm glad you are enjoying it. The Canava Santorini ouzo is characterized by the aroma and the taste of the currants of Santorini's Asyritiko, saffron, and anise. We follow a slow procedure to prepare the drink in a handmade copper still, which enhances its flavor." She waited while the rest of us sampled the drinks. "If you would like a refill, just let me know. I will return shortly." She disappeared through a doorway behind the bar.

After we had finished our tasting of the ouzo and Meze offerings, we purchased a couple of bottles from the gift shop before heading back outside. It was an absolutely lovely day with a bright, blue sky and warm sunshine, and I found myself almost skipping along as we walked to the car. Wills walked up beside me and tried to match my steps.

"You seem quite cheery. Is it the ouzo we sampled or this brilliant day?"

I grinned at him as his skip turned into more of a stumble. "A little of both, I guess." I looped my arm through his, which seemed to please him.

Shelly and Matt were waiting for us next to the car. "Matt was just telling me about an experience he had on one of his tours. It seems he caught the attention of one of the ladies in the group who plastered herself to his side. He finally had to beg her off on his mate."

Matt looked sheepishly at Shelly. "What she neglected to tell you is that the lady was at least seventy years old. Apparently, I reminded her of her grandson, which was a fact I didn't find out until much later. I was certain she had something else in mind based upon the way she was staring at me."

Shelly patted him on the cheek. "Who could blame her if she had?"

The two exchanged a pointed look before Matt opened the passenger door, waiting for her to settle in before closing it and jogging around to the driver's side.

Wills and I glanced at each other with a bemused look. He leaned forward to whisper in my ear. "It seems something is brewing between those two."

I shrugged my shoulders with a grin. "I think you could be right."

He opened the car door, allowing me to enter before climbing in after me. As I scooted across the seat, our thighs brushed, causing a tingle of excitement to travel from my knee up to my throat. I hurried over to my side of the seat and busied myself with fastening my seat belt. Wills did the same, but not before giving me a very intense look. I rolled down the car window next to me, letting the slight breeze flow over me as I attempted to look nonchalant.

Our next stop on the tour was the medieval village of Pyrgos, which was a little southwest of Messaria. The lower part of the village was a mixture of narrow, winding paths, with an interesting assortment of stone houses, domed churches, vineyards, small shops, mini markets, restaurants, taverns, and coffee shops scattered all about.

"It's cute, isn't it?" Shelly asked. "Quaint, almost, but with an obvious influx of touristy places."

Matt turned to her with a nod. "Originally, this area was more residential. But in recent years, the tourists have found it. As you will soon see, the view from the top is pretty impressive."

I leaned forward from my seat in the back. "There seems to be a lot of churches on this island. We've passed several just in the short time since we left the hotel. I noticed the same thing on Andros when we were there. And, of course, in Athens before that."

"Right. You can't go anywhere without coming across at least one church. Especially on the islands. You'll find one or more in every village, each dedicated to a saint. Each saint has a special feast day, and on that day, Greeks who are living in the village have a special celebration in honor of the saint after whom the church is named. At the same time, persons who are named after that saint, which you may have noticed is a common practice in Greece, celebrate what is called their *name day*. Name days in Greece are considered far more important than birthdays."

I looked at Wills, who shrugged with a smirk. "I don't imagine we'll come across any churches that share the same name as any of this lot!"

Matt glanced at him in the rear-view mirror. "Actually, you're wrong. The Greek Orthodox Christians recognize Matthew as one of their main saints, and many men are named after him. The names vary from Matthew, Matt, Mathaios, to Matthias."

Shelly punched Matt in the arm. "Well, there you go then, Saint Matthew. I knew there was something special about you!"

I had been watching their interaction throughout the day and the evening before with some interest. It was true I didn't know Shelly very well, but the fact that she was tossing off compliments to Matt left and right led me to believe that her attraction for him was stronger than she had implied earlier. I also suspected, and hoped, that Matt felt the same way about her.

We continued to make our way up to the pinnacle until Matt pulled to a stop in front of what looked like an old castle. "This is the Venetian Kastelli. It's one of only five castles located on Santorini."

I glanced out at a large, sprawling area covered with the ruins of several beige, stone buildings. "Are we going to get out?" I asked.

Matt shrugged his shoulders. "I'm afraid there isn't much of the castle itself worth looking at as it's mostly in ruins, but there's a nice café inside with an impressive view of the island if anyone would like a drink or a bite to eat?" Matt glanced at the rest of us with raised eyebrows.

"Not for me," I replied, followed by head shakes from Wills and Shelly.

"A little later, perhaps?" Wills said. "I'll need a little more time to let the effects of the ouzo and snacks we sampled wear off."

Shelly nodded emphatically. "Yes, the ouzo hit me a bit harder than I imagined it would, which I suspect is due to the rather early hour. Alcohol in the a.m. is more likely to leave me snockered than later in the day. Not that I'm in the habit of testing that fact."

"It's a matter of metabolism." Wills offered. "Which is why it's customary to hold off on consuming any alcohol until around mid-afternoon, or thereafter."

We drove on for another half hour or so, talking and enjoying the view. At one point, Shelly and Wills got into a detailed description of the area where they grew up, causing Matt and me to fall into a comfortable silence. It was fun to watch the two of them chatting away amiably. I briefly wondered why there hadn't been any other level of interest between the two of them, but I was also glad.

I looked over at Wills while he was busy talking to Shelly and studied his profile. He looked a little like a British dignitary with his sculpted cheekbones and slicked back hair. At least that was the image he portrayed from the neck up. Below that, he looked like a schoolboy in his faded jeans and dark blue t-shirt, an image that was enhanced when a lock of his hair came loose from the gel that was holding it in place and fell over his forehead every time he laughed. I had a sudden urge to tuck it back into place, causing me to sit on my hands to keep myself from acting on that thought. At some point, he must have noticed the odd way in which I was staring at him because he turned to look at me directly with raised eyebrows. I smiled in a way I hoped implied nothing was going on, but he kept looking at me curiously until Matt spoke up.

"I thought we'd stop at Akrotiri next in order to give Shelly a look at the excavations."

"Good idea," I said, anxious to draw Wills' attention elsewhere, although I noticed his eyes continued to study me.

Once we arrived at Akrotiri, we spent some time wandering along the paths overlooking the excavation site before returning to the car. Matt suggested we visit the Akrotiri lighthouse, which was situated on a high cliff above the sea. We drove up the road that led to the structure, stopping to gaze up at it from our vantage point just below.

Matt stepped into his role as tour guide again. "The lighthouse was built in 1892 by a French trading company. It was one of the first lighthouses in Greece. At first, it was manually controlled until it was connected to electricity. It stopped working in World War II until it was reconstructed by the Greek Navy in 1945. These days, it still gives off a bright white light every 10 seconds."

Shelly pointed to a small whitewashed building just below the lighthouse. "Is that where the lighthouse keeper lived?" She asked.

"Exactly," Matt answered. "Although these days it's uninhabited."

We followed the road out of Akrotiri until we reached a black sand beach on the southeast part of the island. The beach area was dotted with sun loungers and umbrellas that lay at the foot of a mountain. Several tavernas and cafés were visible to one side.

"This is Kamari Beach," Matt said. "There are other beaches on the island, as well. Including one mostly covered with red pebbles and sand. But this is the most popular one because of the food and drink availability. Let's go down and reserve some loungers, and then Wills and I can pop up to one of the cafés to pick up some gyros for lunch. There's one spot that serves some of the best I've ever tasted."

We parked the car and made our way to where an attendant stood, giving him payment for four lounge chairs and an umbrella. As we placed our things on the loungers, Matt gestured at the pebbly beach. "Be sure to keep your sneakers on, even when you walk down to the water. The rocks can be very sharp." He and Wills walked off in the direction of the cafés while Shelly and I made our way to the changing rooms.

By the time the guys returned, Shelly and I had settled onto two of the loungers and were chatting away happily. Matt laid down two paper bags he was carrying and pulled off his shirt before plopping down on the lounge chair next to Shelly. Wills placed cups containing iced frappes in the holders on each of our chairs and sat on the chair next to mine, removing his shoes and socks. Matt dug his hand in the paper bags and handed out foil-wrapped packets to each of us.

I unwrapped mine to expose the end of a slice of pita bread filled with chunks of meat in a white sauce mixed with tomatoes and cucumbers. I took a generous bite and groaned in delight. "That is so good!" I said. "They're really fresh. Thanks for the suggestion, Matt."

When we all finished eating, Shelly collected our trash and went to toss it into a nearby bin. "Anyone up for a swim?" she asked.

Matt hopped up quickly. "Absolutely!" He held his hand out to her, and they jogged off in the direction of the sea.

Wills looked over at me questioningly. "Ready to go in the water?"

"In a few minutes. I feel like I need to digest that gyro for a while. I probably shouldn't have eaten the whole thing, but it was too delicious to stop."

He settled back against the lounger and closed his eyes. "Agreed. A little rest in this delightful weather is more my cup of tea right now. Besides, I'll have to change out of these jeans before I can take a swim. But don't let me stop you if you're ready to go in sooner than me. I'll just lie here and enjoy the view." He opened one eye and grinned at me.

"No, I'm good for now." *And besides,* I thought, *there's no way I'm going to have you ogle me while I walk into the water.* Especially since my stomach felt bloated from the gyro.

Just then, we heard a shout of distress followed by a string of curse words. We sat up on our lounge chairs and looked for the source of the sounds, spotting Matt carrying Shelly in his arms as they made their way out of the water. As they came closer, I could see blood dripping from her left foot.

Matt sat her down on her lounger and grabbed a bottle of water to rinse the blood off her foot. "Stepped on a sharp rock. Or maybe a seashell. Either way, it seems to have cut her up pretty bad."

I took a small towel out of my bag and handed it to Matt. "Wrap this around the cut. I'll go up to the attendant's stand and see if they have any bandages.

"I'll come with you." Wills stood up to join me after slipping his socks and shoes back on.

When we returned a few minutes later with some antiseptic cream and a couple of band-aids, Matt was sitting next to Shelly, who was resting her head on his shoulder. I crouched down in front of Shelly and began to apply the cream to her cut. "Does it hurt a lot?" I wrapped one of the bandages around the cut area.

"Only my pride," she said with a grimace. "Matt warned me about the rocks, but I kicked off my sandals because I thought I'd be fine in the water. Silly of me to think that."

Matt patted her hand. "Unfortunately, what happened to you happens to somebody on almost every tour group we bring here. The rocks on the beaches of Santorini are notorious for their sharpness. I guess it's so unusual that people don't take the risk seriously. Not that I'm implying you did anything wrong, Shel. I just want you to know you aren't the first person to think that the bottom of the sea here is smooth like it is on other beaches."

She looked at him gratefully. "Thank you for trying to spare my pride, but I still feel foolish. I'm just grateful to all of you for your help."

Matt stood and began to dry off with his towel. "Why don't you sit awhile and let that antiseptic cream work. I'll go get us some cold water. Jesse, Wills, can I bring you anything?"

We shook our heads, and he trotted off in the direction of a kiosk a little farther down the beach.

I sat down beside Shelly and hugged her shoulders. "The cut didn't actually look that bad once we got it cleaned off. But I imagine it still hurts a lot."

"It's a little better now." She hugged me back. "Thanks. I appreciate your kindness."

Matt returned with two bottles of water and a clean towel, which he handed to Shelly. "I convinced the lifeguard to give us this. I noticed yours caught a good bit of blood before we got you bandaged up."

Shelly looked down at the towel she was sitting on and grimaced. "Yikes. That looks fairly horrendous. Thanks, Matt." She dug the stained towel out from under her and wrapped the new one around her shoulders, drying her hair with the ends. "I'd like to change out of this wet suit before we get back in the car, but I'm afraid I'm going to need help to stay off my foot."

Both Wills and Matt stood up abruptly and moved to the front of her lounger. Matt reached down and held out his hands. "Here. Let me help you up, and then Wills and I will make a chair lift out of our arms to carry you to the changing room. Jesse, why don't you collect her things and meet us up there?"

The guys set about helping her up while I hurried ahead to ready her things. While I was helping her change, Matt went to try and drive the car closer to where we were, while Wills remained close by in case we needed help. Once we were all settled back in the car, we backtracked up the hill to the main road and headed for Imerovigli. The mood in the car was solemn as we each processed what had happened to Shelly. I was looking for a way to lighten the atmosphere when Matt flipped on the radio, bringing forth the sounds of the soundtrack to one of my favorite movies.

"Mama Mia!" I yelled. "I LOVE this music!"

All four of us sang along in unison as we continued our route back to the hotel. What a day it had been! Certainly, an unexpected twist at the end. Nonetheless, it had been a good day overall, shared with new friends and a family member who had become a treasured friend.

I smiled at the slightly garbled harmonies being emitted from my three fellow travel companions before once more adding my voice to the din.

# eighteen

Three days after our beach adventure, we were back on the ferry on our way to Athens with a stop at Andros to drop off Wills and me. Shelly had decided to return to Athens with Matt to allow her foot to heal more completely before returning to London. He had offered her his bedroom since I wouldn't be using it for a while, and after some hesitation, she accepted. I don't know which of us was more surprised by this turn of events: Shelly, Matt, or me. Wills, on the other hand, seemed oblivious that anything out of the ordinary had transpired. In general, he appeared a little distracted, which I chalked up to our pending arrival back on Andros and the work that was waiting for us there.

The rest of our time on Santorini had gone smoothly. Shelly had wisely decided to remain at the hotel, lounging around the pool, and only venturing out when the four of us drove to dinner at one of the local tavernas. Matt was her steadfast companion during that time, rarely leaving her side except to drive to the local mini-market to stock up on supplies. Their constant companionship had freed Wills and me to venture out a time or two on our own.

Our most memorable outing was to Oia. We borrowed Matt's car for the trip, choosing not to attempt to hike the route back and forth. We arrived mid-afternoon and browsed some shops in the main village before scouting out a taverna overlooking the caldera to have a couple of drinks and snacks while waiting for the famous sunset. We had only exchanged light-hearted banter since our tour of the island, and I was beginning to wonder if I had just imagined the spark I had sensed between us.

We chose a cozy spot with a patio that promised a sunset view and grabbed a table along the front railing. Wills pulled out a chair for me to sit and took a seat next to me so that he would also be facing the westerly sky. A waiter brought two menus and indicated he would be back shortly to take our drink orders. The taverna was beginning to fill up rapidly, and he hurried off to seat a party of four that had just arrived. Wills quickly scanned the menu before closing it and leaning back in his chair. "I think we should talk."

His words caused my stomach to clench, and I looked at him uncertainly. "Okay. What about?"

At that moment, the waiter reappeared and Wills ordered a bottle of wine and two glasses of water. *"Ena boukali levko krasi kai duo potiri nero, parakalo."* We waited for the waiter to leave before resuming our conversation. "About us. And your plans to work for my uncle. I wonder if you have any misgivings about your decision?"

Shelly's suggestion about a possible conflict of interest came to mind. "What do you mean? Do you think it would be a mistake for me to take the job?"

He shifted in his chair. "Not at all. I believe it would be a wonderful opportunity for you. But it does beg the question of whether or not it would preclude any further involvement between the two of us. Of a personal nature."

I waited for him to elaborate, and when it was clear he didn't intend to, I shrugged my shoulders in exasperation. "You're going to have to be more precise than that. I'm having a hard time following you."

He sighed and leaned forward to take my hands in his. "You have to know how I feel about you. These past few weeks have been a delight getting to know you and spending time with you. It has taken all of my strength not to act on my feelings, but I'm concerned that if I do, you'll decide you can't both work on the excavation and explore whatever this is between the two of us. I don't want to get in the way of your career. But I'm more than a little bonkers over you."

I pulled one of my hands out of his and placed it over my mouth in an attempt to stifle a giggle. "Bonkers? Is that anything like saying you're crazy about me? Because if it is, I'm afraid I'm suffering from the same malady."

His mouth fell open slightly as a frown appeared on his face. "You are? Are you saying you like me? In that way, I mean."

My barely suppressed giggle burst forth, followed by a fit of coughing. I picked up my glass of water and took a long swallow before setting it down again. "I think we should speak more directly before either of us gets the wrong idea. Yes, Wills. I really like you *in that way,* as you said. And I don't see why it would create a problem for us if I take the job with Simon, which, by the way, I've already agreed to take. It isn't like you'd be my boss or anything. We'd be co-workers, at best. Although I imagine my position would be considered far below your status." I paused before continuing. "But maybe I'm missing the point because for you to even ask that question implies you've already decided that our getting further involved would be a conflict of interest. Is that what you're saying?" I picked up my glass of wine and took a sip.

"No! I mean, yes, I was asking that. But I mostly wanted to be certain that it wouldn't be a problem for you." He recaptured my hands in his. "I'm totally crazy for you, Jesse. In case you haven't figured that out by now. And I'm hoping you feel even a smidgen of the same way about me."

I was again struggling to hold back a giggle. "A smidgen. A ton. A whole lot! Yes, I'm crazy about you, too, Wills."

He stood up abruptly and pulled me to my feet, pulling me close to his chest. "I was hoping you'd say that." He leaned down and captured my lips between his, starting slowly before allowing the kiss to deepen. Suddenly, there was a burst of applause that caused us to pull apart. We looked around the patio to see what prompted the outburst and saw several people at a nearby table grinning up at us. One woman hooted as she jabbed her fist in the air.

"Woo hoo! That was better than any damn sunset!" she yelled, in what sounded to my ears like a Texas accent, followed by a second round of applause and laughter from nearby tables.

Wills and I looked at each other sheepishly before he leaned down and gave me a soft kiss and then folded me in his arms. "I think they approve," he said.

We sat back down and attempted to regain our composure. My heart was beating rapidly, which was partly due to the kiss we had shared and partly a response to the public reaction to our PDA. Wills motioned for the waiter to return. *"Merika meze, parakalo. O, ti proteinete."* The waiter nodded and hurried away. Wills looked over at me with a slight smile. "I thought we could use a few snacks to go along with this wine. I'm afraid it's going to my head. Or perhaps I'm feeling the effects of some other sort of intoxication." He took my hand in his and rubbed the palm with his thumb, causing my heart to resume its rapid beating.

I was relieved when the waiter returned, and I gently pulled my hand from Wills' in order to place a few pieces of crispy *tiropita* on my plate. Everything seemed to be happening so quickly, and I felt I needed a little time to settle down before making a fool of myself.

We munched away on the assortment of tidbits the waiter had brought, sipping wine and looking out at the view of the slowly descending sun. The horizon was beginning to turn into streaks of pastel colors around the orange globe, while the sky surrounding the spectacle began to fade to a deep purple.

I sighed deeply and took another sip of wine. "It's magnificent."

"Yes. Definitely worth a look." He took my right hand in his left, and we sat in silence while we watched the remainder of the setting sun. Soon, the sky had grown completely dark except for an abundance of twinkling stars. All around Oia, a smattering of lights appeared on the various houses and businesses. The air was filled with the sound of laughter and faint music and the clinking of silverware on dishes as the patios and balconies of the nearby restaurants grew even more crowded. It was a magical night. One often written about in novels and poems. And I was beginning to feel more relaxed than I had in a long time.

I glanced over at Wills with a smile, which he returned with a slightly quizzical look. "What are you thinking?" He asked.

"Oh, I'm just enjoying the evening. The weather. The view. The company. Everything is just perfect."

He placed his arm across my shoulders and pulled me against his side. "I'm glad to hear that." We sat that way for another several minutes until the waiter came to ask if we wanted to order anything else. Wills paid the bill, and we headed back to where we had left the car, stopping along the way to share another passionate kiss in the privacy of darkness created by a momentary absence of streetlights. When we pulled apart, Wills sighed deeply. "I don't want this night to end. Perhaps you'd fancy a walk when we get back to the hotel?"

I considered his suggestion. "I think I'd fancy more of an indoor sort of activity." I was a little surprised at my forwardness, and I looked at him to gauge his reaction.

He raised his eyebrows before grinning. "Really? I think I can arrange that. Luckily, I have my own room. Now. The question is just how fast can we get back?" We laughed in harmony as we hopped in the car.

Our first night together was wonderful. There was none of the hesitancy that had marked the time since we'd first met in

Athens and the numerous occasions that followed. Instead, we moved together like a dance where we each seemed to know each other's steps. I had left a text message for Shelly letting her know I would be staying with Wills that night, so she wouldn't worry, intentionally avoiding calling her so I wouldn't have to go into a lengthy explanation of something I couldn't yet explain. She had texted back with a string of emojis that I could only interpret as positive and encouraging.

The entire evening had been like a dream I was reluctant to wake up from. I rubbed one hand over my eyes and yawned as I raised my arms overhead before pushing the covers aside, noticing the bed was empty. I glanced around the room uncertainly, wondering if Wills had made an early exit, when I heard a soft knock on the bedroom door. Wills stepped in, carrying a tray containing a pot of coffee and some breakfast items. He placed the tray on the bedside table before sitting down on the bed facing me. He reached one hand to push my hair back before kissing me on the cheek.

"How did you sleep?" He asked.

I rubbed my hand over my eyes. "Not enough. But I feel surprisingly good this morning."

"Surprisingly?"

"Well, you know what I mean." I threw back the covers and swung my legs over the side of the bed, straightening Wills' t-shirt that I had chosen to sleep in. "I'll be right back." I walked into the bathroom and washed my face before scooping a bit of Wills' toothpaste onto one finger, which I rubbed over my teeth and tongue. I spat out the remains and then grabbed his comb to try and create some order out of my unruly hair. When I returned to the bedroom, Wills was sitting up in bed with the tray in front of him. He patted the bed beside him.

I crawled back under the covers and plumped two pillows behind my back so I could sit upright. "Um. That looks good." I surveyed the items on the tray.

"I noticed you seemed to have a fondness for chicken pies. *Kotopitas.* So, I ordered a few of those. We also have some fresh fruit, yogurt, and rusks with cheese and homemade jam. And, of course, coffee." He lifted the pot. "May I pour you a cup?"

"Yes, please." I picked up a small plate and placed a chicken pie on it. "How did you know I like these? Most places just seem to serve *tiropitas* or *spanakopitas.*" I took a bite and groaned in delight. "Really good."

I noticed when we were at the Green Park, you were eyeing some on a nearby table. Then, the other night when the four of us went to that taverna, you were eating some with what appeared to be great delight. I hope these are satisfactory."

"Are you kidding? Here. Take a bite." I held my half-eaten koto-pita in front of him, and he took a bite that ended up almost finishing the entire thing.

He chewed for a moment before wiping crumbs off his face. "Sorry. I guess I should have ordered more. They're rather small, aren't they?"

I laughed and picked up my cup of coffee, adding a little milk and sugar before tasting it. It was smooth without any of the usual bitterness I had grown accustomed to in Greece. "Good coffee. Thanks for bringing breakfast."

"You're welcome." He placed the tray on the end of the bed before folding his legs beneath him and turning in my direction. "I ran into Matt in reception this morning. I thought he would have a few choice words for me, but he was surprisingly quiet. We arranged to meet him and Shelly in about an hour so we can make it to the ferry on time." He filled a plate with some fruit and a dollop of yogurt and proceeded to eat hungrily.

"Did you see Shelly?"

He shook his head. "No, I didn't. Perhaps she was still asleep." He wiped his mouth and crawled out of bed. "I'd best get a move on. I need to hop in the shower and then finish packing. I presume you'll want to head back to your room to get ready. That is, unless you'd care to join me?" He wiggled his eyebrows at me.

I considered his question. "Despite how tempting that is, I'd better decline unless I want to risk missing the ferry. I still have a lot to do to get ready." I placed my things on the tray and climbed out of bed, walking around to where Wills stood, looking slightly disappointed. I wrapped my arms around him and gave him a solid kiss. "If we weren't leaving soon, you know how much I'd love to stay here with you."

"I hoped you'd feel that way, but it's good to hear you say it." He returned my kiss passionately before pulling back with a moan. "That's enough of that." He patted me on my butt before pushing me gently in the direction of the door. "I'll stop by your room before we leave so I can help you carry your things."

I nodded before grabbing one more kotopita. "One for the road." I grinned as I grabbed my clothes off the floor, quickly pulling on my pants before hurrying out the door.

When I walked into our room, Shelly was just coming out of the shower, humming a tune I couldn't quite place as she rubbed her hair dry with a towel.

"Good morning. What's that song you're humming?"

"*It's a Beautiful Evening,* by Nat King Cole. Do you know it?"

I shook my head. "I don't think so. Can you sing a little of it?"

She started swaying as she sang, "*And as soft as a willow every cloud is our pillow, and all heaven and earth know what we're thinking of. And darling they're so right, so kiss and hold me tight, It's a beautiful evening for falling in love.*"

My eyes opened wide as the words of the song struck home. "Oh! Does that mean what I think it does? You and Matt?"

She stopped swaying and giggled. "A lady never kisses and tells. But I don't suppose there's any harm in hinting." She plopped down on the sofa. "Oh, Jesse. I'm quite smitten with your cousin."

Her use of the same word she'd used to describe my feelings about Wills had me struggling to hold back a giggle again. "I can see that. Well, it seems we have something in common."

She looked at me smugly. "After I received your text, I assumed as much. Things had just begun to heat up between Matt and me, so your timing was exquisite. Was your night as glorious as mine?"

I laughed as I nodded fervently. "It sure was." I glanced at the clock on the kitchen wall. "Oh! We'd better get a move on. Are you finished in the bathroom?"

"Yes. I'll get dressed and finish packing while you're in there. Can I help you pack, too?"

"That would be great. Just toss the rest of my clothes from the closet in my suitcase. I'll add my things from the dresser once I decide what I'm going to wear." We both hurried off in opposite directions. I paused at the bathroom door before going in. "Oh, and Shelly? We have a lot more to talk about."

"We absolutely do." She said with a vigorous nod.

# nineteen

The long ferry ride from Santorini to Andros was a blessing in disguise. We managed to snag a large round table surrounded by curved sofas in the first-class cabin, which allowed us to stretch out and even nap a bit. By the time we pulled into the ferry port of Gavrio, we were all feeling notably refreshed and relaxed. Wills and I said our goodbyes to Shelly and Matt, promising to all meet up again in Athens when our time on Andros was over. Of course, that meant Shelly would have to remain in Athens longer than she had planned, but somehow, after watching the cozy way in which she and Matt had interacted on the ferry, I had a feeling that wouldn't be a problem for her at all. There was the matter of her job, but Matt assured her he had an idea that could bypass that obstacle.

Wills and I stepped off the ferry, where we spotted James Branson waving at us from outside the barriers. We hurried over to where he stood as quickly as possible, given the difficulty in maneuvering our luggage over the rough pavement, and he motioned for us to follow him to a nearby taxi.

"Simon thought it best if someone fetched you from the port. We've shifted our location slightly."

We placed our things in the trunk and climbed into the car. The taxi driver greeted us before he maneuvered his way into the line of vehicles leaving the port. James was seated in the passenger's seat in the front, and he shifted his body so he could address the two of us in the back.

"A lot has happened since you were last here. The Greek government finally saw fit to declare the Bistis Tower a historical site, which meant that funds were allocated for its restoration. Simon was able to step forward and convince the government that the tower was also a significant archaeological site of prime importance for Andros, which meant our team was allowed to begin excavations before anyone mucked up the area. We've only just started the dig, but it's already showing signs of being quite impressive. We've been staying in an old hotel in a nearby village called Apoikia. It's more than a little frayed around the edges, but it will do for our needs."

I remembered the hotel next to the lion's mouth in the village he mentioned. "I've seen that place. It's next to a source of the Sariza Springs, as I recall."

"Correct. At the top of a good number of steps. Wonderful view of the valley and distant sea, and they serve a decent breakfast. The rooms could use a good overhaul, but Simon arranged a fair price for the lot of us."

It struck me that the strong Scottish accent I'd heard from James on previous occasions was gone, and I wondered if he had the ability to turn it on and off at random. It was just one more quirk that had me, again, wondering about his character. I decided not to say anything about it, instead turning my attention to the view outside my car window.

For the next hour, the taxi driver wove his way along the east side of Andros, past the turn-off point for Paleopolis, through the village of Hora, and continuing up a winding road to the village of Apoikia. I was glad I was seated on the side of the car that looked out over the sea with its vision of distant islands, departing ferries, and the rapidly setting sun that cast an array of colors on the horizon. It was so peaceful and full of beauty that I could feel myself settling into a totally relaxed state.

At one point, Wills reached across the seat and squeezed my hand, giving me a subtle but passionate look as I turned to meet his eyes. I could feel my heart rate increase as the warmth from his hand began to fill my entire body, and I quickly turned back toward the window in case James happened to spot our exchange. Luckily, he seemed totally oblivious to anything other than the cell phone he was holding in his hand.

"I've just had a text from Simon. He said we are to meet him at the local taverna once the two of you are settled in. It's just down the hill from the hotel. The food isn't half bad, which is lucky since it's the only one around for some distance. Apoikia's a quaint little village. The owner of the hotel said it used to be considerably more vibrant, but the exodus of young people over the past few decades caused it to become very sedate. Boring, some would say. Although I wouldn't quite characterize it in that manner. It is rather subdued, and it's so quiet at night you can hear the tinkle of goat bells and the chirp of cicadas. They're the loudest things around until the church bells ring. Which they do far too often, for my taste. I can't fathom why they have to ring them so often and for so long. It creates quite a din."

I remembered my discussion about the church bells with Matt and, more recently, with Wills as we hiked on Santorini. "The use of the bells is quite interesting. They apparently tell a story to the villagers to alert them to what is going on. Not only with the church service, but sometimes to things in general."

The taxi headed up a steep but short drive next to the stairs I remembered walking up with Wills when we went to fill the water bottles. The taxi driver pulled to a stop next to a sign indicating it was the entrance to the hotel. The entrance wasn't nearly as attractive as the one I had seen across from the lion's mouth springs. In fact, it was pretty dismal looking.

James hopped out after handing the driver several euro notes. Wills and I climbed out of the back and waited for the driver to open the trunk to retrieve our bags. We followed James inside and up a flight of stairs to the main lobby of the hotel. It was a large area, with a covered balcony on the front, and a small bar tucked away at the far end. A stone fireplace sat against a wall in the middle of the long room, and there was a variety of seating arranged in front of it, as well as at various other spots across the entire lobby. I stepped onto the balcony to admire the view. The sun was beginning to set, casting various shades of pink and gold on the sky above the distant sea. I could see the rooftops of numerous houses scattered around the village, both along the one road that ran through its middle, and across the hills that stretched below and to either side of the hotel. Lights were beginning to twinkle throughout the village, which created an interesting contrast to the star-strewn sky.

Wills stepped outside and walked to where I was standing. "Lovely view. And so quiet," he said.

I turned and smiled at him. "Yes, it is. This would be a nice spot to have a glass of wine. Or a morning coffee."

"I agree. But I'm afraid that will have to wait for another time. James has checked us in." He handed me a key. "We're all on the same level. If you're ready, we can go up now and get settled. James seems in a bit of a rush to have us meet Simon. Apparently, my uncle is growing impatient." He chuckled.

Our rooms were on the same level as the lobby, up a few stairs and to the right. Wills unlocked my door and held it aside for me to step in before placing my luggage beside me. My heart dropped as I glanced around the space. It was small. Even by regular hotel room standards. And the décor was very dated and drab. I walked over to pull aside some curtains that hung to the floor, revealing a small balcony. I stepped outside and was relieved to see the same view I had spotted from the main balcony off the lobby. *At least there's a view,* I thought. Although the waist-high stucco wall in front of the balcony obscured a great deal of it. I stepped back inside.

Wills grimaced as he looked around. "Not much to look at, is it? Oh well. I suppose we've been spoiled by our accommodations thus far. I'll leave you to get settled. Let's plan to meet back in the lobby shortly. How much time do you need?"

I didn't have much to unpack. And I was not anxious to spend any more time than I had to in that dreary room. "I can be down in fifteen minutes. Is that okay?"

"Right-O. See you there." He took a few steps toward the door but then turned back and walked to me briskly, taking me in his arms. "I would be remiss if I didn't take this moment to do this." He kissed me passionately before pulling back slightly to look me in the eyes. "I hope there'll be more time for that later. But just in case, I wanted to remind you how I feel about you."

I felt a little dizzy in the aftermath of his passion, so I just nodded and mumbled something incoherent. He smiled at me before letting me go and walking to the door.

After he left, I glanced around the room again. There was a small refrigerator near the balcony doors and a closet just inside the front door. I opened the door across from the closet and looked in at the bathroom, which was just as outdated as the rest of the room. I sighed and began to unpack my things, determined to make the best of a far from ideal situation.

We arrived at the taverna to find Simon deep in conversation with an unknown man. He spotted us and waved for us to join him. After we were seated, he gestured to the stranger, who looked to be in his late 60s with a prominent mustache and curly white hair. "This is Stavros. He's the mayor of this village, and a taxi driver to boot. In fact, he's in charge of pretty much anything you can imagine." He introduced each of us in turn. "We've just been chatting about the Tower and the plans for it. I have quite a lot to catch you up on since you've been away."

Wills reached to shake Stavros' hand. "*Hero poli.* It's a pleasure to meet you, Stavros." He turned to Simon. "James has filled us in a tad about the new developments with Bistis."

Stavros spoke in Greek, which Simon translated as meaning there was still a lot up in the air about the project. "Stavros has been talking to the government officials and the mayor of Stenies. It seems there's still some question of whether a suffi-cient amount of money will be devoted to the restoration."

Stavros lifted his face upward in an expression that appeared to suggest he agreed, but which I had come to understand meant he thought it might not.

James leaned forward. "Aye. But a nod's as guid as a wink tae a blind horse."

In the blink of an eye, James had shifted into a thick Scottish accent again! I looked at Wills in confusion, but he just shook his head. "Suffice it to say that the mayor believes there's more to tell than what we've been privy to thus far."

Simon flagged down a waitress and placed an order for food and drinks for the table. I leaned back in my chair and glanced around at my companions. It was hard enough to follow a conversation when it was a mixture of English and Greek, but with the occasional addition of Scottish expressions and a little British dialect, I felt like my brain was exploding.

I busied myself sampling the assortment of food that was brought to the table. I recognized some of the usual offerings, which included tzatziki yogurt dip, fried calamari, and Greek salad, but there were also several others I was not familiar with. When there was a pause in the conversation, I whispered to Wills to ask him to describe the rest of what we were eating.

He pointed to each dish in turn. "This is called Briam. Mixed vegetables baked with olive oil. Fava, which is mashed yellow split peas. Soutzoukakia, or a type of meatball, but with different spices than the ones you're probably familiar with. And Yiouvetsi. A traditional Greek dish of lamb and orzo cooked in a rich tomato sauce flavored with cinnamon and some other spices. I suggest trying some of each. If you don't like anything, just pass it over to me." He grinned as though we had shared a private joke, causing me to wonder if he was serious. I scooped a spoonful of each of the dishes onto my plate, sampling them in turn before turning to him with a wide-eyed look.

"They're all delicious! So different, but all so good."

"I'm glad you like them. They're some of my favorites."

The rest of the meal went by in a flurry of conversation interspersed with laughter. The men were eating with gusto. Even Simon, whom I had noticed at other times, ate with some level of reserve. I decided his change in character must be his effort to match the fervency with which Stavros attacked his food, refilling his plate at least three times until all of the dishes were empty. There had also been a copious amount of wine consumed by all of the men, except for Wills, who nursed two Mythos beers throughout the dinner. In truth, I wasn't sure how much wine I had drunk. All I knew was that the waitress kept refilling my glass whenever she passed by our table.

At the end of the meal, a large plate was placed in the center of the table containing what appeared to be small, round pastries. James speared one and placed it on my plate. "'Ere. Take a bite."

I considered whether I should use a fork to eat it or lift the pastry with my hands. Stavros must have noticed my hesitation because he stabbed one with his fork before placing it in his mouth. I imitated his gesture. The pastry was warm and topped with a honey syrup. I chewed eagerly before nodding my pleasure. "I remember these. I had them at the hotel I stayed at in Plaka. Loukou-something, I believe they're called. They're really good."

Simon smiled. "Yes. Loukoumades. These are a special treat for us from the taverna. Traditionally, they are normally served only to coincide with the feast day of a saint, but this taverna makes them every Sunday to serve after the church service is over. The owner is trying out a special recipe that adds pistachios, so he happened to have some available tonight."

"How lucky for us. Please thank him for me." I took another pastry from the plate.

When we had finished eating and drinking, Simon took care of the bill before standing to shake Stavros' hand. The two men had an exchange in Greek, and then Stavros waved goodbye to the rest of us. As he walked down the steps to the street, I noticed he was wobbling a bit. I leaned close to Wills so I could speak to him quietly. "I hope he's not driving the taxi tonight." I giggled behind my hand.

Wills looked at me with a grin. "I should think not. Although Greeks are known for handling their alcohol quite well, which may have to do with the amount of food they consume with it." We watched as Stavros sauntered down the middle of the street, calling out greetings to several people he passed along the way. Eventually, he stopped by a car and got inside, driving away slowly.

Wills turned to Simon. "I thought I'd take a little stroll. Unless you need me for anything else tonight?"

Simon glanced at me before shaking his head. "Let's meet in the morning for a while before breakfast. I want to fill you in on some things before we head down to Stenies. James, why don't you accompany me to the hotel? I want to run something by you on the way."

James looked from Wills to me, a slow grin appearing on his face. "Aye. Be an eejit not to see what's going on here. She's a bonnie lass, Wills."

Wills looked uncomfortable as he shifted from one foot to the other. "Mind your tongue, James."

Simon grabbed James by the arm and pulled him down the steps. We watched until they were out of sight before Wills regarded me sheepishly. "I'm afraid he's caught wind of something brewing between us. I'm sorry if that was uncomfortable for you."

I was surprised by my lack of response to James' offhand remark. "I don't think anyone takes James all that seriously. But I don't think Simon is blind, either. Perhaps you need to talk to him about us in the morning, in case he has any concerns he needs to air."

"Yes. I planned to do just that. Now. How about that walk? I'm a bit too full to take the stairs, but I don't think we'll encounter too many vehicles if we just stroll down the street a ways. Or, another idea is to go up to the hotel and enjoy the balcony off the lobby." He looked at me questioningly.

"Or ... we could take a little walk to let the food settle, and then you could come to my room. That is, unless you think that would be indiscreet."

He smiled widely. "I made certain that neither James nor Simon was on either side of our rooms. They're located farther down the corridor towards the end."

I looped my arm through his. "Well, in that case ..." We set off down the steps.

# twenty

The next day, we left mid-morning for the drive down the winding road to where the Tower of Bistis stood. At least, I hoped it was still standing, given the decrepit state it was in when we last visited. Everyone seemed to be in high spirits. Even Simon was all smiles as he drove along the route, pointing out little churches along the way and other scenes he found particularly notable. At one point, he pulled off onto an overlook that allowed a viewpoint over the entire village of Apoikia, as well as Stenies and the sea beyond. It was a beautiful day, with a clear blue cloudless sky that seemed to blend seamlessly into the turquoise waters. The landscape was dotted with houses of various shapes and designs, tucked into hills and valleys lined with rock walls and greenery of all sorts. I had learned shortly after arriving on Andros that it was one of the few Greek islands with a natural source of fresh water, and that was never more evident than when one looked out across the green expanse below us.

Simon leaned forward in the car and pointed out the side window. "See that stone-looking building down below? That's Bistis. As you can see, there are roads leading to it from two directions, placing it in a prime location for tourists looking to absorb some of the local history. I imagine that's the reason the Greek government finally gave in to the local efforts to restore the tower. It will likely pull in quite a sizable revenue once they set it up as a tourist destination."

I glanced down at the crumbling remains of the tower and frowned. "But won't that take some time before it's even close to a state where someone could safely tour the premises?"

Simon chuckled. "Yes, and that's the beauty of it. For us, at least. It will give us a reasonable amount of time to complete our excavations before they begin work on restoring the structure. I was just referring to the *potential* income that will come to the island. According to Stavros, that's what is driving the decision by the Greek government to invest funds in the project."

We drove on until we reached the closest access point to the tower and parked the car just down the hill. I noticed several people milling about the outside of the building. "Who are all of those people?" I asked.

Simon glanced up. "That's some of our crew, along with a handful of local workers we've hired to assist us. They've been making quite a bit of progress since you were last here."

As we walked closer to the tower, I noticed two people whom I immediately recognized. I leaned over to Wills. "Isn't that the man who had dinner with us last night, standing next to Margaret, whom I met at Paleopolis?"

He nodded. "Yes. Simon told me this morning that Stavros indicated he wanted to make sure to have a hand in the restoration proceedings. Or more precisely, he wants to have his nose in the doings. He's acquainted with pretty much everyone on this part of the island, which couldn't hurt. Simon introduced him to Margaret back when we first began work at Paleopolis. They've grown quite friendly since then. Nothing untoward." He added quickly. "But a close connection couldn't hurt for all intents and purposes."

Margaret waved as we walked up. "Hello, everyone. Fine day, isn't it?"

James strode up and shook Stavros' hand, nodding at Margaret as he did so. "Aye, it 'tis. I'll just go 'round and see what the others are about." He disappeared around the corner of the building. Wills and Simon began a conversation with Margaret, leaving me to fend for myself. I wandered around the opposite direction from where James had gone and came across two men hauling off wheelbarrows full of dirt, which they dumped onto a sizable mound off to the far side. I watched them for a while until one of them noticed me.

"*Yeia sas. Hreiazeste tipota?*"

I looked at him in confusion and then shook my head. "*Den katalavaino Ellinika.*" I hoped I had just told him I didn't understand Greek. My Greek had been improving slightly, but I still could only manage the most basic expressions. What I'd said must have worked because another man standing nearby addressed me in English.

"He say, 'Is anything you need?'"

"Oh, good, you speak English. I'm Jesse. I work with Simon. Or at least I sort of do. He's just hired me to be his assistant. I was curious what you are doing here."

He gave me a sort of half-smile/half-frown, which I thought was appropriate given how incoherently I had spoken to him.

"We dig the floor and move dirt. Make place for archaeologist to find things. Must work slowly so no damage. You are archaeologist, too?"

"No. At least not yet. I'm hoping to study to become one eventually. My job with Simon will be more about recording what is found. Keeping a sort of log of the work that is done here."

He removed the cap he was wearing and wiped his forehead with his shirt sleeve. "Hard work. But my family come here from Albania soon. I want to make home for them. *O Kirios* Simon help." He dug his shovel in the dirt. "Must work more now."

I nodded and stepped around the corner from where the two men were digging, where there were several other men and a couple of women working. Some of them were carefully raking the ground, while others were chipping away at one of the crumbling stone walls. I walked up to one of the women and said hello.

"Hello, love. Have you come to lend a hand?" she asked.

"Yes and no. I'm Jesse Holloway. Simon hired me to help catalogue the findings from the dig." I looked around at the area nearby. "Have you found anything interesting yet?"

She walked over to where there was a small pile of what looked like broken shards of pottery. "We have uncovered several pieces of pottery that appear to have been produced in the proto-geometric style that was prominent between 1050 and

900 B.C. That was the period in Greece that signaled a reawakening of technical proficiency and conscious creative spirit, especially in pottery making. There was a lot of use of circles, arcs, triangles, zig zags, and wavy lines, all derived from the Minoan-Mycenaean representation of life." She pointed to one particularly large shard. "See these horizontal bands? This was where the design elements were typically placed, around the middle or upper part of the vase.

"Proto-geometric decoration was quite a bit different from the Geometric Period, which was the first specifically Greek-style of vase painting that flourished towards the end of the Greek Dark Ages between 900 and 700 B.C. It was characterized by linear motifs, such as spirals, diamonds, and cross-hatching, with abstract forms to represent human figures. If you've visited any of the museums in Athens, you would have noticed some of those vases. They are the most common type you typically see on display. While the designs of the Proto-Geometric Period are not as intricate as those of the Geometric age, in my opinion, they are more fascinating given what they represent about civilization at that time in Greece."

I looked at the large piece she handed me. "But how could this be in the Tower? I thought the earliest evidence of residence here was in the 13th century?"

"True. But they might have been part of a collection. Or perhaps family heirlooms. Either way, the more we uncover, the more we will understand about the people who resided here."

Simon walked up to where we were standing. He placed a hand on the shoulder of the woman named Miriam and gave her a warm smile. "Jesse, I see you and Miriam have met. Good. She'll be able to guide you in your work. Miriam started out with us in much the same way as you. She was in her first year of studies at Edinburgh, eventually obtaining her MA in Classical Archaeology and Greek. But before that, she used to spend her summer months tagging along with our team and cataloging our finds."

I looked at Miriam with more interest. "That's impressive. I'm still planning to do my master's work in archaeology at the University of Berkeley in California, but I've had to take some time off to work on the financial part. Reality stepped in, I guess you could say."

She grimaced slightly. "I know about that all too well. I was lucky enough to get a scholarship that covered my first year at Edinburgh. After that, it was all thanks to Simon here that I was able to complete my studies."

I glanced at Simon with curiosity but was afraid to ask what she meant. Luckily, she didn't seem to have similar qualms.

"He has established a grant that provides financial support for up-and-coming archaeologists. Of course, you have to prove yourself first by achieving superior grades the first year and demonstrating a keen work ethic over the summer months." She studied me through squinted eyes. "But I suspect he has already decided you'll fill that bill. Otherwise, you wouldn't be here now."

I quickly shifted my gaze to Simon and was pleased to find him nodding. "We haven't actually had that conversation in so many words. But you are correct in surmising that Jesse wouldn't have been invited to join our team if I hadn't formed a good opinion of her potential." He picked up a piece of pottery and studied it before placing it carefully back on the stack Miriam had accumulated. "Well then, Jesse, why don't you tag along with Miriam for the rest of the day. Pick her brain about what you'll be doing here. I'll have Wills swing back around for you in the afternoon." He removed a handkerchief from his back pocket and wiped his hands before striding off in the opposite direction from where he had come.

Miriam pulled a bottle of water from a bag slung over her shoulder and took a long swallow. She held it in my direction, but I shook my head to decline her offer. She nodded over her shoulder. "There's more in the cooler under that plane tree. You'll need to make sure to stay hydrated if you're going to spend much time out in this sun."

I reached into my backpack and lifted out a thermos. "I always make sure to pack some. But it's good to know there are more nearby."

For the next few hours, I followed Miriam as she went about carefully raking aside dirt and rocks, which were steadfastly collected by the men with the wheelbarrows I had seen earlier. Occasionally, she would let out a whoop of delight as she uncovered another shard of pottery, which she added to the slowly growing pile. While she worked, she carried on a steady stream of conversation, describing the work she had done as an assistant and what would be required of me. Partway through her recitation, I pulled a notepad and pen from my bag and began to take copious notes on the points she made. Eventually, she stopped her work and gestured to a shady spot under a nearby tree.

"Let's take a break. I want to show you an old notebook of mine. It will give you a better idea of how you should catalog these pieces."

We sat down on the ground and sipped water while she showed me her work and instructed me on how mine should be carried out. When I felt like I had a grasp of the details, I walked over to the pottery pieces and began to create a compilation of the findings that included a rough drawing of the design, the size, and the approximate location where it was uncovered. The work was fascinating, and I continued in the same manner until James appeared, carrying three paper bags.

"Lunch break. I've got gyros from the restaurant below."

My mouth began to water in anticipation, and I realized I hadn't eaten anything in several hours. We each eagerly unwrapped the foil-surrounded treat and bit into the gyros. They were delicious! Full of flavor from the tzatziki and tomatoes layered on the pita, which contrasted well with the seared meat. I was surprised to find that, unlike the gyros I had eaten at the beach, they were also topped with French fries. I commented on that fact, to which Miriam replied that it was a fairly common practice in Greece. When we had finished eating, Miriam lay back on the grass and covered her face with her cap.

"I'll just take a wee kip. Let the food settle a bit before we continue."

James began to gather the trash, which he stuffed into the paper bags that the food came in. "I'd best be off. Need tuh make a dent on that stone wall in the front before we stop for the day."

I looked between the two of them, uncertain whether I should follow Miriam's lead or his, before deciding to walk around the site and see what the rest of the team was up to. A few of the men were lying on the ground in an apparent snooze, while the rest were either on their cell phones or having a smoke. Two of the younger team members were working alongside James, lifting stones from the wall that surrounded the main entrance of the Tower and carefully placing them in a pile a short distance away.

I pulled out my notebook and began to sketch the scene. Drawing was something I'd always enjoyed, and I hoped my attempts to capture what I was seeing did justice to the pieces. I spent the next half hour or so working on the sketches until Miriam reappeared.

"That was a nice break. I couldn't sleep very well last night. Someone in the room next to mine was creating a bit of a ruckus that woke me up, and I had trouble falling back asleep."

My breath caught as it occurred to me I had no idea who was in the room on the other side of mine. Wills had made certain that it was neither Simon nor James, but he hadn't said who else it might be. I ducked my head in an effort to hide my chagrin that the sounds she was referring to may have come from Wills and me.

She shrugged. "Oh well. I'm sure I'll catch up on my sleep once we're on to the next stop. The hotel isn't exactly designed for comfort, is it? Simon has been chatting with the owner of an Airbnb in Stenies to see what he can work out for the remainder of our time here. It would be nice to be close to the sea, although I must say the view from the hotel in Apoikia is lovely." She leaned forward to look at my notepad. "Say! You've been doing quite a bit of work since lunch. Those drawings are impressive. Quite realistic."

Her words pleased me. "Thanks. I'm not much of an artist, but

I just try to capture the overall sense of what each piece looks like."

"You've done more than that, I'd say. Don't sell yourself short, Jesse. If your writing is even half as good as your drawing, I'd say Simon has scored himself a winner."

I heard the crunch of footsteps behind us and turned to find Wills approaching us. He gave a little wave and placed his hand over his eyes to block the sun. "Hello, ladies. Simon sent me to fetch you, Miriam. One of the lads has uncovered a rather large piece of pottery, and he wants you to have a look at it before they dig any further."

"Oh, glorious! I'll be off then. Jesse, why don't you come along, too?"

"I need to speak with her for a few minutes, and then we'll come find you," Wills cut in before I could reply.

Miriam jogged off, leaving me to look curiously at Wills. "What's going on?" I asked.

He reached out a hand to brush a piece of dirt from my cheek. "Nothing really. I just wanted to see how you're doing. I haven't seen you in several hours. It feels like days, actually." He grinned as he stared directly into my eyes.

I was warmed by his touch and the look he gave me, but I was also nervous about anyone catching sight of our exchange, given what Miriam had told me. I took a step back from him and sighed. "Miriam mentioned she was kept awake last night by the noise coming from the room next to hers. Do you think that could have been us?"

He frowned slightly. "Possibly. Although I don't imagine she'd be bothered if it was."

"Why do you say that?"

He hesitated before answering. "Let's just say Miriam has had her share of noisy encounters on previous digs."

I wanted to ask him to elaborate on his comment, but we were interrupted by James calling out to us. "Simon needs to see you, Wills. Straight away," he emphasized.

Wills turned to me with a smile. "All is well. Let's resume this conversation later." He trotted off to join James. I gathered up my things and began walking in the direction in which Miriam had disappeared. *What did he mean about Miriam?* I wondered. *And with whom was she having these so-called noisy encounters?* I tried to put those questions out of my head as I hurried to find her.

# twenty-one

When we returned to the hotel in Apoikia that evening, Simon informed us about the plan to relocate to the Irene Airbnb in Stenies. This was the same new development I had first noticed the day Simon, Wills, and I had lunch at his favorite waterfront restaurant in Stenies. We would spend that evening and the following morning packing our things, then return to the Tower in the afternoon to work, and finally settle into the Airbnb in the early evening.

Wills had seen the Airbnb property up close during one of his previous excursions with Simon, and he described it as clean and well-appointed. I was most interested in learning that it had only been open a few months, which meant it had to be in better shape than the hotel we were to move from. It was unfortunate that the hotel in Apoikia was in such poor condition, because the village itself was lovely, and offered an incredible view of the surrounding mountains and the distant sea. Luckily, I had heard some of the staff speaking one morning about the fact that a new owner was about to step in, who had major renovations to the entire premises in mind as a top priority.

We pulled up in front of the Stenies Airbnb just after six that evening, tired and dirty from the afternoon's work. Simon waited until all ten of us were present, which included me, Wills, James, and Miriam, as well as two young women and four men whom I had met briefly while we were working at the Tower. I looked around the grounds of the Airbnb, spotting a row of freshly painted, white-washed units tucked into gardens spread throughout the property. There was a small house in the front of the grounds that appeared to be the check-in point, and just to its right sat a lovely patio with rocking chairs, tables, and assorted benches, all of which were partially covered by a fabric canopy featuring bright blue and white stripes reminiscent of the Greek flag. A wooden bar stretched behind the seating area of the patio with a placard advertising a variety of drinks and snacks. Simon pointed over his shoulder.

"This is where we'll be staying for the next several days, or at least until we've made progress on the excavations. James will hand out the keys to your accommodations in a moment. I think you'll find them a pleasant change from our last location. Take some time to get settled, and then please join me on the patio just behind where we are standing. There will be drinks and food available starting at seven o'clock. Consider it my welcome to Stenies." He turned and walked away in the direction of the small house.

We all glanced at each other with a curious look before approaching James for the keys to our assigned rooms. There was a sign behind where he stood with a map showing the location of the various numbered units. Wills, Miriam, and I stood in front of the sign for a moment before setting out along one of the garden paths. Apparently, we were in the same general area, and I found myself wondering if that was going to create a problem similar to what had happened at the hotel. Wills had assured me he had discussed our relationship with Simon, who hadn't been fazed by our new development in the least. I wasn't sure what to make of that, if it was even remotely true, but I hoped it meant that Simon wouldn't have any qualms about keeping me on as his assistant.

We stopped in front of the unit to which I was assigned. Miriam glanced at the key in her hand. "I believe mine's just up a bit. I'll be off then. See you at the party." She strode off up the path while Wills stayed behind with me.

He took my key from my hand. "Shall I do the honors?" I nodded, and he opened the door, stepping aside so I could enter first. I looked around with a smile at the small but pleasantly decorated room with its own private bath in the far corner. The furniture was simple but comfortable and reminded me of things I had seen at the IKEA store in Athens one day when Matt and I were wandering around.

"It's nice," I said. "Small, but comfortable looking."

"Yes, it is. He closed the door behind him and took one of my arms, turning me so that I faced him." I've been wanting to do this for hours. "He pulled me into a hug, kissing me longingly until he pulled back with a grimace. "I just realized how utterly nasty I must smell. Forgive me for letting my desire for you override my consideration."

My heart was beating rapidly in the aftermath of the intensity with which he had kissed me, and I wasn't at all sure I wanted him to stop. "I'm sure I'm pretty yucky, too. But I can't say I minded just now." I grinned at him. "Maybe later? If it works out, that is. We'll have to be very discreet and read the lay of the land."

He smirked at me. "Right. Lay of the land. I'll just totter off. Shall I come back to fetch you for the party, or would you rather meet me there?"

I considered his question. "Let's meet there." He nodded and left.

I headed for the party a little before seven o'clock. I knew from experience that the starting time for events in Greece was subject to interpretation depending upon who was doing the hosting. If it were a Greek, things weren't likely to kick off for at least half an hour after the designated starting time. Since this party was arranged by Simon, who wasn't Greek in the least, I assumed the seven o'clock time was accurate.

As I walked along one of the garden paths, I glanced around at the nearby units. I wasn't sure where Wills' unit was situated compared to mine, and I looked around the grounds to see if I could spot him. He was nowhere in sight, but I noticed Miriam wandering along a nearby path, and I waved to her in greeting.

"Jesse! Isn't this delightful? The flowers are so beautiful this time of the year."

She was caressing a bush covered with deep pink flowers I had seen several times since arriving in Greece. I walked over to where she was standing. "What are these flowers called?"

"Bougainvillea. Aren't they beautiful? I love the way they are planted next to the houses so they complement the white washed walls and deep blue doors." She turned to me with a smile. "Are you heading to the patio? I heard that Simon has arranged quite a spread for our first night here. I imagine once we resume our work, we'll have little time for such pleasures, so I intend to fully enjoy myself tonight!"

Her enthusiasm was contagious, and I found myself smiling broadly in response. We continued down the garden path together until we heard the sound of raucous laughter. "Sounds as though we're late to the ball." Miriam nudged me with her elbow. "Can't let these buggers get too far ahead or we'll never live it down."

As we came within sight of the gathering, I could see Wills off to one side talking with two other men. James was also in the thick of things, holding court with one of the young women on the team who was giggling at something he said. I looked around further until I spotted Simon. "There's Simon. I'm just going to say hello."

Miriam nodded. "I'll be at the bar. Come find me later."

As I walked closer to Simon, I noticed he was talking to Stavros. *The man certainly gets around,* I thought. Simon turned in my direction and gestured for me to join them. He picked up two glasses from the nearby bar and held them out to me. "Ouzo? Or would you prefer white wine?"

"Actually, a beer would be nice if they have any. One of those Greek types. Mythos, I believe it's called."

Stavros raised his eyebrows at my request. *"I koritsi* like Mythos. *Oraios!"* He stepped closer to the bar and held up two fingers. *"Theo bieres, parakalo."*

The bartender popped the tops off two Mythos and set them on the bar alongside two frosty glasses. Stavros poured beer into one of the glasses and handed it to me before picking up the second bottle. *"Stin uyeia mas!"* He clinked his bottle against my glass before taking a drink.

I took a sip of the beer, relishing the coolness as I allowed myself to inspect the surroundings. "This is quite a party you've organized, Simon. Everyone seems to be enjoying themselves."

He smiled as he took a sip of white wine. "Yes. It helps to gather everyone at a function such as this. Helps them relax a bit after all the hard work they've been putting in." He studied me for a few seconds. "How have you been getting on with Miriam? She told me you seem to have a knack for cataloguing the finds. Even adding little drawings of each, I understand."

I was pleased to hear she had been saying positive things to Simon about me. "She gave me some good tips, and I've just been following up on her advice. It's a lot of fun, actually. Being part of the team. Seeing how everyone gets on together. I really appreciate you giving me this opportunity."

He shrugged. "It's a mutually beneficial arrangement. I needed the help, and you seemed to need the work. A *win-win,* as you Americans would say." He grinned at me before taking another sip of wine.

Stavros had wandered off while we were talking, and he returned with a plate of what looked like meatballs and some stuffed grape leaves. *"Keftedakia kai dolmades."* He held the plate out to me. "Try. Very good." I looked around for a plate, finally settling for a napkin onto which I placed one of each. Stavros nodded approvingly. *"Bravo."* He walked off in the direction of the two young women from the team who were still surrounding James.

Simon watched him leave with a smile. "Stavros loves a good party. He's quite affable, although you wouldn't think so if you listen to the locals talk. He has a bit of a reputation as being standoffish, although I believe that's just the demeanor he has to adopt because of his position as mayor." He glanced at me. "I take it you and Wills have been getting on rather well."

His comment took me by surprise, and I fought the urge to spit out the meatball I had been chewing, which now seemed to get stuck in my throat. I finally managed to swallow it, and I looked at him questioningly. "What do you mean?"

He peered at me with a slight grin. "Oh, now, don't act as though you haven't any idea. Wills was quite upfront with me when we met on the hotel balcony the morning after you two checked into the hotel. Not that he needed to say much, mind you. Your obvious chemistry had not gone unnoticed. And not just by me, I must add. Miriam has also dropped a word or two about it."

I wadded up my empty napkin and held it tightly in my fisted hand. "Oh, dear. I'm sorry to hear that. I hope we haven't created an awkward situation for you."

He reached out his right hand and placed it on my shoulder, squeezing slightly before removing it. "Not at all. Romance between team members is not unacceptable. In fact, it can help take the edge off the long hours and loneliness that are often an unfortunate part of this experience. I'm quite alright with a work-related romance, as long as it doesn't distract from the reason we are here. As Wills explained things, the two of you are mutually attracted to each other, and also mutually committed to working as members of our crew. I must admit, I wondered how all that would pan out once the summer came to an end. I imagine you'll be heading back to California, and

Wills ... well, Wills will likely be back in England by then. Has he told you of his plans?"

I looked at him with surprise. "No. We really haven't talked about anything beyond Greece. What are you referring to?"

He looked at the ground and cleared his throat. "I think it's best if I leave that conversation to Wills. I'm sure he'll broach it with you in a timely manner."

At that moment, I spotted Wills over Simon's shoulder walking in our direction. I wanted to ask Wills immediately to explain what Simon was talking about, but I knew that discussion was best kept until we were alone.

"Hello, you two. What have you been about?" Wills clapped his hand on Simon's shoulder and gave me a warm smile.

"Talking about you, as it turns out. But I need to go make the rounds. See how everyone is getting along ..." Simon walked off, leaving Wills to look at me curiously.

"What were you talking about?" he asked.

I wasn't sure how much to say. "He brought up our relationship. It seems he doesn't have any problem with it, much to my relief. But he also said something about your plans at the end of the summer. He hinted it was something big."

Wills looked slightly uncomfortable. "Oh, that. I wish he had let me be the one to bring it up. I can assure you it's nothing for you to be concerned about. But it's a conversation that would be best conducted in private, if you don't mind. Please just trust me for now."

I wasn't sure how to respond. My mind had been mulling over several possible scenarios ever since Simon first brought the subject up, and now it was working overtime once I heard that the information would be kept from me even longer. I sighed and nodded slightly. "I can't say I'm comfortable knowing there's some big issue that I don't know about. But I agree we should wait and talk about it later."

"There you are! I've been trapped in a verbal give-and-take with Brian and Yiorgos. They're convinced that the pottery shards we've been digging up over the past two days are from the Proto-geometric era, but I told them they're clearly marked by geometric designs. I'm afraid we'll have to wait and resolve our differences after a few more pieces are uncovered." Miriam stood looking curiously from one of us to the other. "It would seem I've interrupted something. Perhaps I should leave?"

I grabbed her arm with my hand. "No, please stay. You can keep Wills company while I scoot off to the restroom." I turned abruptly and walked in the direction of the W.C. I had spotted at the corner of the bar. Once inside, I locked the door and stood at the sink staring at my reflection. *What have I gotten myself into,* I wondered. First, the new job. Then the relationship with a man I'd only known for a short time. And now there was the hint of a secret he had been keeping to himself that could possibly throw everything off-kilter. Then again, maybe I was allowing myself to imagine the worst when I really had no reason to. Wills had always been up-front with me, as far as I could tell. If there was something going on he had yet to share with me, perhaps he had a very good reason.

I splashed cool water on my face and dabbed at it with a paper towel. "Come on, Jesse. Get a grip on it," I said to my reflection.

When I returned to the party, some of the attendees appeared to have left, and the rest were sitting around the assorted tables under the canopy. The mood was more subdued than before, and I wondered if something had happened in the short time I had been gone. I walked up to where Wills still stood with Miriam. "What's going on? Everyone seems strangely quiet."

Miriam leaned toward me and whispered. "Simon got word that one of the Albanian's children took a fall when he was playing near the Tower. They've rushed him off to the doctor, but he may have to be taken to Athens if he's broken something. Apparently, there's no one on the island who can properly fix him if it comes to that."

"Oh, how terrible!" I said. "I hope he'll be alright."

Wills nodded and sighed. "Well, I for one could use another drink. Can I get either of you ladies a refill?" Both Miriam and I shook our heads. "Okay, then. I'll be back shortly."

Miriam gestured to two empty chairs nearby. "Let's have a sit-down. The day's work has suddenly caught up with me." We settled ourselves into the chairs and accepted two glasses of water from a passing waiter. "Life certainly has a way of keeping us on our toes. One minute, we're laughing about the silliest of things, and the next we're near tears about the unfairness of it all." She sighed deeply. "When something happens to a little one, it's especially difficult to accept. Have you ever thought of having children?" She looked at me expectantly.

"Not really. I've been too caught up in my studies and trying to get out from under my debts to even consider what else life might have in store for me. How about you?"

She seemed to drift off momentarily as she stared at the ground. "I almost did. Have a child, that is. But I suppose it wasn't meant to be." She shook her head slowly. "It's just as well since it wouldn't have been an easy situation for anyone involved. Me, the baby, or the man I became pregnant by. If I were to take that step, I'd rather it be a choice I made. Not just something I stumbled into. And out of."

"So ... you lost the baby?"

She nodded. "After just a few weeks. I knew it was for the best, but it was still hard to take. Especially knowing it may have been my last chance."

I frowned at the implications of her last remark. "But it's not too late, is it? To have a baby, I mean. You're still young."

She wagged her head from side to side. "I have a few more miles on me than you might have guessed. I got a late start at Uni, so I was almost thirty by the time I finished my master's." She sighed and shook her head. "A pregnancy at my age is often referred to as geriatric, which is a horrible expression, but one I've had to come to terms with. No. I think I missed my shot at that."

Wills sauntered up with a small bottle of clear liquid and three shot glasses. "Sorry. I noticed a heavy pall resting over the two of you and thought perhaps a little pick-me-up was in order. The bartender had some of this homemade ouzo from Santorini we sampled while there." He set down the glasses and filled each one before handing them to us. "Cheers. Or I suppose I should say *stin uyeia mas!*" He clicked his glass against ours before taking a sip. "Um. Lovely. Just as I remember it." He pulled out a chair and sat.

Miriam and I exchanged a look before clicking our glasses together. I took a small sip of the ouzo. It was smooth and slightly sweet. "Nice," I said. "Thank you, Wills."

"Don't mention it. But perhaps I should bring a few nibbles to go with it." He started to rise, but Miriam stopped him with a hand on his arm.

"Let me. I want to check with Simon to see if he has any news about the boy."

We watched her leave, and then Wills looked at me with raised eyebrows. "What was that about? The two of you seemed quite gloomy when I walked up."

"Oh, just girl talk. Nothing you need to worry about." I realized I was giving him a taste of his own medicine by intentionally withholding information, but it really wasn't my story to tell, and I also didn't want to bring up a subject that could lead to an uncomfortable discussion. We were still at an early point in our relationship, and there was the unsettled matter of whatever Simon had been alluding to that Wills still hadn't shared with me. "I think I'm going to go soon. It's been a long day."

He peered at me between half-closed eyes. "Are you sure there's nothing else going on?"

"Nothing that can't wait." I stood to leave.

"At least let me walk you to your room." He began to rise from his chair.

"I think it's better if you don't. I could use a little time to myself tonight, and I suspect Simon would appreciate it if you were close by."

He sat back down. "Okay, then. I'll see you in the morning."

As I walked in the direction of my room, I thought about the things that had transpired in the short time since we had arrived at the Airbnb: our passionate embrace in my room,

Simon's announcement that he was aware of our relationship, Miriam disclosing that she had lost a baby, the accident that had occurred to the Albanian child, and the puzzling comment by Simon about Wills' future plans. It was exhausting just thinking about it, and all I wanted to do was climb into bed and allow myself to escape into sleep.

I entered my room and pulled the curtains closed on the window before taking off my clothes and pulling a nightshirt over my head. The room was pleasantly cool, and I set the alarm on my phone before slipping beneath the covers.

## twenty-two

I woke up the next morning before my alarm and lay staring at the ceiling. Thoughts about my interactions with Simon, Wills, and Miriam had invaded my dreams and kept me tossing and turning most of the night. I wished I could just turn off the alarm and try to sleep another few hours, but I knew that would not be the smart thing to do. Work was waiting. And I definitely did not want to jeopardize my job in any way.

I threw the covers aside and swung my legs over the side of the bed, attempting to propel myself into a standing position. A wave of dizziness suddenly came over me, and I sat back down with a thud.

"Wow! What just happened?" I said out loud. I waited another minute and then tried to stand again. Luckily, whatever had caused my temporary dizziness disappeared as quickly as it had appeared. *Must be the stress.* I thought. *Or maybe the heat during the day and the drinks last night dehydrated me.* "More likely the stress of the unknown," I said out loud. I had to admit that the uncertainties surrounding my future with Wills were beginning to get the best of me.

I went to the bathroom, where I filled a glass with water, drinking it thirstily. It was refreshing, and I immediately began to feel better. I set aside the glass and then washed up and dressed in shorts and a t-shirt, tying a sweater around my shoulders in case there was a lingering chill in the air. I pulled on my sneakers and left the room, heading in the direction of the patio where the party had been held the night before. I wasn't sure what time breakfast would be available, but I was hoping there would at least be some coffee waiting for me. I was in luck because I spotted a pot on the bar with a stack of mugs beside it.

Two waiters were scurrying around behind the bar, setting out dishes and cutlery, as well as an assortment of hot and cold food trays. A few other members of the team began to straggle in, and I helped myself to some coffee before choosing a place at a table on the far side of the patio. I was hoping to have some quiet time to enjoy my coffee without talking to anyone. Unfortunately, two of the team members whom I had yet to meet headed in my direction with friendly smiles.

*"Yia sas. Ti kanete simera?"*

Luckily, the young man was saying one of the few Greek expressions I recognized, and I replied in halting Greek, *"Eimai kala. Kai ehseis?"*

He sat down at the table across from me and was quickly joined by another man of a similar age, whom I guessed was close to my own. The second man regarded me curiously. "You speak Greek?"

"Not really. But I think he said hello and how am I doing today, and I tried to reply that I'm well and I asked how he is."

"*Bravo*. You understood him correctly and replied as you should." He held a hand in my direction. "I am Yiorgos, and this is Nikos. His English is not very good, but I can translate for you both."

I shook his hand. "There seem to be a lot of men with your names in Greece. My friend told me it's fairly common since most Greeks are given the name of a saint. I guess there are just so many names of Greek saints to go around."

He grinned. "That is correct. I have two cousins who are also named Yiorgos. It makes it difficult at times to know who they are referring to when someone calls our name. You are Jesse, *etsi dhen einai?*"

"Yes. Sorry, I didn't introduce myself."

Nikos said something to Yiorgos that I didn't catch. "He say everyone know you because you are here to work as Simon's assistant. That is good. We worry when the other assistant had to leave when she fall. The work cannot continue unless someone makes record." He added sugar to his coffee and took a sip before continuing. "So, you study archaeology?"

I shook my head. "Not yet, but I'm hoping to as soon as I can afford the tuition. I have a degree in history, and I'm teaching in California until I'm able to go to graduate school."

He glanced at Nikos and said a string of words in Greek to which Nikos nodded. "We understand this difficulty. Niko finish his undergraduate degree but was unable to continue. Simon arrange so he can return to study after the summer. I in my second year of graduate work in archaeology, and I hope to finish middle of next year. Simon help me also. In return, we both work very hard for him." He looked at me curiously. "You have talked to him about help?"

I was surprised at his question because it reminded me of something similar that Miriam had said. "No, but perhaps that's not a bad idea."

At that moment, a bell rang and one of the waiters called out, "*"To fagito einai ehtimi."* I looked at Yiorgos for a translation. "The food is ready. Shall we see what they have?"

I nodded and stood to follow him, joining the line of team members who had already begun to help themselves to the buffet offerings. When it was my turn, I filled my plate with a slice of an egg dish reminiscent of one I had before that I thought of as a cross between an omelet and a quiche, some roasted tomatoes, two slices of fresh bread, and some apricot preserves. The food was emitting a delicious aroma, and I couldn't wait to taste everything. I returned to the table where the young men were already digging into their breakfast with gusto.

"You try the patates?" Yiorgos asked. "Cooked with lemoni." He used his knife to push a few onto my plate. "Try. You will like."

I forked one of the potatoes and nodded my appreciation before cutting a slice of the egg dish. Everything was delicious, as it usually was in Greece, and we ate in silence for a while. Finally, I pushed my plate back and picked up my coffee mug. "I'm going to get a refill. Would anyone like some more coffee?" The men glanced at each other and shook their heads.

When I headed for the coffee pot, I spotted Wills sitting on the far side of the patio with Simon. I filled my mug and walked to where they sat. They both looked tired, and I wondered if they had suffered from the same poor sleep I had been subjected to. "Good morning. Have you heard anything about the injured boy?"

Simon looked up with a slight smile. "Good morning, Jesse. Yes. Luckily, the child is fine. Nothing was broken, so the local physician in Hora was able to fix him up. It took a while for us to locate the doctor, which made for a long and stressful night. But everything worked out eventually."

"I'm glad. I was so worried about him."

Wills looked up at me with tired eyes. "As were we all. Have you had any breakfast yet?"

"Yes. I'm just having a second cup of coffee now."

Wills stood and pulled out a chair. "Forgive my manners. Please. Have a seat."

I hesitated before sitting in the offered chair. "I didn't want to intrude on your conversation."

Simon waved off my concern. "We weren't talking about anything of substance. Just mulling over the plans for the day." He took a sip of water before continuing. "I've asked Miriam to focus on resolving the origin of the shards she's been uncovering. I suspect you've heard there's some difference of opinion on that?" I nodded. "If you could shadow her again today and record everything of substance, it would be most helpful."

"Certainly. I'm glad to help." I glanced at Wills, who seemed to be staring distractedly off to some distant spot. "Wills, could we talk for a few minutes before the work begins? Perhaps take a walk?"

He looked up as if he had just noticed me. "I'm sorry. What did you say?"

"I was wondering if we could talk. If you can spare the time, that is."

He glanced at Simon and then nodded. "Of course. I have to meet some of the team in about half an hour, but we can talk before then."

Simon pushed back his chair and stood. "I need to have a chat with Stavros before heading to the Tower. I'll see you both later."

He walked away, leaving Wills and me to look at each other uncomfortably. Finally, Wills spoke up. "What did you want to talk about? I'm afraid I'm not in a very communicative mood, so if it's anything important, you may want to hold it until later."

"It is important, so perhaps you're right." I shifted in my chair so I could make sure no one was close enough to overhear. "I just thought we should talk about what happened yesterday. The awkwardness between us, and how we left things last night."

He stared at me directly. "Yes. We should air things out. Why don't we make a date for later? I could stop by your room at say …" He glanced at his watch. "Six?"

"That will be fine." I noticed Miriam walking across the patio. "I should go now and talk to Miriam. I'll see you at six."

He nodded as I walked away. I raised one hand and waved at Miriam as she approached. "Good morning! Simon told me to stick close to you again today. I understand you're hot on the trail of deciphering the source of the pottery shards you've been uncovering. I overheard a couple of the team saying they disagreed with their origin. I'd be more than happy to help with that in any way I can."

She waved her hand as if to brush aside my concern. "I don't think there's much to resolve. I'm almost 100 percent certain that I'm correct in my appraisal. All we really need to do is gather several more pieces to solve the puzzle once and for all." She looped her arm through mine. "Come on, then. Let's get on with it."

By the time we arrived at the Tower, several of the team were already at work. Miriam pulled on some gloves and picked up a hand pick and shovel. I followed her around the side of the crumbling building to a spot where two women were on their hands and knees, carefully raking aside the dirt and rocks accumulated there.

"Hello there. We've come to lend a hand. Jesse, this is Anna and Sofia. They're part of our summer team on leave from Uni in Athens. Jesse is Simon's new assistant."

The young ladies smiled and welcomed me with a simultaneous *yeia sas* as Miriam set her things down and studied the pile of rubble they had accumulated. "Have you come across anything of interest today?" she asked.

The one named Sofia replied. "Mostly very small fragments, although Anna did find one rather large piece a minute ago. Show her, Anna."

Anna wiped her hands on her pants and reached into a bag lying on the ground. She pulled out a fragment of pottery that looked to be about a third of the size of an actual vase, allowing one to get a clear view of the decorative markings. Miriam took it from her, pulling a magnifying mirror from her pocket, which she held close to the piece. She studied it in silence before lifting her head with a smile.

"This is exactly what I was hoping for. As you can see, it is clearly from the Geometric Period as evidenced by the cross-hatching and linear motifs." She held it out to me. "Jesse, why don't you take this and see if you can sketch out the details. Take several photos of it, as well, using your phone camera. When you've finished, bring it round to Simon. He'll want to have a look before it's wrapped and stored to protect it." She looked down at the two girls. "Good work. That's the best piece anyone has located so far."

Anna and Sofia beamed at each other with pleasure.

I spent the next several minutes writing and sketching in my notebook, trying my best to replicate the design of the piece, as well as the location where it was found near the Tower. I shot several photos with my phone, zooming as best I could in order to capture the intricate design and colors. When I had finished, I carried the piece around to the front of the Tower in search of Simon. It took a while to locate him, but I finally found him deep in conversation with Stavros. They looked up as I approached.

"I'm sorry to interrupt, but Miriam asked me to show you this." I held the piece out for him to see. He took it from me, his eyes growing wide as he turned it in his hands, finally holding it up for Stavros to see.

"Wonderful! This is precisely what we need to convince the local authorities to hold off on bringing in the big equipment. Stavros tells me they're intent on expediting the renovation by bulldozing as much of the area as possible. This will hopefully show them how much damage they could do if they follow through with that plan." He looked at me appreciatively. "Well done, Jesse."

"I really had very little to do with this. It was one of the team members, Anna, who found it. Miriam just told me to record the find and show it to you."

"Well, it's a team effort." He took the piece back from Stavros. "Let me have this photographed so we can send it to the officials."

"I've taken several shots with my phone. I can send them to you if you'd like."

Simon nodded. "Yes, do that. But I'll also ask our team photographer to shoot some, as well. It never hurts to gather as much info as we can." He strode off like a man on a mission.

Stavros regarded me with a slight grin and narrowed eyes. "You are an enigma, Jesse Holloway. Simon say you live in California, but here on vacation to visit cousin *Stin Athena*. Apparently, Wills introduce you. Now you important member team. Maybe you stay longer? Not go back to California?"

That was far more English than I had ever heard him speak, and it made me wonder if he had been keeping his command of the language a secret on purpose. Perhaps in an effort to overhear something useful from one of the team members. "I'm afraid I have to return to work in California at the end of the summer. You see, I want to go to graduate school. To study archaeology. But I need to work out the finances first."

He looked at me thoughtfully. "Perhaps another way. Maybe Simon help. Talk to him."

I was reminded of Yiorgos' and Miriam's comments about financial help. So maybe there WAS more we could discuss. "Thank you. I'll think about what you are saying, but I have to go back to work now."

I turned and walked away quickly. I realized that my sudden departure could be interpreted as rude, but I wanted to get away by myself and sort through the messages I had been receiving. I wandered down the hill away from the Tower and spotted a stone wall overlooking the sea below. I sat down and pulled my cell phone from my backpack. It had been quite some time since I had heard from either Matt or Shelly, and I wondered how they had been getting along since our time on Santorini. More than anything, I wanted to hear familiar and friendly voices, and maybe get some help clearing my mind of doubts and worries. I decided to call Shelly first. The phone rang several times before she answered.

"Jesse? You must be psychic. I was just thinking it has been ages since we've spoken. How in the world are you? Is everything hunky-dory on Andros with that hunky man of yours?"

I shook my head with a smile. "I've missed you, you silly girl. How are things with you and my cousin?"

"Hmm. I think that is called *deflecting* the subject at hand. Everything is fine here. Matt is a treasure. We've been getting along famously and having a grand time. He's at work now. We decided we could use a breather from each other. At least for a few hours. Whew! Who knew that love ... or lust ... could be so exhausting!"

Her comment made me slightly uncomfortable, given the images of the two of them that it created. "TMI, my friend. I mean, it's my cousin you're talking about."

She chuckled. "You're right, of course. I get a bit carried away when I think about Matt. Let me reverse gears and get back to my original subject of you and Wills. I take it you are still together? Have either of you talked about what you will do at the end of the summer? Matt and I have been dancing around that subject for the past day or so but not coming to any conclusion. It's a real dilemma."

"I know. Wills and I haven't really talked about it either. In fact, we haven't talked about several things that are sort of hanging over us. Simon hinted that Wills has some sort of plan for the fall, but Wills hasn't said anything to me about it yet. And to top it off, some team members have suggested that Simon could help me out financially when it's time for me to start my graduate studies. I'm hesitant to bring it up to him because it seems as though he would have mentioned it to me himself if it were an option. I'm wondering if the fact that he hasn't said anything means he's not too happy with my work? Or that he's still waiting to decide how he feels about me. Honestly, I don't know what to do."

There was a pause on the line. "It sounds as though you are letting the *what-ifs* get the better of you. My advice is to set up an official meeting with Simon and talk it all out. From what you've said, he seems to be quite straightforward. I'm sure if he has any concerns, he'll express them openly. And if you ask him directly about the possibility of financial help for graduate work, he'll likely give you an honest reply. As for Wills, you seem to be implying there are things you've each been hesitant to talk about. In my experience, as limited as it admittedly is, that never comes to much good. Talk to him, Jesse. Say what's on your mind. With any luck, he'll respond in kind."

Her advice was welcome, although the thought of following through on it made me more than a little nervous.

"I'm sure you're right. Although I'm honestly scared to death to be that direct with either of them. What if it blows up in my face and I'm suddenly out of a job and out of what feels like the beginning of a special relationship? I don't know if I could take that."

"It's scary, I know. But what choice do you have? Think about how you're feeling now. If you don't allow yourself to get to the bottom of these doubts, they'll just continue to eat away at you."

My dizziness in the morning came to mind. I took a slow breath, exhaling it noisily. "I know you're right. In fact, Wills and I made plans to talk this evening. Maybe once I know what he's been holding back, I'll be able to approach Simon with the rest of my concerns. Thanks, Shel."

"You're welcome. Now I must totter off. I'm meeting Matt for a late lunch in an area called Fokionos Negri, and then he promised to show me a bit more of the city."

Her mention of Fokionos Negri reminded me of the incident with the waitress we encountered on my first evening in Athens. I hoped he didn't plan to risk another run-in with her, but even if he did, at least this time it would be clear he'd moved on.

"Well, enjoy yourselves and give my cousin a big hug from me. I'll let you know how things go after I've had those conversations with Wills and Simon."

"Sounds good. Ta for now!"

I pressed the end call button on my cell phone and stared at the screen. Her advice about talking things over honestly with both Wills and Simon made sense, but that didn't mean it felt like an easy thing to do. I tucked my phone away in my back pocket and looked down at the view below me. The sea was painted in broad strokes of blue, turquoise, and deep green, with shadows of the nearby hills along the sides. There was a faint breeze blowing, which was stirring up the waves where they lapped the shore. I could spot the tiny images of people bobbing about in the water or lying on the sand, and I had a sudden urge to join them. We hadn't been able to visit the Nautical club in Hora yet, and the only time I had been in the water was at the swimming pools at the hotels on Santorini. It felt like a shame not to at least take a swim in the sea when I had the chance.

I took my cell phone out of my pocket again to check the time. It was just shy of 5 p.m. That meant work at the dig would be wrapping up soon, and I could discreetly wander off without having to announce my intent to anyone. I decided to text Miriam to let her know I was leaving in case she went looking for me, and then began walking down the dirt path to a series of stone steps that would take me to the beach. Luckily, I had tucked my swimsuit into my backpack that morning. *Must have been a premonition,* I thought to myself. Or just a case of wishful thinking. The idea of dipping into the cool, refreshing water made me quicken my steps, and I smiled in anticipation.

By the time I had finished my swim and walked up the road to the Airbnb, it was almost six o'clock. I hurriedly showered to remove the sand and salt before slipping on a pair of jeans and a cotton t-shirt. I was still towel-drying my hair when I heard a knock on the door to my room. I crossed the floor and opened it, smiling when I saw Wills standing there. Even though I was expecting him, it was still nice to see that it was him. I stepped aside and gestured for him to come in.

He rubbed his hand over his hair with a tired smile. "It looks as if someone has just had a shower."

"Actually, I went for a swim. The water was absolutely lovely."

"I wish I'd had the good sense to join you. Or at least made time for a shower. I'm afraid I haven't been able to freshen up after the day's activities."

I noticed his shirt was wrinkled and the knees of his pants were smudged with dirt. "Would you like to take a shower? I'm afraid I don't have any clothes to loan you, but at least you'd feel a bit better."

He looked around the room uncertainly. "Perhaps we could walk up to my room. I can pour you a glass of wine while you are waiting for me to clean up."

"Sure. Just let me grab a couple of things." I went into the bathroom to brush my hair, glancing in the mirror to be sure I looked okay before returning to the room. I placed my room key and phone in my backpack, adding my wallet before turning to him with a nod. "Ready. Lead the way."

We headed back outside, turning to the right to follow one of the garden paths that led to a room a short distance behind mine. Wills strode forward to unlock the door, stepping aside so I could enter first. He reached past me and flipped on a light switch. I glanced around the room, which looked very much like the one where I was staying. The only obvious difference was the wall color, which was a deep blue, whereas mine was a pale grey. Wills walked to the small kitchenette and pulled a bottle of white wine from the fridge, pouring a generous amount into a glass before handing it to me.

"Why don't you have a seat on the sofa? I'll just be a few."

He began collecting some clothes from the bedroom before disappearing into the bath. I sat down on the sofa and slipped off my sandals, tucking my legs under me before taking a sip of wine. It was cool and refreshing, and I took another swallow before setting it down. I looked around the room some more, noticing how tidy everything appeared. In fact, if I didn't know anyone was staying there, I would guess it was unoccupied except for the suitcase sitting in one corner and a stack of papers placed next to a laptop on the table. Even the bed was neatly made, although I supposed that could be attributed to the fact that a daily cleaning service was provided by the owners of the Airbnb. Still, the space spoke loudly of order and function, in contrast to the lived-in look of my own rental space.

*Huh. Must be a guy thing,* I thought. At least a trait shared by the two guys who were currently featured prominently in my life.

That brought up thoughts of Matt, and I wondered what he would say about how he and Shel were getting along. It made me smile to realize there was an obvious attraction between them, which both surprised and delighted me.

The bathroom door opened, and Wills stepped out wearing a pair of well-worn jeans and a dark navy t-shirt. He was rubbing his hair vigorously with a towel, and I couldn't help but notice the way his biceps flexed with the up and down motion. He must have seen me staring at him because he paused his toweling for a moment with a grin.

"How's the wine?" He nodded at my glass

"Nice, thank you." I shifted in my seat. "Your room is very tidy."

He glanced around with a nod. "A family trait I've apparently inherited. As children, we were taught to straighten up our rooms before doing anything else. I'm afraid I haven't been able to shake off that tendency over the years, even though no one is standing over me expecting me to do it anymore." He walked over to the kitchenette and poured some wine for himself.

I looked at him curiously. We hadn't really talked about his childhood, and, other than his Uncle Simon, I really had no idea about any of his other relatives. "Do you have many siblings?"

"Two older sisters and a younger brother. They all still live in Reading, where we grew up. I'm the only one who fled the nest." He hung his towel in the bathroom before taking a seat on the sofa near me.

"And your parents? Do they still live in Reading?"

He looked down at the glass in his hand before responding. "I'm afraid they both passed a few years back. It was a car accident, actually. They were driving home from dinner one night, and an older gent ran a red light. Turns out, he was nearly blind from cataracts. Shouldn't have been behind the wheel at all, and certainly not at night."

I set my glass down and shifted so I was facing him. "Oh, Wills, I'm so sorry. That must have been terrible!"

He placed his glass beside mine and took both my hands in his. "It was. Harder on my siblings naturally, because they were used to seeing Mum and Dad almost every day. I felt a load of guilt because I had stayed away so long. Especially when it struck me that I would never have a chance to see them again."

I looked down at our hands. "Was there a reason why you left? Other than just getting on with your life, I mean."

He squeezed my hands and nodded. "My father and I never saw eye to eye on most matters. It made things quite tense whenever we were around each other. After a while, it just seemed that keeping my distance would be better for everyone."

"Did your sisters and brother have the same type of relationship with your dad?"

He shook his head. "No. And I suppose that's what goaded me the most. Why me? My mother once told me it was because we were too alike. That seeing me made him have to face what he was afraid to see about himself. When she said that, it made me feel there was something wrong with me. I never managed to get to the bottom of it, although one of my older sisters said something one time about how our father expected perfection out of me because he couldn't get it from himself. It's still a puzzle, I'm afraid, and I guess it always will be."

"Maybe you could talk to your sister again. See if she can shed any more light on what she meant."

"Perhaps. Although it might be better to leave things as they are. Not stir the pot, so to speak. I suppose I'm afraid of getting burned in the process."

I smiled slightly at the analogy between stirring a pot full of boiling water and digging deeper into his family issues. I wasn't unfamiliar with the feeling of being on the outside with one's parents. My relationship with mine had been fairly comfortable over the years. Nonetheless, I always had the feeling they were just waiting for me to get on with my life instead of, as they put it, *treading water while you wait for the tide to recede.*

My parents grew up on the coast of Florida, so an analogy involving the ocean tides was not uncommon for them to use. I interpreted it to mean they didn't approve of my life choices and would prefer it if I would just get back on the track they had imagined for me. Since that would have involved my staying in Nashville, marrying a *nice young man with a good job,* and starting a family as soon as possible, I opted to move to the West Coast to pursue my dreams away from their constant scrutiny. Still, I loved my parents, and I couldn't imagine my life without them around. Even if it was just for infrequent, short-term visits.

"I can't imagine how hard that has all been on you. It helps me understand you a little better. What makes you tick, so to speak. You've had to live with the belief you were a disappointment to your dad, and then to suffer in silence by his sudden absence."

"That pretty much sums it up. Except for the fact that Uncle Simon has played a large part in helping me feel that I'm not all bad. Even before my parents were gone, he always made the time to talk with me, regardless of how far away we were from one another. I guess you could say he was more like a father to me than my own was. They weren't all that alike, you see. My dad always said that Uncle Simon was his scatter-brained younger brother, always off on one adventure or another. He never married or had any children, which my dad chalked up to him being too selfish in his pursuit of his own dreams. But I never saw him that way. To me, his life was admirable and exciting. I guess I always hoped he saw me as a surrogate son. Or at least someone he could relate to like a son." He grew silent for a moment, and I thought I could sense a level of sadness in him that I hadn't seen before.

He shook his head and cleared his throat. "That's enough about me. You indicated you had something you wanted to talk about."

I squirmed in my seat as I let go of his hands, reaching for my wine glass again and taking a long sip before answering. "It's something Simon said. He hinted you've made some major plans for the end of the summer."

He sighed. "That was a conversation he should have let me pursue in my own time." He lifted his glass and took a swallow before setting it back down. "I want you to believe me when I say I had every intention of talking with you about it before things were finalized. I just didn't want to raise any ruckus without due cause."

*Raise any ruckus? Did that mean that whatever he was planning was going to have a negative effect on us, whatever "us" even meant?*

"I think you'd better explain what you mean. The unknown is starting to feel like a huge wall between us."

His hair had begun to fall over his face as it dried from his shower, and he pushed it back with one hand. "Okay. Let me start at the beginning. Hopefully, by the time I get to the end of the story, you'll understand why I've been hesitant to say anything before now."

For the next several minutes, Wills explained how he had been offered an administrative position at King's College in London, which would involve overseeing the Archaeology department and helping decide who would be granted admission. It was a prestigious position and an honor not usually bestowed on someone as young as Wills. Nonetheless, he was hesitant to accept the offer, in part because it would shift his focus from field work to academic administration and limit his ability to travel outside of the London area. Apparently, he had been in the process of negotiating the terms with the college while we were on Andros and had told Simon about it because he was seeking his advice.

According to Wills, Simon wasn't too keen on the idea of Wills making such a dramatic shift in career focus, and he had been trying to come up with an alternative arrangement that would satisfy both of them. Unfortunately, time was running out because the King's College offer was only going to be good for another week, and then it was off the table.

I had listened carefully. Or at least with as much attention as I was able to garner, given the huge knot that had lodged itself in my chest and was threatening to suck the breath out of me. If he were to accept the administrative position, it would certainly end the possibility of anything further between the two of us. There was no way I could even consider moving to London, and the idea of a long-distance relationship, especially with the travel restrictions he mentioned, meant there was very little chance of us seeing each other again. I stood and carried my wine glass to the kitchenette so I could empty the last few sips in the sink and refill it with water. I drank thirstily in hopes of calming my heart, which was thumping so hard I swore I could hear it. I felt Wills walk up behind me.

"Please tell me what you are thinking. This is why I didn't want to say anything until I knew what was likely to happen."

I turned to face him. "Honestly, I don't know *what* to think. It's quite an opportunity for you in many ways, but it also totally changes the direction I thought your career was heading. At least, from what you've told me."

"You're absolutely correct, which is why I've been having such a difficult time deciding. But what you haven't told me is how this makes you feel on a personal level. About us, I mean."

I hesitated before responding. "That's just it. *Is* there an *us*? We've had fun, but we've never talked about anything beyond the summer. Maybe this is all we'll ever have. Especially if you're on one continent and I'm on another. I suppose it was silly to imagine we could be anything more than a summer romance."

He frowned and rubbed his hand over his face as he took a few steps away from where we stood. "It's true that we haven't delved into the possibilities of our relationship, but to be honest, I was hoping for something more. I had even allowed myself to imagine how we could arrange things so we wouldn't be apart after the summer." He stopped pacing and looked directly at me. "Would you consider pursuing your graduate degree in London? I may just know someone on the admissions committee at a rather prestigious university there." He smiled sheepishly.

"You mean at King's College?"

"Yes. It could be a stellar move for both of us."

I sighed and shook my head. "That's a lot to think about. I haven't even decided *when* I'll be able to afford to go back to school, much less where." I remembered my earlier conversations with Miriam and Yiorgos. "I've been thinking that perhaps I should approach Simon and see if he would be able to help in that regard. A couple of people mentioned he sometimes provides financial assistance for team members who are seeking to continue their studies in archaeology in exchange for a longer-term commitment."

"Yes, he has been known to do that, and I'm sure he would be open to considering such an arrangement with you. He thinks very highly of you."

His words pleased me. "I'm glad to hear that. So, to answer your question, I think the first thing I need to do is talk to Simon. After that, I'll have a better idea of my options. In the meantime, you have a rather huge decision to make for yourself, and I don't want whatever I do, or don't do, to be a factor in that."

He walked back to where I stood and took both of my hands in his. "But it is. *You* are. That's a key factor in my uncertainty about the offer. Truth be told, I can't imagine being happy in any place that would prevent me from seeing you. I hoped you felt the same." He looked at me questioningly.

"I think I do. At least, I *thought* I did until you brought up the London offer. Now I don't know what to think. As I said, I don't want to get in the way of your career."

He pulled me toward him and wrapped his arms firmly around me. "You wouldn't be in the way, as you put it. I like to think of it as you being a key part of whatever I do."

I rested my head against his chest. I could hear his rapid heartbeat, which matched the intensity of my own. I wanted to reach up and kiss him and allow my feelings for him to show through my actions, but instead, I pushed back slightly and looked at him apologetically. "I want to be with you, too. But I can't be the reason for whatever decision you make, nor can I let you be the reason for mine." I took a step back. "Let's agree to talk about this again once I've had my conversation with Simon. In the meantime, why don't you examine your feelings about the London position and decide what you truly would like to do? That way, whatever happens, at least we'll know that we chose based upon what was right for us rather than what we were afraid of."

He smiled slightly. "Wise words, although I'm not sure it's what I was hoping to hear you say." He shoved his hands in his pockets. "Alright. I agree to your terms. We'll take a day or two and sort out our situations separately. But after that, I want us to revisit this conversation before either of us arrives at a decision. Agreed?"

I nodded. "Agreed. Now. I'm half-starved. What do you say we walk down to that taverna Simon likes so much and have something to eat?"

He hesitated a moment. Catching my hands in his again before pulling me close against his chest. "Only because I promised to give us a little time to sort things out. What I'm hungry for more than anything is time alone with you."

I could feel his interest growing where our bodies were pressed together, and I had to take a step back in order not to respond in kind. "I feel the same way. But it's better if we give ourselves a little time." As soon as I said those words, I regretted it, although

I knew it was the right thing to do. "I'll just pop into your bath for a moment, and then we can go." I entered the bathroom and closed the door, walking to the sink where I splashed cool water on my face. I looked at my reflection in the mirror. *What are you doing?* I wondered. *Do you really want to just walk out that door knowing you may never have a moment like this with Wills again?* My heart responded one way while my head said I was doing the smart thing. "Being smart isn't always what it's cracked up to be," I said to my reflection before going back out to join Wills.

# twenty-three

When I arrived at breakfast the next morning, I noticed that neither Wills nor Simon was anywhere in sight. I spotted Miriam and walked over to where she sat with a few more members of the team.

"*Yeia Sou*, Jesse. Did you have a good sleep?"

"It was okay. I was wondering if you've seen Simon this morning? There's something I need to talk with him about."

"I'm afraid he's off to Athens with Wills. I've been told they left about an hour ago to catch the first ferry. Apparently, Stavros arranged a special meeting with some officials there in hopes of getting rapid approval for a delay in the planned renovation of the Tower. I'm not sure how successful they'll be since, in my experience, nothing in Greece happens quickly, although I'm sure Stavros' involvement will be useful. Is there anything I can help you with?"

Her words filled me with regret for not approaching Simon sooner, and I wondered how their absence would affect the deadline looming over Wills' decision. "No, thanks. I'll just have to wait until he returns." I glanced around the patio, noticing how relaxed everyone appeared compared to my anxious state. I decided the best thing I could do was to busy myself with work. "I think I'll just grab a bite and head back to my room. I want to finish the cataloguing I started yesterday while it's still fresh in my mind."

"Grand. I'll head back to the site once I finish here. Come find me when you're ready."

I headed to the buffet line, grabbing a slice of bread and cheese before filling a mug with coffee. When I entered my room, I placed the food on the counter, realizing my appetite had vanished. I took a sip of coffee before placing that down, as well. I walked to the window and pushed the curtains aside. A bright shaft of sunlight blanketed the room, and I closed my eyes, soaking in its warmth. *What now?* I thought. It wasn't going to be easy to concentrate on anything until I had the opportunity to talk things over with Simon, and the fact that Wills was also gone meant his decision could well be finalized before we had the chance to see each other again.

Suddenly, the prediction of the old woman at the hotel in Athens, the waiter Yanni's yiayia, came back to my mind once more. Was this what she meant when she said the coffee grounds showed *uncertainty*, the *unexpected*, and *big change* were in store for me? That could easily describe several things I had experienced already, but it could also be a foreboding of what was still to come. I hated not knowing what was going on, but what choice did I have? None. That was the bottom line. All I could do now was distract myself as best I could in order to try and reduce my apprehension.

I walked over to the kitchen counter and picked up my notebook, flipping to the pages where I had begun to sketch the images of the pottery shards. I looked them over and nodded. *Not bad, Jesse. Now, maybe you can put that mind of yours to good use to find more about the history of that era.* I sat down on the sofa and opened my laptop, googling the Geometric Period until I came across what seemed to be a lengthy description. I propped my feet on the coffee table in front of the sofa and began to read.

It was close to noon by the time I finished reading and jotting notes about it all. I had barely lifted my head from the laptop for so long that my head felt dizzy. I glanced over at my untouched food on the kitchen counter and realized I hadn't eaten anything since the night before. I considered eating the now-stale bread and cheese I had picked up that morning before deciding that something more appetizing was in order. I grabbed my notebook and shoved it into a backpack before heading out the door. I stopped by the patio where breakfast was served and looked around in hopes of finding some remaining food items. The buffet was bare, but I noticed a sign with a short list of things that could be ordered. Lunch was clearly not a priority at the Airbnb. I suspected most guests would be out and about on the island during the day, so it would be a waste of time and money to put out a more extensive list. I walked up to the counter and placed my order for a ham, cheese, and tomato *tost*, which had become my go-to meal in Greece, and a cup of American coffee. The waiter handed me the coffee and indicated he would bring the rest to me. I added a little milk and sugar to the coffee and made my way to a table. I had just sat down when I heard someone call my name. I glanced up to see Yiorgos and Nikos heading my way.

"Hello! Are you on a break for lunch?" I asked.

"No. We're on our way to Hora. Miriam asked us to pick up some more plastic containers for the pottery pieces. On our way back, we're to buy pizza. You'll be joining us, I hope?" He glanced down at the *tost* the waiter had just brought.

"That sounds more appetizing than what I ordered. Is Miriam still at the Tower?"

"*Nai.* She's working with Anna and Sofia. They've uncovered quite a few more pieces this morning."

"That's good news. I'll join them as soon as I finish up here."

They waved their goodbyes as they headed to the parking lot.

I took a bite of my toasted sandwich, which wasn't bad at all, quickly finishing it as I realized how hungry I was. I washed it down with the rest of the coffee and stood to leave.

When I arrived at the work site, I immediately spotted Miriam bent over a pile of dirt with Anna. "Hello there. I ran into Yiorgos, who said you've been having quite a bit of luck this morning."

She straightened up with a smile and wiped her arm across her forehead, leaving a dirty streak. "Yes, we have! Look at this." She pointed to a sack that lay just behind the dig site.

I walked over to where she pointed and carefully opened the sack. There appeared to be ten or more pottery shards inside, all in reasonably good condition. I took one out and examined it. "These look similar to the large one you found and, again, clearly representative of the Geometric Period. I've done quite a lot of reading about that era this morning. I can see why you are so excited about the finds."

She grinned and nodded. "These are some of the best pieces anyone has ever found on this island. Maybe on ANY island. I can't wait to turn in the report to the Greek Archaeological Council." She pointed at my backpack. "Do you have it with you?"

I opened the pack and pulled out my notebook, handing it to her. "I think you'll be pleased. I've compiled quite a list of the finds, along with sketches of each, and a description of where they can likely be traced historically. I don't think Simon will have any problem convincing the officials to delay excavating this site until we are certain everything worth finding has been dug up."

"Grand! If you don't mind, I'll keep this and go through it this afternoon. Simon sent word that he and Wills should return on the morning ferry. He'll be thrilled at the progress we've all made."

I was relieved to hear they would be back on the island soon. "Once you have a look, let me know if there is anything else you'd like me to do. In fact, I can give you a hand here if that would be helpful."

She looked around at the ground and nodded. "Anna and Sofia have been loads of help. But if you could take over for me, that would allow me to go back to my room and study the work you've done. Anna, why don't you show Jesse how to use the rake? I don't believe she's had the pleasure of experiencing a true archaeological dig firsthand."

I glanced down at the implement Anna was holding. "No, I haven't. That would be fun."

Miriam chuckled as she and Anna exchanged a look. "We'll see how much fun you think it was in a couple of hours. That's about how long I estimate it will take for you to realize the physical part of archaeology is not nearly as enticing as the mental work." She collected her things and walked off with a wave.

I turned to Anna expectantly. "Where should I start?"

By the time Yiorgos and Nikos reappeared with the plastic containers and pizza, I had worked up quite an appetite, as well as a soaking sweat. My clothes were splattered with dust and dirt, and my hair hung in a straggly mess around my face, which I imagined was streaked with mud from where I had swiped a hand across it in an effort to keep the sweat droplets from filling my eyes. I was tired. But it was a GOOD type of tired. The kind where you feel you've been spending your time on a useful endeavor. Yiorgos called out to let us know the pizza would be available in fifteen minutes on the patio at the Airbnb.

Anna and I collected our tools, placing them in a shed next to the Tower before joining the others as we set off on foot for the patio. We passed a lion's head spouting water along the way, similar to the one I had first seen in the village of Apoikia, and we stopped to rinse off our hands and various other body parts as best we could. The water was cool, and I ducked my head under the spout and drank thirstily. I wiped my mouth and waited while Anna and Sofia did the same, giggling as the water dripped down their faces and soaked their shirts.

"So much for the glamour of archaeology!" Sofia said with a grin.

When we arrived at the patio, the smell of pizza filled the air. My stomach responded with its usual insistent reminder, and I followed the others as we lined up at the counter. There were at least six different types of pizza laid out for our selection, and I hungrily added three different slices to my plate. One was topped with Kalamata olives and feta cheese, the second held grilled mushrooms and chunks of ham, and the third was covered with eggplant and slices of tomato. Pitchers of beer and water were available on each table, and for a while, the only sounds were the satisfied moans of the diners.

When I had finished my second slice and taken a hefty bite of the third, I leaned back in my chair with a groan. "I can't remember when anything has tasted so good!" I grinned at the others at my table, which included Anna, Sofia, Nikos, and Yiorgos, along with James Branson, who had shown up unexpectedly. He crooked his head as he considered what I said.

"Ah dinnae ken a lass as wee as yerself could fill her gob in sech a way!" He grinned at me mischievously.

There it was again: the inconsistency of James' accent. I wasn't sure why it bothered me so much, seeing as how we were barely friends, but I found that it instilled a suspicious caution in me that made me want to hold onto my skepticism about him until he proved me wrong. I narrowed my eyes as I considered how to answer him. "And I didn't know that a man as young as you could be so cheeky. Nice of you to show up just in time to help yourself to the pizza. Where have you been lately?"

He took another huge bite of pizza topped with what appeared to be chunks of calamari and answered as he chewed. "Paleopolis. Brian had me hauling t'ings out the museum. That's until Margaret came 'round. She's quite the auld blether. Dinnae want tuh clipe on her, but listening to it made me crabbit. I thought it best if I set some distance 'tween us."

His accent was curious. Different from the British, and quite a bit different from anything I'd ever heard in the States. Except for those rare times when it disappeared completely. He was definitely an odd one. I couldn't decide if he was a mischief maker or just someone used to saying what was on his mind without worrying how it came across. His comment to me and Wills as we were leaving the taverna in Apoikia came to mind, and I decided it would be best to keep my distance from him. I turned to Sofia in order to stop the conversation between James and me.

"How long have you worked for Simon?" I asked her.

She considered my question for a moment. "Um, about six months all in all. Only in the summers when I'm on school break. Although I wish it could be year-round. I'd much rather be outdoors than sitting in a stuffy classroom."

I glanced across the table where James had his head inclined toward Anna, seemingly regaling her with his attempts at humor. I studied her expression. She appeared to be enjoying his attention, but also held herself back as though she was still deciding whether or not to take him seriously. *Smart girl,* I thought. I stood up from the table with a groan. "If you will excuse me, I'm going to have a rest before we return to the dig.

I'm afraid I'm not used to so much physical labor." Anna and Sofia waved goodbye with promises to see me later, while James leaned back in his chair with a smirk, making me realize that we must share some level of mutual distrust. Of at least a modicum or doubt regarding the other's intentions. I wasn't sure why I let him get under my skin. Only that he did, and I needed to put a stop to it.

I turned and walked away quickly before he had a chance to speak, making my way up the path to my room. Once inside, I headed for the bathroom and stripped off my dirty clothes before stepping into the shower. The water was pleasantly warm, and I let it rain down on my head with my eyes closed before grabbing the bar of soap. I scrubbed vigorously to remove the day's accumulated debris and then rinsed thoroughly before stepping out and grabbing a towel. I wrapped the towel around my body as I walked into the bedroom, searching my closet for another outfit to put on. I suspected we would continue working for another few hours after everyone returned to the dig, and I didn't want to waste one of my better outfits on just getting dirty again. I dressed in a pair of cut-off jeans and a t-shirt, and pulled my hair into a ponytail. Satisfied I had done my best, I plopped down on the sofa for a rest.

# twenty-four

The next morning, I struggled to make myself get out of bed. I had worked at the Tower until almost seven the night before, and my body was aching from all of the uncommon exertion I had put it through. I stretched my arms overhead and yawned. "Ugh. I'm sore in places I didn't know I had." I walked over to the window and pulled aside the curtain, surprised to see that the ground was wet with rain that was still falling. There was a heavy cloud cover that caused everything to look gray, and I turned on a lamp to try and cast off the gloom.

I was dying for a cup of coffee, but I wasn't sure if there would be any on the patio given the weather. I walked over to the kitchenette and searched the cabinets, pulling out a jar of tea bags. "This will have to do." I filled a mug with water, adding one of the tea bags before setting it in the microwave. While I waited for it to heat, I walked into the bathroom and looked in the mirror. The skin on my face held a rosy tint, which I attributed to how much time I had spent in the sun the day before. I turned on the faucet and soaped my hands before running them over my face and neck. My skin was slightly tender, and I touched it gingerly and then toweled off. I heard a ding from the microwave, and I strode back to remove the mug before sitting down on the sofa with my legs tucked under me.

I carefully took a sip of tea. It was hot, and I blew on it before taking another small sip. I heard my cell phone ring, and I set the mug down on the coffee table to reach for it.

"Hello?"

"Jesse, it's Miriam. I hope I'm not disturbing you."

I smiled at the phone. "Not unless you're calling to tell me I have to come out in this weather to dig around in the mud."

"Unfortunately, not. The rain is predicted to continue for another few hours. I'm calling to let you know it's unlikely we'll be able to do anything at the dig today, and to find out if you'd fancy heading down to Hora a little later? There's an archaeological museum there, and I thought it would be fun to visit it. The curator is quite knowledgeable about the history of the area. We could pick her brain about our finds."

"Sounds like fun. When did you want to leave?"

There was a pause on the line. "Perhaps in an hour? I don't imagine there'll be any breakfast on the patio this morning. When the weather's bad, which it rarely is, they usually have bagged pastries available. We could go someplace in the village to eat and then wander around until the museum is open."

"I like that idea. Where shall I meet you?"

I've arranged to borrow a car. I'll be in the parking lot at nine."

I hung up the phone and reached for my mug of tea. It had grown cool while I was talking, and I carried it over to the microwave to warm it again before heading to the closet. Since we weren't going to be working outside today, I decided to dress in something more presentable. I rifled through my meager choices, finally selecting an outfit that I tossed onto the bed before heading for the shower.

I hadn't had an opportunity to spend any time in Hora, or *Andros Town* as it was officially known, since I had been on Andros, and I was looking forward to exploring the area. I knew from talking with Wills that it was a place steeped in history, but it was also the capital of Andros, and the only sizable village on this part of the island. It was built on a small peninsula in the center of the east coast of the island between two long sandy beaches: Nimporio and Paraporti.

We made our way up a narrow road from Stenies to the main road before continuing down a slightly wider road that led to Hora. The road twisted along a steep drop with a to-die-for view of the sea, the village, and the neighboring hills. I hoped that the expression *to-die-for* wasn't prophetic, as we narrowly missed several cars that sped their way past, seemingly intent on claiming as much of the pavement as they could garner. I took a slow breath of relief when we finally reached the end of the road and took a right turn onto the main street that ran alongside Nimporio beach. The right side of the street was lined with cafés and rental units, while the beach lay to the left. I could see a row of thatch-roofed umbrellas along the sand and loungers that were filled with a few beachgoers who were apparently unswayed by the cloudy weather and risk of rain. At the beginning of the stretch of beach, there were several roadside tables shaded by the same type of umbrella where several people were relaxing over drinks or snacks. Miriam pointed out the window to her left.

"We could stop along here if you'd like, although I don't fancy inhaling car exhaust along with my food. There's a better spot up in the old town that's away from traffic."

"That sounds good to me. I've never spent any time here, so I'll go along with whatever you suggest."

Just before the end of the beach, we took a left turn into a parking lot. "We can walk from here. There's another parking lot higher up, but it can get quite full at times. It's probably better we don't chance it."

Luckily, the rain had stopped as we were leaving Stenies, and the sun was just beginning to break through the low cloud cover. I could feel the heat intensifying, and I tossed the sweater I had been wearing onto the back seat of the car and grabbed my hat.

I followed Miriam as we made our way along the backside of several cafés facing the sea before heading up a series of marble steps. Now and then, I paused to catch my breath and to look back at the view behind us. The higher we climbed, the more impressive the view of the multi-shaded turquoise water and white-washed houses that were scattered across the hills surrounding the village. At the top of the steps, we reached a pedestrian street that was, again, lined with cafés, each featuring an outdoor dining area. I was surprised at how many people were sitting at the tables until I realized it was vacation time for most folks, and the rapidly improving weather was also likely to be a factor in drawing people outdoors.

Miriam turned right before stepping into the door of a bakery where several people stood in line, waiting their turn to select from the display cases. The smell of freshly baked treats was wonderful, and I stood on my tiptoes to peer over her shoulder at the available selections. I leaned forward to whisper in her ear. "It smells wonderful in here. What are you going to have?"

Their tiropita is some of the best I've ever had. I'm afraid I rarely order anything else."

"I'll have what you're having then." While we were waiting for our turn, I studied the various offerings on display. There were several shelves along the walls holding bags of cookies or crispy rusks. The side display case held an assortment of sand-wiches, as well as the tiropita Miriam had mentioned, slices of pizza, and hot dogs wrapped in crispy filo. The back case, in front of the cashier, held more sweet and savory snacks and a sign offering different types of hot and cold drinks. Miriam looked over her shoulder at me. "Coffee? Or perhaps a frappe?"

I considered my options. "A frappe, please. With a little milk and sugar."

When it was our turn, Miriam placed our order and was handed two bags and two plastic cups to go. We left the store and turned to our left, making our way up the pedestrian street until we reached a flagstone-covered square with several stone benches. We selected one in a shady spot near the back and took a seat.

I pulled my tiropita out of the bag and took a bite. It was amaz-ing! Hot and crispy, with just the right amount of creamy cheese filling. I took another large bite and then sipped at the icy coffee. The sun was bright, giving a welcoming warmth to the day, while the plane trees surrounding the plaza provided just the right amount of shade. I took another bite of tiropita and let out a small groan. "Thanks for the recommendation. This is SO good!" I looked around the plaza curiously. On the far right from where we sat, I noticed a line of taxis, presumably waiting for customers while their drivers lounged nearby on an assortment of metal folding chairs or stone benches similar to the one where we sat. A kiosk was positioned just in front of the taxi area, offering an assortment of packaged snacks and cold drinks. Directly in front of the plaza was a grocery store. I turned to look over my shoulder at a large building just behind us. "What's that building?"

Miriam glanced behind her. "That's the Embiricos. A retirement building named after the main street we walked down, which is called *Georgiou Embirikou* Street. It was built around 1894 by shipowners who used to populate the town. In fact, this square is named after one of them: Goulandris. It's considered a very desirable spot because it is both peaceful and vibrant. If you come here at dusk, you'll find a good number of residents sitting around on folding chairs, watching children at play, or listening to the hubbub of the town as people pass by on their evening *volta*. That means walk. Sometimes, they have live music playing." She pointed to her left. "That building at the far end of the pedestrian street houses the Andrian Club, which was started in 1925. It's one of the longest-lived and most progressive social clubs in all of Greece."

We finished our breakfast and meandered our way back up the main street into the heart of the town. All along the way, I was struck by the beauty of the landscape that could be viewed between the buildings we passed, or over the edge of the steep roads leading up to the town. The buildings themselves featured a combination of Venetian, Byzantine, or Ottoman architecture, which gave a medieval atmosphere to the town.

At the same time, there was a modern feel to it that was enhanced by the various shops displaying local fare and hand-made items for sale.

We passed several more outdoor cafés as we walked along the street before coming to another square paved in stone with a fountain in the center. There was a large plane tree prominent on one side that provided shade to the many cafés, restaurants, and pastry shops spread around the area. The place felt energetic due to the large number of people sitting around enjoying a coffee or something to eat. Miriam stopped in the middle of the square.

"This area is called *Kairi*. It's named after Theofilos Kairis. That's his image on the bust over there. His philosophy and ideas are also part of the guiding principles of the Andrian Club. As you can see, this square is a popular spot for both locals and tourists looking to enjoy something to drink or eat, or just to catch up with friends. It's also at the center of the cultural area of Hora, where you find the Archaeological Museum, the Maritime Museum, the Museum of Contemporary Art, the Kairios library, and farther back, an open-air theatre where they stage the Andros International Festival, which is a summer-long celebration of the arts." She paused and pointed at an opening between two buildings just ahead of us with enough space for a single car to pass. The opening was surrounded by an arched column of stone, creating an impression of a door. "That's known as the *porta*, which means door. When you pass through that opening, you enter the old part of town. Let's walk over there so I can point out a few more things before we visit the museum."

We made our way just before the entrance to the porta and stopped. Miriam pointed to our right, where there were a good number of stone steps leading down the side with an expanse of sea and sandy beach visible in the distance. "As you are aware, that beach is called *paraporti,* which in English means side door. It's not as popular as *Nimporio* because the water is slightly rougher, and there is only one place to grab a drink or bite to eat. The big draw, however, is that there is ample parking nearby, which, as you saw when we drove through town, is not the case with *Nimporio*.

"On the opposite side, if we climb down the steps next to the Archaeological Museum and the Museum of Contemporary Art, we would come to a small church known as Agia Thalassini. From there, you can see *Nimporio,* the Tourlitis Lighthouse, and the pier of the Yacht Club. We'll take a look at that later, but now let's walk on into the old town to the end of the peninsula."

We passed under the porta and wound our way along the narrow streets of the old town. Along the way, Miriam pointed out the church of Agia Varvara, a movie theatre, and the Maritime Museum. I noticed that some of the buildings we passed appeared to be crumbling into disrepair, while others were impressively well-maintained. Eventually, we reached another square set off to the left of the street with steps leading down to the water to its far right. I looked down over the edge and spotted a stone pier from which several people were climbing into the sea or sunning along its expanse.

Miriam stepped up onto the square and pointed to a bronze statue in its center. "This is Rivas Square, known for that statue of The Unknown Soldier, as well as the ruins of a Venetian castle you can see just beyond the edge of the square. The statue, known to the Greeks as *Afanis Naftis,* is a tribute to the sailors who perished at sea."

We walked to the end of the square and looked out over the ruins. There was a stone bridge just below the overlook that connected the end of the peninsula to the remains of the castle. A few young men were climbing over the bridge, seemingly intent on reaching the other side. I shook my head at their daring.

"There's no way you'd catch me doing that!" I nodded to the men who by then had reached the ruins and were scurrying to the top.

"Nor I. But it's a fairly popular spot for young people intent on peering through the opening you can see on the castle wall, or diving off the other side, although doing either is discouraged by the local authorities. The castle was built in the 13th century, but it was blown up by the Germans in 1943 when they bombed the port of Andros. You see, this area used to be the main port of entry for the island, whereas nowadays that position is held by the port of Gavrio. In Greek, the name of the castle is *kato kastro,* which means lower castle. It was actually built as a residence for a man named Marino Dandolo, who was the leader of the Venetian forces that captured Andros."

I was impressed by the wealth of knowledge Miriam displayed about the village, as well as the island as a whole. "How do you know all these things? Is it part of what you have to learn in order to participate in an archaeological excavation?"

She smiled and shook her head. "No. That's just part of being a history nerd. And spending a good deal of time around Simon, who knows everything you'd want to know about the history of this island and most of Greece. I believe he mentioned you were a history major at Uni. Did you spend much time learning about Greece?"

"Very little, I'm afraid. Although it was enough to pique my interest in wanting to visit here once I found out my cousin, Matt, took a job in Athens. From what I've seen so far, it's a fascinating place."

"That it is. And to show you just how much, let's make our way to the Archaeological Museum now."

We retraced our steps, turning right after we passed under the porta until we came face to face with a tall, modern-looking building with whitewashed walls. It was impressive in size, and for the fact that it was located in such a relatively small village. I turned to Miriam. "I know there's an archaeological museum in Athens, but are there others in Greece besides these two?"

She grinned. "Just a few. Two hundred and ten, to be precise. You can't venture far in Greece without coming across one."

"Kind of like churches," I suggested.

She laughed. "I'm not sure I would draw that conclusion, but yes, the prevalence of museums is similar to the presence of churches, although there are a lot more of the latter. Greece is rich in history, and Greeks love to remind us of that fact."

We stepped into the main entrance, where we were greeted by a young woman who handed us a brochure with a warm smile. "Welcome to the Archaeological Museum of Andros. Have you visited us before?"

Miriam nodded. "I have several times, but this is the first time for my friend."

The woman, whose name badge identified her as Eirini, smiled in my direction. "Please enjoy your visit, and let me know if I can answer any questions." She stepped back to allow us to enter the main room of the museum.

I opened the brochure and read the description of the museum and its contents. I was surprised to learn that it was founded fairly recently in 1981 due to a donation from the Basilis and Goulandris Foundation. I recognized the second name from one of the squares we had visited. I leaned over to Miriam so I could speak in a whisper. "The Goulandris family must be pretty well-to-do."

She raised her eyebrows in the Greek expression of agreement. "They are a shipping family. You're likely to hear that name more than once."

The museum was laid out beautifully, with well-designed rooms containing sculptures and inscriptions from the geometric settlement of Zagora and various sites of Andros. Luckily, the displays were described in both Greek and English, which made it possible for me to understand what I was seeing. I was surprised to read that the displays dated back to a period that spanned from the Archaic era to the Venetian occupation of the island. Among the most striking items was a copy of the Hermes of Andros that was found in 1833 in Paleopolis, a very well-preserved copy of a map of Greece created by Rigas Feraios, and statues of the headless Kouros and the torso of Artemis.

I paused in front of a description of Zagora, which was situated on a peninsula on the south-west coast of Andros. I read that the settlement dated back to the 10$^{th}$-8$^{th}$ centuries B.C., but excavations by Australian archaeologists of the site didn't begin until 1960, with more extensive work taking place from 1965 until 1972. I briefly wondered why archaeologists from the University of Sydney in Australia were involved in such an important dig until I read that they were working under the supervision and protection of the Archaeological Society of Athens.

As I continued to read, I discovered the excavations were reopened in 2012 using more modern methods of geophysical surveying and digital recording mapping. I suspected this was what led to the fact that the later excavations uncovered about 10% of the total settlement, which included 55 definable stone-built rooms representing at least 25 houses organized in neighborhood clusters much like the Greek island villages of today. Miriam walked up to look at what I was reading.

She pointed to one drawing of the site. "The layout of the houses at Zagora suggested they were built in blocks rather than detached buildings. They contained a central rectangular hearth in the floor, with stone benches along the walls that were used for storage. Many houses also had courtyards that separated the front of the houses from the street.

"The roofs were flat, which helped with the capture and storage of water. This was very important since springs or wells were not identified at the excavation sites. The roofs also used heavy, flat stones that helped keep the roofs from being blown away by the strong northerly winds that affect the island year-round."

Her description of the ancient village was exciting, and I was anxious to learn more. "It sounds like a very vibrant life. Is there any evidence why the inhabitants moved away?"

"The settlement appears to have thrived until the 9th or 8th century. After that, it is theorized that earthquake damage caused the underground water supply to be insufficient to support the populace. Earthquakes around that time have been recorded in an area just north of Zagora."

Where would the people have gone?"

"We don't know for certain, but possibly to other existing neighborhood settlements on the west coast, like Ipsili or Paliopolis. It's also likely that some of the inhabitants joined ships heading west to Sicily or southern Italy."

We continued our tour of the museum for a while longer before Miriam suggested we grab a coffee in one of the cafés on the square. When we stepped outside, I was unprepared for the contrast between the cool interior of the museum and the bright midday sun, and I hurriedly pulled out my sunglasses. "Wow. I forgot how bright the sun can get here. I hope we can find a shady spot."

Luckily, there was a vacant table just outside the museum under the shade of a plane tree. A waiter hurried over and took our orders, returning shortly with a frappe for each of us. I looked around the courtyard and marveled again at how many people were out and about. "This is a very popular place," I commented.

Miriam glanced around at the nearby tables. "Yes. It's not only a popular spot for tourists, but quite a few of the locals come here regularly. Speaking of which ..." We looked up to find the familiar faces of Anna and James heading in our direction.

"Hello! What are you two doing here?" Anna asked.

Miriam smiled at them. "The same as you, I presume. Taking a little break while we wait for the ground to dry out. By the feel of this sun, that shouldn't be too much longer. Would you like to join us?" She indicated two empty chairs at our table.

"Don't mind if we do." James pulled out a chair for Anna and then sat down himself. "What's good ta eat 'ere?" He opened one of the menus tucked inside a wooden holder on the table top.

"We're just having coffee, but they have several different pitas to choose from. They're in a display case inside the café if you'd like to take a look."

James put down his menu and stood up. "I'll take a gander."

When he had left, I turned to Anna. "So, you and James?"

She looked down at her hands. "I know it probably seems fast. But we hit it off after the pizza party the other night. He's very sweet, actually."

I scoffed to myself at her description of him as sweet, although I had to admit that if someone as kind as Anna had taken a liking to him, perhaps my skepticism of him was unfair. I turned to regard Anna with a slight smile. "The two of you seem to get along quite well. You must like him a lot."

She nodded vigorously. "Oh, yes. I've never met anyone like him before. At first, I was a little hesitate to open up to him. But he told me about his past, and I realized there was a vulnerability to him that wasn't readily apparent."

I looked at her curiously. "In what way? I'm afraid I don't really know much about him at all."

She seemed to hesitate a moment before responding. "I guess it's okay to talk about. You see, he grew up in an orphanage. He only told me after I questioned why his accent seemed quite strong at times and almost nonexistent at others. He explained that he found out as a young child that he was born to a Scottish father and American mother, and although he never had the opportunity to meet them, he became determined to try and become a reflection of them both. I also believe that's why he comes on rather cocky at times. I guess the abandoned child in him shows itself at times." She looked at me with a slight shrug. "I suppose you could say he's touched my heart. I just hope I haven't given in to my romantic notion of him prematurely."

Miriam patted her on the hand. "If it feels right to you, that's what matters. Just don't let him get away with any fool-ishness."

Anna frowed slightly. "What do you mean?"

Miriam shifted in her chair. "Let's just say he has a bit of a reputation when it comes to summer romances, although I'm sure it's different with you. You seem to have a good head on your shoulders. Just protect yourself."

At that moment, James returned with two coffees. "I ordered some pastries for the waiter to bring out shortly. In the mean-time, Anna, I took the liberty of bringing us an iced cappucci-no." He placed one in front of Anna before sitting down next to her. "Hou's it gaun? What have ye been up to?" He directed the question to me. I took a moment to process what he said because his use of Scottish phrases intermingled with English still tended to throw me off. Although after listening to Anna's description of his past, I was beginning to view him in a different light.

"We just visited the Archaeological Museum. It's very interest-ing. Have you been there?" I asked.

"Aye. It's pure dead brilliant the way it's set about. Did ya see the auld map?"

"Yes. And all the rest. It's very impressive."

The waiter brought a tray filled with various sweet and savory pies and four plates, which he placed around the table. James motioned to them with his chin. "Thought ye mite be hungry." He raised his coffee. "Slainte Mhath!" We all clicked glasses before helping ourselves to the food.

Miriam picked out a thick wedge of crispy filo covering a creamy filling and took a bite. "Um. Galactoburiko. One of my favs." She chewed for a minute before turning to address James. "Has anyone heard from Simon this morning? I believe he and Wills are expected back on the early ferry."

Anna nodded as she chewed a bite of what appeared to be spanakopita. "Sofia said they'll be arriving about midday. She stayed behind to make sure they weren't returning to an empty place. Pretty much everyone else has either gone for a swim or back to bed. It's hard not to take advantage of a few hours off."

I yawned at the mention of bed. "It is at that. I could use a little more sleep myself. Miriam, would you mind if we headed back soon?"

She wiped her hands and shook her head. "Not at all. I have a little work I'd like to do before Simon arrives. Let's clear the bill and take off." She motioned for the waiter to return, but James stopped her.

"It's taken ker of. Me treat."

Miriam looked a little taken aback. Neither of us was used to this version of James, and it was a little disconcerting. "If you're sure, then, thank you." She stood up, and I did the same. "We'll see you back at the Airbnb. I suspect we'll resume work in the early afternoon."

We headed back in the direction from which we had come, finally arriving at the lot where the car was parked. As we drove along the road that bordered Nimporio, I looked out the window at the expanse of sea that featured the Tourlitis lighthouse in the middle, a view of the village and the small chapel of Panagia Thalassini built onto the rocks in the old harbor to the right, and the jutting pier of the Yacht Club to the far left. It was a lovely sight, and I felt so lucky to be able to enjoy it in the company of such a unique group of individuals. Even James, who I was beginning to see in a completely new light.

I was reminded of something my mother said to me one time when we were discussing how surprised we were to find out that a neighbor in Nashville who always appeared happy on the surface actually lived with the pain of having lost a child to cancer at the age of 5. When I asked my mother how it was possible for us not to have seen her sadness, she had replied, "Everyone has their own load of baggage. It's just that some of us are better at hiding it than others. What I've learned in my life is that if you allow yourself to see beneath the surface, you'll find that everyone has scars from some pain they have experienced or are still suffering from."

Her words had escaped me over the years, but after Anna's wake-up revelation about James, I vowed to myself to try and do a better job of looking beyond the obvious.

With that thought in mind, I leaned back against the headrest and allowed sleep to overtake me.

# *twenty-five*

By the time Miriam and I pulled into the parking lot of the Airbnb, I was wide awake again. My nap had been short-lived due to the jostling of the car as we swung around the curvy road leading to the village of Stenies. I noticed that Simon's car was in the parking lot, and I felt my anxiety return as I imagined the conversations that awaited me with both him and Wills. I decided the best thing I could do would be to go to my rental to collect myself before either encounter occurred. I said goodbye to Miriam and headed for my unit. When I stepped inside, my cell phone rang. I looked down at the screen and saw Wills' name. I hesitated before answering, wishing to delay the inevitable as long as possible. I clicked the answer button.

"Hello, Wills."

"Jesse. How are you? Simon and I have just returned from Athens. Are you on the property?"

"Yes. Miriam and I went to Hora. We just returned."

"Good." There was a pause on the line. "I have a lot to talk with you about. I wonder if I could come by in a bit?"

My mind was spinning as I tried to decide how to respond. "Of course. But I really need to talk to Simon first. There's a conversation I've been putting off that I need to get over with."

He chuckled. "It seems there's more than one of those about. Why don't you do what you need to with Simon, and then stop over to my place? I'll be here."

I agreed and hung up the phone, deciding to freshen up before trying to see Simon. I showered and changed clothes, and then headed out the door and up the path that led to his rental. I could hear music as I walked, which I imagined came from the patio. I was tempted to take a detour in that direction, but I forced myself to continue with my original plan. I stepped up to Simon's door and knocked quietly. I was halfway hoping he wouldn't answer, and was just about to turn and walk away when the door opened.

"Jesse! Come in. I've just been on the phone with Stavros. There's good news, I'm pleased to say."

I walked inside his unit and took a seat on one of the chairs near the door. Simon sat down opposite where I was and leaned his elbows on his knees as he faced me. "The town has decided to halt the plans for tearing down the Tower. It seems the government officials in Athens got wind of our recent finds and are keen on seeing what they're worth. We've been given the green light to continue our excavations."

"That's wonderful, Simon. You must be so pleased."

He looked at me curiously and leaned back in his chair. "I am.

But I have a feeling you've come to talk to me about something else. Please. Tell me what's on your mind."

I cleared my throat, attempting in the process to calm my racing heart. "I heard from a couple of people on the team that you sometimes provide financial support to those who want to pursue graduate work. I was wondering if that was something you would consider doing for me?"

He studied me intently. "Yes, it's true we have given financial help to some of our workers. But only those who seem very committed to our endeavor. We require a commitment from them to continue employment with us during the summer months, and often for a period of time after they complete their studies. Is that something you would be comfortable with?"

"I think so. I mean, yes, if I understand what you are saying. I guess I'm hesitating because I'm not sure if you've been pleased with my work so far. Perhaps you haven't had enough time to decide whether or not I'm a good fit for the team. I can understand if you're not ready to decide about that yet. I haven't been here very long."

He regarded me with a smile. "Don't you recall what I told you not long ago about believing in yourself? It seems to me that no one is as much of a critic of your work as you are. For my part, I've been extremely impressed with you. In fact, I would daresay your work has played a key role in swaying the town's decision."

His words both pleased and surprised me. "Really?"

"Really. Now. Let's talk facts. Where do you have in mind to do your graduate work? California? Athens? Or perhaps somewhere else?"

His question took me by surprise. "I guess I've always assumed I'd go back to UC Berkeley because I've been living and working there, and I can qualify to pay in-state tuition. Plus, all my things are there, not that I have that much."

"Of course. But why not allow yourself to think a little broader? I can ask Miriam to present you with a few other options for your consideration." He stood. "Let's continue this conversation after you've had time to talk with her. You'll have more facts on your plate by then, and we can explore your options together."

I stood and nodded. "Thank you. I really appreciate your willingness to help me."

He stepped closer and put one hand on my shoulder. "My dear girl, it is I who should be thanking you."

When I left his unit, I took a deep breath and allowed my mind to sort through what I had heard. He was basically agreeing to help cover the cost of my graduate education and offering me the chance to consider exactly where I wanted that to take place. I realized I had never even allowed myself to question where I would go. I just thought UCB would be the most reasonable choice, both for practical and financial reasons. The idea of attending school somewhere else was both frightening and exciting.

I was about to head to Miriam's when I remembered my promise to Wills. I turned down the path that led to his door, which he opened after my second knock.

"There you are. I've been wondering when you'd arrive. Come in. Can I offer you a cup of tea? Or perhaps a beer or a glass of wine?"

My throat felt parched, so I asked for a beer. He poured one into a glass and handed it to me. The first swallow was so soothing that I had to stop myself from finishing the entire drink at once. I walked over to his sofa and sat down, placing the glass on the coffee table in front of me.

"How did your conversation go with Simon? You looked a little worried when I saw you. Did everything work out?"

"Yes. Better than I expected and more than I hoped for. He's offered to pay for me to go to graduate school, and given me the chance to consider where I want that to be. He suggested Miriam may have some ideas that could help me decide."

He smiled and nodded. "I'm sure she will. I may have a few suggestions of my own, as well."

As he spoke, I remembered his job offer to work for King's College in London. "I'm sorry for not asking sooner, but have you made a decision about working permanently in London?"

"I have. I think it's something I'd like to do. But, truthfully, I've been waiting to talk with you again before I make my final decision. The news you've just shared about Simon's supporting your graduate work helps make that easier."

I frowned. "What do you mean?"

"He's basically given you an open pass on studying wherever you'd like, which means that if I am in charge of admissions at King's, you could easily make that your choice."

I shook my head. "I'm not sure I'm comfortable attending somewhere just because I have an in with the director of admissions. Wouldn't that be somewhat illegal? Or at least unethical?"

His mouth twisted into a grimace. "I hadn't thought of it that way, but I suppose you're right. At least technically. But if I allow the other admissions committee members to weigh in on your application, and their decision agrees with mine, I don't see any conflict of interest."

"Maybe not. But I'd still be inclined not to complicate matters. I thought I'd talk it over with Miriam. And Shelly. See what they think."

He wagged his head from side to side. "Get a woman's perspective and all. I can see the benefit in that." He stood and walked to the window, staring out before turning back to face me. "Let's leave it at that for now. Gather your thoughts and consider your options. We can talk again when you've had more time to sort it out."

I was relieved he wasn't pressuring me for a decision, and I could feel myself relax. "Thank you, Wills. It means a lot that you're willing to be patient with me."

He walked to where I sat and extended his hands to me, pulling me up gently until I was enclosed in his embrace. "You're worth waiting for. Whether it has to do with a professional or personal decision. Right now, I'm more interested in the personal side of it all." He bent his head and allowed his lips to explore mine, slowly at first, and then more intently as the spark between us ignited. After a few minutes, he pulled back slightly and studied my face. "Can we put everything else aside for now?"

I nodded, allowing myself to lean into his kiss again.

Later that afternoon, Wills and I had just emerged from his unit when we came across James and Anna striding arm in arm down the path in the direction of the parking lot. James eyed us up and down. "'Ad a nice afternoon, I see. Anna and I did, as well." He grinned at her, and she punched him in the arm.

Wills gave him a warning look. "We're heading to the dig site. Care to join us?"

"Aye. But ye can ride with us if ya like. We've Simon's car. He went ahead with Stavros and asked me to bring it 'round later."

The four of us proceeded to the parking lot and piled into Simon's car before heading down the road beside the beach and up the hillside to the Tower. When we arrived on site, I was surprised to see that there was quite a bit of activity already taking place. Several of the team were working along the far, right side of the Tower, while the rest were camped out at various spots along the front and left sides. I spotted Miriam on her hands and knees just in front of the main entrance.

"There's Miriam. I'm going to see if I can help her with anything." I hopped out of the car, grabbing my bag before striding purposefully in her direction. When I walked up behind her, she turned and shaded her eyes with one hand.

"Hello, Jesse. Grand you came just now. I'm on the verge of a find that I think will be quite impressive."

I crouched down beside her and peered into the ground where she was carefully uncovering what looked like a piece of metal. The shape was circular, although only half of it remained intact, with a small figurine at the top that appeared to be a horse. I reached out with one finger and caressed the image. "It's lovely. What do you think it was used for?"

"I'm not sure, but I suspect it was a handle off the top of a caul-dron. The metal is likely bronze, which we'll know more certainly once it's cleaned up. These pieces were typically used in tombs and other places of worship."

I felt a strong urge to caress the piece, which I stifled since it hadn't yet been catalogued. "Would you like me to take it for cleaning so I can record the find?"

"That would be great. Sofia has the cleaning solution. Once she's finished, why don't you work your magic on a drawing and photo and then read up on pieces such as this? I'll be 'round soon to fill you in on what I know of the history. Between the two of us, we should be able to fill in the gaps." She stood and wiped her hands on her pants legs. "I'll tell you for certain, though, it's a very significant find. I can't wait to share the news with Simon." Her eyes glowed with excitement.

"The two of you seem very close. But I guess that's to be expected given how long you've worked together. He's a really sweet man."

She smiled as she nodded her agreement. "That he is. And, yes, we've grown close over the years." She hesitated as if she wanted to say more, but just as quickly changed the subject. "You'd best be off, now. Bringing this piece to the attention of the mayor and the other local officials is very important. "It's my hope that this will finally resolve all uncertainty surrounding the future of this site."

I carefully wrapped the piece in cloth before heading off to find Sofia. She was sitting on a rock under the shade of a tree, seem-ingly engrossed in a book, when I walked up. I paused just in front of where she sat, uncertain whether or not I should inter-rupt her. Luckily, she glanced up before I had to decide.

"Hi, Jesse. What have you got there?"

"A metal piece that Miriam uncovered. She said that you have the cleaning solution."

She pushed herself into a standing position and looked down at the piece as I unwrapped it. "Oh! That's nice! I've seen pictures of something similar before, but never close up. May I hold it?"

I hesitated before carefully handing it to her. She turned it from side to side, letting the sun's glow illuminate it before carefully re-wrapping it again. She leaned over and picked up a bag from which she removed a plastic bottle and two rags, handing one to me. "Here. Let me show you how to use this." She squeezed a small amount on one of the rags and began to gently wipe it across the surface of the metal object, stopping to shake the rag free of dirt every few seconds. Once she had managed to clean one side, she handed it to me along with the second rag. "Just wipe it gently, making sure to shake the rag regularly. Otherwise, you can damage the metal if there are any rough pieces in the dirt."

I set to work cleaning the other side of the piece, taking special care with the small horse sculpture that graced the top. When I had finished, I held it up for her inspection.

"*Orea!* It's lovely. Let's set it down over here so you can take a photo." She carried it to a small wooden table off to the side.

I pulled my phone out of my bag and took several shots from various angles before putting it away and taking out my notebook. Sofia wandered off while I set about sketching the object. It seemed funny to try and draw the image by hand when the camera could obviously do a much better job, but there was something about viewing it with the naked eye that tended to bring out unseen elements that the camera couldn't capture. When I finished, I sat back and looked at what I had drawn. Sofia walked up beside me and looked over my shoulder.

"Not bad! I've been looking through some books of that period to see if I could find any similar images. Here's what I found." She flipped open a book to a page that held a photo of a large cauldron with what appeared to be a round handle at the top. I leaned closer to the picture and studied it. There was definitely a similarity between the photo and the piece we had uncovered, except that the small sculpture at the top of the photo seemed to be of a different animal than a horse. I heard footsteps and turned to spot Miriam approaching. I held up the book so she could see what we were looking at. She glanced at the image and nodded.

"Yes. That's from the same period. I've just been looking at a similar photo in this book." She opened the one she was holding.

The three of us glanced from one image to the other and then looked back down at the piece we had found. The resemblance was uncanny.

"It appears that what you've found was the top handle from a cauldron of some sort, as you first suspected. Does it say what it may have been used for?" I asked.

"Sometimes they had a practical purpose, such as to warm or cook food. But the size of this piece suggests it may have been part of a trophy used at theatrical or athletic events. And given the fact that there is a horse molded to the top, my guess would be on the latter."

My mind went to images of horse racing and showing events I had attended in my hometown of Nashville as a child, although I suspected that whatever athletic events had taken place in ancient Greece would be quite different from those I had experienced. I was anxious to read more about that period to try and fathom what such an event may have looked like. I picked up my notebook and tucked it back in my bag. "Would it be okay if I disappear for a while? I'm anxious to read more about that period and see if I can gather any more information about how the bronze piece may have been used."

Miriam nodded her approval. "Of course. Take your time and come find me when you're ready. In the meantime, I'm going to carry this piece back to the Airbnb to see if I can find Simon. He'll be over the moon when he sees it."

As I walked away, I suddenly remembered the conversation I had intended to have with Miriam about graduate school options. I turned back to see if I could still catch her, but she had disappeared. I let out a sigh. *Oh well.* I thought. *I guess I'm just going to have to put that discussion on hold until a better time.* But was it *me* who was procrastinating on dealing with the issue, or was life just getting in the way? I shook my head in exasperation. Whatever the reason, that was one more conversation that was just going to have to wait.

# twenty-six

As it turned out, my opportunity to talk with Miriam took even longer than I anticipated. Once she showed the bronze piece to Simon, it set in motion a flurry of activity that centered around alerting the local officials to the discovery and notifying the Archaeological Institute in Athens. Stavros arrived at the Tower with a carload of local dignitaries whom he marched around the dig site while expounding upon the importance of the work. At least, that's what I was told he was talking about. All I could tell was that he was very excited and seemingly pleased with his involvement in the entire process. Someone compared his physical demeanor as he led the visitors around the site to a *rooster who had just had his way with an entire hen house*. I giggled at the image, although I found it hard to imagine Stavros in that way. Still. He did seem to display a clear amount of pride as he strode around, waving his arms as he loudly addressed the entourage.

Simon and Wills had left that morning to drive to the ferry landing to meet some of the officials from the Athens institute. They were due back in about an hour, and the rest of us had been instructed to tidy up the place and make certain a feast was prepared for their arrival. James and Anna were given the task of picking up food from the local restaurant, or *estiatorio* as it was called in Greece, while Sofia and I were busy making the work site look presentable. How we were supposed to do that in an area that was mostly dirt and rocks wasn't clear, but we did our best under the circumstances.

When we returned to the Airbnb, we could hear music drifting over from the patio. I spotted Miriam in the distance, seemingly instructing the wait staff on how to set up the buffet and arrange the seating. I noticed someone had brought freshly cut flowers that were now gracing the center of each dining table. There was a palpable feeling of excitement in the air, and I found myself picking up my pace as I headed to my unit to freshen up.

When I emerged from my rental, the patio was full of people whose laughter mingled with the sound of the music I had heard earlier.

I walked to the edge of the patio and paused to look around. I recognized several members of the dig team, but there were also many others I hadn't seen before. Miriam caught my eye and gestured in her direction. I walked over to where she stood.

"What a crowd!" I remarked.

She nodded. "They've certainly come out of the woodwork, it seems. I only hope this brings good tidings for the rest of our work here."

James and Anna walked up with a drink in each hand. "We thought you two could use these. It's been quite a day!" Anna said as she handed a glass to me, and James did the same to Miriam. Just then, I heard a murmur from the crowd and looked across the patio to see what the commotion was about. Simon and Wills had apparently just arrived, accompanied by several other people. Miriam nodded in their direction. "That's the mayor of Andros in front, followed by the director of the Archaeological Museum in Athens. I don't know the other two, but I suspect they hold similarly important positions."

As they made their way across the patio, I spotted two other familiar faces. "I don't believe it! That's my friend Shelly and my cousin Matt. I wonder what they're doing here?" I held up one arm and waved in their direction. Shelly spotted me and nudged Matt, who caught my eye and smiled. "I'm going to go talk to them." I set down my drink and walked to where they stood, drawing them both into a hug when I arrived. "What are you two doing here? I mean, I'm thrilled to see you. But a little notice would have been nice."

Shelly nodded as she looked around the patio at the crowd. "Yes. It seems we've arrived at an inopportune time. Perhaps we should leave and come back when things are less busy."

I realized my hesitation in greeting them must have come across as me not wanting to see them. "No! I'm sorry I gave you the wrong impression. You see, things have taken an exciting turn around here, and I'm just a little thrown by it all." I put my hand on her arm. "Please stay. Having you both here makes me feel more relaxed already." I looked at Matt, who was staring at Shelly uncertainly. "Matt? What's going on?"

He looked at me before glancing at Shelly again. "It's just that we came to share some good news with you. But now it seems like it wasn't such a good idea to catch you by surprise."

His words confused me, as did the look on both of their faces. "Come on, you two. You're making me nervous. What's the news you're referring to?"

Shelly looked at Matt, who nodded. "We wanted to tell you we've decided to join forces."

I glanced between the two for further explanation. "You mean, you're getting married?"

They both looked shocked, and then Shelly laughed out loud. "NO! I suppose my comment could lead you to that conclusion, but what I meant is we've decided to become business partners. With my expertise in real estate and Matt's in tourism, we realized we could combine our efforts in a potentially lucrative way. We still have some details to work out, but we wanted to share our news with you right away, and we decided we'd rather do that in person than by a phone call or text."

I felt a sense of something that could be described as both relief and disappointment. It wasn't that I was opposed to the idea of Shelly and Matt getting married. In fact, it would be nice to think about having them both in my life in that way. On the other hand, it seemed a bit too sudden. Or maybe I was just jealous to think their relationship had evolved so quickly, whereas mine and Wills' seemed stuck in neutral.

"I'm happy for you both, and I have a ton of questions. Why don't you grab yourselves a drink, and we can find a table off to the side to chat, although I think I'd better check in with Simon first. He may have some work stuff he wants me to attend to."

Matt waved his hand in a gesture of dismissal. "Don't worry about us. We plan to stay around for a few days, so there'll be plenty of time to talk. Go take care of whatever you need to, and come find us when you can."

Shelly nodded. "In fact, we need to sort out our rental first anyway. There weren't any rooms available here, but we found a spot just up the road. We rented it sight unseen, so I'm anxious to make sure it's acceptable."

"Okay." I reached over to hug each of them in turn. "I really am happy to see you both. I have some things I'd like to run by you, as well. Hopefully, this soirée won't last all night, and we can find some time a little later."

When they left, I looked around again for Simon, who was standing next to the bar talking to the two men Miriam had identified as the mayor of Andros and the director of the Athens Archeological Institute. Simon noticed me looking at him and gestured for me to approach.

"This is one of the young women who was responsible for our recent discoveries. Jesse, I'd like to introduce you to Mayor Stephanopolis and Professor Drakao. Of course, you know Stavros, the mayor of Apoikia. Gentlemen, this is Jesse Holloway, my assistant and the young woman responsible for much of the information I have provided you about our archaeological finds here on the island."

I nodded to the men and glanced at Simon with a look of both surprise and gratitude. "I'm afraid Simon exaggerates my role, but it has certainly been my pleasure to work alongside him and the other members of his team.

Simon smiled at me with a glint in his eye. "I was just about to suggest that we take a walk up to the Tower so they can see our progress. Perhaps you can join us?"

"Certainly. But I was hoping for a moment of your time first."

He looked at me curiously. "I'm sure these three would enjoy a beverage first anyway." He motioned at a passing waiter whom he addressed in Greek before turning back to the three guests. "This young man will show you to a table. Order anything you would like. I'll join you shortly." The three men followed the waiter agreeably, with Stavros leading the way. Simon turned to me. "Shall we take a walk in the garden?" I nodded and followed him as we made our way around the side of the patio. We walked in silence for a few moments before he stopped and turned to face me. "Tell me what you have on your mind. It's clear that whatever it is, it's important."

I looked at the ground as I attempted to collect my thoughts. "I'm sure you're aware of the offer Wills has had to work in admissions at the Archaeology Department at King's College in London. He has suggested that I consider enrolling there for my master's. I've been wondering what you would think about that."

He looked over my shoulder before answering. "It's a very good program and an excellent opportunity for Wills. I realize you may be having mixed feelings about attending there yourself because of the history between you two. I can only advise you to explore your reasons for considering studying there. Is it something you would look forward to, or do you feel compelled because of your personal feelings? Or perhaps you are hesitant because you fear you would be admitted based upon your relationship rather than your merits as a potential graduate student?"

I was surprised by how accurately Simon was able to pinpoint the reasons behind my hesitancy. "You pretty much hit the nail on the head. I would have to say all of the above."

"I see. Then I would suggest you give yourself a little time to think about it further. Perhaps speak to Miriam. She has quite a bit of experience with the program at King's, as well as other institutions around the world. She may have a suggestion regarding the best fit for you." He started to walk again. "Whatever decision you make, just know I will support you. Both financially and personally. Although I must admit a preference for you to remain close at hand rather than choose to study some place far away. It would simplify your return to our team."

The fact that he was so supportive of me regardless of what decision I chose to make was wonderful, and I looked at him gratefully. "Thank you, Simon. That means a lot to me. I was planning on talking with Miriam, but I'm glad you suggested it too. That will be my next step."

He stopped walking and looked at me again. "Good, good. Just be certain that whatever decision you make is based upon facts, but also resonates in your heart. If that is the case, you can't go wrong." He looked at me carefully. "I have a feeling your mind will not be fully on anything else until this matter is settled. Why don't you head off to find Miriam now? I'll pull aside a couple of other members of the team to join us at the Tower. You can come around when you're ready."

"I appreciate that, and I will take your advice seriously. Thank you, Simon."

He smiled warmly. "I'd best get back to the others. There's no telling what fanciful stories Stavros has concocted by now."

I watched him leave before turning back in the direction I had last seen Miriam. When I approached the patio, I saw her sitting at one of the tables talking with Anna and Sofia. I walked up and stood next to where they sat. "Miriam? I was wondering if you have a few minutes to chat with me? Simon just left for the Tower, and he suggested I come find you."

She looked up at me curiously. "Sure. I was just going over a few things that I'd like the team to follow up on back at the dig." She turned to Anna and Sofia. "Why don't the two of you go on ahead, and I'll join you in a little while?" They stood up to leave, and I sat in one of their vacated chairs. Miriam pointed at the mug in front of me. "Would you like a coffee? Or perhaps something more substantial?"

I glanced at the mug. "Coffee would be great."

She gestured to a waiter who came over promptly with a pot from which he filled both our mugs, returning shortly with a small plate of cookies. I had noticed that in Greece, when you ordered an unsweetened coffee, cookies were served with it, whereas nothing was offered if you ordered a sweet drink. That made sense.

Miriam studied me intently. "What's on your mind? I have a feeling it's something important."

I took a sip of my coffee. "I've been wanting to talk with you about a Master's program in Archaeology. Simon has offered to cover my expenses, but I'm having trouble deciding where to apply."

She nibbled a cookie. "Which ones are you considering?"

I picked up a cookie and then laid it back down. "I always thought I'd return to UC Berkeley. Now, I'm not sure. Wills has been encouraging me to go to King's College in London, and Simon said he'd like it if I studied somewhere not too far away. I wonder what you'd recommend."

She smiled slightly. "I can't help but wonder if your uncertainty has anything to do with Wills' job offer at King's? That could potentially present you with both an opportunity and a conflict."

Her words took me by surprise. "You knew about that? Why haven't you said anything?"

"Oh, I rather thought it was something you'd either approach me with or prefer to decide on your own. I didn't want to intrude in any way."

I shook my head. "I've been spinning around in my head about it for days. I honestly don't know what to do. I've been wanting to talk to you and get your thoughts, but things kept popping up that have kept me from approaching you. I believe Simon sensed my confusion, because he actually told me to come find you and talk it out."

She smiled and nodded her head. "Simon has an uncanny knack for doing that. He's very perceptive. When I was trying to decide whether or not to join the dig here, he knew before I did what was holding me back."

I looked at her curiously. "What was it?"

She wagged her head from side to side. "Let's just say that something, or someone, was distracting me from reaching a decision. Perhaps we have that in common."

Her comment reminded me of our earlier discussion about her lost pregnancy, and I couldn't help but wonder if the person she had been involved with had been a member of the archaeological team. I wanted to ask her more about what had transpired, but I decided the time wasn't quite right to bring it up. I decided to stick to the topic at hand. At least for now.

"I'm worried that if Wills helps sway my admission into King's, it will give everyone the impression I couldn't get admitted on my own merits. On the other hand, if I decide to go somewhere else, what will that do to our relationship, not that I'm at all certain what that is. He can keep things pretty close to the chest. Sometimes I feel confident about his feelings for me, and the next moment I'm not sure at all."

"Maybe you're giving too much weight to what HE feels. Have you asked yourself honestly what YOU want to do?"

I sat back in my chair with a forlorn expression. "That's just it. I don't know WHAT I want. I mean, I know for certain I want to pursue a master's in archaeology. I love this field, and I can't think of anything else I would want more. But I guess my personal life is clouding my judgment about it."

She looked off in the distance with a thoughtful expression. "Let me suggest this. Close your eyes and try to put any thought of Wills out of the equation for a moment."

I looked at her with disbelief before following her suggestion.

"Now. Imagine yourself back in school. What do you see?"

"A classroom full of kids."

"Oh. I meant, see YOURSELF back in school. Not in the role of a teacher."

I opened my eyes to look at her. "That's just it. The first thing that popped into my head was teaching kids. Do you think that means anything?"

She looked at me curiously. "Let's try again. Close your eyes and allow yourself to imagine you're in graduate school. What do you see?"

I did as she instructed, but once again, the images of my classroom in California filled my mind. "All I see is my old job. Do you think that means I really just want to be a teacher?" I wasn't sure if the thought of that was pleasing or distressing.

"Would that be so bad?"

I considered her question. "I guess not. But I've always had the idea of going to grad school, and teaching archaeology to young kids just isn't an option."

"No, it's not. But what makes you think teaching young kids is your only choice? There are students at every age who need good instruction."

I considered what she was saying. I truly loved teaching. I loved the idea of introducing topics that spurred someone to want to know more. But it was also true that I wanted to learn more myself, which meant I would need to allow myself to be challenged by knowledgeable professors, as well as fellow students, who could help me expand my horizons. I paused as I allowed myself to really consider what I was thinking. "I guess the truth is that I want both. I want to teach, and I want to be taught."

She nodded with a slight smile. "I could tell that digging in the ruins was not what excited you. You always seemed to be more fascinated by learning as much as you could about the finds, so you could draw an image and write up a report. Have you ever thought about combining art history and archaeology in your future plans?"

Her question reminded me of something one of my high school teachers once said to me. We had been given an assignment to write about the history of the Civil Rights Movement in Nashville. Since it occurred far before my time, I spent a lot of hours in the local library, where there was an entire section devoted to the topic, including quite a few photos from the various events that took place in Nashville at the time. When I turned in my report, the teacher remarked that my sketched-out impressions of some of those photos added a unique twist to my writing. At the time, I just thought she meant they were interesting. Now I wondered if what she had really meant was that I had shown a special talent at including them in my report. If the A+ I received on the paper was any indication, the latter seemed to be the case.

"You know, I've never really thought about that. But what you're saying makes a lot of sense. I've always enjoyed scribbling little drawings of the things I was reading about. And I have to admit that sketching the finds from the dig at the Tower has been a lot of fun. Almost as much fun as learning everything I could about the history."

"Exactly. So, I'll ask you again to close your eyes, and this time try and imagine yourself in your ideal job."

I did as she instructed. It took a few minutes for me to quiet my mind, which was bouncing all over the place with the possibilities. Finally, an image began to form in what I could only call *still life*. "I see myself in a large room. I'm up on a stage with a screen behind me that is projecting something. In front of the stage are several rows of chairs filled with people."

"Good, good. Now, try and see what is on the screen."

I attempted to peer at the image until it began to become clearer. "There are a lot of words, and alongside the words are drawings of things. Things like the pots the shards likely came from at the Tower." I paused as I tried to fill in more of the image. "A lot of the people in the audience are writing. Taking notes, I guess. Some are just staring at the screen, and others are raising their hands." I opened my eyes. "It's a seminar. I'm giving a seminar to someone. Students, or colleagues from the profession." I looked at Miriam gratefully. "I think I know what I want to do."

She clapped her hands together. "Wonderful. Do you want to tell me now, or would you rather wait until you've had more time to think it over?"

"Let's wait. Not because I don't want to tell you, but I want to explore a couple of possibilities first."

She stood up from her chair. "That makes a lot of sense. Now. What do you say we go and join Simon? I, for one, am very anxious to find out more about what he's worked out with the officials."

# twenty-seven

By the next morning, I had made considerable progress sorting out my thoughts on my next step. At least, professionally speaking. I had yet to talk with Wills about what I had in mind, in part because I was reluctant to allow anything he might say on the subject to influence my decision. I guess, on some level, that indicated I wasn't 100 percent confident in my plans.

After talking with Miriam, I had spent a lot of time searching the internet before finally arriving at what seemed to be the right choice. I stopped by Simon's unit later that evening to discuss what I had in mind. To my relief, he seemed as enthusiastic about my decision as I was. That helped bolster my confidence that I was finally on the right path.

I gathered my things before heading out of my rental, turning right to walk in the direction where Wills was staying. I stood outside and took a slow, deep breath before knocking quietly on his door. It opened almost immediately.

"I thought I heard someone rummaging around out here. Come in!" He stepped aside to make room for me to enter before closing the door behind me. I glanced at him appreciatively, taking in the fact that he was barefoot and wore only a pair of jeans and an unbuttoned shirt, which showed off his toned abs and tanned skin. He grinned at me teasingly. "I was just getting dressed when I heard you knock. Have you had breakfast yet? I can make us a pot of tea. Or coffee, if you prefer."

I turned my back on him and walked to the sofa and sat down. "Coffee would be great."

He gave me a curious expression before walking to the kitchen counter to fill the coffee pot. "What have you been about lately? It feels like I haven't seen you in ages."

"A couple of days, at least. Things got a bit hectic after the most recent find at the dig and the distinguished visitors that you and Simon brought here as a result of it. I did manage to find a little time to chat with Simon and Miriam about my next career step. Oh, and Shelly and Matt showed up unexpectedly! They're staying nearby, and we met up for a couple of drinks late last night. I was hoping the four of us could get together sometime later today. Perhaps for dinner."

He carried two cups of coffee to where I sat, placing them on the cocktail table before taking a seat beside me. "I'd like that. But first, I want to know what you've decided about grad school. Do you know where you'd like to apply yet?"

*How's that for getting right to the point!* I took a sip of the coffee and nodded. "I'd like to attend the University of Cambridge. Miriam helped me realize I would like to pursue a combined degree in art history and archaeology. Teaching is something I'm passionate about, as well as learning all I can about the history of Ancient Greece. I enjoy creating sketches of the finds from that era and producing a detailed account of how each piece likely fit into life at the time. Then, I want to teach others about it so they can understand how important it is for us to embrace the past in order to appreciate the present.

"I've been reading how the University of Cambridge offers a master's degree program that combines research seminars, skills training, and supervised individual study. The main focus of the program seems to be to prepare students for academic teaching and research. I guess I've realized recently that those are the things I am passionate about." I noticed Wills had been studying me intently as I spoke, and I was anxious to hear his response to what I said. Luckily, he didn't keep me waiting.

"The Uni at Cambridge is certainly impressive. Their archaeology department is ranked first in the world. It's an excellent choice and one in which a recommendation from Simon should prove quite beneficial." He leaned back against the sofa. "I must say I'm a little disappointed you haven't chosen King's College, but I can understand your reasoning. Plus, the two institutions are less than two hours apart by car. Less by train. That's certainly preferable to the distance between London and California."

I breathed a sigh of relief. "I'm glad you feel the University at Cambridge is a good choice, and I have to admit that the reasonably close proximity between London and Cambridge factored into my decision. We wouldn't be able to see each other every day. Perhaps not even every week. But it doesn't have to mean we would never see each other again."

He reached for my hands, enclosing them in his warm grasp. "That pleases me greatly. I've been more than a little worried about what you would decide and how that would affect us. I believe I've made it quite apparent how I feel about you, and even though we've a lot of things to sort out, I've always hoped we would have enough time to see where all this is leading us." He grinned at me as he squeezed my hands. "And it just so happens I have a flat picked out that can easily accommodate two. That is, if you would agree to our living together. It's near the train station, so you could be in Cambridge in under an hour and a half. Less if you take the express line. You could use the time to study or prepare your assignments, and we could share dinner together most evenings. And breakfast on those days when neither of us has to be anywhere early." He smiled at me hopefully. "What would you say to all of that?"

His suggestion filled me with an odd combination of excitement and anxiety. It was one thing to take a leap of faith and apply to a graduate program in a country I'd never even visited, but it was quite another to consider moving in with a man whom I was still sorting out my feelings about. I gently removed my hands from his as I scooted back against the sofa cushions. "Frankly, I don't know WHAT to say. I'm happy you would even consider our living together. But isn't that a bit too soon? I mean, I don't even know yet if I'll be admitted to the master's program at Cambridge. Why don't we take things one step at a time and delay making any major decisions until I have my ducks in a row?"

He looked at me thoughtfully. "Ducks in a row. If what you mean by that is until you've made sure everything is in order, I agree with you. I've still got some things to sort out, as well." He placed one hand on my thigh and caressed it gently. "What's important to me is for you to know how I feel about you, and that I want you in my life. We can figure out what that will look like when the rest is sorted out."

I was relieved he wasn't pressuring me to decide on the spot. "Thank you, Wills. It's all pretty overwhelming to me, and I just need some time to think things through." I suddenly remembered my conversation with Shelly and Matt. "When I saw Shelly and Matt yesterday, they told me they are going into business together. In Athens. If I study in the UK, I'd be close enough to visit them sometimes. Shelly said there are direct flights between London and Athens every day. That would also mean I could pop over to see what's happening with Simon and the team when there's a school break."

He smiled and nodded. "It sounds like those ducks you were referring to have already started to line up. Which brings me to another point. What would you say to spending the afternoon touring a bit of the island with me? We could invite Matt and Shelly to tag along. There are a few places you haven't seen yet I'd like to show you."

I smiled. "I'd say that's exactly what I need! Let me just give Shelly a call and make sure they're available. How should I tell her to dress?"

He shook his head with a grin. "Only a woman would think to ask that question. Tell them to dress comfortably, but to also bring swimming costumes." He stood up. "Why don't you go collect your things, and I'll come 'round to your place in an hour? I'll stop by the patio first and gather some bottles of water and snacks."

I quickly made a call to Shelly and, after confirming their availability, arranged to meet them in the parking lot in a little over an hour. I tucked away my phone and turned to Wills. "We're all set. I'll see you soon." I reached up and kissed him on the cheek, then turned to leave, until he stopped me with a hand on my arm. He pulled me back against him and kissed me firmly on the mouth. As I responded with a quiet moan, his kiss softened and his tongue caressed my lips. I was just about to suggest we delay the outing to a later time when he released me and took a step back.

"I just wanted to remind you of what's important. All the rest can be sorted out in time. Now, go on with you, woman, before I change my mind!" I giggled and hurried from the rental unit, practically skipping down the path.

He had succeeded in reminding me of just how intense the spark between us was, and how easily it could be set off. Exactly what that meant in terms of my professional plans, I wasn't sure. But I also didn't feel the need to figure it out right at that moment. For now, all I wanted was to have a little fun. And that was what I intended to allow myself to do.

———

The island of Andros was a lot larger than I realized. Most of what I had seen so far was spread across the middle of the island from the western port of Gavrio to the eastern villages surrounding Hora. We started our tour by heading up the road past the village of Apoikia, stopping to fill our water bottles at the lion's mouth fountain outside the Sariza Springs Hotel. From there, Wills drove north along a winding road that eventually led to a former monastery overlooking Hora and the surrounding hills. He pulled the car into a parking spot just above the monastery, and we headed down a set of steps.

"This is the monastery of Saint Irene. It was founded in 1780 by two monks from Apoikia, who were also brothers. The building fell into ruins in the 1800s during the Ottoman regency. It remained that way until a man named Eleftherios Polemis purchased the 13-acre estate, which included the monastery, in 2006. He and his family saw to the restoration of the buildings and the temple over the next ten years or so. These days, it is best known for hosting camps for orphaned children, but it also has an impressive museum."

We made our way through an arched entrance and into a courtyard. There was a stone-faced area just to the left with a pipe spouting fresh spring water. Above it stood two bell towers. Another bell tower was visible to the far right, and the entrance to a temple was directly in front of us. The walls surrounding the entire monastery were made of weathered stone, as were the faces of the rooms within the walls. Wills pointed to the right of the temple.

"There's a museum next to the temple with an interesting collection of writings, a display of traditional musical instruments, geological collections of rocks and minerals, and a botanical collection from the region. Let's take a look at the temple first, and then we'll visit the museum."

We followed him inside the door to the temple, which featured a domed roof made of slate. The inside was filled with arched areas made from the same stones with multiple crosses and icons tucked into their recesses. The floor in front of the altar had an image of a bicephalous eagle made out of what appeared to be marble. There were also several white, marble-faced areas, including a large wall across the back that contained several of the icons. It was an impressive place, and I couldn't help but be moved by its peaceful beauty, enhanced by the lovely scent of what I guessed was incense. Shelly leaned over and whispered in my ear.

"Which of those images do you imagine is of Saint Irene?"

I glanced at the icons she was referring to. "Since only one of them appears to be female, I'd guess that one." I pointed to the one just to the left of what appeared to be an altar.

She nodded her agreement. "Funny isn't it that there's only one image of her. I would think there would be several more."

We stepped back into the courtyard and spent several minutes browsing the museum before walking to the rear, where it was possible to step up onto a stone wall and gaze down at Hora and the turquoise sea far below. As we stood in awe of the beauty, a woman walked out of a doorway just below us.

"*Yeia sas! Boro na sas voithesete?*"

Wills walked to the edge of the wall just above where the woman stood smiling up at us. "*Ohi. Eimaste apla koitazoume ti thea! Einai omorfi.*"

Shelly and I glanced at Matt for a translation. "She asked if she could help us with anything, and he said no, that we were just looking at the beautiful view."

The woman nodded at us appreciatively. "*Nai. Einai. Tha thelete enan kafe?*" Wills turned to us to ask if we would like coffee, and all three of us nodded eagerly. The woman gestured with one hand for us to follow her inside. We hopped down from the wall and followed her into what appeared to be a kitchen with a large, oblong table on one side. I noticed a small window cut into the stone wall at the rear of the dining area. I walked over to peer out of it and was rewarded with a lovely view of the sea and houses scattered down the hillside and across the distant hills.

"*Katheiste.*" She gestured to the table. We each took a seat as she brought over five small cups into which she poured coffee from a briki. "I just made." She nodded at the pot.

"Oh, you speak English!" I said.

She wagged her head from side to side. "*Mono leego.* Only little." She returned to the kitchen area and filled a plate with an assortment of cookies that she placed on the table in front of us before sitting down herself. "*Apo pou eiste?* Where you from?"

Wills explained in Greek that two of us were American and two English. "*Eimaste archealogists kai einai stin taxidiotiki epixeirisi.*"

"*Kala!* You like Greece?" she asked.

I decided to test out a few Greek words. "*Para poli. Einai toso omorfo!*"

She looked at me with surprise. "*Bravo! Poli kalo.* Very good."

I blushed with pleasure at her compliment.

The five of us sipped our coffee and munched on the cookies for another half hour or so, during which time we alternated back and forth between Greek and English. She seemed to be just as eager to test her use of English as I was of Greek. While we enjoyed our drinks and snacks, she explained, with Matt's help in translating, that she was the sister of the man behind the renovation of the monastery. Apparently, he had passed away a few years prior. I could see the sadness in her eyes as she spoke.

"He was GOOD man. Good brother. *Mou leipei para poli. I miss very much.*"

Her words touched me, and I reached across to place my hand on hers, squeezing it gently. Neither of us spoke, but we exchanged a look that needed no translation.

When we finally got up to leave, she disappeared behind a door, returning with a paper sack which she handed to me. "You take. For the road!" She laughed at her use of the English expression.

"*Efharisto poli.*" I took the bag gratefully. Everyone thanked her and made their way out the door and up the hillside to where the car was parked. After we were settled, I turned to Wills with a smile.

"That was nice. Thanks for suggesting it."

He smiled in return. "I thought you'd enjoy seeing the place. I've been there once or twice before, but I was never invited inside for coffee. That was a special treat, and I think the woman we met, Xenoula, really enjoyed trying to speak English with us."

"She was pretty good. Better than me, at least."

Shelly spoke up from the back seat. "Where are we headed next?"

"There's another monastery farther up this road. We could stop there, or venture down a bit to a remote beach. It will require a hike after a point, but I can assure you the effort will be worth it."

Matt leaned forward. "I vote for the beach. And a hike sounds like just the ticket to walk off those cookies I just stuffed down."

Shelly nudged him in the ribs. "I noticed you didn't hold back on helping yourself to quite a few."

He grinned. "I don't know what it is about Greek snacks, but I always find them hard to resist."

Wills glanced at me and then at the two of them in the rear-view mirror. "If everyone is in agreement, we'll head to Achla Beach. It's about a thirty-minute drive to where we can leave the car, and then another thirty minutes or so on foot.

We drove on along the road that wound up the hills above Apoikia, passing the monastery Wills had mentioned along the way, before turning to the right onto a narrow dirt and gravel road. The terrain made for a bumpy ride, but the view outside our windows of the surrounding hills and distant sea was well worth the slight discomfort. Eventually, Wills pulled off into a parking area and stopped the car.

"We'll walk from here. Grab your swimming gear and water bottles, then we'll set off."

We piled out of the car, collecting our things before trooping off down a dirt path. As we walked, we were treated to the sight of magnificent, tall trees planted alongside streams of water flowing out of the slopes of the hills surrounding the village of Vourkoti, eventually creating a river that led down to Achla beach. Several small waterfalls dotted the hills and made little lakes. We stopped next to one of them and stripped off our sweaty clothes, changing behind the nearby bushes into our swimsuits. After enjoying a refreshing dip, we sat in the sun, sipping water before pulling on our shoes and setting off again, unanimously choosing to finish the hike in our swimsuits.

Wills took my hand as we resumed walking. "Are you enjoying this?"

I nodded happily. "It's lovely. And the stop at the waterfall was so refreshing. I can't wait to reach the beach. I'll bet the water is really nice this time of year."

Shelly came skipping up beside us. "Did you notice how many birds there are? And dragonflies! I don't believe I've ever seen so many."

A short while later, we arrived at Achla beach. It was covered with countless white pebbles layered on top of sand, which made a lovely contrast to the emerald waters of the sea. At one end sat a small chapel with a lighthouse on the hill just above it. Wills pointed in that direction.

"That's the church of Agios Nikolaos and the Gria lighthouse. They are popular resting spots for hikers who venture down the path we've just taken. They provide a bit of shade."

I noticed there were several boats moored in the water, including a couple of large yachts. Matt walked up beside me and pointed to one of the larger boats. "You can hop a ride here from Hora on that boat. It makes the trip a couple of times a day, and stays long enough for the passengers to swim and enjoy the beach before heading back. I've tried it a couple of times."

I looked at the boat where I could see several people lounging on the deck or swimming in the sea just off the side. "That would be nice, but I kind of liked walking down here. It gave me a different perspective that I don't think I would have gotten if we'd just arrived by water."

Wills nodded. "They're both unique experiences, although I must admit that the view from the sea is rather magnificent. There are several caves and islets along the way, including one where it's possible to see a bird called *Mavropetritis* at times. Especially in September. It's a rare species of hawk that nests nearby to reproduce before it starts its journey to Madagascar, where it will stay the winter."

We made our way over to the pebbly shore and spread our towels. "Who's up for a swim?" Shelly looked at us with raised eyebrows.

We all hurriedly kicked off our shoes and tucked our socks and other items safely away in our packs. I pulled a tube of sunblock out of my bag and slathered it on my exposed skin before handing it to the others. Wills came up behind me and began rubbing some of the cream on my back and shoulders. "Wouldn't want you to get burned." When he finished, he handed the tube to me and turned so that his back was to me. I hesitated slightly before slathering some of the cream on my hand and rubbing it over his exposed skin. His back was warm to the touch, and it sent a tingle up my arm. His back was firm, and I was enjoying tracing the contours of his muscles when he glanced over his shoulder at me. "Perhaps we should get in the water?" His look told me he was enjoying my caresses as much as I was enjoying giving them. I nodded and handed the sunblock to Shelly, who was regarding me with a smirk.

Wills grabbed my hand and we walked gingerly on the rough beach before stepping into the sea. The water was slightly cool, which surprised me given how hot the day was. I shivered as my body attempted to adjust to the chill.

"The waters flowing down the mountain keep it cool all year round. It's a bit of a shock when you first get in." He pulled me into his arms as we moved deeper into the sea until we were floating in the waves. I wrapped my legs around his hips, noticing that he was as excited to be close to me as I was to him. I leaned against his chest and groaned. He chuckled slightly and pulled me firmly against him. "I think we can do something about that." He moved us farther away from the others until we were standing in water up to our necks. With a swift movement, he tugged aside my swimsuit so he could enter me. The up and down bobbing motion of the waves did an excellent job of hiding our behavior, and we both quickly reached an intense, but silent, orgasmic peak, before relaxing against each other again. He reached down and shifted our swimsuits before giving me a soft kiss on the lips. "I hope that was okay. I'm afraid I got a little carried away being so close to you."

"It was mutual. Although I hope nobody noticed what we were up to." We glanced around, but it didn't appear that anyone was paying any attention to us at all.

"I think we're safe. Now. How about a swim? I need to cool off a bit. In more ways than one."

We separated and began paddling our way along the shoreline. After several minutes, I headed for the beach where our towels were located. Shelly and Matt were already sitting on theirs, and they looked up when I walked toward them.

"Having fun?" Shelly looked at me with a grin, causing me to wonder if she'd seen more than I intended her to.

I pulled out a small hand towel and began to dry my face and hair. "The water's lovely. Did you two go for a swim?"

She and Matt exchanged a look. "We went over near the lighthouse and then swam back."

I wondered if she was hinting that they had done more than just swim, but I decided not to pursue it. Wills walked up and plopped down on the towel next to me, shaking his head, which caused water droplets to fly out in all directions. I punched him in the arm. "You remind me of a dog I once had. Whenever we would get near water, he would dive in and then shake himself furiously once he emerged." I handed him an extra towel from my bag, and he proceeded to rub himself dry.

Shelly reached over for the sack the woman at the monastery had given us, pulling out four squares wrapped in wax paper. She opened one and took a bite, rolling her eyes in delight. "Spanakopita. Delicious!" She held the other three out so that we could each take one, and then pulled out four bottles of water from the bag and passed them around.

Wills leaned over and looked inside the bag. "It appears that there's a thermos of iced coffee also," Wills announced. He lifted out the thermos and four plastic cups.

Matt reached past Shelly and took the thermos from Wills. "Fantastic! I could use a shot of caffeine about now. Anyone else?" He held up the thermos and wiggled it. We all nodded, and he twisted open the thermos, filling the four cups before handing them out.

We sat in silence for a few moments, munching happily on the pies and sipping the iced coffee. When we had finished, Shelly stood and wiped her hands on her towel. "I'm going to take a stroll over to the chapel. There's a porta-potty there I could use about now. Anyone want to join me?" She looked at me pointedly.

I stood and began collecting our discarded papers and cups. "I will. Anyone else have anything to throw away?" The guys added their napkins to the collection and then lay down on the towels as Shelly and I strode away. When we were out of earshot, she leaned close to speak quietly in my ear.

"You and Wills seem to be quite happy together. I take it you've worked out some sort of plan for your studies?"

"Sort of. Or at least we've talked about my options. I still have to go through admissions, but Simon seemed confident I won't have any problem getting in once he's made his recommendation known." I dropped the pile of trash in a nearby receptacle. "It's still a bit overwhelming, to tell the truth. So many potential changes. I'm having trouble wrapping my head around it all."

"I can well understand. That's pretty much how I've been feeling since Matt and I decided to go into business together. I've a lot to do, closing up shop in London and then arranging to transport my personal things to Athens. I've been thinking that perhaps I should sublet my flat for a while. At least until I see if this cockamamie plan will sort itself out." She suddenly looked at me with a gleam in her eye. "Say. What would you think about staying in my place? It's in a lovely area. Not far from the center of London, but also near a metro station. You could easily get back and forth to Uni without much trouble. And it's a stone's throw from where Wills lives, which would be another plus." She looked at me with a grin. "That is, if I've read things correctly between the two of you."

I considered her suggestion seriously. "That might not be such a bad idea. At least, it would give me time to figure out where things are going between Wills and me without putting too much pressure on either of us. I still need to make sure I can be admitted to the program, and then find out how much stipend I'll receive."

She waved her hand. "Don't worry about the cost of the apartment. I'm sure we can work something out. But for now, let's keep this idea between us. At least until your plans are more certain."

We made our way to where the port-a-potties were located. "Shelly stopped and looked at them with a shake of her head. "I don't really plan on using these things. I just mentioned it so we could have a few minutes to ourselves without the guys listening in. Go ahead if you want to. I'll be out here."

I hesitated before stepping inside, looking cautiously down into the seat to make sure I couldn't spot any snakes or undesirable critters of any kind. I quickly shook my head and decided that taking a whiz in the sea was far more preferable to taking a chance on having an undesirable encounter. When I stepped back outside, Shelly was sitting under the shade of a nearby plane tree, staring at the sea. I walked up and sat beside her.

"Quite a view, isn't it?" She asked.

"I never get tired of looking at it." I sighed. This has been an amazing summer. It feels like ages since I first arrived. It's hard to realize it's only been a couple of months. So much has happened."

She nodded. "I agree. I never would have dreamed I'd be planning on moving to Athens. Or that I'd have met someone as special as Matt. He's such a dear fellow. Funny and sweet, and SO interesting. Just think, all this started because we happened to sit next to each other on the airplane."

I laughed. "You mean, because you just happened to move next to me while I was asleep. Yes, that was quite a serendipitous meeting." I shifted so I could face her more fully. "Will you regret moving out of the UK? From what you've said, it's been your home for a long time."

She looked thoughtful for a moment. "Surprisingly, no. I believe I've been hungry for a change for some time. I just didn't know what kind of change I was looking for. In this case, it seems that the stars have aligned in many interesting ways. It's a bit scary, I'll admit. But, more than anything, it's terribly exciting."

"I agree. I can't wait to see how things will unfold. For both of us. Let's make a pact to stay in touch."

"Absolutely. Friends to the end."

I pushed up from the ground and held out a hand to Shelly. Once she was also standing, we embraced briefly before heading back to the beach.

# twenty-eight

I peeked out the window as the plane touched down at the Athens International Airport. It wasn't the first time I had made the trip since ending my summer work on Andros three months earlier. In fact, I had returned regularly to see how things were going with Simon and the team, as well as to check in on Shelly and Matt. Their business merger had been going well, as anyone who knew them could have predicted. Combining Shelly's real estate knowledge with Matt's knack for anticipating his clients' tastes had helped them land several sizable sales, both in the city and in neighboring towns.

It was one sale in particular that was bringing me back to Athens this time. Shelly had caught word of a house that was going on the market along the Athens Riviera, and she was eager for me to see it. From everything she had said, it sounded like a great deal, although she had been a little vague about what she had in mind for it.

I hurried into the terminal in the direction of the taxi stand, hopping into the first available car. I rattled off the directions

Shelly had given me and then pulled out my mobile to phone her. She answered on the second ring.

"There you are! I've just been telling Matt we have to hurry or you'll arrive before us. Are you on your way?"

"Yes. I've just left the airport. The driver said we should be there in about thirty minutes." My Greek had been improving slightly since I had been spending more time in Greece, and I was now able to have short and simple conversations. That is, as long as the speaker was willing to talk slowly, which wasn't always the case with native speakers. "When will you and Matt be at the house?"

I could hear muttering before she replied. "Matt says in about 20, so we should arrive before you. We'll see you soon." She hung up before I could ask her anything further.

The drive from the airport to the Riviera reminded me of the first time I had visited the seaside area with Matt. It seemed so long ago, although it had really been only a handful of months. It was during my first week in Greece, and I recalled wistfully how eager I had been to absorb every bit of the culture of the area that I could. That tendency of mine—to throw myself wholeheartedly into whatever I was doing—had both served me well and put me in the middle of untoward predicaments from time to time. Most recently, it had helped me navigate my way through my graduate studies at Uni, which, so far, had been going surprisingly well.

The taxi pulled up in front of a building on the main road just across from the seashore. The driver looked at me in the rearview mirror. *"Fitasame. Eikosi euro."* I pulled out my purse and dug out a twenty euro note, which I handed to him, adding another five as an afterthought. It was still uncomfortable for me not to tip when I was in Greece, and I knew from experience that very few people minded being paid a little extra. The driver thanked me before driving off.

I turned to look up at the house in front of me. It was two stories tall, with a porch that spanned the entire lower front. A bright blue fence created a separation between the sidewalk and a patch of lawn. I opened the gate that marked the center of the fence and followed a line of large, flat stones leading to the front door. I was just about to knock when the door opened.

"You're here! Come in!" Shelly grabbed me in a hug before ushering me inside. "Did you have a good flight? I hope the turbulence wasn't too bad. We've had a lot of wind lately."

"It was fairly calm all the way here." I turned at the sound of footsteps.

"Hey, Cuz! Glad you've arrived." Matt pulled me into a hug and then stood back expectantly. "Well? What do you think of the place?"

I looked around curiously, taking note of the well-groomed flower beds lining the front walkway and the tidy paintwork on both the outside and inside walls. "From what I can see, it's lovely. Why don't you show me around?"

I followed them as they led the way through each room of the first floor before climbing the steps to the second floor. While the downstairs included four good-sized rooms, a bathroom, and a kitchen, the upstairs was less impressive, with three modestly sized rooms, no closet space, and only a half bath. A small porch at the back of the upper floor overlooked a modest patch of lawn. I stepped out onto the porch and nodded.

"This is nice. I could see someone enjoying a cup of coffee or a glass of wine here and just relaxing."

Shelly stepped out onto the porch behind me with a pitcher and three glasses. "I'm afraid we'll have to make do with some cold water this time around." She set the glasses down on a small metal table in the middle of the porch and gestured to one of the metal chairs. "Have a seat, Jesse." She filled the glasses with water and passed them around. Matt sat down to my right, and Shel took the chair beside him.

I took a sip before turning to regard the two of them.

"I can see a lot of potential in this place, but I'm still waiting for you to tell me why you were so anxious for me to see it?"

They glanced at each other before Matt gave a subtle nod at Shelly. She smiled slightly before turning to me. "We have in mind to make the main floor a business, combining our real estate venture with a small touring company. Matt has missed the tourism side of things, so we thought adding a little of that trade would round things off nicely. The real estate business is booming in Athens of late, particularly in this area. If we focus on sales that emphasize the seaside and nearby hills, we should do quite well."

I took another long drink from my glass before setting it aside. "I'm glad things have been going so well for you, although I'm not surprised. You're both so talented." I paused for a moment as her description of the house registered with me. "You haven't said how you'll use the second floor. Do you plan to add more offices up here? Or perhaps make it more livable? It's quite a long commute for you to drive here every day from your apartment in Athens, Matt. Perhaps you'll use it as a place to live during the week, and return to your existing place on the weekends?"

He cleared his throat. "I'm going to let go of my flat in Athens. You're right that it's too long a drive to do very often. Shel and I plan to have the upstairs here renovated so that it's fully livable. We'll have a kitchen added, along with a full bathroom. That will still leave space for a nice-sized bedroom and living area. The downstairs will become our workspace with separate offices for each of us, and a gathering area where we can entertain prospective clients. We plan to put in a small bar area to one side of the kitchen and an island to prepare snacks for prospective clients. We'll also add an entertainment center in the gathering area where we can show films of properties we have for sale, as well as special tours that we will be promoting."

I could begin to see the place coming together as he was describing it, and I found myself growing increasingly excited for them. "That all sounds wonderful. I guess it also means that the two of you have decided to try and make a go of it. Not just the business side, but your personal relationship, too. Is that what I'm hearing?"

Matt took Shelly's hand in his and smiled at her warmly. "Yes, to all of the above. We want to make this permanent. In fact, there's something Shel's been wanting to show you." He took her hand and turned it so that the top was exposed. I gasped as I spotted a shiny diamond ring.

"How did I not see that before? I'm so happy for you!" I stood up and wrapped my arms around Shelly's neck before leaning over to give a peck to Matt's cheek. "Way to hide the lead story!" I wagged my finger at them teasingly.

"Sorry to bring you here without revealing our news, but we felt it would be more fun to do so in person," Shelly explained.

"I understand. So, when will all of this take place? The move, the wedding, everything!"

Matt spoke up. "We've hired a contractor who has lined up the work on the house. The renovations will begin in a few days and are scheduled to be completed by the end of the month. The lease on my current apartment is up around that same time, so we should be able to make the move in early November or thereabouts. As for the rest, we were thinking a holiday wedding would be fun. Perhaps just before or after Christmas. That is, if our families can fit it into their schedules."

I considered what he was suggesting. My semester would be wrapping up in mid-December, which would certainly allow me to plan a trip back to Greece.

"That works for me. Have you run your plans by any other family members?" My chest clenched slightly as I realized what that would mean for Matt.

He shook his head. "I haven't mentioned it to either of my parents yet. I guess you could say I'm procrastinating. Although, in truth, I really wanted to talk to you first. The time we've had to get reacquainted these past few months has made me realize you're the closest thing to a sister I have. Shel's family is all on board with both the wedding and the timing of the ceremony. And now that we know you're available, it seems things are on track."

"Except ..." I looked at him pointedly.

"Except for talking to my mom and dad." He sighed. "I'm planning on doing that later today. Or at least by tomorrow."

"Are you worried they won't come to the wedding because they're not together anymore?" I asked.

"Maybe. But mostly I'm wondering if they can manage to be civil to each other long enough for the ceremony to happen, or if their rancor will cause things to get uncomfortable." He reached to take Shelly's hand. "Shel says I should be optimistic, which I'm really trying to do."

I felt a twinge of envy as I saw the warm look they exchanged. Wills and I had been trying our best the past few months to navigate the demands of his job, my studies, and our separate living arrangements, but it had been trying at times, to say the least. I had hoped that things would smooth out as time passed, but I was beginning to wonder if the constant stress of our circumstances would result in our undoing. Just recently, Wills had suggested taking a little time apart to give ourselves a break. On the one hand, his suggestion made sense, but on the other, it felt like a prelude to the end.

"Well, however things work out with your parents, THIS family member will be ready to dance in delight at your wedding!" I smiled at the two of them.

Shelly pulled me into a hug. "That's grand, Jesse! Now, why don't we go somewhere to celebrate? There's a cute little taverna nearby where we can look at the sea and toast one another. That will give you a chance to fill us in on your news, too. I suppose Wills will be joining you for the wedding? Or perhaps his work will prevent him from attending. As I recall, you mentioned that something was up between the two of you. Why don't you tell us your news?"

I had mentioned on the phone to Shelly that Wills and I were considering a change, but I didn't elaborate. By her reaction, I was guessing her thoughts went in the opposite direction from what I meant. "Oh, let's keep the focus on the two of you for now. There'll be plenty of time to talk about the rest of it before I head back to London."

Shelly gave me a questioning look but refrained from asking anything further, which I greatly appreciated. It was hard enough to try and figure out for myself what was going on with Wills, but to try and describe it to anyone else, even someone as close to me as Shelly had become, was just too much to wrap my head around.

Shelly took my hand and squeezed it. "I'll just pop into the loo before we leave. Matt, why don't you show Jesse what you have in mind for the backyard?"

He nodded and took my elbow, steering me in the direction of the back door. We stepped out through an area that was sometimes called a mud room in the States, where one could shed shoes and jackets to avoid mussing up the indoor area. Three stone steps led onto the lawn that I had spotted from the upstairs porch.

Matt stopped and waved his arm from one side to the other. "I realize it's not very large. But try and imagine how it could look with a row of shrubs along the fence line that would block the view of the other houses, and a garden area on either side of the back of the house where we could grow herbs, flowers, and even a few tomatoes or something. It would liven up this entire area."

I attempted to envision what he was describing, nodding as the image took form in my mind. "I think that would be lovely.

You could even put a couple of chairs and a small table out here so you could relax, but still stay close to the kitchen. You know, when you're cooking, or expecting guests to arrive."

He smiled as he surveyed the area with a nod of agreement. "Great idea." He turned so that he could look at me more directly. Now. Why don't you tell me what's really going on with you? The few times we've spoken by phone over the past month, something seemed off. I wanted to ask you about it, but I decided to wait for you to offer it up on your own. Is everything alright?"

I hesitated to answer his question because I really didn't know what to say. *Was everything all right? Or were things about to take an unfortunate turn for the worse?* "I wish I could say. School has been going great, but things between Wills and me are a little confusing right now. I honestly don't know what's going on."

He frowned at my explanation. "Have you asked him? You know, I found myself in a similar predicament with Shel a while back. I started imagining she was losing interest in me, and I felt myself pulling back. Luckily, she's very astute about those things. She pulled it out of me before I could do anything stupid. Perhaps Wills needs a similar nudge?"

I stared out at the yard for a minute before turning back to face him. "You could be right. I just haven't known how to approach him with my concerns." I patted him on the arm. "I've really missed talking to you. Phone calls just aren't a good substitute for being face-to-face. I'm so glad you've kept me in your life."

"Are you kidding? Reconnecting with you has been a gift. There's no way I'd lose that. At least not on purpose. I was a little afraid we'd drift apart when you left for London, but luckily, our mutual love for Shel has helped keep us close."

"Speaking of that, I'm so happy for the two of you. I guess it's proof that taking a chance by sharing your insecurities can work out for the best. Maybe I should take a page from your book."

Just then, Shelly appeared at the top of the steps. "What book? Are we going to the taverna or not?"

Matt smiled at her as he abruptly stood up. "Absolutely! Just let me find the keys to the lock up, and we'll be off."

## twenty-nine

The next several weeks flew by in a whirlwind of exams, wedding plans, and change. Wills and I had decided to table any further discussion of our relationship—pros and cons—until things had settled down a bit. For my part, I was just glad for the opportunity to put it out of my mind so that I could focus on wrapping up the semester. My grades had been good so far, and I was hoping to end things on a high note. Specifically, I wanted to post scores that put me at the top of my class so I could feel justified in continuing to ask Simon for financial support.

Shelly and Matt had made significant progress on their renovations and wedding plans. The former was proceeding smoothly, and the latter was as good as they could have hoped for. Matt finally reached out to his parents, and they indicated their intent to call a truce and attend the ceremony. My parents had also promised to come to Athens for the occasion. They thought it a little odd that the wedding would take place in a country where neither the bride nor groom had family, but I explained that since both Matt and Shelly would need to continue working up to the day of the event, it made more sense for the ceremony to take place near to where they lived.

Shelly had managed to find and reserve a small chapel in Plaka, which would allow the visiting family members to stay in hotels close by. I was excited to return to the area from which I first became acquainted with Athens. I reserved a room in the Hotel Central for myself and one for my parents and Matt's mother. Matt's father had chosen to stay at a small Airbnb nearby, which everyone thought was a good idea. Shelly was planning to spend the night before the wedding with her mother, whereas Matt would drive in that morning after overseeing the final touches on their newly renovated living space.

I wasn't sure what Wills was going to do. He had been uncertain whether or not he could get away from London to attend the wedding. Something about a conference call that might force him to stay in the city past the time when the ceremony would take place. I had to admit I was disappointed. I had actually been looking forward to having him close by to share such an important event with, and I was a little miffed that he would choose to make work a higher priority.

That was one of the things that had been getting between us for the past several weeks: his tendency to become totally wrapped up in work to the extent that he had little time to attend to anything else, including our relationship. When I talked to Miriam about it during one of my visits to Andros to check on the progress of the excavations on the Tower, she said something to the effect that Wills was a member of the "old school" that tended to place work first in the order of things. I can't say that her explanation reassured me. If anything, it worried me even more.

The day of the wedding arrived with a promise of clear, sunny weather and a warm breeze. The ceremony was to take place at a church called the Holy Church of the Holy Unmercenaries of Kolokynthis – Metochion of the Holy Sepulchre, or in Greek, Ιερός Ναός Αγίων Αναργύρων Κολοκύνφη – Μετόχιον Παναγίου Τάφου.

The name was quite a mouthful, but the place itself was a beautiful little church with icons of Saints Constantine and Helen, and benches in the courtyard that provided a shady spot to rest and relax.

There was a small plaque just outside the doors of the church that described how it was first opened in the 17$^{th}$ century as a convent when owned by the prominent Kolokinthi family. Later, in the 18$^{th}$ century, it became an embassy church, or *Metochion*.

"It is the place to be in Athens on the night of the Holy Resurrection."

I turned to look at the man who stood just behind me.

He smiled apologetically. "Forgive me. I am Christos. A friend of Matt. And you are?"

"Jesse. Jesse Holloway. I'm Matt's cousin."

His eyebrows raised in surprise. "I have heard of your visit. Matt is very happy you are here."

I was pleased by his words. "It has been good to see him again, although now I'm living in London while I work on a graduate degree."

"Are you also studying tourism?"

"No, archaeology and art history." I looked at him curiously. He was an attractive man around Matt's age or a little older with black hair and piercing black eyes that were softened by the friendliness that he directed at me. "Do you work with Matt?"

He lifted his head to indicate a negative response. "We are competitors. At least, we used to be, although I am more focused on international tourism, whereas Matt works with the local sector. Now that Matt and his soon-to-be wife will start a new venture, our focus will be even farther apart."

We turned to look again at the small church. "You said this is a popular place on the night of the Holy Resurrection. I assume you mean Easter?"

"Yes. Many visitors come here at that time. Obviously, there is very little room inside, so the courtyard and nearby streets are filled with people. It is believed that this is the place where Jesus died, was buried, and rose from the dead. In fact, there is a place inside where the Crucifixion is believed to have occurred. The Rock of Calvary is encased in glass at an altar. It is the most visited area of the church."

Hearing his description made me wonder if this was an appropriate place for a wedding, given its association with death, and so forth. Although I suppose the idea of resurrection certainly fits anyone's hopes for a new life with someone they love.

"It's a wonder they are allowing a wedding here. Especially between non-Greeks. Is that fairly common?"

"It is not something that usually happens, but my brother is the priest here. The Greek Orthodox community would like for more people to make use of the church at times other than Easter and not to view it as just a place for tourists to visit. Of course, since neither the bride nor the groom is Greek Orthodox, the wedding will have to be what is called a civil ceremony. That is okay, because my brother has arranged for a friend of his to officiate. It will take place outside of the church, as well, which will allow others passing by to witness the event. It is hoped that allowing a wedding to occur here will bring positive attention to it as a place for celebrations of all types, and at all times of the year."

I could tell that what he was describing was highly unusual. Un-Orthodox, you could say. Especially for a place as religiously oriented as Greece. His mention of a wedding reminded me why we were here, and I glanced around to see if I could spot Matt. "Have you seen my cousin? He was supposed to be here by now."

Christos looked over my shoulder. "I believe he is here now. Just over there." He pointed to the right of the church, where I could see Matt emerging from a small door on the side with a man clad in a black robe. I raised my hand to give him a wave, and he returned it as he pointed in our direction.

"He is with my brother. Let's go speak to them." Christos began to walk in their direction, stopping just in front of where they stood. He embraced the black clad man before stepping back and gesturing at me. "My brother, Yiorgos. This is Jesse Holloway, Matt's cousin."

I bowed in what I hoped was the proper gesture when meeting a Greek Orthodox priest. "Father Yiorgos. It's a pleasure to meet you."

He smiled at me warmly. "*Kai ego*. I have just been going over the plans for the ceremony with your cousin. The person who will perform the ceremony will be here shortly. He has been held up in traffic, which is not uncommon in Athens." He chuckled as his eyes darted back and forth between Christos and Matt.

Matt stepped forward to embrace me in a hug. "I'm so glad you're here, Jesse. Have you seen Shel this morning? I'm told it's bad luck for me to see her before the wedding, but I really want to make sure she's here, and that everything is alright. I guess I'm a little nervous." He grinned. "Well, actually, I'm a LOT nervous, but only because I'm so happy to be marrying the woman of my dreams. I never thought this day would come." He looked at the two men with a slight shake of his head.

I patted his shoulder. "Certainly. I'll go find her, but try not to worry. If my intuition is correct, she's just as happy to be marrying you. The two of you are so right for each other. It makes me a little jealous."

Matt glanced around at my comment. "So, Wills didn't make it?"

I looked down at the ground. "No. He got tied up at work." I turned and walked away abruptly. The last thing I wanted was to inject any bad vibes from my situation onto what should be a wonderful occasion for Matt and Shelly.

I walked to the side door of the church and stepped inside. The room was comfortably cool and lit by the soft glow of candles. I noticed a little movement at the back and headed in that direction.

"There you are! My maid of honor." Shelly smiled and pulled me into an embrace, keeping her arm around me as she turned to the other two women standing beside her. "Jesse, this is my mother, Olivia, and my aunt Ava."

I looked at her with surprise. "I'm your maid-of-honor? You didn't mention that."

"Sorry. With all the preparations, I guess it slipped my mind. I hope it's okay. I mean, I hope you'll agree to stand up for me?"

"Of course! It's just that I wasn't expecting it. But it's a NICE surprise." I looked at the two women standing beside her. "It's so nice to meet the two of you. Shelly and I haven't known each other very long, but we've become fast friends."

Her mother reached out and took my right hand in both of hers. "Shelly has described you in a similar way. I'm so happy to meet you. Your cousin, Matt, seems like such a nice man, and I'm thrilled that he and Shelly met, which, I understand, is all thanks to you."

I squeezed her hand and turned to Shelly. "Speaking of Matt, he's outside, and he wanted me to come find you and make sure you're alright. I believe he's a little worried you may have developed cold feet all of a sudden."

She glanced down at her feet, which were clad in high heels. "I have to admit they are a bit chilly in this weather, but if he's referring to that American expression that implies I may have changed my mind about marrying him, not a chance! I'm the luckiest girl on the planet to have found a man like him." She suddenly turned to me with a slight frown, "I'm sorry. I suppose Wills hasn't arrived?"

I raised my shoulders in a shrug. "Nope. He texted that he got caught up in something at work. But let's not talk about him. This is your day." I glanced at my watch. "I need to make sure my parents are here. We had dinner together last night, and they said they'd find their way to the ceremony this morning." I walked back out the door I had entered and looked around the courtyard. I spotted my parents standing next to Matt, who was talking with the priest and another formally attired man who looked vaguely familiar. As I walked closer to them, I realized who it was. "Why, hello, Mr. Stephanopolis. How nice to see you again." It was the mayor of Athens whom I had met on Andros when he and some other dignitaries had arrived with Stavros to give their approval for our team to continue work on the Tower.

He smiled at me. "Ms. Holloway. When *Pappas* Yiorgos told me who the couple was that would be getting married today, I gladly agreed to help. Simon and your entire crew are to be thanked for saving us from destroying such an important historical site."

"Thank you so much for being here. Have you met my parents yet?" The three nodded, and Matt explained he had made the introductions earlier. At that moment, Father Yiorgos spoke up.

"Jesse, please go inside and tell the bride we are about to begin. The church bells will signal when she should come out."

I hurried back inside and instructed Shelly's mother and aunt to join the others before taking Shelly by the arm. "Ready?"

She nodded with a smile. "Now, and always." We stood silently for a moment until we heard the insistent sound of the church bells. They had been ringing steadily since I arrived, and had been increasing in intensity as the ceremony grew closer. I led Shelly to the door, and we stepped outside.

The priest and mayor stood in the middle of the patio beside Matt and Christos, who I assumed must be his best man. I recognized Matt's mother and father in the small crowd of people who stood just behind them, along with Miriam and Simon, who must have arrived while I was inside. There were a few other members of the group who I guessed included co-workers of Matt or Shelly, and I even spotted James and Sofia standing just behind Miriam and Simon.

I caught Miriam's eye and waved hello, noticing as I did so that she had her arm looped through Simon's. The image puzzled me for a moment because I had never noticed any signs of physical affection shared between the two of them before, but I guessed that weddings brought out nostalgia in most of us in predictable ways. I was certainly finding myself struggling to handle the feelings of loneliness and sadness in Wills' absence, and I glanced for a moment at Christos, who winked when he caught me looking at him.

As the wedding party gathered in front of Father Yiorgos and Mr. Stephanapolis, I noticed several curious tourists had stopped to watch the proceedings, likely drawn by the sound of the church bells and the gathering of nicely clad attendees. As I glanced at them, one in particular caught my eye. I struggled for a moment to recall where I had seen the face before, when suddenly it dawned on me. It was Kiria Makris! The grandmother of the waiter at the hotel who had read my fortune from my coffee grounds. She caught me looking at her and waved slightly. I waved back, which caused a grin to break out on her face.

As she continued looking at me, I suddenly had another real-ization. That was the same face I had struggled to see in the dream I was having just before landing in Athens for the first time! My breath caught with the realization. She must have seen the look of astonishment on my face because she nodded at me with a soft smile and patted her heart before turning to disappear into the crowd.

I stood on my tiptoes to try and catch another glimpse of her, but she was nowhere to be seen. At that moment, Christos walked up beside me and patted me on the shoulder. "Forgive me for disturbing you, but you look like you have seen a ghost. Or perhaps a ghostly spirit."

I gave him a wide-eyed look. "Perhaps I did." I shivered as I hugged my chest." I guess we'd better get into position. The ceremony should begin shortly." He looked at me question-ingly before nodding quietly.

The sun was high in the sky by the time the ceremony began, and its warmth helped to cast aside the chilly December air and the chills that still shivered up and down my spine as I struggled to allow the images I had seen to register. There was no explanation for the old woman appearing at the wedding, or for the fact that her image had appeared in my dream before I had even met her. It was spooky. But as I thought about the sweet look she gave me, I felt a sense of calm settling into my chest.

I glanced over to where Matt and Shelly stood in front of the church, preparing to enter into matrimony. They both looked so happy, and I noticed Matt was wiping a stray tear from his eye as he looked lovingly at Shelly. The official part of the cere-mony moved quickly after that. The mayor spoke first in Greek and then translated his words into English since most of the attendees were non-Greeks. There was the usual reciting of vows followed by the exchange of rings before the mayor pronounced them husband and wife.

The crowd erupted in a burst of applause and a few whoops of delight as Matt and Shelly leaned in for a kiss. At that moment, a small group of women emerged from the church carrying trays laden with an assortment of snacks and drinks. They offered them to the bride and groom first before circling the crowd. I took one of the small glasses of clear liquid, which I assumed was tsipouro. My first taste confirmed my guess, and I gladly had a second sip.

Christos walked over to where I stood and clicked his glass against mine. "*Stin uyeia mas!*"

"Yes. *Stin uyeia mas.* What does one normally say to wish the bride and groom a happy married life? I heard the expression once, but I can't recall it now."

"*Na zisete.* Which means 'to your life.' Or sometimes we say, '*I ora einai kali.*' The time is good. That is perhaps the most common."

I took another sip of my drink and considered what he said. "Greek has the most interesting traditions."

He looked at me curiously. "You like Greece?"

"Yes. Very much. I hope to spend more time here in the near future."

And now you are in London?"

I nodded. "I'm just finishing up my first semester. In the summer, I will return to Greece to join a team of archaeologists headed up by Simon Harris. The last time I was with them, we were working on the island of Andros. I'm not certain if that's where they'll be next summer, but I imagine so."

Christos stopped a woman with a passing tray and selected two more glasses before handing one to me and collecting my now-empty one. "Would you like something to eat? I believe I saw some assorted pitas."

"That would be nice. Thank you." I watched as he walked off. He seemed to be a nice man. And, certainly, a very attractive one. As that thought went through my mind, I felt a sense of guilt toward Wills. It was true our relationship had been struggling, and I was more than a little miffed that he hadn't made attending the wedding a priority. But it still didn't feel right to entertain any thoughts of attraction toward another man.

I looked around the patio to see where Shelly and Matt were. I spotted them standing off to one side with their arms around each other as they nodded gravely at the man and woman standing in front of them, who I recognized as Matt's estranged mother and father. I hoped neither of them was causing a scene, and I walked quickly in that direction. The woman turned as I approached.

"Why, hello, Jesse. Matt told me you'd be here. How are you these days? It's nice that your mother and father came. It has been ages since I've seen them." Her tone was friendly, but her eyes looked guarded.

"Hi, Aunt Evelyn. I'm fine. I'm so happy my parents were able to attend the wedding. It's been a while since we've seen one another, since we're on different continents now. They're still living in Nashville, although they often talk longingly about returning to the East Coast—Florida, or somewhere nearby. How have you been?"

She bristled slightly before answering. "Fine. Although I suspect Matt has filled you in on the details. I'm only here today because John promised to be on his best behavior." She glanced over her shoulder to where Matt's father, my Uncle John, stood chatting with Shelly.

"I'm sure that's been tough. I was surprised to hear the two of you had separated."

"Yes, well, things are often different from what they seem." She pulled her purse up higher on her shoulder. "If you'll excuse me, I'm going to find the powder room. Although I imagine they have some other name for it in this godforsaken country, if they even HAVE such a place."

I cringed internally at her obvious displeasure with the Greek culture, which, by the way, I suspected she knew little to nothing about. "I noticed a sign for a bathroom just behind the church. You'll see the letters WC and an arrow. Oh, and as you may be aware, you're not supposed to drop paper in the toilet. There are little metal cans next to the toilet for that."

She rolled her eyes as she strode away. I decided to take a chance and approach my Uncle John to see if his attitude was any more positive. He turned to me with a wave and a big grin as I walked up.

"There's my girl! How are you, Jesse?" He held out one arm and pulled me into a hug.

*Wow! What an opposite reaction*, I thought. I allowed myself to be crushed against his side. "Hi, Uncle John. It's nice to see you again."

"Matt here has been filling me in a little on your recent activities. Archaeology. Grad School. And a blooming romance, I understand. Your momma and daddy must be beside themselves with pride."

I blushed at his mention of a romance. "Let's just say they'd be a lot happier if I were in the States. They don't much care for the fact that I didn't return after what was supposed to be a summer vacation visiting Matt. This is the first time we've seen one another since I moved to London. I've been trying to convince them to visit more often, but they don't seem particularly interested in that idea."

He waved one hand. "Oh well, to be honest, they've always been a bit of sticks-in-the-mud. Maybe they'll come around eventually." He turned to regard Matt and Shelly, who were engrossed in conversation with another couple who seemed to have come out of the tourist part of the crowd. "He sure looks happy, doesn't he? And why wouldn't he be? Shelly seems like quite a catch." His eyes narrowed as he looked at her in a way that made me slightly uncomfortable.

"Yes, she's great. And head over heels for Matt. Can I bring you another drink? I think I saw someone with some beer if you'd prefer that."

"Sure. Just point me in the right direction, and I'll fetch one for myself."

I indicated which way he should go before turning back to Matt and Shelly. Shelly was regarding me with a smirk. "Odd one, that. I hope the apple falls very far from THAT tree!" She giggled behind her fingers.

"Yeah. He's always been a little odd."

"At least he's friendly. I can't say the same for Matt's mother."

Shelly nodded with her chin as we spotted her coming around the corner of the church.

"How anyone can call this a civilized country is beyond me!" She was wiping her hands vigorously with a sanitizing wipe. "Luckily, I thought to bring several of these with me!" She wadded up the one she was using and dropped it unceremoniously on the tray of a passing waitress, who looked at it in surprise before hurrying away.

I glanced at Shelly, who appeared to be struggling to keep from laughing. I suppose that was preferable to the opposite, which is what I found myself trying to resist. "I'm going to go find Miriam and Simon. Shelly, why don't you join me?" She nodded, and we quickly walked away from Matt's mother, who didn't even seem to notice we were gone. She was glaring at a couple of young men in the crowd who were being noticeably affectionate with each other. In fact, from what I could tell, they weren't the only ones who seemed to be romantically affected by the ceremony they had just witnessed. To be honest, seeing their response made me feel a little jealous and more than a little sad. *If only Wills could be here*, I thought. But then I immediately shook my head as I realized that if he was, we would likely be feeling at odds with each other, given our current state of uncertainty.

I linked my arm in Shelly's and squeezed her in a hug. "I'm so happy for you! It was a lovely ceremony."

She turned to me with a smile. "Yes, it was, wasn't it? Better than I anticipated." We stopped next to where Simon stood chatting with Mr. Stephanopolis and Father Yiorgos. From what I could tell, he was talking about the latest archeological findings that were slated to be on exhibit in the Athens Archeological Museum. Miriam stood quietly at his side until she spotted Shelly and me. She quickly walked over to us and embraced Shelly in a hug.

"Congratulations! Although I believe it is customary to congratulate the groom and offer good wishes to the bride." She released Shelly and looped an arm through one of mine. "It's good to see you, Jesse. I suspected you would be here. Our attendance was rather last-minute or I would have reached out to you so that we could coordinate our plans. Will you be staying in Athens long?"

"I'm not sure. A few things are up in the air right now."

She glanced around before giving me a knowing look. "I see. Well, we'll catch up about all of that in a few."

At that moment, Matt appeared and threw his arms around Shelly from behind. "There you are! I was beginning to wonder if the disaster of my parents being here had caused you to run off."

She laughed slightly as she clasped his arms in front of her. "Not at all. If anything, seeing them has given me new appreciation for the man you are."

He released his grip in order to step in front of her and looked deeply into her eyes. "What do you say we get out of here? I believe we're due for a honeymoon."

"That sounds lovely, which reminds me. You never told me what we have planned. We could just go back to our apartment since it has such a lovely view. It would be like going someplace new since the renovations have just finished."

"We could. But I have something else in mind. A surprise I've been keeping to myself." He looked at Christos. "Is everything in order?"

Christos nodded. *"Vevaios.* As we discussed." He turned and began to walk away.

"Jesse, can I count on you to run interference for us with my parents? Just tell them we left for our honeymoon, and I'll phone them sometime tomorrow."

The thought of having to talk to either of them again filled me with dread, but I decided it was the least I could do for Matt and Shelly. "Of course. As long as you let me in on this secret get-away you have planned."

He glanced at Shelly before answering. "Let's just say we'll be close by yet far away. Shel can fill you in on the details later. I want to keep it a secret for now."

"That makes sense. You two go on, and I'll speak to your parents. Shelly, do you want me to say anything to your mother and your aunt?"

"Thanks, but I already told them Matt and I would take the rest of today to ourselves. We made plans to meet up for a late lunch tomorrow. In fact, you can extend the same offer to your parents and Matt's as well if you'd like. Although I'd truthfully rather avoid another scene like the one we had today. There's something definitely at odds between the two of them. Something beyond the fact that they are divorced. I sensed animosity bordering on anger in his mother, whereas his father seemed to be trying to gloss things over with a nonchalant attitude. I could be wrong, of course. I barely know them."

"Actually, I believe you're spot on from what I could tell. But why don't you put them out of your mind for now? It seems this husband of yours has planned some sort of surprise."

Matt nodded vigorously. "On that note, let's go! Christos went to get the car. He should be waiting for us about a block from here. I already gave our thanks and a generous donation to Father Yiorgos and the mayor. I think we can safely head out without any fanfare. Walk with us, Jesse."

The three of us headed toward the back of the church. Just as we were almost out of sight, the crowd broke into applause and began tossing handfuls of rice in our direction. Shelly and Matt let out a laugh before picking up their pace, with me close behind. When we reached the corner of the street, I spotted Christos leaning against a shiny, black Mercedes. Matt opened the passenger door for Shelly and then jogged around to the driver's side. Just before stepping in, he turned to me with a grateful look. "Thanks, Jesse. We owe you one." He climbed inside the car and sped off. I watched them go with a smile tinged with a pang of regret that my own love life hadn't worked out as well. I shook those thoughts out of my mind as I remembered my promise. I started to head back in the direction of the church when I heard someone call my name.

"There you are! I was afraid I had missed you."

I looked up to see Simon approaching me rapidly with Miriam at his side. "Hello, Simon. I'm surprised to see you. I assumed you would be off at a dig site somewhere."

"I was. Or, at least, I have been. I wanted to get here sooner, but our ferry was delayed arriving at the port. Miriam and I arrived just in time for the wedding. Was that the bride and groom I saw leaving? I'm afraid I got so caught up talking with the mayor that I didn't have a chance to extend my wishes to them."

"Yes. I'm afraid you just missed them. I didn't realize you were close to Matt and Shelly. Or maybe it was the mayor's presence that motivated you to make the trip."

He grimaced with a slight smile. "Well, you aren't totally wrong. Although in this case, my intentions were more honorable. Wills told me you would be here, and I wanted to explain something to you. Something he should have told you himself. You see, the reason he isn't here today is because of a promise he made to me. We had a frank discussion a while back, and he let on that things had been a bit rocky between the two of you due to his work demands. I did some exploring and found what I thought might be a solution. Or, at least, a sort of compromise. Things began to come together just about the same time as the wedding plans, which prevented him from attending."

I gave him a puzzled look. "I'm afraid I don't understand. Wills said he couldn't come because of work demands, but you seem to be implying there was another reason."

"I suppose he was accurate in the sense that he was trying to sort things out in a way that would lessen his work demands. You see, I was able to assist him in shifting his responsibilities so that half of his load would be covered by an assistant. We were able to justify that by explaining he would be needed at the dig sites in Greece to help gather material for several publications that would feature the university in a positive way. Material that you would play a major part in compiling, I should add."

My eyes widened as I gazed at him. "So … you're saying he didn't attend the wedding because he's finalizing arrangements that would free up more of his time and allow the two of us to work more closely together? Am I understanding you correctly?" I glanced at Miriam to gauge her reaction, and she gave me what appeared to be a nod of affirmation.

"Precisely. Although I felt he should explain the situation to you himself so there wouldn't be any misunderstanding. Apparently, he didn't take my advice."

"No. I got the impression he felt his work was more important than being here with me. I thought he was giving me a signal that things were winding down between us. That he wanted to break up." I could feel tears welling in my eyes as I spoke.

Simon put one hand on my shoulder. "Oh, dear girl. Nothing could be further from the truth. Wills is totally devoted to you. He has felt terrible that he hasn't been able to show you in the way he would have liked. We are both optimistic that this latest change will remedy that. At least in time."

I wiped away my tears and gave him a slight smile. "You have no idea how much it means that you came all the way here to explain things to me. I'm still confused. But at least now I have a glimmer of hope that things can work out between Wills and me. Frankly, I haven't been at all sure I wanted them to, the way things have been going lately. Now I'm beginning to understand that a major factor has been a lack of communication between us."

"Yes. I'm afraid Wills has inherited a tendency to keep things close to the chest, so to speak. A tendency that I'm sad to say I suffer from myself." He glanced at Miriam. "It has been a sore spot in every relationship I've ever attempted, even to the point of ruining things that could have been quite wonderful if I'd only had the presence of mind to discuss how I felt." Miriam squeezed his arm, causing me to wonder again if there was more between them than I had ever imagined. "That's something Wills will need your help to remedy. That is, if you are still interested in pursuing a relationship with him?"

I considered his question carefully. My relationship with Wills had been hesitant in the beginning, smooth in the middle, and tumultuous in recent times. Now I could see that a lot of the difficulties had to do with a tendency for each of us to avoid talking about tough issues until we had sorted through them on our own. For a relationship to work, I knew we would both have to be willing to take a risk on revealing our thoughts and feelings to each other before they were totally resolved. That would take a lot of work. On both our parts. But now I was feeling a renewed sense of hope that we could weather that storm together.

"You have no idea how much your candor has helped me. I can't wait to talk to Wills. Or, better yet, to see him face to face. We have a lot to talk about."

Simon grinned and clapped his hands. "Grand! I was hoping you'd feel that way. I've arranged for Wills to fly here immediately after he ties things up in London. He should be here sometime tomorrow, or by the next morning at the latest. I assume you'll be staying that long?"

I shrugged. "I hadn't decided how long I would stay, but I don't have anything pressing that would prevent me from delaying my departure until after the holidays."

He rummaged in his coat pocket and pulled out a card, which he handed to me. "I've taken the liberty of arranging accommodations for the two of you at a property owned by a friend of mine. I think you'll find it comfortable. He's expecting you sometime tomorrow, but you can delay it by a day if you prefer. I wasn't sure what your plans would be with Matt and Shelly."

I took the card and glanced at the name: Hotel Astir. "Matt and Shelly are off on a honeymoon. I plan to have dinner with my parents tonight and catch up with Matt and Shelly sometime tomorrow. We don't have any set plans yet, but I'll have time to check in at this hotel before then." I looked at him gratefully. "Thank you, Simon. You have no idea how much I appreciate this. How much I appreciate you." I leaned in to give him a slight hug and was surprised as he pulled me tightly against his chest.

"You are family to me, Jesse. I felt it from the first moment I met you. The fact that you and Wills are a couple. At least, I HOPE you still are and will remain so. It's just a bonus. Either way, I would still hold you in high regard."

I smiled at him through a new onset of tears, which he gently wiped away with his handkerchief. Miriam stepped forward and embraced me firmly. "We'll talk soon. There are a lot of things I have to explain to you. At least, I hope you'll give me that chance."

I looked at her in confusion as I nodded slightly. "Of course. Just give me a call when you can. We could even arrange a time to meet in person if you'll be in Athens long enough."

Simon stepped forward. "Miriam, why don't you stay and visit with Jesse now. I arranged to meet the mayor for coffee shortly. I can text you when and where we can meet later." He turned to leave at that point, waving goodbye with a smile before climbing into a nearby taxi that had been idling at the curb. As I watched him go, I shook my head in disbelief. Just when I started thinking that things with Wills were coming to an end, Simon flipped a switch that had me feeling hopeful again. Or, at least slightly less pessimistic.

I looked at Miriam with a shrug. "Wow. That's a lot to take in. I'm not sure what's going on with you, but I have a feeling it's pretty significant. Just let me take care of something, and we can find a place to talk. Maybe over a coffee or something stronger." As she nodded her agreement, I took a deep breath and headed to where Matt's father stood, flanked by Matt's mother, who had positioned herself at a safe distance away. Talking to them was at least one thing I could take care of. After that, it was anyone's guess where things were headed.

# thirty

To say that Simon's idea of what classified a hotel as *comfortable* was a far shade removed from mine was an understatement to the extreme! I had thought the hotel on Santorini was the epitome of luxury. But the Four Seasons Hotel Astir took that word up another few levels.

It was located on the Athens Riviera at the tip of the pine-clad Vouliagmeni peninsula, not far from the lake that Matt and I had visited one afternoon. That placed it about a 30 or 40-minute drive from the center of Athens, but it felt like a world away.

As my taxi driver made his way to the front of the hotel, I gaped out the window at the stunning scenery. The resort was spread out over several acres. Close to 100, if I were to guess. I could see a few private beaches with cabanas encased in greenery that faced a line of yachts docked along the shoreline. There were two main buildings on the property, both situated so that they faced the sea and curved around a bay before trickling down to the waterfront. The first one we passed was designed in a chunky, modernistic block shape with a sea-view terrace and verdant gardens surrounding it. My taxi driver pulled to a stop in front of the second building, which appeared to be the more glamorous of the two.

"*Nafiska*," he announced, nodding at the entrance. It was fronted by a glass-walled lobby with a curved roof. I noticed a boardwalk jutting out from the side that appeared to continue all the way to connect with the first building we had passed.

Before I could step out of the taxi, my door was opened by a young man wearing a pair of tan shorts and a button-up jacket bearing the name *Four Seasons Hotel Astir*. A pair of headphones was strapped to his head with a small mouthpiece on one side. He smiled at me as he held open the door. "Welcome to the Hotel Astir. If you will follow me, I will show you where to check in."

I noticed another young man jog past us to the rear of the taxi, where he quickly removed my bags from the trunk.

I stepped out of the car and proceeded to follow the first man inside. As we walked, he gestured to the sides of the lobby. "Here you will find a saltwater pool. It is a little cool this time of the year, but there is also a spa with an indoor heated pool, a sauna, and a steam room where you can warm up." He gestured outside the window to our left, where I had spotted the boardwalk. "Along this walkway, you will arrive at an adults-only infinity pool at Arion. It is less crowded. At either location, someone will assist you with towels and bottles of water.

"If you choose to go to the pool here at Nafiska, you may prefer to go down to the pontoon or rent a cabana next to one of our private beaches. At the pontoon, ladders make it possible to step directly into the sea. There are also jet-skis and kayaks available, as well as inflatable devices for a relaxing time." He stopped in front of a long desk manned by a woman wearing a jacket with the same hotel logo and a broad smile.

"Welcome to the Hotel Astir, where we strive to make your every wish come true. May I have your name, please?"

I told her my name and waited while she typed something into her computer.

"Ah, yes. Mr. Harris has informed us to expect you this morning." She handed a key card to the young man who was standing just behind me. "Petros will take you to your accommodations and acquaint you with some of the special features of the hotel along the way. Please let us know if you need anything else. I hope you enjoy your stay."

As we walked through the lobby, Petros pointed out the location of a couple of restaurants and an all-day, complimentary coffee station. Opulence was evident everywhere I looked. The floors were a shiny beige marble that reflected the framed prints and ornate décor. Comfortable seating arrangements had been placed in various areas to allow either a private space to rest or a larger area to congregate with friends. The air smelled of flowers and herbs, which likely came from the numerous vases that sat on tables throughout the lobby. I could hear the subtle strains of acoustic music as we walked, which added to the calming ambiance.

Eventually, Petros stopped in front of a door marked with the number 25, which he opened with my key card, and stepped aside to allow me to enter. The first thing I noticed was that my luggage had already been placed inside, next to a table that contained a basket of snacks and assorted drinks.

The room was fairly large and was laid out in such a way that a folding screen separated the living space from the bed. The entire room was decorated in light wood tones with a plush carpet, both leather and rattan furniture, and a row of floor-to-ceiling windows at the far end. Petros picked up a remote control and an iPad from the table. He punched a button on the remote, and the blinds covering the windows began to roll upward, revealing a view of the sea. He set down the remote and held out the iPad. "You can use this to order room service or book a reservation at any of our restaurants. There are six restaurants and four bars in total. The Taverna 37 offers tradi-tional Greek food and is located next to the water. The Mercato, serving Italian fare, is open all day. It can be very busy, but the homemade pizza or spaghetti with clams is worth waiting for.

"For lunch, you can eat at Helio next to the pool here at Nafiska. It is Mexican style. I highly recommend trying the mango and mezcal drink along with the tacos al pastor. For something more upscale, we have a Michelin-star restaurant called Pelagos. They offer a four, six, or twelve-course tasting menu."

He strode across the room and opened a door. "This is the bathroom."

I walked over and peered inside. It was a good-sized room with marble walls and countertops, a deep, egg-shaped tub, and a rain-shower similar to the one I had seen on Santorini. A generous supply of toiletries lined a glass shelf above the vanity. "It's beautiful." I stepped back into the bedroom and glanced around. The bed was king-sized and covered with a monogrammed comforter pulled partly back to reveal neatly pressed sheets. A chest of drawers stood against one wall at the end of the bed, and two recliners were placed on the side nearest the windows, facing a very large TV.

I shook my head in disbelief. "It's all very impressive. And beautiful!"

He smiled and handed me the key card. "Please let me know if there is anything else I can assist you with." He bowed slightly and walked quickly to the door, closing it quietly behind him.

I sat down on the edge of the bed and looked around in awe. "This must have cost Simon a pretty penny!" I was momentarily embarrassed that he would spend so much just to allow Wills and me to reconnect. At least I hoped that's what would happen between us. But I shook those thoughts aside as I set about unpacking my things. I heard my phone ding at one point, and I hurried to dig it out of my purse. The message showed a text from Shelly asking if I could meet her and Matt in the early afternoon for a drink. Apparently, they were going to have dinner with Matt's parents and her mom and aunt, and they were looking for reinforcement prior to facing that encounter. I texted back that I was available and asked her where and when. She replied that it would be around 5 p.m. and said she would get back to me about the location.

I finished unpacking my things and decided to take a walk around the grounds. It was only noon, so I had plenty of time before I would need to get ready. I still had no idea when Wills would arrive, but I had heard from Simon that it would be sometime the next morning, so I was glad to have something to do in the meantime to distract me.

The weather was mild outside, especially for late December. I wandered down to the pool and spotted the restaurant called Helio that Petros had mentioned. I took a seat at a sea-view table on the patio and ordered the mango and mezcal drink he had recommended. It arrived accompanied by a small bowl of tortilla chips and salsa. I took a cautious sip. It was delicious! And strong. I decided I'd better pace myself if I was going to stay awake long enough to meet Shelly and Matt. I helped myself to several of the chips.

By the time I had finished my drink and roamed around the rest of the resort, I decided to rest a while on the patio just outside my room. I had just settled onto a cushioned lounge chair when I heard giggles and what sounded like amorous stirrings from the patio next door to mine. I tried to block out the sounds, but it seemed impossible. I was just about to go inside to avoid eavesdropping on what should be a private moment when I heard the unmistakable sound of Matt's voice. I listened again to be sure, and I heard the name *Shel* spoken out loud. I stood up and walked to the edge of the patio. "Matt? Shelly? Is that you?"

I heard the scraping of furniture before Matt's voice called out. "Jesse? Jesse, are you there?"

The patios were separated by a wall that provided viewing privacy but was obviously not soundproof. I walked to the end of the wall and peered around just as Matt came to the end on his side. He stopped abruptly and shook his head in surprise. "How did you know we were here? I thought I'd kept our honeymoon location a total secret. Even from Shel."

"You did! I had no idea you were here. Simon showed up at the church in Plaka just after you and Shelly left. He told me some things about Wills that I didn't know, and informed me he'd booked a room for us here. Wills is supposed to arrive some-time tomorrow."

Just then, Shelly peeked over Matt's shoulder with a sheepish grin. "Hello there, Jesse. Fancy meeting you here!"

I noticed her blouse was partially unbuttoned and that Matt's shirt was inside out. I looked away in embarrassment. "I'm sorry to interrupt your honeymoon. Perhaps I should ask the front desk to move me to another room."

The two of them looked at each other and shrugged with a grin before Shelly answered. "No! It's wonderful that you're here. Matt and I have been having a splendid time, and now we'll be able to share some of the rest of our vacation with you. And Wills, I understood you to say? What's that all about?"

I shook my head in bewilderment. "I wish I knew. Simon said he and Wills have been trying to work something out so Wills would be able to spend part of his work time on site with the rest of the dig team. Apparently, he has been as unhappy with our distance as I have. At least that's what Simon indicated. I'll have to wait and talk to Wills to find out if that's true."

Matt looped his arm around Shelly's shoulders. "We'll hope for the best. And now that we're all here, let's make plans for where we'll meet to have that drink Shel texted you about. I'm starting to dread the thought of seeing my parents again. I need something to take the edge off my anxiety."

I nodded. "I understand. I heard there's a nice taverna next to the water. Why don't we meet there? Or we could just walk over together."

"That sounds perfect. We'll knock on your door a little before 5 p.m. and head over together. We're meeting the others at 7 p.m. at a restaurant called the Mercato. It's supposed to be Italian. Say, why don't you join us?"

I considered his offer, then shook my head. "I think not. I had dinner last night with my mom and dad before they left, and I could use a little time to myself before Wills arrives. I'm still trying to sort out what Simon told me."

"Okay, then. We'll see you at five."

The two of them disappeared around the corner of the wall, and I headed back inside my room.

# thirty-one

The next morning, I slept in a little later than I was used to. Sharing drinks and laughs with Shelly and Matt had been a lot of fun, but once I returned to my hotel room, I found I was too stirred up to relax. Eventually, I gave up trying and went for a walk around the hotel grounds, returning just before midnight. When I finally fell asleep, it was close to 2 a.m.

I reached over for the remote control on the bedside table and raised the window blinds, quickly regretting my decision when the sun hit my face full-force. "Good grief!" I quickly lowered the blinds halfway and turned so my back was to the windows. I picked up my cell phone to take it out of airplane mode and saw that two text messages had come through earlier in the morning. One was from Simon asking if I was pleased with the hotel, and the other was from Wills saying he was arriving at the Athens airport around 10 a.m. and would be at the hotel about an hour or so later. This news jolted me awake, and I quickly got up and began to straighten the room in preparation for his arrival.

I was just coming out of the bathroom after showering and preparing to dress for the day when I heard my cell phone ring. I hurried over to where it sat on the bedside table and picked it up.

"Hello?"

"Hi, Jesse. It's me."

I felt my heart begin to race at the sound of Wills' voice. "Oh, hi. Are you here?"

"Yes. I'm in the lobby. I thought perhaps you'd like to meet me here. I can pick us up a couple of coffees so we can talk. There's a sitting area just past the coffee station that's in a quiet location. It's next to some windows looking out on the patio to the side of the hotel."

I remembered the area he was referring to. "Okay. I'll be there in a few minutes." I carefully selected my clothes and ran a brush through my hair, adding a little lipstick and powder before grabbing my room key card. As I crossed the lobby, I spotted Wills standing looking out the windows in the area he had mentioned. I stopped to look at him before continuing. Despite our struggles, I still felt an intense attraction to him, and I had missed being with him. I walked up behind where he stood.

"Hi."

He turned around with a smile. "Jesse. You look wonderful." We both stood awkwardly facing each other. Neither one of us made a move toward the other. He gestured at two chairs to his right. "Would you like to sit? I've brought you a coffee the way I remember you like it."

I took a seat and picked up the Styrofoam cup on the table in front of me. I lifted the lid and took a sip. "Um. It's good. Thank you." I blew on the coffee in a pretense of cooling the hot liquid, although I was really just trying to buy myself some time before we delved into what I imagined would be an awkward conversation. Wills looked at me with a slight smile before taking a seat in the opposite chair.

"How have you been?" he asked.

"Good. Matt and Shelly's wedding was really nice. They left for a couple of honeymoon nights right after the ceremony. In fact, they surprised me by popping up on the patio immediately next to my hotel room. Apparently, this is where they've been staying."

His eyebrows raised in surprise. "Really? Well, I shouldn't be surprised. Uncle Simon mentioned how popular this place has become. I was amazed he was able to book us a room here with such little notice." He paused to sip his coffee. "I guess you were rather taken aback by him appearing at the wedding, and the news he shared about me."

I nodded. "More than anything, I was surprised you hadn't told me anything about your plans, which wasn't the first time you've kept something so important from me. It occurred to me that this has been part of our problem all along. We don't talk about the things that really matter until we've worked them out on our own. And by then, a level of distrust has come between us as we struggled to figure out what the other wasn't saying." I paused as I considered what else I wanted to say.

"Frankly, I don't understand why you didn't tell me what was going on. Didn't you think I would like to know that you were trying to change things so we could have more time together? You just let me believe that your job, your work, was more important." I was a little surprised at how openly I was expressing my feelings. I guess things had been building up in me even more than I realized.

He leaned on his knees and looked at the floor between his feet. "You're absolutely right. I've been foolish not to talk to you about what I was thinking, and what I was hoping to do about it." He looked up at me with a woeful expression. "For some reason, I have a difficult time letting you, or anyone, be privy to my innermost thoughts until I've sorted them out on my own. I'm afraid that has been an unfortunate pattern of mine for a long time. Simon has been telling me it was going to create trouble at some point. I just couldn't see my way around it before his forebodings came to fruition."

I couldn't help but smile at his use of what I gathered was a very British expression. "When I saw him after the wedding, he tried to explain what you had been worrying about, which helped a little. Unfortunately, I wish I had heard it from you first, and much sooner than I did."

He ran his hands over his face and shook his head. "I'm really terribly sorry, Jesse. Please understand that I never intended to hurt you or cause you distress. In fact, I THOUGHT I was doing the opposite: trying to work things out so we could spend more time together without my job always getting in the way. I'm afraid I've botched that up royally." He leaned back in his chair with his hands splayed to the sides.

"It's not all your fault. I haven't been exactly up-front with my feelings either. I was afraid of pushing you away if I told you how frustrated I'd become, when in fact my reticence probably had the effect of pushing you away even further."

He shook his head with a grimace. "What a pair we are. Do you think we can find our way out of this mess? Together?"

I was touched by how sincerely distressed he appeared. "I hope so. I'd really like to. We can try a fresh start. That is, if you'd like to?"

He leaned forward and grasped my hands in his. "More than anything. I'd love for you to give me a chance to make it up to you."

I could feel tears welling in my eyes, and I freed one hand to swipe them away. "I'd like that, too." I glanced at where his suitcase sat. "Why don't we drop your bag off at the front desk and have a bellman take it to the hotel room, and then we can take a walk. The grounds here are lovely, and there's a nice spot next to the beach where we can have a drink or a bite to eat. I actually haven't had any breakfast yet."

He grinned broadly and nodded. "That sounds perfect. I haven't been able to eat anything yet either." He stood and picked up the handle on his roller bag before holding out a crooked arm to me. "Shall we?"

---

We spent the next couple of hours wandering the hotel grounds and enjoying a little breakfast on the patio at the Mercato. The restaurant was much quieter than it had been the previous evening when Matt, Shelly, and I had met there for drinks. The peaceful ambiance gave Wills and me a chance to talk things out much more thoroughly than we had in a very long time. If ever!

By the time we had finished, we strolled along the beach for a little while before returning to our hotel room. Maybe it was the mimosas we had enjoyed with our meal. Or the fact that we had connected in a way that was far more intimate than we'd shared in a long time. Whatever the reason, we flew into one another's arms the second we stepped inside and reached a slowly building crescendo of harmonious passion. Afterward, as we lay in each other's arms amidst the tumble of bedcovers, I marveled at how quickly things had changed between us. Over the previous two hours, we had found our way past misunderstandings and pain to a new level of sharing, which was both physically and emotionally intense.

I shifted in his arms so that I was facing him. His eyes were closed, and I wondered if he was asleep until I saw him open one eye partway. "Hi there." He smiled.

"Hi, yourself. That was wonderful."

He closed his eyes again as he shifted slightly so our bodies were pressed together. "Um hum. Beyond wonderful."

I hesitated before speaking, unsure if what I was about to say would be misunderstood. "I don't want to go back to the way things were. I want a change."

He opened his eyes wide as he stared into mine. "What do you mean?"

"I want us to live together. I don't think we can survive living apart. There are too many distractions with my studies and your work. Even if you're in Greece and I'm in London, or vice versa, if we can still come back together in our own place, I think it will make a difference."

He shifted in order to lean his head on one hand. "I agree wholeheartedly. In fact, I was hoping to ask you if you'd be willing for us to find a place somewhere between our two flats. Since I'll be splitting my time between London and Greece from now on, I thought we could actually find something closer to your school so you wouldn't have far to travel. That would be nearer to the airport, too, for those times when I have to fly out. And during school breaks, you could travel with me. What do you think?"

What he was describing was close to the arrangement I had in mind, as well. "There's a place I know about that fits what you're describing. It's a nice flat, in a quiet area, a short bus ride from campus. There's a park nearby, and a few bars and restaurants, so we wouldn't need transport to go out some evenings and weekends. There's also a metro stop very close by with a direct line to Heathrow, where, as I'm sure you know, there are several non-stop flights a day to Athens. I've had my eye on it for a while, and I checked with the rental agency after talking with Simon. They said they'll hold it until the beginning of the week." I looked at him hesitantly. "I wasn't sure if I would even bring this up as a possibility until we had a chance to talk things out."

He sat up and took my hands in his. "I think it sounds like a grand plan. Why don't we call the agency today and finalize the rental? I don't have to be back in London until Tuesday, so I hoped we could fly back together. That would give us the rest of the holiday to sort things out."

It was a wonderful turn of events. Almost losing each other. And then finding our way back together with a closeness we hadn't quite experienced before. It felt wonderful. And more than a little scary. But I was determined to get past my hesitation and move forward to wherever that brought us down the road.

As I thought back to the path we'd been on so far, I was reminded of my conversation with Miriam a few days prior.

"I need to ask you something. Were you aware of what has transpired between Miriam and Simon? In the past, I mean."

He looked at me hesitantly. "I'm not sure what you mean. Has Miriam said something?"

"Just recently. But she hinted at something a while back without disclosing exactly what she was talking about. Apparently, she and Simon had a thing. A fling, I suppose you could say. But it ended rather badly. As I understand it, Miriam discovered she was pregnant with Simon's baby. He was pretty freaked out about it and turned tail before they could sort out their feelings together. Unfortunately, or perhaps fortunately, given the circumstances, she lost the baby very soon after she spoke to Simon.

"As she described it, he felt a load of guilt that kept them at a distance from each other for some time, except for their professional dealings. She told me it was only recently that they began to talk again about what happened and start to sort out their feelings toward each other. By the look of things at the wedding, it seems they've made a good deal of progress."

He nodded with a slight smile. "That's another thing I've been hesitant to talk with you about, although it really wasn't my story to share. I spoke to Uncle Simon recently, and he indicated that things had begun to shift for them in a positive way. He actually said that our relationship—yours and mine

—has been a significant factor in causing him to open up again."

I frowned. "What do you mean?"

He hesitated as he appeared to collect what he wanted to say. "He told me he watched how my reluctance to open up to you, about what I have been both thinking and feeling, has driven a wedge between us. He thought that was very unfortunate because he believes we are absolutely right for each other. Seeing what was happening with us caused him to take a serious look at his own life and the mistakes he's made.

"He said that led him to reach out to Miriam in an attempt to explain what happened between them and see if she was willing to allow him to try again. As he explained it, at first she was extremely hesitant to listen to anything he had to say on the matter. But she eventually came around, and now they seem to be in a good place. Better than at any time before. Frankly, I've never seen my uncle look so enchanted."

I smiled at his description of an enchanted Simon. It was a hard image to fathom. But no harder than the one I was seeing in front of me. "That's wonderful. For both of them. And it pleases me that watching us go through our trials and tribulations has helped them reach that point." I placed my hands on his arms and squeezed them slightly. "Do you really think we still have a chance? Are you certain you want to try?"

He pulled me into an embrace and looked into my eyes. "Absolutely. In fact, I feel certain of it, which is an odd state for me to be in, given my tendency to keep my guard up. You've gotten under my skin in the best of ways. I can't imagine my life without you, and I hope you feel the same way."

We exchanged a kiss at that moment that grew in intensity with each passing second. Finally, we pulled back with a sigh. "Why don't we try out that rain shower I noticed in the bath earlier? I could use a little freshening up, but I'm not ready to let you out of my sight yet either." He looked at me with a smug grin.

"I say that's a great idea."

---

That evening, we met Matt and Shelly at the Michelin-starred restaurant on the hotel property and treated them to a post-wedding celebration that had all of us groaning with pleasure and pain at the multi-course feast. It was a lovely night, full of laughter, a few tears, and many toasts to the joys of our present and hopes for the future. We would all be embarking on significant changes in our lives. Changes that I felt optimistic would work out for the best for each of us.

Wills and I had been able to secure the rental property in London and would be able to move in before the new year. We phoned Simon to tell him our news, who sounded as ecstatic as we felt. Now, it was up to us to continue our efforts at opening ourselves up to communicating more thoroughly. A plan that filled me with equal measures of anxiety and eager anticipation.

As for our future together, let's just say that if this were a Hall-mark movie, everything would go smoothly. But as I knew only too well, that wasn't what usually happened in life. There would be ups and downs ahead for us, both separately and together. I could only hope that the ups would be more plentiful. For the moment, I planned to give my heart and mind entirely to the experience of getting to know this wonderful man. And I was committed to getting to know myself just as well.

I fished inside my backpack for a tissue to dab at the tears that had begun to well in my eyes, touching instead a scrap of folded paper. I opened it and recognized it as the one where I had made note of the coffee cup predictions the waiter's grandmother had made while I was staying in the hotel in Plaka. I glanced over the list. *A trip. Unexpected love. Friendship and big change.*

"Huh. That about covers my last few months." The trip in reference could be Andros, Santorini, London, or just Greece in general. Unexpected love was what I hoped was happening with Wills. And friendship—well, that definitely made me think of my renewed connection with Matt and my newly formed friendship with Shelly, who was now my cousin-in-law, and Miriam, whom I had grown to admire and respect the more I learned about the challenges she'd faced in trying to prevent her personal life from interfering with her professional one. From what I could gather, she and Simon had made significant progress on putting a positive twist on things between them, and from all accounts, they seemed to be on the road to rediscovery of each other.

I glanced back down at the piece of paper in my hand. All-in-all, it boiled down to the last thing on the list, *big change.* Change that had already happened, and change that was still ahead for all of us in both life and love.

I was reminded of a quote I'd once read: *You have to love yourself first before you can love someone else.* Did I really believe that? It made sense because if you don't know yourself, truly and honestly, then you can't be fully present in a relationship with anyone else. Not that knowing who I really am meant I would be able to love myself with all of my various idiosyncrasies. That would take time. But time is one thing I have.

Just then, my quiet rumination was jarred by a familiar sound. I glanced over at Wills, who was standing next to the front steps of the hotel, waiting for our ride to the Athens airport. We looked at each other in shock for a moment before bursting out in delighted laughter. Wills pointed across the street to a nearby hill where we could spot the white edifice of a tiny chapel. A handful of people were standing on a small patio out front while a few others were making their way inside.

I walked up to stand next to Wills, who looped his arm around my waist. "I'll take that as a good omen and assume the church bells are ringing on our behalf. A sort of send-off on this next phase of our journey, together and apart." He leaned down and gave me a gentle kiss on the lips, causing me to rise on my toes to meet him halfway.

That's how I wanted it to be from this point forward: each of us meeting the other halfway with love and respect.

A taxi pulled up at that moment, and we scurried to place our bags in the trunk before climbing inside. The driver glanced at us in the rearview mirror. "*Pou pate*?" he asked. "Where are you going?"

"Home," I said, after exchanging a happy smile with Wills. "We're going home."

THE END

# about the author

*Photo credit: Frank Dolen*

Annell St. Charles was "born and raised" in Nashville, Tennessee, where she spent most of her life before making a permanent move to Hilton Head Island, South Carolina in the early 2020s. Her professional "working" years were spent in health care and health education, focused in the areas of Health Promotion, Exercise Physiology, and Nutrition Science, in which she holds a Doctorate degree. She has written several continuing education booklets on numerous topics for health professionals. Upon her retirement, her writing shifted to more fictitious creative endeavors, which she describes as a "sort of regurgitation" of what had been festering in her spirit and gut her entire life.

Her first two novels – *The Things Left Unsaid* and *The Choices We Make* – were set in Nashville, and the latter two – *The Chances We Take* and *The Hearts We Trust* – feature Hilton Head. The key character introduced in the first novel, named Georgia Ayres, can be found in all four books, along with her good friends and significant other. Annell often refers to the latter two books of this series as Gullah Ghost Stories part one and part two because of their intricate portrayal of the Gullah-Geechee heritage of Hilton Head Island, and Georgia Ayres' foray into the spirit world as she discovers this fascinating culture.

In her most recent novel, Annell has taken a shift in focus to the country of Greece, where she has spent a significant amount of time for many years due in large part to marrying a Greek-born man, Costas Tsinakis. Most recently, they took on the task of overseeing the renovation of an old stone stable located on land owned by Costas' family. The stable is now a lovely, livable stone house.

Annell has also published three books of photography, the most recent of which is titled *Hilton Head Island: Sunrise, Sunset, and the Beauty Between*. When she is not writing or thinking about her next story line, Annell can be found logging many walking steps, either alone or with one or more of her like-minded walking buddies.

Loved *When The Church Bells Ring*? Please consider leaving a review on Amazon and Goodreads—your support makes a huge difference in helping new readers find it.

www.ingramcontent.com/pod-product-compliance
Lightning Source LLC
Chambersburg PA
CBHW021951120726
47898CB00001BA/71